Love's Call

Book Two
The King's Riders Series

Other Books by C.A. Szarek

<u>The King's Riders — Epic Fantasy Romance</u>

Sword's Call (Book One)
Rogue's Call (Book Three)
Fate's Call (A Novella from the World of the King's Riders)

<u>Highland Secrets — Historical Fantasy</u>

The Tartan MP3 Player (Book One)
The Fae Ring (Book Two)
The Parchment Scroll (Book Three)
The Princess and The Laird (Prequel to Highland Secrets) — *Coming 2017!*
Highlander's Portrait (A Highland Secrets Story) — *Coming Jan 2017!*
Highland Valentine (A Highland Secrets Story) — *Coming Feb 2017!*

<u>Crossing Forces — Romantic Suspense</u>

Collision Force (Book One)
Cole in Her Stocking (A Crossing Forces Christmas) — *FREE read!*
Chance Collision (Book Two)
Calculated Collision (Book Three)
Collision Control (Book Four)
Superior Collision (Book Five)

<u>Anthologies</u>

Deep in the Hearts of Texas — *FREE read!*

Story: Promise (A Crossing Forces Companion)

THE NORTH

Dragon's Tail
Mountains of Aramour
Elfin River
Terraquist
Coire Isle
Greenwald
North Ascova
Penial Valley
Tarvis
Hadrian's Place
Berat
Elfin Islands
South Ascova
Dalunas
Southern Strait
Penal Territory

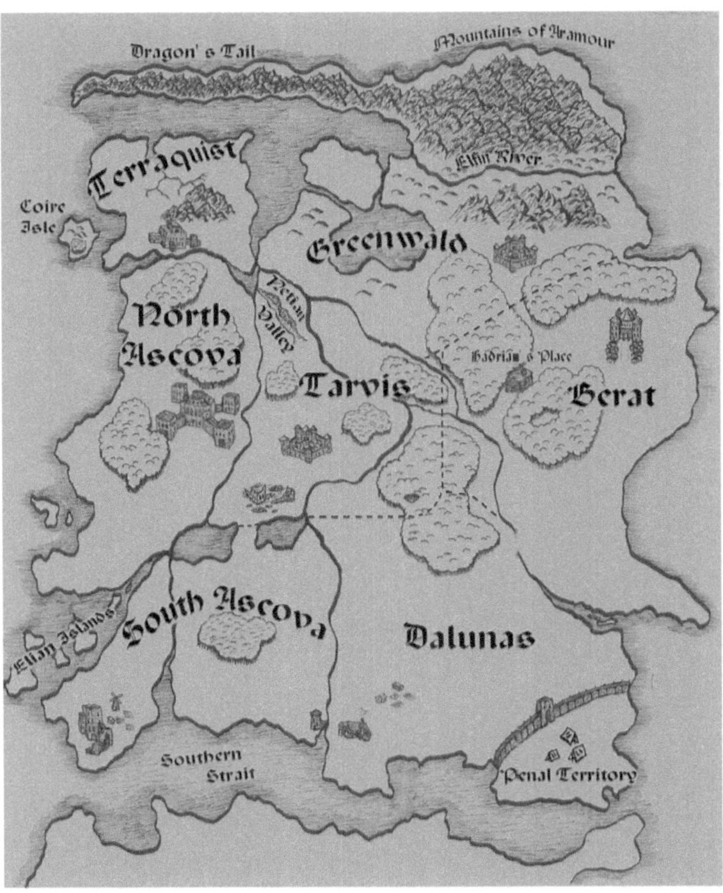

Dedication

This one goes out to all my girls in the Tomb!

Chapter One

Ansley rode hard. She leaned into Caide, holding tight to the reins and squeezing the saddle with her thighs. She wasn't worried about losing Ali. Her wolf would keep up; she always did.

Night had fallen hours before, and she'd ride four more before she reached the center of Greenwald. She'd entered the Province some time ago, but this journey was long and arduous.

She'd left Terraquist right after supper, and the hearty rabbit stew sat in her stomach like a brick.

Ali, stay close, love, she thought-sent to her bondmate, sucking in a breath as the hood to her Senior Rider cape slipped off her head. She pulled it back into place, covering her ears against the rushing wind.

Her bondmate's only answer was a mental grunt, but it was reassuring. The wolf's black coat was hard to see in the dark, but Ansley could sense her at the horse's side through the magic that joined them.

They moved down the road, encountering no one; she stuck to the main thoroughfare, her sword sheathed at her waist and the message she carried safe in her belt-pouch.

At least we're making good time.

There'd been no time to prepare for this overnight run assignment. Fatigue was encroaching. Her back throbbed; her legs were heavy, despite the stirrups taking most of her weight.

Her captain, Sir Artair Moray, had summoned her after evening meal. When she'd arrived, the king was present, as well. She'd been charged with orders to deliver a message to the neighboring Province of Greenwald.

It was urgent, King Nathal had said. Nay, it wouldn't hold until dawn.

Captain Moray had already ordered her white gelding readied to await her in the courtyard.

Ansley wouldn't question her superior or her king. She'd hidden her surprise.

Worry had seized her gut, but King Nathal had promised nothing was amiss. He commanded her to take her time at her destination, giving leave to visit with both Lady Cera, the Duchess of Greenwald, and her other good friend, Lady Aimil, who also resided at the dukedom stronghold, Castle Aldern. Both ladies, newly married, were former Senior King's Riders.

Cera was carrying a child due any day now, so the king had encouraged her to stay for the birth.

Time away from her duties as one of the king's messengers was unusual and welcome. Ansley would enjoy herself. Take her time coming home.

Even her father, captain to the king's personal guard, had encouraged her. He'd met her in the courtyard and given her a long hug goodbye. She'd scratched their cat, Xander, behind the ear, ignoring the hiss he directed at her bondmate.

Caide had carried her well into Greenwald now; they were perhaps an hour from the gates that surrounded Greenwald Main.

Ali came to an abrupt halt in the middle of the road.

"Ali!" Her shout did nothing to move her bondmate.

Ansley yanked Caide's reins, and he stopped short, throwing his head back and whinnying, but it kept him from mowing down her wolf. Her steed's muscles rippled, and she squeezed her thighs to keep her seat, whispering to calm him.

Ali. The wolf didn't respond to her mental scold.

The large she-wolf's posture was tight.

Sighing, she threw her leg over her gelding's back and slid down his side. Her feet throbbed with the jarring impact of the ground. She patted Caide's sweaty neck and apologized.

He snorted and tossed his head, as if he was blaming Ali.

She bit back a smile. Her constant companions only *tolerated* each other. When she stepped beside her wolf, she ran her hand down the length of Ali's back.

Her bond's ears were perked, head tilted to one side. "What do you hear?"

Ali didn't acknowledge Ansley's voice.

With a curse, she drew her sword and looked around. The wolf's gaze was locked toward the woods that lined the road, but Ansley's human eyes couldn't penetrate the darkness.

She buried her hand in the thick, black fur at the back of her bondmate's neck, muttering a spellword one of the king's mages had taught her when they'd bonded. Instantly, her own sight sharpened as she shared Ali's eyes. Colors were off a little, but her vision had never been clearer. Where she could only see shadow on her own, the wolf's eyes allowed her to take in shape, make out so many more things in the night.

Her bondmate blinked, as she absorbed the feeling of Ansley's mind slipping into hers, but she didn't fight her. They were bonded, and Ali was used to Ansley's presence in her mind. The spell temporarily deepened their connection.

She didn't have much magic, so she couldn't maintain the link for long. Using spells, even simple ones, exhausted her.

A low growl sounded in the wolf's throat, and Ansley tightened her grip. Soft, thick fur grazed her palm and pushed through her fingers.

But she spotted what Ali had.

There was a lump lying in the underbrush about six feet from the road. It moved. Then moaned.

The she-wolf startled, but Ansley stopped her from

jolting forward with a quick mental command.

She released her hold and the spell, lifting her sword. Sweat broke out on her forehead and her heart thundered as she edged forward. A too-cool breeze for the fall evening made a tremor shoot down her spine.

Her bondmate darted in front of her. Ali would let Ansley check out the mystery, but the wolf would always act without order to protect.

"Blessed Spirit," she whispered, hitting a knee. The tip of her sword scraped into the dirt making a small high pitched screech she ignored.

Ali lifted her head, catching the poor creature's scent, then whined and pawed the ground. Her wolf lost her defensive posture and inched closer. If Ansley could smell the blood—and she did—no doubt her bond did, too. She sheathed her sword and pulled off her riding gloves, tucking them into her belt.

"Help." The word slipped from damaged lips.

Ansley leaned down, shoving her thick plait over her shoulder when her hair fell forward. Digging in her belt-pouch, she felt for a magic-activated light. She said the spellword to bring it to life as soon as her fingers closed around it. It wouldn't last long because her energy was almost spent, from the long ride as well as the magic she'd used with Ali.

She gripped the small sticklike object. It was designed by the king's mages for a single lighting. All Riders carried them on runs. Handy for emergencies, but even a mage of great skill could only make them work—and last—about two hours.

The slight figure made another noise, and her stomach lurched. She reached out, gently moving matted hair.

What had to be instinct made the girl move away at the same time the gasp fell from Ansley's mouth.

There was no way the woman could see her. One eye was swollen shut, the other open only a slit. Her lip was split, and there was gash across her right cheekbone. Her nose was broken and bloody. No area was left untouched.

The girl was young and small, eight and ten at the most. Her tight, ebony curls were disheveled and several spots soaked in blood. Her clothing, a ragged scrap of a dress, was soiled and torn, as was the thin cloak she wore. The light fabric could never warm her adequately on a Greenwald fall night.

"Shhh, I won't hurt you. Promise."

Ali growled long and deep.

Hooves pounded down the road.

Ansley shot to her feet, dropping the magic light. She stomped it to extinguish the glow and redrew her sword.

Caide neighed and fidgeted from the road.

Ansley whistled and he bolted toward her. Twigs snapped and leaves shifted under his hooves. The moonlight highlighted his white hide. She had no doubt the party of riders had spotted them.

"Halt!" The call went up before she could react, confirming her fear.

Her heart sank to her gut, as Ali rushed in front of her, hackles raised.

Ansley's eyes darted over the dozen or so men. She spared a glance over her shoulder, widening her stance to hide the girl from view. She'd protect her, if need be.

There were only a few possibilities of who could be on the road at the late hour. The group was too large to be other Riders—their captain never sent more than two—three if they were training—on a single run.

Brigands or a troop of men-at-arms on patrol were the only other logical choices. Perhaps she was closer to Greenwald Main than she'd realized.

Blessed Spirit, let it be the latter.

"Who goes there?" a deep voice called out.

She cleared her throat. Needed to harden her tone. Sound male as well. "Who goes *there*?" Ansley returned, flexing her grip on the hilt of her sword.

A rider moved forward from the back of the group, the other horses parting way to let him through. It was too dark to see his face, but a drawn sword glinted in the moonlight. His long dark hair shifted in the frigid wind.

"Sir Leargan Tegran, Captain of the Aldern personal guard." His breath floated around his words.

Her heart flipped.

Leargan.

Ansley chided herself and squared her shoulders.

He doesn't know you're alive, remember?

She strode forward and sheathed her weapon. "Good. I need some help."

Leargan stared at the tall *female* figure coming toward him in the dark. "And you are?" he prompted for the second time.

"Senior King's Rider Ansley Fraser," she said, and stopped in front of Fia, his buckskin colored mare.

"Captain!" Roduch's yell kept him from answering the Rider.

The knight dismounted the large, blue roan stallion, rushing off the road and skidding to his knees in the dirt. "Who did this to you?" he shouted. The big man leaned over a barely-visible figure lying on the ground.

There was a moan as his friend and fellow guardsman lifted something — no, some*one* — into his massive arms.

A woman.

"What's going on?" Leargan demanded. He dismounted improperly and almost fell on his face, but the King's Rider was at his side in seconds, commanding his attention. Embarrassment rolled over him, seared his neck as his boots hit the dirt. He straightened and squared his shoulders. Hopefully, it was too dark for her to be aware of his near mishap.

"I found her, thanks to my bond. She saw her first." The girl gestured to a large, dark wolf. The beast growled, yellow eyes catching the moonlight. "Ali, easy." The messenger buried a hand in the fur behind the wolf's head, and it appeared to calm.

"We need some light," one of his men called.

"I'm coming, Sir Roduch." The leather of the man-at-arms' saddle creaked as he dismounted. He muttered something under his breath, and his hands lit up with an amber glow. He bent over the big knight.

"What happened?" Leargan repeated, tearing his eyes away from the two men and the magic on display.

"I found her like that. She's in bad shape. Looks like someone beat her." Her voice was deep for a woman but not unpleasant. She was obviously worried, wringing her hands in front of her.

He wished he could see her in more light than the moon could provide. "We will get help for her."

"Good." She nodded and her hip-length plait shifted, dancing over the hood resting against the shoulders of her Rider cloak.

The girl had said she was a Senior King's Rider, so the cloak would be a deep green color, denoting the highest messenger rank, even though the darkness of the night made it seem black.

Roduch made it back to their group. The female form in his arms was tiny, with long, dark—or dirty curls in her matted hair. The big knight shifted her closer to his massive chest, and the man-at-arms raised his glowing hands to illuminate her face.

Leargan winced and heard the Rider's sharp intake of breath beside him. There were murmurs from a few of his men.

She was damaged, her face bloodied and broken. And *damn*, she was young. Inadequately clothed for the weather, too. Her gray dress was ripped, hanging off one shoulder; the light cloak failed to cover her body. Her pale skin was evident in the moonlight, but her skin was tinged blue. She was too cold.

The poor thing wasn't moving. Had probably had passed out. Not a bad thing, considering what she'd been through.

"She's alive, but barely just." Roduch's words were pained, as if the girl mattered to him.

Who's this lass?

Leargan threw a look at his longtime friend, but Roduch was looking down into the girl's face, wide jaw clenched. "Let's get her to Tristan. Now," he ordered.

Alasdair, another knight of the personal guard, barked at the men to remount.

"She doesn't look too good, Captain," one of the men said.

"Aye. The sooner we get back, the better." Leargan looked at Roduch. "Do you want me to take her?"

"Nay," Roduch said, pulling her closer to his chest.

Leargan quirked a half-smile. Whoever she was, the lass suddenly had a champion. His friend's expression screamed *mine.* "At least let me hold her so you can mount up."

Roduch looked at her face again before meeting Leargan's eyes. The other knight didn't want to give her up.

"Let him take her," the Rider urged.

"I won't hurt her, my friend."

"I know," he said, his tone about as gruff as Leargan had ever heard. He shot a look at the King's Rider.

Leargan stared as the big man shifted on his feet, shoulders tight.

After a heavy sigh and a look that could've slayed him, Roduch laid the unconscious girl in his arms.

He held her as gently as he could, grimacing when he couldn't avoid another glance at her face. Every inch of her skin was marred. Bruises, cuts and blood. Lord Tristan Dagget, healer as well as the Duke of Aldern's Second, would keep her from scarring when he healed her wounds, but Leargan's heart clenched.

Who would do something like this to someone so young and small?

She didn't weigh much, just a feather in his arms. He settled her into his chest, and the girl groaned but didn't awaken. That was for the better, sleep would spare her pain.

Soon, she was returned to Roduch's arms, and Leargan remounted Fia. He grabbed the reins and turned his mare, facing the group of his men, a mix of castle men-at-arms and knights of the personal guard.

Tonight was supposed to have been a training patrol to show the new men how to keep their eyes peeled. It was supposed to have been an easy task, a normal training exercise.

We have to expect anything. Always.

He cleared his throat. "Alasdair, you've the lead. Stay on patrol. See if you can find out where she came from or who did this to her. Report back as soon as possible," Leargan ordered, meeting his friend's eyes.

The other knight gave a brusque nod.

The King's Rider pulled her large, white gelding abreast with Fia. "I'll ride with you."

"Oh?"

"I'm headed to Castle Aldern. I have an urgent message from the king."

Chapter Two

"She should sleep for a while. Not my doing with magic, though. Exhaustion. Blessed Spirit only knows how she was strong enough to make it to the edge of the road," the healer, Lord Tristan Dagget said, his face pale with concern, as well as expended magical energy. Healing was physically exhausting and dangerous to the untrained, as Leargan understood it.

The lord was dressed casually, in just a tunic and breeches. No usual doublet or belt, not to mention a sword, in sight. Then again, everyone had been called in from their beds.

The duke himself, Lord Jorrin Aldern, pressed him into a chair, but he waved everyone's attentions away.

Tristan's wife, Lady Aimil, hovered. Her long dark locks were in two thick plaits and swayed with her movements.

There was really no need to worry, but the healing lord always saw to his own needs last.

Leargan smirked as he just flashed a smile to everyone.

Morag, the castle's headwoman, fussed over Roduch's refusal to leave the foundling girl's side. He was posted in a chair flush against the bed.

They'd settled her into one of Castle Aldern's many large guest suites, and the warrior was holding one of her pale hands, ignoring the woman in charge of all the castle's female staff as she muttered about decorum.

Her glare demanded he be dismissed, but when Leargan and the duke both ignored her, she huffed, barking at her two maids as they bustled around the room.

The very pregnant duchess, Lady Cera, stood arm and arm with the Rider. The missive from the king to the duke was in the messenger's hand.

Lord Aldern had assured her he'd be with her in a moment.

The Rider waited patiently, her worried eyes darting over the scene before them. Every once in a while, she and the duchess would whisper to each other, heads bent together. Her hair was red like the duchess' but a lighter shade, more orange than Lady Cera's deep auburn.

Lady Aimil had been in on their conversation as well, before she'd left them to be at her husband's side.

The messenger's name had clicked in Leargan's mind. The moment light of the castle had allowed him to get a better look at her.

Senior Rider Ansley *Fraser*. Daughter to the captain of the king's personal guard, Sir Murdoch Fraser. His former captain and longtime mentor.

She favored her father to a tee, bright red hair and teal eyes. The smattering of freckles across the bridge of her nose gave her an air of innocence. Her body was partly obscured by her cloak, but she was tall and slender.

Absolutely *gorgeous*.

Leargan could barely tear his eyes away, even though he *should* be paying attention to their very serious situation.

Morag and the maids shuffled out, the headwoman closing the door quietly. She was discreet. Hopefully the two maids would exercise the same care. Events like tonight tended to spread over the castle like a contagious disease.

"Did you get her name?" The duke's voice took his attention, and Leargan glanced at both of his lords.

"No," Tristan answered, voice low. His eyes shot to Roduch and the ladies, before the healer looked back at Lord Aldern. "I touched her mind with mine when I began to heal her, but hers snapped shut, probably defensively. She's been through hell. More than once."

"What do you mean?" the duchess asked, one hand on her swollen stomach and moving closer to Tristan's chair.

The Rider was on her heels.

Jorrin threw his arm over his wife's shoulders, but she ignored his whispered admonition to get off her feet.

The group was in the sitting area of the large room, but the bed wasn't far enough that Roduch wouldn't hear them. He had some of the sharpest senses of the personal guard.

"I sensed tons of half-healed wounds, old scars, and bruises, inside and out. Even two broken ribs that had knitted wrong. I fixed all that, though, too."

Lady Aimil gasped and took a step closer to her husband.

Tristan took her hand.

"Blessed Spirit..." the Rider whispered, her eyes misting over.

Leargan's heart skipped, and he was overcome with the desire to comfort her. Touch her in some way. But he planted his hands at his sides and stayed where he stood, just inside the door, watching. Listening.

"And..." Tristan's voice dropped even further. "I sensed evidence of repeated rapes. Fresh...bleeding...there that needed healing, as well." He winced.

Ansley Fraser gasped. She stared at Roduch's new charge. Her mouth wobbled, as if she was fighting tears.

For a girl she didn't know?

Leargan was intrigued. He scooted closer.

Lady Cera uttered an un-duchess-like curse.

When he tore his gaze from Ansley Fraser and met the duke's blue eyes, Lord Aldern shoved a lock of black hair behind one slender tapered ear, revealing his mixed heritage—his father was human, and his mother elfin. His hands were jerky, and he made a fist. His jaw was tight.

"I will find whoever did this to her and kill the bastard," Roduch vowed. The big knight turned toward them, fists clenched.

"We need to talk to her first," Tristan said, tone gentle.

Leargan went to Roduch, placing a hand on his shoulder.

His friend looked up at him, saying nothing. He squeezed, when he read the anguish in the pale blue eyes.

"Captain…" Roduch whispered, shaking his head.

Leargan glanced at the girl asleep in the large bed. Dark curls covered the pillow. She was ethereally beautiful, her small hand engulfed by the big warrior's. Pale skin now clear of bruises, her expression was serene, from delicate brows to full lips. Thick sleeping furs swallowed her small frame, but he could see the rise and fall with her deep, even breathing.

Peaceful innocence.

Who hurt her?

"We'll deal with it, Roduch, I promise," the duke vowed.

"Thank you, Lord Aldern," Roduch said. His broad shoulders heaved, as he relaxed, and Leargan patted his back.

"Greenwald has the same laws as the rest of the kingdom," Lady Cera said. "Whoever it was *will* be brought to justice."

Leargan met the half-elfin duke's eyes again and gave a curt nod, which Jorrin returned.

"Do you think she's a servant who has run away?" Lady Aimil asked.

"Her clothes were poor, at best," Leargan said.

"But just soiled, their quality was not all that poor," the duchess said. "They were irreparable. I've had the offending things thrown out. Even if she *is* a servant, she should've been better cared for. She can't be very old."

"No. Seventeen or eighteen turns, no more," the Rider

said, biting her bottom lip.

Tristan nodded. "Age is hard to determine even through magic, but I agree."

"I will take care of her," Roduch said.

Another vow.

Although Leargan hadn't moved from his side, Roduch's back was to them again. The knight caressed the back of the girl's hand with his thumb, leaning in to push the ebony curls from her face with a gentleness that belied his size.

"I know you will, my friend," Leargan said.

Tristan and Jorrin exchanged a look with their wives, and Ansley Fraser shifted on her feet, when Leargan met her eyes.

He shrugged and looked back at the two lords. He'd never seen Roduch like this either. This girl—she meant something to his fellow knight.

Roduch only had eyes for her.

"When will she wake?" his friend asked.

"Hopefully in the morning, but I wouldn't be surprised if it was early afternoon. Her body's healed. She won't be scarred or sore anymore, but sleep needs to finish the job," Lord Dagget said.

"I will stay with her."

No one contradicted him.

Leargan nodded and met Roduch's eyes. The big knight relaxed into the chair even more.

"When she wakes, I want to be summoned," Tristan ordered.

Roduch nodded over his shoulder before turning back to his charge.

"Morag will tend to anything she needs," Lady Cera said. "Don't mind my headwoman, if she fusses at you, Roduch. She will. If you think your place is here, it is. And you have the healer's blessing or you wouldn't be permitted to stay."

Tristan nodded as he gained his feet, pulling his wife

to his side.

"Good night," Roduch whispered.

After murmured goodnights, the six of them stepped out into the corridor.

Lady Aimil closed the door quietly, before slipping her arm around Tristan's waist. He'd gotten his color back, but he looked drained.

The healing lord swallowed back a yawn no one missed, but he smiled.

"Blessed Spirit, he's awfully protective of someone he doesn't even know," the duke whispered.

"I'd noticed," Leargan said.

The Rider stood close to him, and he forced himself to look at his lord, and ignore the urge to yank her to his side.

Where's that coming from?

Both couples stood arms entwined, and he tried to ignore the picture of him and his old captain's daughter touching in his mind.

"But…" tumbled out of Leargan's mouth.

"But what?" Jorrin asked.

"Roduch has a little magic."

"Go on…" Lady Cera prompted, gray gaze sharp.

The duke's eyes narrowed. *Why did I not know this?* His eyes asked.

Leargan bit back a wince. Roduch wasn't comfortable with his gift. How many times had he heard that as a lad? Even when his magic had been helpful, and one of Roduch's visions had saved them.

Despite keeping secrets for a close friend, he should've told his lord. Jorrin had a right to know what *all* the Knights of Greenwald were capable of. But somehow, Leargan was still leery of revealing Roduch's secret. He forced words out of his mouth. "He sees things. Visions. Since we were lads. He can't control them. Sometimes the past, sometimes the future. He's told me it's hard to discern. He's not comfortable. Never willingly accesses his magic. It's physically disorienting. Roduch has told me he doesn't know what brings it on, but they've saved my hide—my men's and the king's—a time or two, so I keep his secret. I'm not sure even the rest of the guard knows. Perhaps he sees something of the girl he has yet to reveal."

Five sets of eyes stared at Leargan.

Jorrin didn't look angry as he absorbed his speech, but said nothing.

Tristan and the women all looked pensive.

"My aunt has visions," Lady Cera said. "But she's very powerful and always in control. My mother, as well, had them, though not as strongly."

Leargan nodded; he'd heard that Lady Lenore—Duchess of the Province of Tarvis—was a powerful oracle, among other things.

"He's never trained?" Tristan asked.

"Only the sword." He met the healer's hazel eyes.

"Unhoned magic can be dangerous," Jorrin said, dark brow drawn.

"I'd agree, if it was more than visions, but it's not," Leargan said. "Especially since he doesn't use it. Or try to."

"I agree." Tristan nodded.

"We can sort the rest out in the morning," Lady Aimil said, tightening her grip on her husband's waist as he swayed.

Leargan took a step forward to assist, but the healer put a palm up.

"I'm fine, but seeking my bed is necessary." With further assurance he needed no assistance, he slipped his arm around Lady Aimil's shoulders. The couple headed down the corridor away from them.

"I'd like to say the same, but it seems I've other business." Jorrin turned to Ansley Fraser and gave a half-bow, offering a charming smile.

The girl blushed scarlet and something akin to jealousy tightened Leargan's gut. He pushed it away and chided himself.

"You've a message for me?" the duke prompted when

she said nothing.

"Aye." The Rider produced a small scroll, placing it in his outstretched hand.

"I've heard so much about you, Mistress Fraser. It's so nice to finally meet you."

She touched her cheek and smiled. "And I of you, my lord, but please call me Ansley."

"Please call me Jorrin."

"Oh, Ansley, I'm so glad to see you!" Lady Cera hugged her friend. "When are going back to Terraquist? You have to stay until the baby comes."

"The king has given me leave for a visit."

"Wonderful!"

The two women chatted for a few moments, and Leargan couldn't tear his eyes away from the vision that was his captain's daughter. Her blue-green eyes and gorgeous face lit up, as she laughed with the duchess.

"It's late, love. You need to get off your feet. Tristan said it'll help with preventing more false labor," the duke said.

"False labor?" Ansley's voice was concerned.

Lady Cera scrunched up her nose and nodded. "We were up all night last night. No baby, obviously." She patted her distended tummy.

"Oh my. By all means, get to bed then, Cera."

Jorrin slipped his arm around his wife's shoulders and pulled her to his side. "I'll review the message tonight. The king said it was urgent?"

"He did." The Rider nodded.

Leargan was intrigued with the change in her expression. Concern for her friend melted into seriousness, as she discussed the scroll; her duties. She cared deeply for her role.

She squared her shoulders and her green cloak shifted. When she caught him looking at her, Ansley smiled shyly.

His stomach fluttered, and he made himself look

away as heat crept up his neck.

"Goodnight, Leargan."

Jorrin's voice made him jump and he swallowed.

The duke shot him a knowing glance, and he bit back a groan.

"I'll brief you on the scroll in the morning if need be," his lord said.

Damn empathic magic.

Leargan was transparent, whether he wanted to be or not.

The duke's gift allowed him to literally *feel* other people's emotions. The closer he was to a person, the more he felt for them, the stronger his ability. They were like brothers, really. As he was with the guard, so Jorrin knew him very well, indeed.

"Understood." Leargan forced a nod.

"I'll call a maid to show Ansley to a room and order her a bath," Lady Cera said.

"Don't go to any trouble." The Rider gestured and shook her head.

"It's not trouble. You need to rest as much as the girl in that room. A bath will loosen your muscles. I remember long runs well. It's hard on the body."

The duke laughed. "Don't argue with her."

Ansley smirked. "I know all about that."

"I'll do it." Leargan's voice startled him and he almost fidgeted

The duchess smiled. "Put her on the far end; it's the nicest room."

Leargan nodded.

The Lady and Lord of Greenwald slipped down the wide hallway, their conversation too low to hear.

"Thank you, Sir Tegran. I don't want to be any trouble."

"You're not. *At all.* You saved that girl's life tonight. If you hadn't found her, she wouldn't have lasted until morning."

"Well, Ali found her. But thank you." Again, a shy smile curved her lips, her cheeks stained pink.

She's blushing? Why?

And why did it please him?

She glanced at the door to the girl's room. "Will she be all right?"

"She's safe, and Roduch will protect her."

"That I believe."

The black wolf sidled up to them, leaning into the Rider's thigh and destroying his concentration on her mistress's lovely face. The beast put him on edge, though he was long comfortable with wolves in the castle. Both of his ladies were bonded to wolves.

Ansley's Ali didn't like him. Leargan could feel it in his bones. The hair stood up at the back of his neck. He made split-second contact with Ali's yellow eyes, but forced his away, not wanting her to think he was challenging her.

Ali growled.

"Ali, no." Ansley's voice stopped the noise coming from the beast, but it took all he was made of not to shift on his feet. She patted the wolf's head, but it was admonition, not caress.

"She doesn't trust me."

"Sorry, Sir Tegran, she doesn't trust anyone but me."

"Leargan. Please call me Leargan."

Her cheeks went crimson again and he smiled.

Leargan took her hand and tucked her arm into his elbow. "Let's get you to your room. It's late."

Ansley looked around the lavish guestroom Leargan had shown her to.

A young maid had met them at the door and introduced herself as Daicy. She was a pretty and petite, with dark honey locks and brown eyes. Even at the late hour, her clothing was crisp, her hair partially covered with a white linen kerchief. Her skirt and tunic were tan in color, covered by a white apron.

Daicy promised she would be back with hot water.

The large tub had been placed in front of the fireplace for warmth, instead of in the sizable privy in the corner of the room.

Sir Leargan had taken his leave then. Ansley had had a hard time *not* staring at his retreating figure, especially the tight breeches that hugged his rear and muscled legs.

She rubbed her arm, and the touch reminded her of his fingertips brushing her skin.

The knight's presence in Greenwald wasn't a surprise. Her father had told her he was the captain of Cera and her husband's personal guard, but she'd never imagined he'd be one of the first people she'd meet.

He has no idea who you are.

Ansley sighed. It didn't matter anyway. Sir Leargan Tegran had nothing to do with her assignment.

Leargan had been a girlhood crush. Over the turns, she'd tried to forget her childish fantasies regarding the handsome knight. *And failed.*

He still made her heart flutter and her stomach jump with only a thought. And why was she thinking of *him* anyway? Ansley should be focused on that poor girl.

Repeated rapes.

More beatings than what had been evident on her body tonight.

Thank the Blessed Spirit Lord Dagget had been able to heal her.

"Who hurt her?" The phrase reverberated in her mind as worry seized her gut.

The girl's body was healed. But her mind?

Moving passed what she'd been through would take a long time. Ansley shuddered, wrapping her arms around her waist.

Cera had magic at her disposal. Surely, her men would find the person who had hurt the dark-haired girl.

Hopefully when she woke, she could give Cera's husband information.

Ali wuffed, and Ansley threw her a glance. Her bond had claimed the large bed, lying at its center.

She went to the trunk at the foot of the ornate bedframe, laying her hunter green Senior Rider cloak down with care. After plopping down on the bed, she threw her arms around her wolf. "You growled at him, you naughty girl," she chided, smiling into Ali's soft mane.

Her bond whined and licked her ear. The she-wolf whimpered and nuzzled her side before curling up against Ansley's body.

A knock on the door made her sit up. "Come in."

Ali lifted her large head, but Ansley's bondmate made no move to exit the bed.

Stay. She thought-sent the command. If the she-wolf remained still and visible, it would probably make Daicy feel better.

The staff at Greenwald should be used to seeing wolves, since there were two in residence, but Ansley wanted to be safe.

Being bonded to a wolf, or any other kind of beast, wasn't uncommon, especially among the messengers of the King's Riders. Even Senior Riders tended to be young and were expected to travel vast distances, most of the time alone.

Any beast with relative intelligence, sharp teeth and claws, was handy for protection, even though Riders were all trained with the sword and bow.

Ali had been a gift from Ansley's father three turns before, when she'd achieved the rank of Senior Rider.

Daicy was back, along with the headwoman and two lads about twelve. They all carried steaming buckets of water and filed into the room.

Morag was pleasantly plump, rather pretty and had her graying, brown hair in a thick neat plait down her back, just like Ansley's own.

The lads, one blond and the other his opposite, with black hair, both displayed lopsided grins she couldn't help but return.

Was everyone chipper, despite the late hour?

Maybe Cera ran an overnight shift of servants regularly.

They dumped the water into the large tub, and Daicy smiled at Ansley. "That should do it, mistress."

Steam rose idly from the tub. *Inviting.* Ansley couldn't wait to get into it. *So, a bath isn't a bad idea after all.* Her limbs and back ached. Cera was right. She needed a good soak.

The lads scampered out of the room, their wooden pails knocking together.

Ansley bit her bottom lip to keep back another grin as Morag muttered something about rascals being worse late at night.

"The beast is on the bed?" The disapproval in the woman's voice swung Ansley's gaze back to her. Morag wiped her hands on her white apron, glaring at Ali.

She bit back the urge to gulp. With squared shoulders, and mouth a hard line, the woman was the picture of authority but different than she'd been when caring for the injured girl. This expression was irritated.

"Mistress, shall I stay to assist with your bath?" Daicy asked, a knowing glint in her brown eyes.

"Oh, no, that won't be necessary," Ansley answered, but she wanted to thank the maid for the distraction.

"Shall I bring you something to eat?" Daicy asked.

"Thank you, but not now. I want to bathe and get some sleep. I rode all night from Terraquist."

Both women nodded and took their leave.

Ansley's breath exited on a whoosh as she slipped into the water. The warmth enveloped her, and she sank against the side of the tub, arms resting on the edges. She let the heat take the tension from her hard ride out of her muscles.

Leargan.

His handsome form danced into her mind. Ebony hair hung past his shoulders in soft waves she longed to touch. His eyes were the darkest brown she'd ever seen, and always so warm.

Like honey at midnight.

His naturally golden skin, denoting that he was originally from the Province of Ascova, made her want to run her fingertips over every inch of it.

Everything appealed; chiseled face, muscular body, height. Not as tall as her father or the king, but he was probably an inch or so past six feet. *Perfect.*

Looks aside, he was every bit a knight. A wonderful, chivalrous, honorable warrior. And Ansley wanted him as much as she ever had.

Her stomach flipped.

A huge yawn and a wave of fatigue washed over her. She needed to wrap up her bath before the water cooled.

She scrubbed her hair with sweet-smelling soap and rinsed it from her body.

After drying off with a linen bath sheet, she slipped into the soft chemise Daicy had left for her, caressing the diaphanous fabric as it settled over her body.

Ali wuffed a complaint when Ansley shoved the wolf over so she could climb into the oversized bed, but she grinned and ignored her bond's bluster.

With another yawn she couldn't hold back, she yanked up the thick sleeping furs.

So soft and warm.

The she-wolf curled into Ansley's body, as soon as they both settled.

She glanced up at the carved decorative ceiling of her temporary quarters. Armored and mailed knights sat on powerful steeds, preparing for an unknown battle, flags waving.

Perhaps she would dream of her own knight, Sir Leargan Tegran.

"It wouldn't matter anyway. *Not* yours," Ansley

whispered.

Blessed Spirit, she was doomed.

chapter three

Roduch's visions had come to life. She lay peacefully on the bed that dwarfed her form. Memories of images teased his mind, the picture in his head so different from the woman in front of him. Even healed, her skin lacked the luster of happiness she'd always exuded when he'd dreamt of her.

No matter what he tried, he couldn't get the pictures out of his head that had woken him just that morning. The vision rocked him with disturbing clarity, the girl's smooth pale skin begging for a caress as she threw her head back and laughed at something he'd whispered in her ear.

What he'd said was a mystery, but his eyes had been locked onto the hollow of her throat. He'd burned to kiss her there. And then he'd pressed a kiss to her lips.

One kiss normally would lead to two, and… He'd done that, and much more in other visions.

Tonight…he'd finally met her in reality.

Beaten.

Bruised and broken.

Raped.

Mixed emotions hit him in a wave, his stomach twisting, grinding his heart into pieces. The organ that should be in his chest had taken up residence in his gut from the moment he'd seen her in a tattered, damaged ball on the side of the road.

This girl, beautiful enigma, was supposed to be his wife. His heart told him as much, though his dreams had never confirmed it.

She'd been in his visions — his cursed magic — since he was a lad, but he didn't even know her name.

Since he'd come to live in Greenwald—accepting the position as one of the Aldern personal guard the very moment Leargan had asked him—the images had been much more frequent.

Roduch used to get a flash, a tease. The past several months had left him with whole scenes—as if he was reading a book, with occasional conversation, though he couldn't always make it out. If they weren't speaking, or she wasn't laughing, Roduch would see them making love, her face flushed pink, her lithe body bared beneath his. Desire would overwhelm him, even when awake.

Each was a reminder of what he didn't have, and since he'd recently begun his twenty-fifth turn, he was convinced he'd never meet her. It was odd, how much he could ache to hold her in his arms and not even know her.

A place that was never fulfilled, even by the occasional lovers he'd taken. He might have held them close momentarily, but this girl—dark curly-haired beauty—would always hold *him*.

He sighed, stubble grazing his palm, as he dragged a hand down his face.

Now that she was in front of him, Roduch felt farther away from her than ever before. His gaze rested on their joined hands. So small, her palm resting against his. Soft. Pale. In need of protection.

Cursing under his breath, he clenched his jaw. Pain shot up into his teeth. He'd find who had *dared* hurt her and rip them to shreds.

Nonnegotiable.

No one would hurt her again.

When she woke, he'd voice his vow.

Roduch must've fallen asleep in the chair, because the rustling of bed linens jolted him awake. His lower back and neck ached. After shifting and taking a breath, he met the greenest orbs he'd ever seen, even more so than the Greenwald knighted mage, young Lucan.

She gasped when she realized he was awake, yanking

her hand out of his and scrambling back against the carved headboard, knees drawn to her chest. She wrapped her arms tight, making herself smaller, and glancing around the room frantically.

She's going to bolt, first chance she gets.

"Wait." Roduch kept his voice low, raising flat palms. "I won't hurt you."

The lass froze and stared. "Where am I?" The whisper was so low he'd almost missed it.

"Castle Aldern. We found you in the middle of the road. You collapsed in my arms. Asked for help," he spoke softly, making no moves. He was a large man, but she had nothing to fear from him, *ever.*

She whimpered. Her gaze was locked onto his hands, and she trembled.

Damn, she's scared.

His heart flipped, and he forced another breath. She *couldn't* fear him. "I won't hurt you," he repeated. "*Ever.*" He wanted to touch her, but she'd just shy away. She wasn't ready.

The girl looked around the room again, this time a bit slower. "What's your name?" she whispered, but avoided his eyes.

"Sir Roduch Grantham, one of the twelve knights of Lord and Lady Aldern's personal guard." He gave a small bow from his seat. Standing was a bad idea.

She was likely nervous of his size while seated, so he'd terrify her if he straightened, all six-feet-five-inches of him.

"You're a knight?" Gorgeous green eyes wide, the girl looked torn between horror and awe.

"Aye. I'm from Terraquist, formerly one of King Nathal's knights."

"I was rescued by a knight?" She glanced at him sharply when he chuckled, but her shoulders loosened, and she let her legs fall to the bed. She was still pressed into the corner, but she reached for the furs, snatching them away when Roduch leaned in to help.

He tried not to be offended that she made sure they didn't touch. "Actually, you were rescued by a Senior King's Rider, several knights, a half a dozen men-at-arms, and a squire in training. Mistress Ansley Fraser found you first. The men and I were on patrol when we rode up on the both of you. I got to you as fast as I could."

The lass finally looked at him, and he fell into her eyes. He swallowed. Her black curls were disheveled, but it didn't take away from his instant attraction to her. Her face was still flushed pink from sleep, and Roduch ached to touch her. "What's your name?" he breathed, ordering his hands to remain in his lap.

She shook her head, and her front teeth sank into her full bottom lip.

He reached for her hand, but she scooted even further away from him. "It's all right. I promise you're safe here. *No one* will hurt you ever again." After berating himself for reaching out when he'd known better, Roduch threaded his fingers together and planted them on his thigh.

Silence descended, and he called himself every curse word he could think of. He'd ruined what tiny bit of progress he'd made with her.

"Avril." Her voice was barely above a whisper, and she averted her eyes.

"Avril," Roduch echoed, one corner of his mouth lifting.

My wife's name is Avril.

But as he met her gaze, he saw the long road ahead of them. She wouldn't be his until she healed. He'd be by her side, no matter how long it took. As much as he detested his magic, it was never wrong. Avril was meant to be his.

She spread her fingers, then hands, looking at her arms. She touched her face, her stomach, small breasts lifting with one breath, then two as she inhaled deeply. Avril closed her eyes and stretched like a cat.

He watched as memories from his past visions teased.

Roduch had seen her move like that many times.

Naked. With him moving over her, with her. He gulped.

Wretch.

She'd been through hell, and all he could think about was her being bared to him?

"My wounds...they're gone. I'm not hurting now. Where are my clothes?" Avril whispered, staring down at the soft beige chemise. She reached for the fabric, as if it was the finest gown. "Who...who...dressed me?" Her cheeks went an adorable shade of pink.

He couldn't hold back his smile. "The Headwoman, Morag. Lord Dagget healed you. Lady Aldern threw your clothes out. She'll have them replaced. They were beyond repair."

Avril's hands stopped their exploration of the linen. Her eyes went wide again. "A...a...*lord* healed me?" she whimpered. Her small fist balled up the chemise at her stomach, her already-pale skin as white as the bed linens.

"Avril? Are you all right?"

She ignored him. "*The* Lady of Greenwald will get me new clothes?" Muttering, she shook her head, dark curls bobbing, and her knuckles blanched from her tight grip. Then she quivered. As she met his eyes again, she jolted, as if she remembered she wasn't alone. Avril cleared her throat. "I am fine, Sir Grantham." Her voice was steady, and he had to admire that she'd gotten herself together so quickly, even if she really had nothing to fear.

His instincts tingled. She was far from *fine*. It was all a mask. They'd just *officially* met, but it bothered him she wore it with him. *Immensely.*

"Just Roduch," he whispered. He reached for her hand. She didn't pull away, so he squeezed gently.

Her eyes darted there and then back to his face.

He offered a small smile, but her shoulders didn't relax. Roduch wanted her to open up, needed to find out who'd hurt her, but she had to trust someone first. They'd made progress, but not nearly enough.

Would she answer him if he discreetly questioned her?

"What happened to you?" he whispered.

"What do you mean?"

"Who hurt you, Avril?"

Silence descended again.

He cursed under his breath. Being direct had pushed her too far. He loosened his hold and her fingers slipped away.

She wrung her hands and scooted as far away as possible. Avril paled out even more and drew her knees to her chest like she had before. She studied the bed linens, her small frame heaving. "My husband."

His chest ached when she wouldn't look at him. Sharp daggers pierced with each breath. Rage boiled his blood. He was torn between anger and crushing pain.

She was already married.

Belonged to someone else. She was supposed to be *his*.

A man who should've sheltered and protected had harmed her.

He growled. "I *will* kill him," Roduch whispered.

Avril scooted to the edge of the bed, kneeling in front of him. She grabbed his arm, pulling him back to reality when her nails bit into his skin.

Damn, he must've spoken aloud.

"Kill him?" she croaked, tears spilling down her cheeks. A tremor racked her diminutive body. "You would do that for me?" Awe and admiration wrapped her words.

He froze, every fiber in his being wanted to pull her in his arms, but he couldn't. She'd recede even further. Even though her expression was the most open he'd seen it. He couldn't overwhelm her like that. "Did he rape you?" Roduch demanded. He bit back a groan as she winced.

Cheeks very red, Avril looked down, took a breath, then met his gaze. Her jaw was tight. "Yes," she whispered. "Ever since I was fourteen." The toughness in her expression faltered. Tears cascaded again, and he couldn't take it anymore.

He slid onto the bed and pulled her into his arms as gently as he could. "Dammit," he whispered.

She didn't wrap her arms around him, but she didn't yank away, either. She buried her face against his tunic, but sobs reached his ears as they shuddered through her.

He held her, rubbing her back tentatively at first, then with more soothing pressure when she didn't protest. She was so tiny and perfect.

How could someone hurt her?

Roduch didn't tell her not to cry. Avril deserved the reprieve the tears might bring. Instinct told him she never cried over what'd happened to her. Her mask, her inner toughness, wouldn't allow it. She needed to grieve, as sure as she would if someone had died. He bit back curse after curse, plotting the murder of the man she called husband.

The bastard would die. And it wouldn't be pleasant.

A dull sword, hell, maybe just a shovel and a stake. His bollocks would be the first to go.

Her tears were hot on his skin as her arms shot around his neck, and she pulled herself even closer.

Roduch tucked her under his chin and rested his cheek against her dark curls, inhaling her scent. Small, firm breasts pressed into his chest, and he threatened to lop off his manhood if it so much as stirred. "You're safe with me, I promise," he whispered to distract his thoughts — and his blood — from diving into forbidden territory.

Blessed Spirit, he wished he was holding her under different circumstances.

Avril's body shifted against his, as if she'd taken a breath, and she met his eyes. His fingers itched to wipe her tears. However, he didn't want her to pull away from him, so he kept his hands still.

"Will you really kill him?" she whispered.

"I would kill anyone who dared hurt you," Roduch said.

A vow.

Does she understand?

She gasped. "Why?"

He stared, his tongue thick. Couldn't very well tell her of his visions. Magic was commonplace, but what would she think if he admitted he'd been dreaming of her for turns? Even if she had magic, she'd think he was daft.

"I will always protect you," he forced out finally.

Her cheeks went crimson again. Avril sniffed and swiped at her nose. She closed her eyes as if she was trying to gather her thoughts.

He beat her to it, words tumbling from his mouth. "How old are you? You don't even look old enough to have a husband."

She made no move to leave his embrace, and her lips twitched.

His heart skipped. It wasn't like the brilliant smiles in his visions, but it was start.

"I've been eighteen for two months, but I married when I was four and ten." Her voice shook, and she made a fist against his chest.

Fourteen? Married at *fourteen*?

Roduch *would* kill the bastard. His blood simmered and he tamped a growl so he wouldn't scare her. "Four and ten is not legally old enough to marry."

"It is when your parents arrange it." Her eyes narrowed. For the first time, her voice had an angry edge.

Good. He wanted her angry instead of weeping. "They forced you?"

Her eyes welled up again, and Avril bit her lip, nodding.

Roduch waited for her to compose herself. "You do not wish to stay married?"

"I have a choice? No one…has ever asked me that." She sniffled and shook her head. "Nay, I do not."

He swallowed the breath of relief he was about to release. She couldn't know just yet what her answer had meant to him. "Good. You don't have to remain married to him anymore."

Chapter Four

"What do you mean?" Heart pounding, Avril stared into the huge knight's crystal blue eyes. His heat surrounded her, but she forced herself to sit still. Instinct told her to burrow into him. He would keep her safe. *Forever.* She reared back, chiding herself for foolishness.

Am I crazy?

Maybe she'd finally lost her mind, like Tynan always accused.

Why was she practically on the man's lap anyway?

Letting him hold her?

She gulped, but couldn't bring herself to scoot away. She hadn't felt so safe in turns. *Four* turns to be exact. The very amount of time she'd thrown away to a husband who did nothing but abuse her.

Why had she admitted that to Sir Grantham?

The words had fallen from her mouth. Like he'd used truth magic on her. She couldn't *not* tell him. But she sensed no magic from the oversized knight.

She *always* sensed magic. Especially since they were touching. It was a part of her powers. The *blasted* part Tynan valued.

The only thing she had of worth, since she'd failed to give him children. Avril shuddered, slamming the door shut on those thoughts.

Sir Grantham studied her, as if he could tell he'd unsettled her.

No, this man had good instincts but no magic.

His warm hand still rested on her back. He made no move to draw her closer, but she had to shout a mental command for her body to remain where it was.

She wanted to snuggle into a man she didn't know.

What is wrong with me?

His pale hair resembled straw, shaggy, could use a haircut, but she liked it. Wide, sculpted jaw was in a need of a shave, but the growth new, he normally went clean shaven.

How could she know that about a handsome knight she'd never met? Avril looked into his light blue eyes. *Beautiful.* High cheekbones and a cleft in his chin that added to his attraction.

Attraction?

She'd never been *attracted* to a man. Experience spoke that men hurt, men controlled. Especially those who were physically large.

Despite the fact he was sitting, she could tell he was very tall, broad shouldered. Being up against his chest told her his body was packed with hard muscle. Like a wall.

She'd look like a dwarf—or an elf—standing next to him. No chance of fighting him if he wanted to rape her.

Nay.

He wouldn't do that.

Confidence rose up and wrapped around her with a vehemence she didn't dare question. Avril had her own instincts. And they told her Sir Roduch Grantham had spoken the truth when he'd said he wouldn't harm her.

"Do you live within the Province of Greenwald?" Sir Roduch asked. His voice was firm and even. Grounded her.

"Yes," Avril whispered.

"You were married underage. Now that you're eight and ten, you can declare yourself to your duke—Lord Jorrin Aldern—that you were unable to consent to your marriage, and you no longer want to remain married to the bastard."

Bastard was putting it mildly where Tynan was concerned.

"I can do that?" she croaked. Her pulse thundered in her ears.

"Aye. It's the law. He cannot force you to stay wedded to him."

Her vision wobbled as his words washed over her.

Tynan can't force me to remain his wife.

Avril bit her bottom lip until the tang of her own blood greeted her tongue. She shook against the large man's warmth, sucking in one breath, then two. Had he not been cradling her against him, she would've passed out.

"Avril. Avril. Avril."

Swallowing a sob, she met those pale eyes. Her name on his lips was just as jarring as his revelation. Words evaporated, and she sank into his intense gaze, reading all sorts of emotions that didn't make sense. *Feelings* Avril refused to acknowledge. *You don't know me* was on the tip of her tongue, but the phrase wouldn't pass her lips.

When his hand restarted the slow soothing circles along the length of her back, she let him, moving closer instead of away. Somehow, she was helpless to do otherwise, resting her cheek against his heart. The steady *thump thump* made her feel even better.

Tynan had never tried to hold her—not that she would've wanted him to, even at the beginning.

Suddenly, everything clicked in Avril's mind. Her husband had kept her virtually locked up since her birthday two months before. The beatings and rapes had increased. He'd been angrier with her, though she'd been a model wife, doing whatever he'd ordered. She'd stayed out of his way, and hadn't met his gaze more than once.

She'd forced premonition after premonition, and done anything else he'd commanded requiring the use of her magic. Anything to keep his hands off her and his manhood out of her. Not that it'd helped—much. Her husband took her whenever he wanted. If she so much as whimpered, Tynan reminded her it was his *right*.

When her monthly had started yet again, he'd beaten her until her ribs cracked. The pain had made her pass out. She'd woken in a pool of her own blood the next morning.

Avril had lost count of how many times that'd happened. None of the servants ever cleaned her up, lest his rage be turned onto them.

Yet another month and she'd still failed to conceive. There was no hiding it from him. She'd never gotten pregnant over the course of her marriage, but she'd thanked the Blessed Spirit every month when her bleeding started.

Tynan would eventually kill her. He was cruel to the servants he kept in his household, and even to the animals he owned. His dogs cowered. Children would be no different, no matter blood ties. And he'd promised if she delivered him a girl-child, the babe wouldn't have more than one breath anyway.

She shivered, squeezing her eyes shut against Sir Roduch.

He squeezed his arms around her, saying nothing. But he didn't have to; his heartbeat was as soothing as his caress.

Safe. Warm.

He would actually kill Tynan.

Avril swallowed.

"I would rather make you a widow than have you renounce your marriage," he murmured, as if he'd read her mind.

What can I say to that?

She could have justice. He was a knight, lived by a code. She had witnesses now to what'd happened to her. There'd be no legal consequences if Sir Roduch killed Tynan.

Plotting a man's death — her husband no less — should make her feel guilt, sorrow, something…but Avril was only greeted with relief. Tynan would never hurt her again.

Had she finally slipped into evil, also as the man had accused her time after time?

Heartless…frigid?

No.

She wouldn't let him be right about *anything* concerning her. Her husband's death would be justice.

Won't it?

The door opened, and she flew out of the knight's arms, heat creeping into her cheeks. An apology hovered on her lips when her back touched the wood of the headboard, but she couldn't push it out. Her body chilled without his warmth surrounding her.

Their gazes collided, and her face burned even more.

Sir Roduch's eyes were wide, but he smiled gently. Something flickered in his gaze, and Avril's heart skipped. But it was gone so fast, she'd probably imagined it.

She ignored the urge to reach for his hand, her stomach jumping.

"Oh, she's awake," a female voice said brightly.

Tearing her eyes away from her knight, she took in the older woman. Ample hips, graying brown hair in a long plait, and soft green eyes went well with her friendly smile.

Behind her was a younger woman, a girl really, not much older than Avril. She had dark hair in braided pigtails and tugged the white kerchief on top of her head straight as she curtsied.

Avril relaxed and let Sir Roduch take her hand when he reached for it. His calloused fingers brushed her wrist, and she felt a calming rush. Her eyes shot to his. How had he done that with no magic?

His tentative smile made her squirm.

The older woman bustled around the room, pouring steaming water into a small wash basin. "Go fetch Lord Dagget," she told the girl.

The maid's pigtails bounced with her nod, but she turned to Avril. "I'm Meara and I'll be right back. I'm for you." The girl grinned, flashing dimples.

"Oh, go, troublesome lass," the older woman said, but the tone of her admonition was affectionate. "You'll have time to visit later."

Sir Roduch chuckled, the deep sound making Avril glance at him. The sound was appealing. She wanted…to smile. He winked, and her cheeks seared.

"I'm Morag, Headwoman here. Your name?" The woman continued to move around the room, opening the heavy drapes over two floor-to-ceiling windows.

She squinted against the new brightness. "Avril."

This woman was in control of her surroundings, duties.

Avril couldn't refuse. As she watched her work, she sensed magic from the woman. Nothing specific to reveal the headwoman's main talent, but she felt heat, so the woman probably had a good handle on fire magic.

"Nice to meet you, Avril-lass," Morag said. Her soft expression faded as she turned to Sir Roduch. "You can go now. See to your duties. The men are already about the yard."

Avril bit back a wince. Headwoman or not, how could Morag order a knight about?

His jaw locked, and she shivered, tugging her hand out of his.

Sir Roduch let her go, without looking away from the older woman.

Her earlier confidence that the large man wouldn't hurt her danced into her mind. Would he get angry? Was the headwoman now in danger?

Panic rushed. But she chided herself when she recognized she wasn't afraid he'd hurt Morag—he wouldn't. She couldn't fathom him leaving the room, leaving her. A shout of '*no*,' threatened to jump out of her mouth.

"I'm staying here," he said the moment she opened her mouth.

Avril's breath exited on a whoosh.

He won't leave me.

Her knight's long arms were crossed over his broad chest, and his tone was even and calm. He wasn't angry at the headwoman, just irritated. His fair brow was furrowed, his shoulders tight.

Tynan had lost his temper for much less. A woman ordering him about would've been a death sentence.

Morag tsked, but turned away from him, gesturing dismissively. "Anything you need, lass?"

Avril blinked. She pushed away the chaos relating to Sir Roduch.

Get it together, Avril.

She bit her bottom lip. When was the last time someone asked her what *she* needed? "I..." she cleared her throat. "I could use a privy." Her voice shook. She wiped away tears when Morag smiled.

"Of course. This great brute didn't show you where you can relieve yourself?" she asked, shaking her head.

The low growl Sir Roduch emitted shook Avril.

When she met his pretty eyes, one corner of his mouth lifted. He was amused. The headwoman was just a fusser.

"Oh, leave off him, Morag. He's been worried." A dark-haired man stepped into sight, shaking his head and laughing. His embroidered, brushed leather doublet was dark brown, his breeches a shade lighter, and the pale green tunic beneath had to be silk. Even his tan boots were impeccable.

"As you say, milord," Morag answered, bowing.

The maid Meara came in whistling and carrying a heavily laden tray. The scent of fresh sweet bread and rich broth tickled Avril's nose.

Her stomach growled, and Sir Roduch smiled.

"You can eat soon," he whispered, squeezing her hand.

"Come, lass. Lord Dagget can look at you when you're done, then we can get some food into you." The headwoman gestured for her to follow, and Avril scrambled off the bed.

She didn't need the healer. Her cursory stretch had told her all was well in her body. Her side, which had plagued her for months after some of Tynan's kicks, didn't even hurt anymore. She felt better than she had in turns.

When she was done in the privy, the low tones of the two men greeted her ears before she shut the door, Morag on her heels.

"...hasn't told me everything I need to know," Sir Roduch was saying.

Heat crept up Avril's neck. How much had he told the healer? Would everyone know all about her? She winced and ended up tripping over her feet.

The large knight was at her side in seconds, his hand swallowing her upper arm. But his grip didn't hurt. "Are you all right, Avril?"

She met his crystal eyes and her heart thumped as her gaze trailed his frame. "I'm...I'm fine, thank you." He was huge indeed. She barely came up to his shoulder.

Sir Roduch lifted and carried her to the bed as if she hadn't answered him.

Her face burned even more when he set her down as if she weighed nothing. Avril met the healer's eyes.

He smiled, and amusement rolled off him.

She looked away as her magic surged in reaction to his. He was *powerful.* More so than any other healer she'd ever met.

His aura was bright and pale, and it glowed around his tall, slim form.

Most of the time, she had to concentrate to read an aura, but the healer had so much magic it was overt, as if it rested on the surface of his skin. It was thick, almost gold. This man was not only a healer, his soul was clean. He cared for people and had a pure heart.

A good man.

"Avril, this is Lord Tristan Dagget. He healed you last

night. He won't hurt you," Sir Roduch said, his voice low and gentle. He must've misinterpreted the reason she'd shied away.

"Thank you," she whispered, meeting the lord's warm hazel gaze. This man was gentle, too. Strong of body and mind, but a healer through and through.

The lord nodded and reached for her hand.

She couldn't refuse him. Calm washed over her the moment their fingers touched, and Avril sighed.

"How are you feeling this morning?"

"Good. Better than before," she said, looking down. He *knew*.

His magic would've told him every bit of her physical history. Embarrassment warred with the artificial serenity his healing powers were pushing on her.

It's all right. Let the magic relax you.

His mental speech tickled her mind with the thought-send. Soothing, like his words moments before.

I'm sorry, Avril thought-sent back.

His kind smile dismissed her need for an apology. The healer's skin glowed as he probed her, gripping both her hands.

Heat washed over her, and Avril sank into the softness of the bed, letting Lord Dagget search for what he would.

"There we are," he said, pulling her into a sitting position what seemed hours later.

Her limbs were languid; her whole body was warm, as if she'd just gotten out of a hot bath. Comfortable and safe, Avril sought out the one person who'd been by her side, showing her she wasn't alone anymore.

Sir Roduch.

Lord Dagget took a step back, breaking their physical contact.

Her knight looked nervous.

Avril scooted closer to him, reaching for his hand.

"She's thoroughly patched up," the healer said.

Sir Roduch's broad shoulders shuddered, as if her health mattered to him.

She swallowed. Their eyes locked, and Avril smiled.

He froze, his blue eyes intense.

Her heart sped up when she saw unshed tears.

After entwining their fingers, he brought her hand to his lips, pressing a kiss into her knuckles.

Avril shifted on the edge of the large bed. She forced her gaze away, but looked at the healer. "Thank you, Lord Dagget." She fought for composure, ignoring the emotion her knight had on display.

I don't even know him.

"You're very welcome." His warm smile was infectious, and she smiled for the second time.

"Well, Avril, is it? Nice to meet you. I'm Cera." A very pregnant—but still striking—redhead stepped forward, a smile on her full lips. Her tan gown was plain, but she carried herself with elegance, despite the large tummy.

The duchess.

Beside her was a small woman with dark hair almost as long as she was tall. She wore a shimmery dark green gown with gold leaves embroidered on it. It was fancier than Lady Aldern's.

Who was she?

There was a third woman, also a redhead, but a lighter hue than the duchess', and her hair in a thick plait that fell to her waist. She wore brown breeches and a simple tunic covered by a hunter green jerkin.

The Rider.

Avril owed her thanks for finding her.

When had they entered the room?

She hadn't even heard the door. Her eyes darted over her surroundings. The healer, the three ladies, two maids, plus her knight.

Everyone was looking at her.

Her head swam, and she gripped the bedding with her free hand until her knuckles whitened.

Lord Dagget exchanged a look with Sir Roduch Avril didn't miss, then the knight squeezed the hand that still rested in his.

She took a breath. The small gesture calmed. The room stopped spinning.

"Aimil-love, Cera, Ansley, give her some space," the healer admonished gently, stepping toward the women. "She hasn't even eaten yet."

"I apologize," Lady Aldern said. "I was eager to meet you, and see how you are this morning."

Avril scooted closer to Sir Roduch, wishing he was still on the bed so she could tuck herself into him, which was ridiculous, because none of the ladies meant her any harm.

"I'm...I'm fine." *Manners, Avril.* "Good morning, Lady Aldern? Mistress Fraser? Lady—" She inclined her head to each woman.

Both redheads nodded, confirming Avril's assumption.

"Aimil," the dark-haired girl said. "I'm Tristan's wife." She smiled and gestured to the healer, who reached for her hand.

"I'm sure Avril and Roduch are hungry. They've had a long night. Let's let them eat, and give Avril a chance to bathe," Lord Dagget said.

The knight's shoulders loosened.

She too relaxed a little. Soon, she'd be alone with him again. She could get her bearings. And a bath would be heavenly.

"Of course," Lady Aldern said. "Meara?"

"Yes, milady?" The girl hurried away from the tray of food and curtsied before the duchess.

"Why don't you head down to the stores and find a few things for Avril to wear."

Meara beamed, dimples visible, and nodded, her pigtails bobbing. "Yes, right away, milady."

Lady Aldern's smile lit up her beautiful face.

Lord Dagget and the Rider grinned.

Lady Aimil had her hand to her mouth, as if she was hiding mirth.

Even Sir Roduch looked amused.

Avril studied the girl. She didn't sense much magic, but as she concentrated, Meara's aura flickered into view. Its pale pastels revealed the girl was pure of heart and content. Bubbly. No doubt she rarely went without a smile.

Envy rolled over her. How could a young maid, whose duty was to serve people, be so happy?

"What's your favorite color?" Meara asked, looking straight at Avril.

Gazing into the open, sincere expression, she let go of her ill feelings. The maid was lovely.

Perhaps we can be friends?

Sir Roduch chuckled, the ladies were all grinning again. Only Morag had tsked, but none of the others seemed to pay her any notice.

Avril struggled for words, biting back a gulp. No one had *ever* asked her preferences before. Tynan had bought her three new dresses when they'd gotten married, but he'd picked them out. They'd been what *he'd* wanted her to wear.

Dark colored, drab, and too old for her in style. She'd hated them every time she'd donned one. He'd even thrown out all the gowns she'd brought from home. She'd had the same three garments for four turns. Mended time and time again. Lady Cera had thrown out the gown Avril had worn the most.

"Go on, lass, you can answer her," her knight said, amusement in his tone.

Her eyes darted to his before meeting Meara's light brown orbs. "Umm…I like blue. Light blue."

The maid nodded curtly and left the room whistling.

"I'll have to have a word with that one," the headwoman muttered.

"She's fine, Morag," Lady Cera said.

Morag said nothing, but her brow furrowed. Then she bowed and slipped into the privy room with a bucket of fresh supplies.

"Th-thank you, Lady Aldern," Avril said.

"It's nothing, but you're welcome." She rested a hand on her swollen belly.

"I'll be back to check on you later," Lord Dagget said.

Heat rushed her cheeks, but Avril nodded.

Surreal.

A *lord* had healed her. *The* Lady of Greenwald was getting her new clothes. What could they want from her in return? She couldn't pay them.

"Roduch will send someone to find me, should you need anything," Lady Aldern said. "Morag has already ordered you a bath. You're safe, Avril."

No doubt everyone in the room knew all about her.

Her stomach churned, appetite dissolving.

"Don't worry about anything right now," her knight whispered, as if he could read her mind.

The healer and his wife entwined their hands and took their leave.

Mistress Fraser waited, smiling when Avril's gaze rested on her.

"I'll be back later with Jorrin," Lady Aldern said to Sir Roduch.

He nodded, rising to retrieve the tray of food.

"It was nice to meet you, Avril." With an awkward bow, the duchess excused herself, the Rider on her heels.

She gasped. "Lady…*Lady* Aldern bowed…bowed to me."

Sir Roduch chuckled, returning to his seat and placing the tray of food between them. "You'll find out rather quickly we do things a bit differently around here."

"Oh," she said, but the steaming broth caught her attention, so she didn't mull over his words.

"Ah, good, you're eating. Sir Roduch, give me or Meara a shout when you're both through and we'll get her all cleaned up," the headwoman said, drying her hands on her apron as she exited the sizable privy room. "The tub is ready to go. I'll have the lads bring hot water."

"Thank you, Morag." Her knight inclined his head and the headwoman nodded before heading from the rooms.

Silence descended, but Avril could finally breathe again. She was comfortable with the knight. Being alone with him was natural. Like they'd been acquainted for turns. She watched his hands when he ripped fluffy bread open and spread butter all over it. He was warm and large and safe.

"Hungry?" he asked.

Her eyes shot to his face. One corner of his mouth lifted, and Avril chided herself to calm down. "Yes. Very."

Sir Roduch nodded and handed her a spoon for the broth. "I'm sure Lord Tristan ordered a light meal. Later we'll get something more substantial, if you wish. Some meat."

"It's fine," she said, closing her eyes as she savored the rich taste on her tongue. "It's very good."

He laughed, and she looked up from her bowl, forgetting to take a bite of the sweet bread.

The sound of his deep carefree chuckle was as appealing as he was.

Avril grinned.

Their gazes locked.

His pale eyes blazed with the emotions she refused to name yet again, and Sir Roduch reached for her hand, pressing a kiss into her knuckles without looking away. "Avril," he breathed.

"Yes?"

"Don't stop smiling, all right?"

Her heart thundered. "I'll try not to."

His chest heaved, and the apple of his throat bobbed. "Good." Her knight grabbed a hunk of bread and grinned.

Avril stared.

What had this man done to her?

Chapter Five

Leargan couldn't get any decent sleep. Ansley Fraser was never far from his thoughts, and she haunted his dreams.

Dreams as real as visions, where she writhed naked beneath him as he touched and tasted every inch of her tall, slender form.

Over and over.

If he closed his eyes, her phantom moans would drift into his mind.

He should be concentrating on Avril's situation, but Roduch had things under control. They could do nothing until the girl told all.

Tristan had urged that they not push her, and Jorrin and Roduch agreed.

So now, they waited. She was safe, but they needed *Avril* to recognize that. She would. Eventually.

Unfortunately, Leargan could use a distraction from the Senior King's Rider. Waiting wasn't satisfying. His fantasies had only worsened since meeting with his duke regarding her message.

"What's so amusing?" he'd asked from his seat across from Jorrin in the lord's ledger room the other day.

"See for yourself. I'm not sure you'll like it…but perhaps you will," the half-elfin duke had said. One corner of his mouth shot up, his blue eyes dancing. His lord and friend had leaned forward in his ornate chair—his desk between them—and handed Leargan the small scroll Ansley had delivered.

King Nathal's red wax seal was broken but visible.

What does the missive have to do with me?

Jorrin tapped his cheek with a long finger, then brushed a strand of his too-long coal black hair past a slender, tapered ear.

Leargan glanced at him before looking at the scroll again, ignoring the duke's eager amused expression. He read the words again and again, his eyes more frantic with each pass. Repetition didn't help his comprehension...or his denial. Sweat broke out on his brow, and he tugged at the tunic collar that lay nowhere near his neck. He swallowed hard.

Jorrin,
You are the recipient of this missive as a ruse more than anything.

Young Ansley Fraser has been a daughter to me as much as my own little Mallyn. Her father, my captain, Sir Murdoch Fraser, and I were raised together and I owe him my life many times over.

Ansley has been a member of my Riders for several turns, and at the age of two and twenty, it is time for her to settle down. She is well past the age for marrying, and both he and I agree that Leargan would be a good match.

She is unaware of the reason she was sent to Greenwald.

This perhaps, is the best course for the time being, but I shall leave that up to you and, of course, your captain.

Knowing Leargan as I do, he may be resistant to my plans, and the **order** *to marry. But I am sure Ansley's fair countenance will be a sufficient persuader.*

Murdoch and I shall depart Terraquist in two or three sevendays to arrive in fair Greenwald for their wedding.
Regards,
Nathal

I'm supposed to marry *her?*

He stared at the words. When they didn't change in any way, he looked at his duke. "I can't believe he's doing this to me." He muttered a few choice words and shook his head.

Jorrin chuckled. "You sound like Cera. She, too, had issue — however temporary — with the king's *plans.*"

Frowning, Leargan met his lord's eyes. "You had the advantage of already being in love with her, and she with you."

"I'll have to give you that one. Although, Mistress Ansley Fraser *is* no hardship on the eyes." His gaze sharpened and Leargan forced himself to sit still.

"He's ordering me to marry her." He flicked the word on the scroll. "So it doesn't matter if she was a bearded troll."

The duke laughed long and hard. "Would it be so horrible? Ansley would fit right in. She already knows everyone, even Tristan. She's very close to Cera and Aimil, and seems very sweet. I realize you don't love her, but do you think you could?"

Had he not seen Jorrin with Cera, and Tristan with Aimil, he wouldn't have acknowledged believing in romantic love. He'd never planned on love for himself; he was a knight, a warrior. Leargan never had problems with getting a woman when he'd wanted one, but Ansley was different.

Innocent, wellborn…his former captain's daughter.

"She *is* beautiful." The admission slipped from his lips after several moments of silence.

And she makes my heart do funny things.

Jorrin shot him a look, but said nothing.

"Somehow I don't think she'd be any happier than I with King Nathal's games. Although, her father is in on the plan as well," Leargan said.

"Perhaps not. But you don't have to tell her now. Even the king says so."

"Then when? After the wedding? Which is apparently only a few sevendays away."

The duke's lips twitched as if the he was fighting another smile. "Keep the scroll. It's more yours than mine.

Why not show it to her? Maybe she'll just agree to marry you when she reads it." He cocked his head to the side.

"What would you do?"

"Oh, no. The king says my part in this is a ruse." Jorrin put his palms up. "Anyway, it was just a suggestion. Not my fault if you don't like it."

Leargan scowled, then and now. Air rushing from his lungs yanked him from his memories. He stumbled. He'd run into someone in the corridor. At the muttered exclamation of surprise, he blindly reached to steady the other person.

"I'm so sorry," she said, meeting his eyes.

The Blessed Spirit is laughing at you, Leargan Tegran.

He fell into her blue-green orbs. Swallowed and shook himself. "Are you all right?" He screamed at himself to focus, sucking in a breath. His shoulder smarted, but with the jarring impact, Ansley had probably bruised her cheek. Leargan's hand rested on her upper arm, and he stared there for a moment before withdrawing it. He smiled at the blush that lit her cheeks.

She was charming. The mix of innocence and toughness was intriguing.

Perhaps he wouldn't be opposed to having her as his wife. King Nathal had chosen well for him. But could Ansley even fathom it?

The suggestion — or *order*, as it were — would be out of the blue to her. She thought she was in Greenwald simply to visit old friends.

What the hell *are you thinking?*

Obviously, Ansley wasn't the only one affected by their collision.

Visions of her crimson cheeks, heavy-lidded eyes and naked body flitted through his mind.

His damn dreams.

The too-short period of only three days since they'd been introduced on the road in the dark, did nothing to prevent his lust for her. Even the innocent touch on her arm made him want more. Pull her to him. Feel her lush curves against his chest. Kiss her. Touch her.

Leargan shifted his boots. Only strong restraint kept him from tugging her into his arms and kissing the blush off her cheeks. Then he'd capture her lips properly —

"I'm fine. Are you?" Her soft voice pulled him from his desires.

His neck burned. "Aye." He cleared his throat. "You hit my shoulder. Are you sure you're all right?" He cupped her face, tilting her cheek up so he could examine it. His gaze slid to her lips and his throat went dry as her tongue darted out.

Pink. Wet.

Every fiber in Leargan's being wanted to kiss her. He tore his eyes from her mouth and met hers.

"I...I...I'm fine...*really*." She gently pushed his hand away.

"Should we find Lord Dagget?"

"No, no. I'm fine, Sir Tegran, honestly."

"Leargan."

"W-w-what?"

"I believe I told you to call me Leargan," he chided.

The crimson on her cheeks went a deeper shade, and he thanked the Blessed Spirit right then and there for the sunshine coming in the wide corridor windows. He wouldn't have wanted to miss the expression on her beautiful face.

"Sorry, Sir Te — I mean, Leargan."

"Are you sure you didn't bump your head?"

Ansley looked down, and his stomach roiled. He'd not meant the tease to hurt her feelings.

He guided her face back up; his apology evaporated on his tongue. He sank into teal eyes again. Leargan lowered his head, brushing his lips against the cheek that'd slammed into his shoulder instead.

Her eyes widened, but she didn't move away, so he gave in to his desire to kiss her.

Leargan drew her close, jumping when she slipped her arms tentatively around his waist. He captured her lips, trembling at her softness. The gentle sweep of their mouths previewed how she tasted.

More. I need more.

He molded her to him. Full breasts flattened to his chest, her firm stomach against his abdominal muscles, her pelvis against his. His blood sang and his manhood stood at attention, straining against his breeches as desire stole his thoughts. Leargan traced her lips, holding back a moan when she finally let him in.

As she timidly touched her tongue to his, he plunged into her mouth, exploring her sweetness. Ansley mated her tongue to his, and he groaned.

The innocence in her kiss made his heart pound.

Mine.

She was meant for him. She just didn't know it yet.

Ansley tightened her grip around his waist, as if otherwise unable to stay on her feet. Her whole body quivered.

Leargan pulled her even closer, reveling in her softness. His erection twitched. No doubt she could feel it. "Ansley," he whispered. He cupped her face and placed a second, but gentler, kiss to her lips.

She looked dazed, her eyes heavy and cloudy.

Moments passed and she said nothing, so he took her mouth again.

Starting off slow like before wasn't enough this time. He kissed her harder.

Ansley rubbed her tongue against his, whimpering. She gave and took as much as he did, sucking, nibbling, tongues dancing and dueling.

Leargan pushed her against the corridor wall, mapping every inch of her tall slender form. His fingertips brushed her bare neck, following the vee of her tunic, and he wanted to dip his hand inside, but he cupped her breasts on the outside of the soft fabric instead.

Ansley arched against him, moaning.

His erection pulsed while he struggled for control. Need was burning him from the inside out.

She snaked her arms around his neck and buried her hands in his hair.

He lifted her leg, slipping his hand to the underside of her thigh, and nestling his pelvis against hers. The feel of her leather breeches made him pause. Too bad she wasn't wearing a skirt. He would've been touching her skin then. But it wouldn't be long. He *had* to touch her.

She pressed even closer, gasping from the intimate contact.

Leargan groaned and rocked his hips. He reached for her belt. Her hot bare skin was only inches from his fingertips.

"Leargan," Ansley breathed.

Her voice snapped him out of the passionate fog. His name on her lips...*Innocent.*

What are you doing?

This was Ansley Fraser, not some whore or willing maid. He had her against the wall of a lit corridor in the middle of the day, where anyone could see them.

Leargan had been about to take her, for Blessed Spirit's sake.

She was no doubt a virgin.

Disgust shot his desire to hell and his gut roiled. He never lost control, let alone with a woman. He needed to get away from her before he did something that couldn't be reversed, something they'd both regret.

He released her, stifling a groan when his gaze raked her face.

Ansley's eyes were hazy and confused, her lips swollen from their kisses and cheeks flushed. Her red hair was pleasantly mussed, and it took all he was made of not to draw her back to him and kiss her again.

His neck tingled from her touch and his whole body throbbed. "I'm sorry," Leargan panted.

Her brow knitted and she straightened against the wall.

He tore his gaze away.

Coward.

"I need to see to some…duties." One boot in front of the other, he forced himself to walk away while he still could.

Chapter Six

Ansley put her fingertips to her lips. She could still feel him there, taste him. The corridor blurred, and tears scalded her cheeks before she could stop them.

He apologized.

For kissing her. Then walked away.

Her chest ached. Had she just been stabbed in the heart?

Leargan's apology ruined what they'd shared.

She'd been thinking about him when they'd collided in the corridor.

Wide enough that two warhorses could walk it abreast, yet she'd run *into* him. Her cheek had smarted, but she'd been fine.

Was it fate? Ansley ignored the notion. Just because he finally knew who she was didn't mean he was for her. A man as handsome as Sir Leargan Tegran could have any woman he wanted. Why would he even consider freckle-faced Ansley Fraser?

But he'd kissed her. Twice.

She'd never experienced longing like she had at the first touch of his lips on hers. The feel of his hard body pressed against hers. Protected, but consumed at the same time. It was an odd contradiction that left her wanting to get even closer to him. She'd had to hold onto him to remain on her feet, but Leargan hadn't seemed to mind — at least at the time.

When he'd lifted her leg and pushed himself into her, something had shouted for her to stop him, but she couldn't. She'd waited too long for him. Ansley wanted

Leargan, and the evidence against her told her the feeling was mutual.

Could she have been so wrong?

Tears cascaded and she sniffled, swiping at her nose with the back of her hand.

Nay. Don't think about it.

Ansley made a fist. She'd enjoy the rest of her visit and head back to Terraquist as planned. She regretted officially meeting Leargan. It was easier to accept that he didn't know she was alive than be crushed by knowing he didn't want her. Especially now that she'd been introduced to the joy of being held in his arms, have his mouth moving over hers.

Squeezing her eyes shut, she willed the hurt away.

"Ansley?"

She wiped her eyes again and plastered a smile on before she turned to Aimil. "Hello. Just came from visiting Avril. Was on my way to check on Cera. Want to come with?" Words rushed out, and she fought for control. Her cheeks flushed.

Her longtime friend studied her, head cocked to one side. "Is Avril all right? Did something happen?"

Ansley met Aimil's dark eyes and shook her head. "No, no. We shared a meal and spoke with Meara. Avril didn't say much, but she looks well. She even smiled. I think she misses Sir Roduch. He's on the fighting yard today." She forced her smile wider, trying not to squirm under the appraising gaze.

Please believe me.

She'd never admitted her feelings for Leargan to Cera or Aimil, despite how close they were. The whole story would probably come out eventually, but Ansley didn't want to talk about it now.

Too fresh. Hurts too much.

"I suppose you'll tell me when you want to." Aimil gave a curt nod, slipping her arm in Ansley's and looking up at her. "But I'm glad you've spent time with Avril. I don't think she's comfortable around me."

"I wouldn't say that. She's been through a lot. She's not comfortable around anyone."

"Right. These things take time. I shall visit if she'll have me. Let her know we can be friends?"

"Good idea."

Her friend smiled. She was petite, and had to look *up* at Ansley. Her raven hair hung loose to her waist in waves that shone blue in the sunlight streaming in through the corridor windows. It framed her beautiful face. Her gown was dark gray and simple, belying her rank.

Cera called for them to enter her rooms at Aimil's knock.

Ansley reveled at the time she'd been given to visit with Cera and Aimil. It was as if growing up, moving on, had never happened. She'd missed her friends. Much more than she'd realized.

The duchess had changed since the death of her family, but her husband seemed to have helped her heal, and Ansley was already fond of Lord Aldern. She'd been on a message run to the Netian Valley when Cera and Jorrin had married, so she'd missed it, but was grateful for the chance to get to know him now.

As soon as she'd seen them together, it'd been obvious that Jorrin was perfect for Cera.

He was half-human and half-elfin, the most handsome man Ansley had ever seen, with sapphire eyes and hair as dark as Leargan's. Taller than the captain, but just as broad and muscled.

Tristan, too, was perfect for Aimil, but she'd known Lord Dagget for several turns, and Aimil had loved him for much of that time. He was on the quiet side, but there was no doubt the lord loved her friend. Their wedding had been moved up, but when she'd seen the slight rounding of Aimil's tummy, Ansley had guessed the reason, though Aimil hadn't confirmed. Despite the apparent secrecy, she was happy that both her dear friends would soon be mothers.

Aimil and Tristan's baby wouldn't arrive for several months. Cera and Jorrin's, on the other hand, would be here any day. She was excited to be able to witness the joyous occasion.

"How are you today, Mama?" Aimil asked as they entered Cera and Jorrin's vast sleeping room.

The duchess rested in the center of the large bed, her white wolf lying beside her. Auburn brow furrowed, the disgruntled look on her gorgeous face lightened when she saw them. She smiled, and Trikser's tail thumped. "I'd be better if your husband didn't worry mine," she grumbled.

Aimil laughed and Ansley shook her head, biting back a grin.

"I'm sure Tristan's just concerned about you and the baby." She stepped on the stool and sat up on the high bed, her dark hair swaying.

Cera smiled sweetly, her gray eyes twinkling. "Hello, Ansley," she said, apparently ignoring Aimil. She tucked a lock of dark red hair behind an ear and patted the bed. "Come sit with us."

Ansley grinned, climbing onto the large bed. She leaned over and patted Trikser's head. The white wolf rewarded her with a lick to her hand.

Cera laid a hand on her belly and spared a look at her bondmate. "Where are the girls?" the duchess asked of her friends' wolves.

"Hunting, I think," Aimil said, glancing at Ansley.

"They left together?" Cera asked.

"Aye." Ansley nodded.

Their bondmates were often inseparable at Rider Headquarters, and being in Greenwald wasn't proving any different.

"I was surprised Trik didn't go with them," Ansley said.

"He won't leave me when Jorrin's gone during the day. He goes out at night to handle his needs and eat, then comes right back. Either he or Jorrin is with me at all times. It's like they've teamed up." Her voice was half-amused, half-annoyed.

"He must know your time is soon," Aimil said.

"Sooner than later, I hope. But I still don't need to be confined." She scrunched her nose.

"I'm sure Tristan is convinced it's best," Aimil said.

"Hah. I'll have no problem reminding you of that when *your* time is near." Cera beamed.

Aimil groaned, but grinned back.

Ansley chuckled, then met her friend's dark gaze. "I had noticed that, but no one said anything."

One corner of her mouth lifted. "Sorry I didn't tell you; it wasn't for any particular reason. It's not really a secret." She put her hand over her womb and looked down. "We weren't supposed to get married for two more turns. I thought my father and brothers were going to kill him…" Her cheeks shone bright red.

"Well, you're married now, it matters not," Ansley said, taking one of Aimil's hands. "But I had no idea you and Tristan…"

Prior to their marriage only a few months before, Aimil had been living in Terraquist at Rider Barracks, like any other Senior Rider.

Cera had also been a Senior King's Rider before she'd married and made her husband a duke, taking her place as the Duchess of Greenwald.

"Oh, we hadn't before. Honestly, we'd both been content with kisses for the most part. We hadn't seen each other in a while. He came to Terraquist to see me…it just happened." She giggled. "Effectively, obviously." She patted her stomach with her free hand.

"The first time?" Ansley asked. She ignored the voice that reminded her of what could've happened in the corridor with Leargan.

"Aye." Aimil dropped her voice to a whisper. "Don't tell him I told you, but it was his first time, too." She winked.

Cera laughed and shook her head. "I can't say the same for Jorrin, but the same thing happened to me, too."

"Wow." She should thank Leargan for walking away from her, no matter how it hurt. How much worse would it have been if she'd given herself to him, *then* had him walk away? Even more so if he'd left her with child.

What are you thinking? They'd shared a few kisses. *Nothing more.*

He hadn't even wanted that. Ansley sighed.

"Something wrong, Ansley?" Cera asked.

"Nay. Why?"

Her friends exchanged a glance that didn't escape her notice.

"You look upset," Aimil said.

"Not at all. I'm so happy for you two, and I like your husbands very much." She tried for a diversion.

"They both like you very much, as well," the duchess said.

"Are you happy?" The whisper fell from her lips, unintended. Ansley tried to imagine herself married and expecting a child. She didn't want anyone but Leargan, so she probably wouldn't marry. How could she settle for someone else now that she'd had a taste of him?

And isn't that just pathetic.

"I'm very happy with Jorrin. The baby was a pleasant surprise. Now, I can't wait to meet him." Cera rubbed her distended tummy in wide circles.

"I'm also very happy with Tristan. I always knew I would be. I don't regret our inability to wait until we were married or the result," Aimil said, eyes shining.

She forced a smile, and her friends exchanged another look of obvious worry. Questions were written on both their faces. Ansley silently begged them to drop it.

Why do I always have to be so obvious?

Cera took one of her hands, and Aimil reached for the other.

She was doomed. Tears hovered; she didn't have a free hand to wipe them away.

"What happened, Ansley?" Cera whispered.

Soon the whole story poured out, starting with the fact that she'd had an affinity for Leargan for turns. Cera didn't look surprised at all, and Aimil had nodded.

Typical that she'd been transparent to the both of them. The compassion in their gazes when Ansley admitted she loved him caused more tears. She finished with their kisses in the corridor. Sobs took over when she relayed his apology.

Aimil wrapped her in a hug and Ansley crushed her eyes shut. "I'm sure it's not as bad as you think." She smoothed wisps of hair that'd escaped her braid.

Ansley wiped her tears away and sat up.

"I haven't known Leargan well for a full turn yet, but I can tell you one thing." Cera tilted her head to one side. "He doesn't easily show emotion, beyond a smile here and a laugh there. He's always in control. When he kissed you, he lost it. I've *never* seen him like that."

"What does that mean?" Ansley met her gray eyes.

"That he probably feels like he insulted you," Aimil finished.

"Men don't like to lose control," Cera continued, "and when a woman is the cause of it, look out. I know him well enough to assure you; he didn't hurt you on purpose. Leargan's not like that. He's one of the most honorable men I know."

"That's how I think of him as well." She sniffed and dabbed her nose with the square of linen Aimil had offered.

"So much so, that the fact he kissed you may lead to a proposal," Aimil said, tapping her bottom lip as if she was thinking.

"No…" She gasped.

"You're a wellborn lady, he just might," Aimil insisted.

Ansley glanced at Cera, who shrugged. "I only kissed him. I won't marry him because he feels he insulted me, which he didn't. It'd be trapping him into something he doesn't want. I couldn't do that…" She swallowed.

No matter how he made me feel, he doesn't want me. Foolish lass.

Her heart thumped and pain spread from the hole in her chest, threatening to choke her.

"But you just told us you love him." Aimil's dark eyes widened.

"Exactly. I wouldn't want to marry him unless he wanted me."

"I understand." The duchess' expression was somber, thoughtful. "One more thing about men, in general."

"What's that?" Ansley asked.

"They are usually pretty oblivious to feelings." She paused, flashing a lopsided grin. "Unless they possess empathic magic."

"Leargan has no magic."

"Which makes him pretty daft." Aimil flashed a grin, too.

The three women shared a laugh, and Ansley's spirits lifted…a little.

Chapter Seven

The sword slammed into his, knocking him off balance. Hard ground slammed his back, taking the breath from his lungs.

He heard some gasps and several comments from his men.

Leargan was *never* caught off guard in a sparring match, let alone in a real fight. Even Roduch, who he'd been training with, had frozen, then reached a hand down to help him to his feet.

"Captain?" His friend's face was a mask of concern.

He cursed and grabbed the large blond man's arm with a bit too much vigor, but Roduch didn't appear bothered. The knight pulled him to his feet with little effort.

Leargan restrained himself from stomping his foot like a spoiled child. His mind had been on Ansley.

Had the fight been real, he'd be dead.

She *would* be the death of him.

"It's all right. Spar with Niall." Leargan sheathed his sword and brushed himself off. His back and arse ached as much as his pride. After a glare to each of the men who'd stopped to gape, he jogged to the edge of the training grounds.

His men busied themselves with their previous tasks. *Smart of them.*

He nodded at his Second, who hopped the wooden fence that surrounded the training grounds.

Niall wasted no time rushing Roduch, and Leargan heard the clash of metal on metal before he'd even reached the place Niall had been standing.

Leaning on the top rung of the fence, he lifted his foot and rested it on the bottom, studying the two men. At first glance, one would think Roduch would be the winner. The warrior was almost as tall as King Nathal's six-feet-seven-inches. Just as broad shouldered and muscular.

Dark-haired Niall on the other hand, wasn't quite six feet tall, but he was equally muscular, yet graceful. Quick on his feet and skilled with his weapon.

Roduch was also very good with a sword. All his men were, or they wouldn't have been selected to be a part of the Aldern personal guard.

He watched them for a moment, then allowed his eyes to sweep the rest of the fighting yard. Some of the men were sparring with swords like Niall and Roduch, others with spears, and even a few practiced with bow and arrow.

The Duke of Greenwald strode over, sheathing his sword before wiping the sweat from his brow. He too, had been sparring with the men. He leaned against the fence next to him, saying nothing as he passed a skin of water over.

Leargan nodded thanks and took a long drink.

Finally, Jorrin cleared his throat. "I'm surprised Roduch's here. He hasn't left the castle in days."

"I guilted him a little. Told him he owed it to the lads." The big knight was in charge of training the younger men-at-arms with the sword, as well as his special lessons with Leargan's squire, Brodic. "He's patient with them."

"Alasdair doesn't relish the task in his absence."

"Aye," Leargan said, but didn't look at his lord.

"Has she said anything yet?"

"Not that Roduch shared with me. She'll talk when she's ready. She's taking short visits from the ladies, that's something."

"I agree." Jorrin paused. "Leargan, are you all right?"

"Aye. Why?" He swung his head around and met the duke's sapphire eyes.

He quirked an eyebrow. "I've never seen you

knocked on your arse before, that's why," he said, tone half-amused, half-concerned.

Leargan fought the urge to squirm. "I wasn't aware watching me was a part of training."

"Just marry her, Leargan. It's been a sevenday. King Nathal said no more than three...and he'll *be* here with Ansley's father."

"I remember what the scroll says." He scowled.

Jorrin crossed his arms over his broad chest, gaze appraising. "You're not known as a cruel man."

He cocked his head to the side, holding his breath.

"Yet, you've been stalking about the castle for the better part of this sevenday, barking orders and making maids cry. Even Brodic has been staying out of your way."

The better part of this sevenday.

After he'd kissed Ansley in the corridor. Behaved like a lustful beast.

Leargan looked into his friend's eyes and knew better than uttering a denial. Jorrin's magic would've called him a liar even if the duke did not. "I know..." He grimaced.

"So, tell her about the scroll, or ask her to marry you, even demand it."

"Aye, because *demanding* anything of a Senior King's Rider would get me far."

Jorrin smirked. "Well, I suppose you have a point there."

"I don't want a marriage without love," he admitted, looking away. "Your fault, of course."

"My fault?"

When he met the duke's gaze again, his breath exited on a whoosh. Kindness made up his friend's expression. "Well...you and Tristan and your lovely wives. Yet, I'm trapped, *ordered* to marry. I've never disobeyed the king before."

"Are you planning to?"

He didn't sense judgment or censure in the question. "Nay." He paused. "I don't know."

"King Nathal is nothing, if not sensible. Can you explain things to him? I don't know her father, but I'm sure he wouldn't want his daughter to be unhappy." Jorrin's tone was reasonable, but something flared within Leargan.

"Are you saying I can't make her happy?" he barked, then flushed cold. He was addressing his lord, and had no right to speak to him in such a manner, even if they were close. He wouldn't blame Jorrin if he knocked him on his arse.

But the man laughed. "No, not at all."

Calm yourself and stop jumping to conclusions. Leargan took a breath.

"Do you want her?"

"*That* is about the only thing not in question," he murmured.

The duke shook his head, chuckling again. "At least *that* won't be lacking in your marriage then," he teased, but there was knowledge and acceptance in his eyes.

He grinned.

Silence descended, but it was companionable.

"I ambushed her…shamed her…I've been avoiding her ever since." Leargan winced.

Why did you say that?

"Tell me what happened," Jorrin ordered, suddenly the picture of authority.

Bollocks.

The look on his face didn't bode well.

Leargan had chosen his words poorly.

The story tumbled out, Jorrin visibly relaxing more and more with every sentence. "I wouldn't call that shaming her. She didn't smack you, or scream for you to get away from her?"

"Nay. Quite the opposite. That's why I'm so ashamed of myself. Jorrin, I would've taken her, right there, in the corridor…she's not a common whore."

"No, she's not. She's the woman that'll be your wife. Though the time and place may have been a bit off, wanting her is not wrong. She has feelings for you, as well."

He shot his friend a look. "What? Do you sense something?"

"Blessed Spirit, man. I don't *have* to sense anything. Don't you see how she looks at you? I saw it from day one. Tristan, too remarked." Jorrin shook his head, one dark brow arched higher than earlier.

His heart skipped. Ansley might feel something for him?

He'd said nothing to her since he'd kissed her in the corridor. Couldn't look her in the eye.

"Don't you think apologizing and walking away from her, never looking back, might've hurt her some? Even if she didn't have feelings for you, I think it would've had a bite…"

"Ah, I…never thought of that."

Jorrin winced. "I think you owe her an explanation…or an apology…for your apology."

"If I hurt her, it was unintentional. She probably hates me now."

"Let me tell you something about women." The duke threw an arm around Leargan's shoulders. "We often hurt them with our inability to think *of* them, so my wife reminds me all the time. Think about her perspective for a moment."

He'd left her, as far as *she* knew, without another thought about her. Their encounter was likely the first of that kind for her, and he'd not even looked her way since. Leargan had been too absorbed with himself to even check on Ansley.

She'd have no idea he'd been able to think of little else than her lips against his. How she'd felt in his arms, her curves melded to his body.

He'd never meant to hurt her.

And now Jorrin thought she had feelings for him?

It's too much.

"Oh, hell. Now she'll never marry me."

He chuckled. "You have about a fortnight to convince her."

Leargan scowled and ignored the grin on the duke's face.

Cera was easing her body to the edge of the bed just as Jorrin made it through the doorway of their bedchamber. He'd caught her getting up.

"Where do you think you're going?" He shook his head.

"To the privy, unless you'd prefer I soil our bed." She smiled sweetly, then glared when he laughed.

"You know, love, I never would've described you as even-tempered before the baby, but—" Jorrin couldn't finish his jibe, because a big fluffy pillow hit him square in the face, before tumbling to the floor. He retrieved it, going to his wife and kissing her.

"Help me up or get out of my way," Cera ordered, but a smile played at her lips.

He pulled her into his arms, and she sighed against him.

"Wretch," she whispered, her warm breath ticking his neck.

He chuckled again and held her to him; her arms slid around his waist. "Just teasing, love." Jorrin stroked her hair.

"You're still a wretch," Cera said, apparently ignoring his grin. "I have to go, help me?"

"Of course."

When she'd seen to her needs, he intended to help her back into their bed but she shook her head. "I want to sit by the fire, and I think you need to let Trik out before he has an accident." She eased into the oversized chair near the hearth.

Jorrin opened the door so her bondmate could go out

for the night. He didn't lock it, to stave off being woken in the middle of the night at the wolf's return.

Trikser was insistent about being by Cera's side. But locked door or not, he somehow always managed to get back into their rooms.

"Did you have a good day, love?" He pulled a chair next to hers and slipped onto it.

Cera sighed and nodded, resting her head on his shoulder after Jorrin scooted his chair closer. He threw his arm around her. "I won't lie. I'll be happy when the baby arrives."

"I know, love. I can't carry him for you, but I feel what you do." His wife's love for him and their child, as well as her heavy exhaustion, washed over him through his empathic magic when her beautiful gray eyes met his gaze. Jorrin swallowed back a yawn; his limbs suddenly weighed a ton.

"It makes me feel better that you can really feel us," she said.

"I love you both."

"We love you, too." She flashed a smile that had his heart accelerating.

He rested a hand on her swollen stomach. His baby responded to his touch.

Her palm landed next to his, and she leaned up to brush her mouth against his.

Jorrin cupped her face and deepened the kiss, tracing his tongue at the seam of her lips until she opened for him.

She sighed into his mouth, and he tamped down his libido, as he tasted her for the first time all day. Cera was exhausted, but his body didn't care. He wanted his wife.

They hadn't made love in a few sevendays, but not because she didn't want to. The further her pregnancy advanced, the more fatigued she was, so he didn't push her. But they'd had fun being inventive with positions as her belly had grown.

Breeches already tightening, Jorrin broke the kiss

before his blood started singing. He held her as close as he comfortably could, considering their seating arrangement.

"Did you see Avril today?" Cera asked.

"No. But Leargan said she's willing to see you and the girls?"

She nodded. "Ansley mostly. She's been visiting daily. I think Avril feels a connection with her since Ansley found her. Men make her leery, except Roduch."

"Understandable. I really want to know who the bastard is, so I can hunt him down."

"I agree, but we need to wait for her to be ready. If she talks to anyone, it'll be Roduch."

Jorrin sighed. Duke or not, he didn't have the heart to order the battered girl to bare her secrets.

"I'm enjoying Ansley's visit. I wish she could stay longer." Cera snuggled into him.

The longing in her tone made his magic tingle, and he pressed a kiss to the crown of her dark red curls. "You might get your wish."

She lifted her head and met his eyes. "What d'you mean?"

He'd intended to keep the scroll a secret but he told Cera everything. "Promise you'll keep quiet? I mean it."

"Of course."

The whole story poured out, including what Leargan had told him regarding what'd happened between the captain and his wife's friend.

Cera didn't look surprised about them kissing. "Leargan is an even bigger idiot than I'd suspected," his wife mused.

Jorrin's laugh faded as she explained the depth of her friend's feelings for their captain. "Damn…" He shook his head. "It's worse than I thought. I told him he probably hurt her."

"Looks like my empath husband isn't so oblivious." She winked, and one corner of her mouth shot up.

He chuckled. "Aye, but our captain is. What to do?"

"Nothing. They need to work it out, love," Cera whispered, caressing his cheek.

"In a fortnight, I suppose."

"Damn King Nathal's *plans*..." She shook her head.

"I've told him to apologize." He shrugged.

"That's all we can do."

His wife didn't want to play matchmaker?

Well, it was for the better, but on the other hand, Jorrin was worried about Leargan. His captain could find happiness with Ansley, as he'd found with Cera. Although, he'd had to confront her and demand she admit her feelings for him.

He smiled. That day in the elf wizard, Hadrian's barn was like yesterday. Jorrin couldn't imagine his life without her.

Perhaps Ansley would have to do the same with Leargan. His magic told him there was something more to Leargan's feelings than perhaps the captain even knew.

The Senior Rider was a stunner. It wasn't a surprise people mistook his wife and her friend, though she was an inch or two taller than Cera. Red hair and similar build—prior to her pregnancy, anyway. They were also the same age, almost to the day.

Ansley had had him grinning when she'd mentioned her freckles were a distinct difference. His magic told him she was self-conscious about them, but freckles added to her charm.

Even though King Nathal was meddling, she was perfect for Leargan.

Was the king rushing it? They'd be better off if they could come to things on their own. Jorrin chided himself. Meddlesome as the king—or worse, a woman.

Cera was right. Leargan and Ansley needed to work things out on their own. Of course, he'd be there for his friend as much as he could.

He really needed to be focused on Avril's demons. Jorrin would have to act when the girl decided to let him in on her secrets. He was a tad rusty on all the laws he needed to be familiar with. He'd have to ask his wife if there was a specific way they needed to proceed.

Cera had been raised for running a Province; he was still learning.

Then again, the king was coming. Jorrin wouldn't be opposed to letting King Nathal handle things.

He glanced down at his wife. "Cera?"

She'd fallen asleep, head on his shoulder, face tucked into his neck.

Smiling, he kissed her cheek when she muttered his name in her sleep.

Chapter Eight

Where the hell was his little bitch wife? It'd been a sevenday.

Tynan slammed his fist down on the wide arm of his ornately-carved mahogany chair.

Magda jumped, and he glared at the wench. Cooking was about the only thing his steward's wife was any good at.

He'd only parted her thighs once, but she'd made such a fuss about it, he'd not bothered to try again. Harlan hadn't found out, though one had to wonder why she'd not prattled to her husband.

After that, he'd wed Avril and sunk into her sweet little body, so he didn't need Magda anyway.

The harder Avril fought, the better he got off. Damn shame she'd consistently failed to take to his seed. When he got her back, he'd try again. Get a child on her after he punished her for running off.

"May I get you something, sire?"

The tremor in her voice made him snarl and rethink mounting her again. He liked the timid ones.

Staring, Tynan said nothing.

Magda's whole frame shook. The side of her face was sucked in, as if she was biting her cheek. The contents of the basket of cleaning supplies on her arm rattled.

Although passed her prime, her body was slender. Gray had started at her temples, but most of the hair in her long plait remained black. She was probably five or six turns his junior, and her skin was still smooth. Her breasts remained high enough, and she had a nice curve to her hips from bearing Harlan's get. Two...or three sons they had, only one not fully grown. Too bad they'd no daughters.

Her face was pretty, high cheekbones keeping her from being considered plain. Brown eyes. Not green, like his little wife.

His cock wasn't even tempted.

Dammit.

He needed Avril. Now. His bollocks were bound to fall off from lack of use. Tynan would beat her until her eyes rolled back into her head, before...no, *after*...burying himself inside her. She had some nerve. Leaving him.

He *owned* her.

And he needed some coin. He was sorely missing her magic as much as his cock missed her sweet cunt.

He was expecting two visits this sevenday. Needed to know what his wife saw about them. Hosting was tiresome enough without knowing all the secrets he required.

Tynan had enough in the coffers to be comfortable, but he didn't like *comfortable.* He needed *more.*

"Lord Mont!" Harlan sauntered across his grand room, the poor excuse for a great hall.

For now. Only for now.

He'd expand. Make it wider, larger. Higher ceilings. Carvings, maybe some art. Tynan had already consulted a mage who could shape and expand wood. The man was working on an extravagant plan than would make his home a castle when the mage was done.

Too bad he wanted so much gold. He'd have to contemplate things. Make a way for the mage to disappear.

Damn Avril.

He needed her foresight so he could know the man's weaknesses.

"What it is?" Tynan forced boredom into his tone, stopping himself from leaning forward. No need for Harlan to know how eager he was to locate the little bitch.

Chest heaving as he struggled for breath, Harlan

bowed after skidding to a stop, his shaggy salt and pepper hair flopping over his wide forehead. Tall and lanky, the man's face was scarred from all the fighting he'd done as a youth. Since his nose had been healed over and over by weak magic, it was bulbous and angled, even more obvious at the center of his gaunt cheeks.

He wasn't even fifty, but after working the fighting circuits that'd taken him all over the continent to put food on his table, the man looked older than his turns. Haggard.

His gray tunic and black breeches were dusty, as if he'd come in from a hard ride.

He'd been Tynan's cousin's steward for only a few turns before the family's unfortunate demise. Since Tynan had inherited the staff along with the holding, the Pelham family had stayed.

Blackmail had Harlan and his wife indentured to him now. With no end in sight, of course. He smiled slowly, steepling his hands.

"Mistress Avril is not with her family." The apple of the steward's throat bobbed and he shot a look to his wife.

Magda busied herself by mending the tapestry she'd just cleaned, and Tynan ignored her furtive glances to her husband.

He frowned, leaning forward. "You spoke to her father?"

"Yes, milord. He swore she'd not come home."

"Did you search his premises?" Tynan narrowed his eyes, staring until his steward shifted on his feet.

"They allowed me to look everywhere."

"The barn?"

"Aye. Mistress Avril was nowhere on the Larange holding."

He swallowed back a curse, making a fist that made Harlan wince. His blood heated, settling into a rolling boil. He sucked in a breath. Normally Tynan didn't mind a healthy display of anger in front of his servants, but he needed to maintain control now.

Concentrate. Find your wife.

Where else could she have run, if not her family? The girl had no one. He'd made sure of it.

"There was…"

"What?" he barked.

Harlan swallowed hard again. "There was another…"

"Another *what*?"

"A lad on the road, one of the Kenrick lads."

Ah, the son of his *tenants* from the next property over. They were beholden to him, thanks to his little wife's magic.

"Well, go on," Tynan snapped.

"He swears he saw her yesterday at market."

"Market, as in Greenwald Main?"

"Yes, sire."

"Did you believe him?" The man nodded.

"Aye."

"Where was she?"

"He said he saw her coming out of an inn."

An inn? She'd not taken even one coin with her when she'd left; he'd counted every last piece of gold. How did she get a room at an inn?

If she was selling her body, Tynan *would* kill her.

Cheating bitch. He wouldn't be cuckolded.

"Get Ferd and Han to ready my coach."

"Sire?"

Harlan dared question him? Growling, he shot to his feet. "I'm going to go get my wife."

"Roduch? Coming, my friend?" his captain called.

After managing a smile and a nod for Leargan, he allowed the shorter man to clasp his forearm in a familiar and affectionate gesture that he returned in kind.

His brother's eyes shot up and down his body, and it was all he could do to keep from stiffening. "You all right?" he asked.

"Aye." Roduch bit back a sigh as the appraising gaze didn't lessen. "Avril." He might as well tell the truth. His little foundling consumed his thoughts. He probably should thank his captain for ordering him back to his duties, but with or without her, he could think of nothing else. However, being away from her during the day made him cherish the time with her at night even more.

Leargan's eyes sharpened. "Anything I need to know about?"

"She hasn't spoken yet." He shook his head. Not about what they needed to know anyway. But her shy smile was more common, and made his heart miss beat after beat.

Little by little, she was opening up to him. Holding his hand, moving into his touch instead of away. Last evening she'd even reached for him first, while they strolled in Lady Cera's garden after supper.

"Ah."

"Sorry I knocked you on your arse yesterday," he said quickly, desperate for a distraction. Talking about Avril — thinking about her — made him crave things she was nowhere near ready for.

Besides, she still had to formally renounce her marriage to the duke and at least two witnesses. Until then, she belonged to someone else. Roduch ordered his jaw to unclench, but his gut was tight, pained.

Relax. Speak with your friend. You are fine.

The captain's expression was sheepish. "You were in the right. I was distracted. Dangerous. I for one am glad we were just sparring."

"So am I." He gave a genuine grin. "I would hate to have been the one to kill you."

Leargan grinned and shook his head. "That *would've* been unfortunate."

He chuckled. "Bath and then supper?" Perhaps he could even convince Avril to leave her rooms and dine in the great hall with residents of Castle Aldern.

The previous night she'd explained she couldn't stand the worry in every gaze, so he'd not pressed her. They'd eaten in her rooms—where Roduch had taken up residence, despite the headwoman's protests. He was growing tired of sleeping in a chair, though. He didn't mind the privacy. Enjoyed time to get to know her and loved putting a smile on her face. Or making her laugh.

"Definitely. I could use a good soak. My rump will be sore for days." Leargan winced.

"Don't ask me to rub it for you," Alasdair, one of their other longtime friends, and fellow guardsman, said as he passed by, a grin on his face.

"I don't recall requiring that service of *you*," the captain bit back.

"I suppose you could ask Senior Rider Fraser. Gorgeous piece."

Leargan's face darkened and he sprinted after Alas, throwing a punch and a half-tackle, like they had many times when they were lads.

Roduch chuckled again and shook his head. He ran his hand through his disheveled locks and watched his brothers banter. He needed a haircut; it was getting too long.

Alasdair was widely known for his womanizing ways, but there'd been real emotion in Leargan's expression.

What's that about?

Aye, the man was a tease, like normal. Besides, he stuck to whores. He'd never sully an unmarried maid, especially their former captain's daughter.

By the time Roduch sank down into one of the few wooden tubs big enough to accommodate his large frame in the public bathing room, he could've fallen asleep right then and there. The warm water enveloped and soothed aches from the long day of training, and the chair he'd slept in since the night they'd found Avril. His back had never been so sore.

He focused on Bowen and Dallon—two more of the twelve—when one of them called his name.

"Want to head into town later?" Dallon asked.

"I could use a good tumble," Bowen added, running his hand through his shaggy sandy locks.

"Not tonight," Roduch answered, shaking his head. "I'm not up for anything but meat in my belly and my bed." *And Avril.*

Dallon raised a dark brow. "Not even a tall of ale?"

"We've ale in the castle," Leargan said. "But—"

"I'm in," Alasdair interrupted. "Where'd you want to go? I haven't seen Mali at the *Flying Flask* in a long while. Damn, the woman has fantastic hands." His expression was wistful as Dallon, Bowen and a few of the others scoffed.

"I don't want to go into Lower Greenwald," Dallon complained.

"No?" Alas asked. "What about *White Sage Pub*? It's in a better area, for sure. And I could do as well with Betha as I could with Mali, though her talents are different to be sure." He cocked his dark head to the side as if he was reasoning hard, his long dark hair shifting around his broad shoulders. He usually kept it bound to fight, but no doubt intended to wash it now.

Leargan smirked. "Blessed Spirit, Alas. Do you have enough lasses?"

The oldest man of the personal guard, at thirty, wore a grin that could have split his face. "No, my dear captain, there are *never* enough lasses."

"Name a tavern and he has one," Kale put in, scrubbing soap into his short dark hair.

"They'd all rather be with me than you," Alasdair said.

Roduch shook his head at the men who were more like brothers than fellow soldiers. They started swapping stories, and verbally comparing *long swords* as Alasdair so eloquently put it. Not everyone was present, nor were the lads, Brodic and Lucan, so the more Alas spoke, the more reprobate his tales became.

"I've no time to be concerned with you scoundrels anyway," Niall, Leargan's Second said, pulling up a fresh pair of breeches.

"I told you I'd take your duties tonight." Leargan fastened his belt.

"Truly? Lyde would much appreciate it. She's complaining I haven't seen her all sevenday." He spoke of his new wife. Beautiful, petite and fair, she was a maid for Lady Cera in the castle.

"Night patrol?" Roduch asked, leaning forward in the tub.

Both men nodded. "Aye, it's my turn to lead."

"But I'll handle it," Leargan said. "Spend the night with your wife. You too, Paddy. The rest of you go rut where you will on your night off." The captain smirked at the catcalls their brothers gave.

Niall beamed and thanked him.

Padraig, also newly married, smiled and nodded. His red hair, newly shorn close to his scalp, matched his stained cheeks as he looked away, wrapping a bathing sheet around his waist. He was a quiet, private man, and the second oldest of the personal guard.

"I'd offer to help you out, but..." Roduch said.

"No, no. Stay with your lass, it's not your rotation," Leargan said.

Your lass.

His heart wanted nothing more.

"Lucan has been itching to talk to me all day. My gut says he and Brodic will want to come along. Both could help with the new men-at-arms. I've the newest ones on rotation tonight. Greenwald at night is different than during the day. They need to learn the area. The lads already know it well," the captain said.

Roduch had always liked the young mage, Lucan, as well as Leargan's squire, Brodic. He was often put in charge of the younger ones for training. His captain had always praised his patience with them.

The youngest of the personal guard, Laith and Teagan, had been paired with him consistently until reaching knighthood about two turns ago.

He didn't mind in the least. Introducing the young and eager to the art of the sword reminded him of his days as a lad, trained by Captain Fraser.

Most of the knights of the guard had shared the grounds with Roduch then, as they now shared the protection duties of Lord Aldern and his family, as well as the Province of Greenwald. The twelve of them were honored to do so.

The captain glanced at Alasdair. "Thought you were on night patrol this rotation anyway."

"Dammit, I think you're right."

Dallon muttered something about giving Alasdair's regards to Betha and ducked when Alas threw a punch.

Everyone laughed.

Chapter Nine

Leargan heard the laughter before he spotted Ansley and Lady Aimil. He couldn't help but smile when he saw them at the table on the dais. The carefree look on Ansley's face made his heart stutter. He'd never seen anything so beautiful in his life.

He was hit with a rush of guilt. *Fool. How could you fail to consider you might've hurt her?*

"Leargan."

He glanced over his shoulder and offered an easy smile to Tristan. "Evening."

"Nice night." The healer strode up to him.

Leargan found it difficult to keep his eyes averted from the table on the dais.

The healing lord followed his gaze and flashed a lopsided grin. He leaned into him, as if about to impart a secret. "You have a seat at that table, you know." His hazel eyes danced.

"I haven't forgotten…"

"Oh. It looked to me as if you'd still be standing here come morning." Tristan dashed away, quickly jogging up the three steps onto the dais and then sliding onto the seat next to his wife.

Ansley met Leargan's eyes as he slipped onto the chair next to her. Hurt flickered in the blue-green depths. She was quick to disguise it with a smile, but he wasn't fooled.

He wanted to reach out to her, but what was he supposed to say? His tight stomach had nothing to do with hunger.

"Good evening, Sir Tegran." She reached for her

goblet and averted her eyes as she sipped.

"Leargan," he corrected.

A curt nod was all he got in response to his smile. Disappointed flooded him.

All other conversation had stopped. Eyes of their tablemates burned him with every stare.

Ansley's blush said she'd also observed the collective gaze.

He took a breath. "Good evening, Lady Dagget." Leargan inclined his head.

"Evening, Sir Leargan," Aimil said formally. His fellow South Ascovan offered him a much-too knowing smile, dark eyes twinkling.

"Tristan," a lad called, as he strode across the great hall. Lucan's dark brown hair was windblown and clear green eyes bright. He'd just turned fourteen, and was growing like a weed. He'd always been especially attached to the healer, but the feeling was mutual.

"Hello." Tristan waved.

The lad also had a normal place on the dais, because he was the head mage—the only mage really—of Greenwald, although, both the Alderns and the Daggets also had strong magic. His youth didn't matter; he was the most magical being Leargan had ever met.

Leargan's men started to file in, taking their various seats in the hall. Evening supper was always as populated as morning meal. Everyone wanted a hearty meal to wrap up their busy day.

Roduch was notably absent. No doubt he was with Avril, sharing a meal in her guest suite. The lass wasn't ready to venture into the public eye. He didn't blame her. Residents and staff of Castle Aldern were full of genuine friendless and concern, but it could be suffocating.

Niall caught his eye and gave a nod. His Second had his wife on his arm.

Lyde smiled sweetly at Leargan before her husband seated her. She was gorgeous. Diminutive, but just the right amount of curvy, flaxen hair and hazel eyes. His friend was crazy about her.

Leargan ignored the pang that could only be envy.

Now that they were becoming really settled in Greenwald, a couple of his men had taken wives. They were young, handsome knights that many a family recognized as good catches. The rest of his brothers would no doubt follow Niall and Padraig's lead.

Would Leargan? With his former captain's daughter as his bride?

"Something wrong?" Ansley asked, head cocked to one side.

Besides pleasantries, it was the first she'd spoken to him since he'd kissed her in the corridor days before. Then again, he'd been avoiding her like the plague, so there'd been little chance of conversation.

"No, not at all." Leargan cleared his throat.

Tristan shot him a curious look as he overheard them, but he ignored the lord.

"I wonder if Cera will be down," Lucan mused.

Distraction, thank the Blessed Spirit.

"I saw her after midday meal," Tristan said. "She said she's feeling up to it. So, I'd expect so."

"Good, I'd like to see her." Lucan smiled. The lad was extremely close to Lady Cera.

Together they'd defeated an evil man, a former archduke named Varthan, who'd killed Lady Cera's family and coveted her father's magic sword. The weapon had been integral in his plot to kill the king.

Tristan had been working under disguise for Varthan, posing as one of his shades—extensively trained mages— to try to gather proof against the evil man. He'd found Lucan, Varthan's favorite shade, and promised to get him away from the man, when he'd discovered the lad was not evil.

Jorrin and Lady Cera had fought together, along with Jorrin's father, Braedon, an elf wizard named Hadrian, and

Lady Cera's cousin, Avery. They'd defeated Varthan and his shades, along with freeing Lady Cera's aunt and uncle—Lord and Lady Lenore. Her only remaining family had been held hostage in their own home, Castle Lenore, in the Province of Tarvis.

In fact, Lucan was the one who'd killed Varthan, though Leargan would've had a hard time believing had he not seen it with his own eyes. The lad was sweet and honorable and wouldn't hurt a fly. But there was no doubt he'd do it all over again, if he was doing what was right and protecting what he loved.

Leargan, along with a small army led by the king himself, had arrived in Tarvis just in time to witness the end. Many had died at Varthan's hand, but he'd not gotten the magic sword.

Had Lucan not turned on him, things could have ended very differently, very badly. Lady Cera may even be dead, instead of happily married and expecting her first babe.

"Evenings are so lively around here. Almost like being at Rider Barracks, first meal after a long run." Amusement wrapped Ansley's words.

"Aye, yet mornings are even more sc."

She laughed. The sound was heaven.

The Alderns entered the great hall. All of the personal guard stood, Leargan included.

Jorrin smiled and motioned for them to sit as Lady Cera also smiled before resuming a scowl in her husband's direction.

Leargan chuckled and glanced over at Ansley's bark of laughter.

"I think she'll be much more pleasant when the baby finally decides to show up," she whispered, winking. She leaned in to him and the floral scent of her hair tickled his nose. The smile curving her lips made him dizzy.

Blessed Spirit, she was gorgeous.

He swallowed.

She was so delightful and playful. How could she be so nice to him after he'd obviously hurt her? Jorrin had to be wrong. Could an empath *be* wrong?

He *had* seen the flash of hurt in her eyes when he'd come to the table. Doubt made him shift on his feet. "I would never remark on such things," he teased back, reaching for composure with both hands.

"Ah, smart man." Tristan remarked, grinning.

Ansley smiled at the lord and a ridiculous wave of jealousy washed over him.

He tamped it down, berating himself. That was the second time where his old captain's daughter was concerned. He had no reason for his…*feelings*.

Lady Aimil's greeting to the duke and duchess took his attention as Jorrin helped Lady Cera into her seat on his right. She tried to shrug his hands off, but he wasn't having it, the lord maintained his grip on her forearm. The duchess obviously didn't like anyone showing too much concern for her condition, but she'd always been independent.

"Good evening, everyone," she said, ignoring her husband and smiling sweetly at Lucan when he handed her a goblet.

Servants poured in with more food, and Leargan surveyed the room. Most of the castle guard was present, as well as the late shift, who would serve the last postings of the day. His eyes swept over it all.

He saw so many different people, some he knew, some he didn't. All looked content. They laughed and joked, some of his men a bit too rambunctiously, but their energy would serve them well as they ventured into town. He smirked. Alasdair would be grumpy on patrol, no doubt.

"My lady, how are you feeling this evening?" Morag, the headwoman asked.

Leargan swung his head around in time to see the older woman at Lady Cera's side, setting a full basket of sweet rolls, especially for the duchess, on the table.

"Fine, Morag, thank you." Her voice was guarded, and she avoided looking at the other woman.

"Shall I call for the midwife?" The headwoman didn't approve of the idea of Tristan delivering the babe, though he was much more skilled than any midwife.

Lady Cera had told her on many occasions—at least in Leargan's presence—that she had no need of Peg, the midwife.

"No, Morag," his lady said evenly. Her eyes narrowed as she looked back at the headwoman.

"As you wish, milady." Morag's brow was knitted. She said nothing more but bowed and excused herself from the dais.

Lady Cera sighed, and Jorrin leaned over to whisper something in her ear.

Leargan reclined into the back of his chair as she smiled. No one wanted the lady of the castle upset, especially a pregnant one.

"Leargan, can I go on overnight patrol tonight? Sir Niall said you're leading." Lucan's green eyes were wide and sincere when their gazes collided.

He'd been waiting for the question all day. Brodic had broached the subject that morning, and he'd no doubt the lads had come up with the idea together.

His squire was about to take the next step in his training to become a knight. Leargan had gifted him with his first sword to celebrate the lad's fifteenth birthday a month before, so it was no surprise Lucan didn't want to be left behind.

The mage had been officially knighted by the king due to his bravery in saving Lady Cera and the kingdom from the former archduke, but he'd been dying to be considered a skilled, *real knight*—in Lucan's words.

Leargan hid a smile. "Aye, lad. There's no reason you can't. Then tomorrow, you will meet the personal guard and men-at-arms alike on the fighting yard to begin your training. But, no magic."

The lad nodded seriously, his face losing some of its youthful edge.

Tristan caught his eye and nodded approvingly.

"Thank you, Leargan!" Lucan pumped his fist.

"You don't need to thank me, lad. You need to work hard. I know you can do it, *Sir* Lucan."

Lucan nodded again, his mouth a hard line of determination.

Leargan swallowed a laugh lest he offend the boy.

Ansley's breath caught as he addressed the lad. Stern, but caring. And didn't that just make her admire him even more? Leargan spoke to Lucan as an equal. Even mentioned his title. Her knight cared for him very much.

It was already difficult enough sitting next to him, teasing and talking; pretending she was fine. Her chest ached every time she looked at him, only to worsen when he glanced back at her. But this was the first time he'd said more than *hello* in days.

She wanted to be near him…speak to him. Nothing had changed for her. All the self-deprecation in the world wasn't affecting her heart.

As Ansley watched him interact with everyone else at the head table, Cera's words echoed in her head. He did smile and laugh a bit, but with an aura of reservation. Leargan held himself back. He was always observing something or someone as if he knew where everything and *everyone* was, at all times.

The warrior in him required it so he could react if necessary. Her father was like that, too. It was hard to tell if either man ever truly relaxed. Also like her father, Leargan cared deeply for everything he was in charge of protecting. She could tell by the way he carried himself.

Could she be included?

Lord Dagget teased him at the table, as did the duke.

He appeared to laugh easily, which made him even more handsome.

She wanted to see more of *that* side of him. To be close to him. To be considered his friend. *More* than just his *friend.*

Had their kisses truly meant nothing to him? Pain stabbed her chest.

"Now, it's my turn to ask *you* if something is wrong," Leargan said.

Ansley jumped. His soft voice was so close to her ear.

He dipped closer, their faces only inches apart.

As she looked into his eyes, her heart sped up, words evaporating. Her gaze slid to his lips. Memories teased of how they'd felt moving against her own. "N…n…nothing…" *Stuttering?* That was a first.

His eyebrow shot up, so she forced words to keep tumbling out.

"I'm fine. Just thinking."

Leargan nodded and moved away.

She wanted to stop him. Wasn't the least bit offended by his closeness — as a matter of fact, she craved it.

He doesn't want that with you.

"Ansley…" The hesitation in his voice had her meeting those dark eyes again. His tone was un-knight-like and, therefore *un-Leargan-like.*

"Aye?"

He shook his head, full mouth a hard line, broad shoulders tight.

She didn't have the guts to push him, but curiosity ate at her. Turns of watching him flitted through her mind.

Leargan *always* exuded confidence.

What's this?

Ansley stared. She could fall into him. She needed to. It felt *right.*

Neither of them spoke, but he stared right back.

Minutes passed, she jolted back to herself, suppressing the tremor that shot down her spine. They were in the great hall. It was *public,* but everyone else had faded away from the moment their gazes had locked.

No one existed but him.

"Are you sure you're well?" Leargan's voice invaded her thoughts.

Back to normal, steady and sure. As if she'd imagined his uncertainty.

Idiot, get yourself together.

"Aye." She nodded for effect, and forced a smile.

"Leargan."

Sir Niall's voice made her jump in her seat.

"Aye?" Leargan asked his Second.

"Are you ready?"

"I'll be there shortly. But you can retire. I'll handle it."

"I was going to brief the new ones," Niall said.

"Very well. Please have Fia readied for me."

"The day is late. Is something wrong?" Ansley asked, worry creeping up.

"Nay. As Lucan mentioned, I'm leading our overnight patrol. Normally the guard would leave such things to the men-at-arms, but we've new men."

"Ah. Be careful, then."

Leargan smiled, and heat burned her neck, scorched her cheeks. "Always." He inclined his head and pushed his chair back.

Irrational panic swept her, and she had to stop herself from reaching for his hand. Anything to keep him from leaving her. Although their conversation wasn't wholly comfortable, he *had* spoken to her. Ansley wanted more. "Will I see you in the morning?"

His gaze found hers, eyes wide, and his hand was still on the back of his chair. "Aye." Leargan's chest rose as if he'd taken a deep breath. He shifted on his feet and leaned closer. "Can you make time for me tomorrow? I'd like to speak to you in privacy."

Her cheeks flamed and Ansley fought the urge to press her lips to his.

He was so close.

Nod. Just nod. Act like his request is normal.

"Ah…all…right. Aye."

"Thank you." He reached for her hand and squeezed.

She stared at his warm fingers over hers. Alone. With *Leargan?* Her stomach flipped.

Leargan took his leave, and Ansley watched him walk out of the great hall, trying not to be too blatant as she admired the way his brown breeches hugged his rear end.

After forcing her eyes away, she glanced around the hall. Most were filing out, maids starting to sweep in to clean up, removing trays and empty plates. Dishes and silverware clattered and clinked.

Lords Tristan and Jorrin stood collectively, and Ansley didn't miss both ladies assuring their husbands they'd meet them in chambers. Aimil even promised to escort Cera.

Ansley piped in that she'd also make sure the duchess came to no harm, ignoring Cera's grumble that she was not a child.

Both men eventually left the dais, and she was alone with her two best friends at the long table.

"What did he say?" Aimil's dark eyes were curious.

"He wants to speak to me in private." She shook her head, disbelief washed over her. What could Leargan have to say to her?

"Then do it," Cera said.

Ansley nodded absently, trying to calm her heart. "What could he want?"

"You." Aimil giggled.

She blinked. "No. He doesn't want me." She ignored the familiar rush of pain.

"Give him a chance." Cera smiled gently as she rubbed her distended tummy.

One corner of Ansley's mouth lifted. Did her friend even realize what she was doing?

"Just tell him what you want, Ans. Tell him how you

feel," Aimil urged.

"I couldn't..."

"You might be surprised with what he has to say," Cera said.

Ansley narrowed her eyes, studying the other redhead. Cera's tone had been odd.

The duchess's gray eyes held something unreadable, but her friend schooled her expression—almost too fast.

"What do you know?"

Her shrug was casual—too casual. "Nothing. Just...like I said before, I've known him a while now. He's a good man."

"Aye, he is." Ansley nodded.

The duchess said nothing more, and Ansley continued to appraise her.

Her friend might've told her a bit about Leargan the other day, but what *hadn't* she said?

Chapter Ten

Leargan yawned and stretched. He was going to end up oversleeping in the morning; he felt it in his bones. It was past three o'clock, and his troop had finished their rounds, nestling their horses in the stables and leaving the rest of the night watch—early morning, really—to reliable men-at-arms.

Blessed Spirit let me get them all trained soon.

It'd been almost a turn since he'd taken over in Greenwald. Even with the best help—which he had in each of his knights—they probably had several more months before he'd feel comfortable leaving things to others.

He'd yet to choose a man to be in charge of the castle men-at-arms. Jorrin hadn't pressured him, but perhaps they needed to speak of candidates. He and the personal guard couldn't pull double duty forever.

Young seemed to be a common trend at Castle Aldern, but Leargan didn't mind. They were shapeable, trainable, and proving to be loyal and competent. Sometimes experience wasn't everything. Besides, he wasn't exactly a grizzled old warrior, either.

Lucan and Brodic walked ahead of him, whispering excitedly to each other.

"Goodnight, sir." Brodic whirled and bowed deeply, his blond locks falling into his eyes.

He couldn't help but smile. *Young* was refreshing. Made him remember his own training days, and how good it felt to learn; have a purpose.

The lad had been his—first as page, then squire—since the tender age of eight. He idolized Leargan. Most of the time that wasn't hard to live up to; it made him want to be a better man, a better knight. Although, he was only three and twenty, Brodic looked to him like a father more than anything.

"Goodnight, lad." He ruffled his squire's fair hair and winked. "Goodnight, Sir Lucan."

The other lad beamed and Leargan chuckled, inclining his head as Lucan returned his gesture.

"Good job tonight. You both did excellent. I've some news I haven't shared with anyone just yet, but you two will have another joining your lessons with Roduch."

Both young men watched, waiting for him to continue.

"You're familiar with the stable boy, Alaric?"

"Aye, sir." Brodic nodded. "He's our friend."

"Good. Sir Niall will take him to squire. He'll start tomorrow, or today, depending on how you look at it."

Lucan whooped and Brodic grinned.

"I'm glad you're both excited for him. However, he'll have an advantage over you lads."

Brodic and Lucan froze, shoulder to shoulder and stared Leargan down.

He bit the inside of his cheek to keep from laughing. "Relax. I only mean he's been able to sleep all night, and you two only have about four hours until the morning meal."

The lads looked at each other and made a dash for the castle, leaving him chuckling in the courtyard.

Leargan headed toward the servants' entrance through the kitchens instead of the main doors to Castle Aldern like the lads. He always did a final round of the castle innards before climbing into bed. It made him feel more secure.

A familiar voice made him pause.

Ansley.

What the hell was she doing awake, let alone outside at this time of night?

His stomach fluttered.

"Ali, come on! Why do I have to be with you?"

He relaxed a tad at the annoyance in her voice. So nothing was *wrong*. Her bondmate was just demanding her attention.

The wolf heard his steps.

His eyes met her yellow ones when he rounded the corner.

She crouched, with her ears pitched forward. A low growl sounded.

Leargan tensed, tempted to draw his sword. Ali was about to rush and pounce. But he couldn't harm her. Her life was Ansley's, and the opposite was also true. If one perished, the other would soon follow. It was how the magic between them worked, and why animal bonds weren't to be taken lightly. They were permanent, as well.

"Ali?" Ansley's voice held alarm.

"Only me. Leargan." He put palms out flat.

Aye, like that would help. Just gives her something to sink her teeth into first.

The she-wolf didn't pause, and his heartbeat kicked up. Was she going to attack?

"Ali, stop!" Ansley came around the corner with wide teal eyes.

The beast froze.

Leargan flexed his grip on the hilt of his sword, his pulse thundering in his ears. His temples throbbed. He cleared his throat when he looked at Ansley, but didn't want to take his attention off her bondmate.

"I'm so sorry, Leargan." She slid in front of the beast.

At least she'd finally dropped the *Sir*.

Ali made a noise in her throat, but her mistress ignored her.

"It's fine. She's protecting you. Her job."

"She overreacts. We're within the castle gates, there's nothing to fear. You're in charge here, we're safe."

Pride at the compliment rolled over him, and he smiled. "Thank you. I appreciate your faith in me."

"I mean every word." She smiled, and his heart flipped.

Gorgeous.

He needed a distraction; he burned to snatch her up and kiss her. Ali would no doubt take issue with that.

The area was lit by a magic orb attached to the castle wall. Lucan had installed the lights all over the Castle—inside and out. They sensed light and dark, only coming to life when necessary. Their magic wore off every few months, and the mage would have to cast his spell again. He was getting stronger, and so was the power of the lights. Lasting longer.

Leargan inclined his head. "I'd ask what you're doing up, but I guess you've a finicky bondmate?"

Ansley came closer, the large she-wolf at her side. Her hand was buried in the fur at the back of the beast's neck.

The gesture was something he'd witnessed often since her arrival. Evidently, the immediate way to calm her wolf.

"Aye. She insisted I come outside with her. Not sure why, she's already been hunting with Trik and Isair. I was up anyway, with Cera and Aimil in the Duchess Solar. Avril stayed for a while, too. Until Sir Roduch collected her."

"Ah. Glad she's relaxing and making some friends."

Her shoulders loosened when Ali's did. Ansley's wolf leaned into her thigh. "The lass kind of clings to me. I don't mind, but I've told her Cera and Aimil want to be her friends, too. Since they're noble, my guess is she thinks of them differently than me."

The thin material of her shirt clung to her body, and Leargan tried not to stare. She wore no jerkin, just a soft tan tunic untucked from her dark brown breeches and hanging mid-thigh. Her braid looked hastily made and messy, quite the opposite of normal. Strands escaped, red locks dancing around her face, and he itched to touch her.

"You're wellborn." He forced words out, clearing his throat.

"Right. But no title. I think it helps her."

"You found her."

"That, too." Ansley nodded. "But you found her, too."

"You're female. She won't let any male near her except Roduch."

"Sir Roduch is a good man. If she can move passed everything, he'd be good for her, though I know it will be a long while."

He nodded. Leargan didn't want to talk about his friend and the girl. He wanted to kiss Ansley. He planted his fists at his sides, chided himself to focus on their conversation. Discussing someone or something else was for the better.

They were supposed to meet in the morning. He needed time to gather his thoughts. Apologize.

Why'd she agreed to speak privately?

Even if he mustered the guts to apologize, how could he keep his hands to himself if they were alone? The struggle was on right now. They were outside.

Contained in a room? It wouldn't be good for his self-control.

Jorrin had advised telling her about the scroll. Could he? Perhaps propose?

Right. She'd think you're crazy.

Ali growled and darted after something in the shadow the light cast.

Ansley groaned and it made his cock twitch. Her gaze was locked in the direction of her wolf. "I'm tired. I'm about to leave her out here."

"One of the guards will let her back in. The night watch often has to keep an eye out for Trikser and Isair."

"I've thought-sent my threat; we'll see." She smiled.

Leargan met those teal eyes and smiled back. "All right. I'll escort you to your chambers."

She nodded, but jumped when he looped his arm in hers. However, she didn't pull away.

His heart sped up again. It was *right* to have her at his

side. "Ansley," he croaked.

"Aye, Leargan?"

He cleared his throat. "When we get back to your rooms, may I speak to you tonight instead of tomorrow?"

Nay. Wait 'til tomorrow when you're calm. When you know what the hell you'll say.

The blush that lit her cheeks made his mouth go dry.

He needed to kiss her more than he needed to breathe.

Please say no.

He'd never be able to keep his hands to himself if she allowed him into her chambers. Maybe they *should* wait for Ali. At least the beast's distaste of him would help. Fear of remaining in one piece might give him something to focus on other than the memory of her taste.

"Aye," Ansley said.

Leargan was doomed.

Her heart raced as her pace matched his. Even though he had no interest in her, it wasn't proper to see Leargan in her chambers.

So why had she agreed when he'd asked to escort her?

She should've been asleep hours ago, anyway. Instead, Ansley, Cera, Avril and Aimil had gone to the Duchess Solar to lounge around a cozy fire after evening meal, settling into overstuffed chairs and wrapped in warm furs.

Sir Roduch had come to get a sleepy Avril several hours later.

The three of them had remained, talking as they hadn't since they'd been young girls bunking together at Rider Barracks.

All three of their wolves had joined them, napping near the fire until the need to hunt had had Aimil letting the small pack out.

Ansley concentrated on putting one foot in front of the other, trying not to be too obvious as she glanced down. It'd be just like her to trip and fall on her face in front of him. Heat crept up her neck.

Leargan's words at evening meal tickled her mind. What could he possibly want to talk about that required them being alone?

They should've kept their assignation for the morning.

Privacy could've meant the great hall after breaking their fast, a sitting room, the Duchess Solar, a ledger room…any place without a *bed*. The thought jolted her, and she jumped beside him, inadvertently tugging his arm.

He paused, shooting her a concerned look. "Are you all right?"

"Aye." Ansley looked away, her cheeks searing. She'd embarrass herself for sure.

Ali had taken her threat to leave her outside alone seriously. Her bondmate dashed in front of them, stopping by the servants' entrance and glancing over her shoulder. She grumbled mentally to Ansley, unhappy feelings washing over her. The wolf didn't like Leargan's hand on her.

She ignored her bondmate, and they went inside, Ali plastered to her thigh. Ansley chided her because it making walking difficult, but Ali wouldn't break physical contact.

Leargan said nothing when they arrived at her room. He gestured for her to enter, following inside and closing the door.

The lack of sound was like her pulse, pounding in her ears. She had the jitters.

Her bond immediately lay by the banked fire, claiming the hearth. The big she-wolf looked at the captain, her deep growl reverberating.

"Hush," Ansley admonished, glancing at the man who'd stolen her heart.

His shoulders were stiff; his chest rose and fell as if he'd taken a deep breath.

Ali wuffed, her thoughts a small argument, but Ansley reinforced her command mentally, softening it with love, and her wolf whined, thumping her tail.

Never hurt him, Ali. I love him, as I love you, she thought-sent.

Her bondmate's big body relaxed and she lowered her head to her paws.

One corner of her mouth lifted as she watched yellow eyes slip closed, and Ali gave a large sigh. After dragging her all over the gardens and courtyard, it figured her bondmate would be the exhausted one.

Leargan shifted on his feet.

Panic washed over her. She'd not guarded her thought-send. Could he communicate mentally? Had he heard her?

"I'm sorry." Words tumbled out. "She's possessive of me. She even growls at my da once in a while, so she's not singling you out. If that makes you feel better."

"I don't blame her." His gaze was intense, and Ansley couldn't look away.

What does that mean?

Her heart stuttered. "Do you—" She cleared her throat and tried again when her voice faltered. "Do you want to have a seat?" She gestured to the small table and two chairs by the fireplace, but his dark eyes hadn't moved. Her body heated, limbs tingled.

The captain wasn't looking at her like someone with *no* romantic interest.

Calm down, clear your head of nonsense and get this over with, whatever it is.

She pulled out a chair and winced at the screech it made on the stone floor. "Anyway, Ali won't hurt you. I'd never let her, so you don't have to worry about it." *Babbling? Really?* Ansley swallowed, chiding herself.

"I'm not afraid." Leargan's voice made her freeze. He hovered near the door. "I've been living with Isair and Trikser for almost a turn."

"She won't hurt you," she repeated, forcing herself to relax her arms and shoulders.

"I realize that." He came toward her, every step making her heart pound harder.

Ali made a noise in her throat and Ansley sucked in a breath. She needed to calm herself before wild emotions affected her bondmate. When she glanced over her shoulder, her wolf lifted her head, studying them both.

She commanded her mentally to stay put. "What...what did...you want to talk to me about?"

Leargan took a seat, pulling the other chair closer to his and gesturing for her to join him. He cleared his throat right after her bottom hit the cushion, wringing his hands together.

Should she feel better or worse that he was nervous, too? Ansley shifted, grasping both chair arms. His knees were close enough to touch hers, and she could feel the heat coming off his body.

"I wanted to explain myself to you. The other day, in the corridor—"

"You don't have to. It's fine." She spoke quickly, shaking her head. Didn't want to hear it. Her chest ached. She couldn't take the hurt and humiliation of his rejection again, even in privacy.

"No...please. I've some things I need to say to you," he said softly, meeting her eyes.

She blinked away sudden tears, averting her gaze.

Ali whined, and they both looked in the wolf's direction, but neither said anything, and her bond made no moves.

"You don't have to explain yourself to me."

"Ansley." He rose from the chair, pulling her to her feet and into his chest.

She yelped, but Leargan tugged her closer, and her arms shot around him of their own accord.

Ali rose to all fours and growled.

Leargan didn't release her, but he stilled.

"I'm fine, Ali." She made eye contact with her bondmate. *Lie back down. Don't move. Leargan will not hurt me, love,* Ansley reinforced mentally.

Her wolf huffed but did as ordered.

His warmth enveloped her, and her heart thundered. She could feel his echoing hers, just as fast. "She won't move, Leargan."

"I never meant to hurt you." He nestled her closer, and she wanted to melt into him.

"Oh..." she whispered.

What's worse? His apology, or the fact he knew he'd hurt her?

"Leaving like that, I didn't think of how you might react. I'm sorry. I acted impulsively, and...I didn't know how to handle myself." With every word, he inched closer, until his lips were hovering over hers, the heat of his breath tickling.

A tremor shot down her spine and she tightened her grip on his waist. Ansley tilted her face, brushing her lips against his.

Leargan groaned and crushed his mouth into hers. Kissing her harder, he forced her mouth open, but she met his every move. He devoured her, their tongues dueling. She moaned, and he swallowed it, deepening the kiss even more.

Ansley's legs wobbled, desire settling low in her belly. She wanted to get lost in him.

Forever.

But...what did Leargan want?

He grunted a protest as she pulled away.

She stayed close—couldn't help it—resting her forehead against his shoulder. Hurt threatened to swallow her whole. "You *left*. Kissing me was a mistake." Her voice shook, and she concentrated on not crying; her emotions were awry. Ansley wanted to be honest with him, but did she have the guts to do so?

He leaned back, cupping her face. "It's not like that,"

he whispered.

"You apologized…I thought…"

Leargan silenced her with his lips.

She pressed back into him, shooting her arms around his neck. Ignoring questions and doubts, Ansley kissed him back with all her might. She felt his body's response, and her core warmed even more.

He *did* want her.

When he parted their mouths, it was much too soon. Her body was hot; she throbbed between her legs. They panted, chest heaving against breasts.

"Ansley. My Ansley. What am I going to do with you?"

She froze in his arms, staring into his dark eyes.

My Ansley?

He tugged her braid and smiled.

Her stomach somersaulted, but then his expression slid into something serious, his eyes pools of midnight. "I apologized for shoving you up against the wall, pushing myself on you…shaming you."

"Shaming me?" Ansley gasped. *Cera and Aimil were right.* "You didn't shame me, Leargan."

"You don't understand. I was about to…" The apple of his throat bobbed as he swallowed.

"I wanted you. I would've let you." Warmth engulfed her face. Had she really just admitted that aloud?

Leargan blinked. Understanding settled into his expression and her stomach fluttered. Color lit his high cheekbones, olive slipping into red.

Blessed Spirit, I made him blush?

He shook his head, dark hair swishing about his shoulders.

She wanted to reach up and touch the stubble on his cheeks, it'd felt like heaven against her skin when they'd kissed. Gorgeous, like always, his full mouth was swollen from their kisses. A tiny scar above his top lip stood out, white against the golden hue of his skin. She'd always wanted to ask him how it'd happened. "Leargan," she whispered.

His eyes slid to her mouth before he met her gaze again, and she shivered. "I apologized because of what I almost did. It wouldn't have been reversible. And, it wasn't right, against a corridor wall."

"It wouldn't have mattered." Her stomach jumped. Relief washed over her with the confession.

So what if he knows you want him?

"What?" He gaped, eyes wide.

Ansley gripped her newfound bravery with both hands. "It wouldn't have mattered, because it was *you*." Doubt ate at her and she had to avert her gaze. Why had she just admitted she would've given him her innocence without a backward thought?

"Look at me, Ansley, and tell me what you mean."

After squeezing her eyes shut, she took a breath and finally met his eyes. Words fell from her mouth. "I wanted you that day. And...I...want you still..."

Leargan grinned.

Her heart tripped over itself, but she had no recovery time, because he claimed her mouth again. She molded her body to his and opened for him, rubbing her tongue against his.

He kissed her until her legs gave out, and he groaned against her lips. Leargan held her up, plastered to his chest and explored her mouth. Urgency was still there, but he guided their kiss with a languorous heat that melted her heart and soul.

She would do *anything* for this man.

He rocked his hips into hers, and she wanted to be naked with him. Ansley broke away panting and pulled him toward her bed. Embarrassment and insecurity didn't matter anymore. Leargan was in her room, in her arms, and kissing her senseless.

It can't stop here.

Reason, reminders, right from wrong, were all

pushed away, replaced by desire, need, and her body aching in places she'd never experienced before.

"Ansley, we can't," he gasped, locking his feet in place by the table. He must've read hurt in her expression, because he tugged her back into his arms, holding her, stroking her hair.

Her braid had been worked loose, her long red locks flowing down her back. Her heart beat against his, and she hid her face against his neck, tears threatening.

He kissed the top of her head, squeezing her against him. "I'm not rejecting you."

"Then why...?" She met his eyes. Her stomach fluttered at what she saw there.

Tenderness...and desire.

"I won't dishonor you like that."

Ansley trembled. "What if I chose it?"

"I would love to say *aye. Now.* Blessed Spirit knows I want you that badly. But I can't do that to you."

The hardness in his breeches pressed into her.

She swallowed. "I want you, Leargan."

Leargan closed his eyes and made a noise in his throat. "Your virginity is for your wedding night." His arms shook as he held her.

"My virginity is for whatever *I* choose." She glared.

Honor be damned.

She wanted him. She was offering herself to him. Her body demanded it. His hands and lips all over. Ansley needed to feel his weight on top of her, inside her. "And I choose to give it to you." She sucked in a breath and waited for his answer. Rejection would crush her, but she steeled herself for it.

Leargan guided her face back to his, kissing her softly. "I'll never receive a greater gift. But not tonight. Like I said, it's for your wedding night. *Our* wedding night."

She gasped, swaying on her feet. "What're you saying?"

"I'm saying, marry me, Ansley."

Her mouth hung open. *No words. Why* was the man of her dreams proposing?

Don't question it. Just say 'Aye.'

Hot tears cascaded down her cheeks. His handsome face blurred.

He smiled and kissed them away, his lips brushing hers again. She tasted the saltiness of her own tears and blinked.

Was this really happening?

How can this be real?

Leargan had said he wanted her, but that was far from love. Was he asking for physical needs? Because she was innocent?

Surely not. He could find another woman if it was only that. Right? A tavern, even a maid in the castle.

Don't think about this. Respond.

*It's too good to be true…*a voice chided.

Ansley ignored it. Listened to her heart, not her head. She couldn't help it. She *loved* him, more than she'd ever thought possible.

Could she marry him without the same from him? Was physical desire enough to sustain her?

She also disregarded the voice that asserted she needed *all* of him, as well as the voice of reason that there had to be more to this sudden proposal. Perhaps for now, she'd take what she could get.

His expression was open, expectant.

"Marry you?" Ansley stumbled out.

"Aye. Ansley Fraser, will be my wife?"

"Aye." Was there really any other answer? She clutched the front of his leather jerkin as her head spun.

Blessed Spirit, please don't let me wake if this is only a dream. I want to stay here. Forever.

"You said aye?" Leargan whispered, wonder in his tone and his eyes wide.

She nodded, feeling his arms tighten around her.

He gave her a brilliant smile and pulled her closer.

"You thought I wouldn't?" She'd never seen Leargan…vulnerable. Ansley should reassure him, but she liked him this way. It made him more reachable, not so much the perfect knight.

More *hers*.

"Aye…nay…I don't know…" He looked away. "It's out of the blue…"

I love you.

She bit her lip to keep the words inside, panic washing over her.

Ali whined, and they both shot glances to the she-wolf.

I'm fine, Ansley thought-sent. *Stay. He's not hurting me.* She turned back to him, taking a breath and forcing words out. "I will marry you."

Leargan pressed a kiss to her mouth, then rested his forehead against hers. He flashed a grin that had her heart galloping all over. "I'm glad. There's nothing I want more."

"Is this really happening?" she whispered.

He laughed and she jumped. He caressed her cheek, and rested his palm against it; the movement of his thumb caused a shiver to slide through her whole body.

"Aye, it's happening." He kissed her nose.

Ansley smiled, burying her face against him and closing her eyes.

Ali made a noise, but she was only relaxing. The wolf rolled to her side and closed her yellow eyes.

"She let me kiss you," Leargan whispered against Ansley's hair.

She nodded, her cheeks burning. "I threatened her."

He laughed and she grinned.

The captain didn't laugh nearly enough. The sound washed over her, warmed her.

Leargan grabbed her hand and kissed her knuckles. "Will she ever like me?"

"I don't know. We'll just have to see. We have a

lifetime, right?" Ansley slid into the heat of his dark gaze.
"I suppose we do."

Chapter Eleven

ynan cursed as colorfully as he could manage, spitting in the dirt and stomping his foot. He'd been to every inn and tavern near the market center, and then worked his way out, ending up in the slums of Lower Greenwald.

Nothing.

His little wife was nowhere he could scent out.

Had the Kenrick boy lied?

His steward shifted on his feet at Tynan's glare but pretended not to notice his ire. "The boy said what tavern?" he barked.

"The *White Sage Pub*, sire."

"That is *not* in Lower Greenwald," Tynan growled.

She'd no coin, and the tavern and inn in question was in Greenwald Main, the better part of the city center. If his wife was there, unless she sold her body like barmaids at many a tavern, she'd gain no room and board.

"Aye, sire. But Mistress Avril is not there." Harlan's knuckles were white on his horse's reins as the beast stood beside him. His steward fidgeted; only the large gelding stood still.

"You looked at all the wenches as well as spoke to the proprietor?"

He nodded. "Even looked in the kitchens. They've not seen a dark-haired lass that fit Mistress Avril's description."

"Where the hell is she?"

"Shall I have Ferd and Han rove the market again?"

"Do it now."

The man shouted for his two oldest sons and relayed

Tynan's orders.

Without a word, both young men mounted their horses and took off toward the city center, only a ten minute ride from the slums.

Tynan glared up at the disheveled sign announcing the *Dragon's Lair*. Supposed to be shaped like a shield, the wood was split and hung at an angle above the entrance, the other nail long rotted through. The fire breathing dragon on it used to be green. It was chipped and half gone.

The stupid bartender swore he'd not seen Avril, either. Tynan had checked all his whores. Every last one was older and haggard; none could hold a candle to his wife.

In the very least, she was attractive. If she'd have been trying to work there selling her body, the other women wouldn't have had it. She would've been tossed to the street for taking all their *visitors*.

He snorted. If she was trying her sweet little bottom at being a whore, Tynan would kill her. No matter where he ended up finding her. Then he'd demand her stupid father repay her dowry or replace Avril with her younger sister.

A slow smile spread across his mouth. Perhaps that wasn't such a bad idea. The girl was at least four and ten now, would be pretty too, because she looked like her older sister.

He could have another virgin. Maybe the younger sister could do what Avril had not, and give him a son. Although his wife was the only one known to have magic in her family, it was in the blood, wasn't it? Her sister's son could be just like Avril.

"Let's go, there's nothing here," he snarled at his steward.

"Aye, sire." Harlan tied his horse to the back of Tynan's coach and climbed into the driver seat.

"Take me to the *White Sage Pub*."

"Sire?"

"We're staying in Greenwald until we find her. She's around here somewhere. I *will* find her and bring her home."

The more Avril spoke, the more Leargan's blood boiled. His blunt nails were biting into his palms as he squeezed tight fists, but that was about the only thing that kept his sword in its scabbard. He wanted to tear the bastard from limb to limb.

Ansley's teal gaze and wide smile kept dancing into his mind, making him see even more red. Even the thought of someone hurting her like Avril had been hurt made him want to run something through. He would *kill* anyone who'd attempt to hurt Ansley like that.

The duke, too, was angry, fists clenched, jaw tight.

Tristan was also present to witness what the girl had to say, but he sat silently, pale. Knowing what she'd been through because of his magic, and hearing her talk about it were two different things.

Lady Cera had expressed concerns that a female should be present, but Roduch protested it would be too many people for Avril, so the ladies had been excluded. No doubt, Ladies Cera and Aimil, as well as Ansley were awaiting Avril in the Duchess Solar.

Roduch sat, his chair plastered to hers, her small hand in his. But the more she spoke, the closer the lass moved to the big knight, until he'd finally pulled her onto his lap, holding her as her voice shook and she fought tears.

Leargan was proud of how long Avril had held it together.

Tears didn't course down her cheeks until she'd finished her recital. She promptly buried her face against his friend's broad chest and started to sob.

Still, he admired her. It wasn't easy to show emotion in front of virtual strangers.

Jorrin winced and exchanged a glance with Tristan. The duke's empathic magic would cause him to feel what Avril was. That'd be *uncomfortable* at best.

Leargan shifted in his chair, taking a breath.

"Let's go arrest the bastard," Roduch growled. The girl in his arms whimpered, but the knight just held her tighter.

The duke cleared his throat, holding a palm up. "Calm, Roduch."

Leargan pushed to his feet and moved behind the taller man, squeezing his shoulder, smiling slightly at the grateful look Roduch shot him.

"Avril," Jorrin said softly. He waited for her to compose herself.

She lifted her head and looked at him, her green eyes as wide as saucers.

"You were married at age fourteen, correct?"

"Yes, Lord Aldern," she whispered.

"Do you wish to remain wed to Tynan Mont of Greenwald, now that you've come of age?"

Avril shook her head vehemently. "No!"

Biting back a smile, Leargan stood taller. She was small, but strong. It was nice to see some spirit. Her former husband hadn't ripped it all from her.

"He needs you to say it, lass." Roduch squeezed her hand.

She looked into his friend's eyes for so long, Jorrin and Tristan shifted in their seats. Then Avril squared her shoulders and sat taller against Roduch's broad frame.

Leargan didn't miss the softness in his friend's gaze. He could already see a bond forming between his friend and the girl. They both deserved happiness. If they could find it together, so be it.

Blessed Spirit guard their hearts.

He spared a glance at the duke. Jorrin's expression was serious, but Leargan could tell his empathic magic saw it, too.

"I, Avril Larange, formally renounce my marriage to Tynan Mont." With every word, her voice rose, more clear and confident. When she finished, her face was radiant.

"Witnessed by Lord Jorrin Aldern," Jorrin said.

"Also witnessed by Lord Tristan Dagget," the healer seconded.

"Also witnessed by Sir Leargan Tegran." He added his voice, as did Roduch, vehemently. Probably more witnesses than legally necessary, but it couldn't hurt anything.

Avril looked overwhelmed, but allowed Roduch to kiss her knuckles. She relaxed against his friend, a smile playing at her lips.

Good.

Leargan hadn't seen her smile yet.

"Gamel drew up this parchment. We'll sign it. It decrees that your renouncement is official, Avril. We'll go arrest him, and then the king can deal with him."

"I still want to kill the bastard," Roduch muttered.

"The king?" the girl breathed, paling.

"Aye," Roduch said.

"He should be here soon," Jorrin said, one corner of his mouth up. He caught Leargan's eye.

"Don't remind me," Leargan mumbled.

"Why is the king coming to Greenwald?" she whispered.

"For Leargan and Ansley's wedding," the duke said, much too brightly.

Leargan glared, and Tristan coughed, but it was really poorly disguised laugh.

Roduch shot him a glance, but he just shrugged.

He hadn't told his men about his betrothal.

"Oh," Avril said, looking at Leargan. "Congratulations, Sir Leargan. I like Mistress Ansley very much."

"Thank you," Leargan said. "She's fond of you, as well."

The lass' lips upturned slightly. It was shy and sweet and had him smiling in return.

Who was this girl that she could say congratulations regarding marriage, considering the one she'd endured?

"What happens next? Now that the decree is signed?" Roduch asked Jorrin. "Can we go arrest the bastard?"

"Very soon, Roduch. Very soon." The duke nodded, his blue eyes earnest as they regarded the knight. "We have more to discuss, but Avril is safe here, and welcome to stay as long as she wants."

Roduch pulled her closer.

Was *forever* an option? Leargan smirked. No way Avril was going anywhere.

"Am I done?" she whispered.

"Aye, lass. Let's go get some air. I'll take you to Lady Cera's garden again. Even in the fall, the place is peaceful and beautiful."

She smiled — a genuine one — as the big knight stood in one fluid motion and put her to her feet.

Leargan tried not to stare.

Avril's face lit up. *Beautiful* slid into *gorgeous*. And his friend was already obviously lost to her as he stared down.

After tucking her small hand into his elbow, Roduch bowed to the lords and inclined his head to him before taking her from the room.

"Wow," Jorrin whispered as soon as the door to his ledger room had closed.

"There's certainly something between them," Tristan said.

The duke came around to the front of his desk, perching on the end and crossing his arms over his broad chest. "You're not kidding. My magic lit up from the inside out."

"Speaking of magic, did you notice something about her recital?" the healer asked.

"What's that?" Leargan leaned forward as he took a seat in the ornate carved chair across from Jorrin.

"Not once did the word '*magic*' come out of that girl's mouth."

"So?" The duke cocked his head to the side, blue eyes intense.

"Could you not feel her magic, Jorrin? When I healed her…I knew it was there."

"I felt nothing." His brow furrowed.

"Exactly. She has great power. *Great power.*"

"Of what nature?" Leargan asked.

"That, I cannot tell you. She's too guarded. When I touched her mind with healing magic, a vault slammed shut on me. I sensed magic, a lot of it. But nothing more."

"Do you think she knows she has magic?" Leargan asked. Having none himself, the only knowledge he had of magic was from those around him. He could thought-send if he concentrated, but it gave him an instant headache. Having someone else's voice in his mind always made an unmanly tremor shoot down his spine, but he'd received thought-sends from others on occasion.

"Aye." The healer nodded, taking a breath. "There's no way she has that much control and doesn't know she has it. She's hiding it. Avoiding it at all costs."

"I agree. Control suggests training. But why hide?" Jorrin mused, shoving his hand through his dark hair.

"We need to find out. *Before* we go traipsing to Tynan Mont's holding," Leargan said.

The duke threw him a look. "You don't think it's a trap?"

"Nay. Not with those kind of wounds," Tristan said before he could speak.

"I just mean, we need to know what we're riding into."

"Well, you're my captain. Tell me what you need," Jorrin said.

"Knowledge."

"I can't order her to divulge her magic." He blew out a breath. "I mean, I *won't*. Not after what she's survived."

"Only one person can get her to talk." Tristan's hazel eyes were keen, and he tented his fingers.

"Roduch," Leargan and Jorrin said at the same time.

Chapter Twelve

Roduch assured him he could get the girl to open up to him about her magic, but he'd begged Leargan and Jorrin to give him some time. People overwhelmed her.

Avril still took most meals in her room, and the big knight only left her side for training.

Tristan checked on her daily, and the ladies visited briefly—now she would see all three of them regularly—but for the most part, the lass was a hermit of her guest suite.

If Roduch—more anxious than anyone to apprehend Avril's husband—could be patient and wait until she was ready, so could the rest of them. It would happen all in good time. She was being taken care of, safe. Leargan was content with that, until it was time to lead his men to get the bastard.

Jorrin had put out feels, magic as well as sending a few men, to discreetly see if Tynan Mont knew his former wife's whereabouts. They'd received no confirmation, other than the man was angry beyond all means that she'd disappeared. None of the men had approached him, but he'd been spotted in Greenwald Main.

He didn't even try to play the grieving husband, though he was promising a reward of gold for her return. Wouldn't Tynan Mont be surprised when he received an armed escort of knights instead?

Despite the plan in regards to Avril's former husband, the next few days passed quickly, with Leargan grabbing Ansley and kissing her senseless every chance he got.

He had to concentrate not to skip down the wide

corridor.

When had he ever been happier?

Leargan could only grin at the looks he received from servants he passed on the way to the kitchens. He didn't care. Nothing could bring him down.

"Captain, I've everything you asked for. And the bread is still warm. I put sweet spread on it and wrapped for you both." Daicy inclined her head, grinning. Her brown eyes danced as he took the picnic basket.

He smiled. "Thanks, Daicy. Did you give her my note?"

"Aye, sir. I also made sure one of the lads readied your horses. Mistress Ansley should be in the courtyard waiting for you."

His stomach jumped. A free afternoon was rare, but Leargan wanted to take time to get to know his betrothed.

Alone with Ansley—really alone—away from the prying eyes of Castle Aldern was going to be a test. He was determined to be honorable by her. She'd make it to their wedding night with her virginity intact.

Even if it killed him.

And with the way she pressed against him, caressed him, and kissed him back, it just might. Ansley wasn't just responding to his overtures anymore. She'd started initiating contact; she'd reach for his hand, touch his arm, and kiss him, too.

The fact that she wanted him as badly as he wanted her was challenging his resolve—and self-control.

Daicy bowed and returned to her duties with a parting smile.

Leargan whistled, grinning like an idiot as he headed out of the castle.

She looked up, as if her eyes sought him as he crossed the main courtyard. The smile that lit Ansley's face made his heart skip.

He ordered himself to keep it together and thanked her for minding Fia when he reached her and their horses.

"Afternoon." Leargan pressed a kiss to her cheek.

Grinning, she leaned into him. "Afternoon." She glanced at the well laden basket. "A picnic, Leargan?" Her blue-green eyes were wide and eager.

"Aye, if you're up for it."

"Oh, aye." She slipped her arms around his waist and squeezed. "You could've just asked me, you know. The note suggested something clandestine."

Leargan chuckled. "And here, I thought my Senior Rider betrothed would have appreciated my efforts, message and all."

She giggled. "I do, I really do. Thank you."

When she bowed, he could hardly keep from beaming. What was this woman doing to him?

Ansley's eyes swept the courtyard, and Leargan's gaze followed, seeing a tiny Avril on Roduch's arm, headed toward the gardens. When she looked back at him, her expression sobered. "Maybe we shouldn't go. There's a lot going on right now."

He caressed her cheek. "We'll get Tynan Mont when the time is right. I think an afternoon to ourselves is fine. She's safe here, with Roduch especially."

She bit her bottom lip, but nodded, squeezing his hand. "Do you have a place in mind?"

"Aye, if you're up for a long ride."

Ansley patted her white gelding's neck. "Of course. Long rides are what Caide does best."

"Good." Leargan secured the basket to his saddle, giving Fia a pat. She nickered, bumping his hand for more affection.

Ansley ran her hand down her long muzzle. His buckskin mare bumped her hand when she went to move away. "You're a greedy lass, aren't you?" Her tone was amused.

He rubbed his horse's jowls and laughed. "She likes you."

She glanced over her shoulder. Her bond was slinking

toward them, head down, as if she was stalking prey. She sighed. "I wish I could say the same for how Ali felt about you."

The beast sprinted the last twenty feet, coming to a stop only seconds before plowing Ansley over. She leaned into her mistress's thigh, the look in her yellow eyes screaming, *Mine.*

Leargan shook his head, then met Ansley's teal gaze. "I hope she'll change her mind at some point."

After scolding her bondmate, his betrothed pushed her off and patted the wolf's rump. "Be nice, Ali, I mean it." Her expression was full of chagrin. "Well, I like you, so that's all that matters."

His heart thundered and he fell into her eyes.

She *liked* him? Liking him was one thing, but couldn't it be more? It shouldn't bother him, because he *liked* her, too. He ignored the voice that suggested it was more.

He'd been lucky—and a coward—in the way he'd asked her to be his wife. Leargan still didn't understand why she'd said yes. But she *had.* So he was going to make the best of it—of her, of *them*—until he mustered the guts to tell her about the king's order.

He didn't want to think about that right now.

His hands reached for her of their own accord. Ansley came to him, ignoring Ali's protest. He disregarded her bondmate as well, claiming her mouth.

Just one kiss and then they'd go.

She pressed closer, opening for him like she always did. Her lush breasts flattened against his chest. She wrapped her arms around him, her hips pushing into his.

Leargan felt every inch of her tall frame, and his manhood stood up straight, threatening to punch through his breeches. Her taste exploded in his mouth as their tongues dueled. He kissed her harder, swallowing her moan. He pulled away gasping when he caught himself cupping her bottom and thrusting against her.

Looking at her face was a mistake. He groaned at

heavy-lidded teal eyes, full kiss-swollen lips and pink flushed cheeks.

He wanted to make her truly his. Leargan would never survive until their wedding night. "We—" He cleared his throat. "We should go. I want to take you to the lake."

Ansley nodded, slipping out of his arms and taking a breath that made her delectable breasts rise and fall. She brushed red wisps out of her face. "Are you bringing a blanket?"

Planting his fists at his sides was the only thing that kept him from grabbing her when he saw the twinkle in her eye. She wasn't half as worried about her virtue as he was. He bit back another groan. She was going to kill him yet. "Aye."

"Good." Ansley winked, and swung herself into Caide's saddle.

He stood staring at her fine breech-clad long legs.

Numbly, like an idiot.

"Are we going?" she asked sweetly, one delicate flame-colored brow arched.

Shaking himself in his boots, Leargan managed a nod and scrambled onto Fia's back. His mare whinnied; like she was asking if he was all right.

He ignored the amused look on his betrothed's gorgeous face, muttering a prayer under his breath.

The last thing he needed her to know was how tightly wound she had him.

The fall day was bright and clear, the sun high in the cloudless sky. The air was unusually warm; an occasional breeze shifted the colorful leaves on the trees along the road.

Ansley should've been able to appreciate a beautiful afternoon in Greenwald, but nature couldn't hold her attention.

She couldn't stop staring at her betrothed.

He wore no helm, his thick black locks loose and moving around his shoulders with the wind. Leargan's olive skin flushed pink—from their kiss, as much as exposure to the outside, and had her heart thundering with every step of Caide's hooves.

It was a good thing her horse was experienced and able to guide his rider. Otherwise, she would've fallen off his back, because she wasn't paying attention to the road or the ride.

Or her bondmate, who either jogged ahead or lagged behind their horses, sulking no matter her position.

"Enjoying the scenery?" Leargan asked.

"The company, for sure." Ansley slapped her hand over her mouth. What had she said? Her cheeks burned. His grin relaxed her shoulders, and her breath exited on a whoosh.

"I like being with you, too."

"Good." She swallowed, forcing her eyes ahead.

Idiot. You can let him kiss you until your toes curl, but you can't talk to him? Fine marriage you'll have.

"We're just about there. Over that hill." He pointed, and she followed his gaze.

"I noticed the lake on my ride in." The moonlight had reflected off the water, even at a distance. "Thank you for bringing me here. I'll love the chance to get a better look." She clung to his distraction, ordering herself to calm.

"I love it here." Leargan smiled. "I discovered this place not long after coming to Greenwald. The lake is vast, so open, yet so private, if that makes any sense. No one lives within sight. Breathtaking view."

Good, they'd have privacy. But did they need it? Every time Ansley thought she was breaking down his block on making love before they got married, he'd pull away. He was driving her mad with desire.

Why didn't *she* have a say? It was her body, after all. Or did he not want her as badly as he'd claimed?

Cera was right about one thing, Leargan had more than his fair share of control.

Her breath caught at the moment they crested the small hill he'd pointed out. The lake extended as far as the eye could see, the water moving gently with the breeze. Surrounded by forest on one side, and open field on the other, the sight was serene. Not a soul around, but she heard ducks calling to each other.

Ali wuffed and rushed toward the water, several large birds taking flight as her bondmate disturbed their rest. She leapt after them, powerful jaw snapping air as she failed to make purchase. Undeterred, the large she-wolf jumped again and again, tail wagging.

Leargan chuckled, pulling Fia to a stop next to Caide. "Well, I'm glad she's enjoying herself."

"Finally." Ansley grinned.

Her wolf sent playful thoughts and pictures.

At least you're done sulking, she thought-sent.

Exercising the selective comprehension she was so good at, Ali ignored her.

"Let's find a spot. Fia is probably eager to graze."

She dismounted beside him, nodding. "Caide feels the same, I'm sure."

Following his lead, she tugged her gelding toward a small copse of trees. Her betrothed unloaded their horses. She spread out a thick brown sleeping fur, setting the picnic basket down on one end.

She removed her cloak and took a seat, reveling in the softness of the blanket. Ansley leaned back, spreading her palms out. She closed her eyes as the warm breeze caressed her face and shifted her long braid. Loose strands tickled her face. "What a lovely day."

"What a lovely lass."

Ansley met his dark eyes, her face warming at the intensity of his stare. "Thank…thank you."

Kneeling, he took one of her hands and pressed his mouth to her knuckles. "You're welcome, but I only state the truth."

She smiled, shifting on the furs and averting her gaze. "You're not so bad yourself, you know."

Leargan chuckled and released her. He opened the basket and reached inside.

She glanced at him as he took a seat next to her. Very close, their thighs almost touching. Her body heated, limbs tingling.

"Are you hungry?" he asked.

"Aye." *Not for food.* She wanted Leargan.

After inching even closer, she took the red grapes he offered and popped a few into her mouth.

He stared at her lips.

Desire settled low in her belly, and Ansley shook herself. How much longer could she endure this game they were playing?

The apple of his throat bobbed, but he tore his gaze away. His side brushed hers as he leaned into the basket.

A tremor slid down her spine.

"Daicy did us well. We've two kinds of meat, buttered bread, more fruit, a full skin of wine, and even sweet rolls."

"I'll have to thank her," she forced out. Food was the last thing on her mind. What would he say if she declared she just wanted him for midday meal?

"Ham? Or venison?" Leargan's dark eyes went wide as he turned back to her. He gulped. "Ansley…"

She dropped the grapes and snaked her arms around his neck.

He met her halfway with a groan, crashing his lips into hers. The tartness of the fruit mingled with their kiss, and she scooted closer, shoving her tongue into his mouth.

His hands on her made her shiver, and she pushed him down into the softness of the blanket, only to yelp as he flipped them and landed on top of her.

The thought of making love in an open meadow should've given her pause, but if she didn't get naked beneath him soon, have his hot skin against hers, she'd just die.

Leargan dragged his tongue down her neck, and she tilted her head to give him more access, moaning at the heat of his wet kisses washing over her. When he pushed her tunic up, she cried out at the first touch of calloused hands on the skin over her ribs.

Cool air on her bare flesh made goosebumps, but she wasn't cold. She wiggled so he could pull her shirt up even more, her nipples peaking even before he enclosed his hot hands over her breastbands. Her whole body was on fire as he spread kisses across her belly.

His hips rocked into hers. She could feel his erection through breeches and wanted nothing between them, bodies unencumbered. Her sex throbbed.

Leargan pushed the fabric covering her breasts up and over, exposing her.

Ansley called his name, burying her hands in his long dark locks when he enclosed a nipple with his mouth.

His tongue teased and tortured while his hands kneaded. "You're sweeter than I could've even imagined," he murmured, the vibration of his words against her breast making her tremble.

"Blessed Spirit, don't stop," she breathed.

He froze, then lifted his head. His eyes were at half-mast and black with desire. "Ansley, you're killing me."

"I want you."

Growling, he pulled back, closing his eyes. "I want you, too."

"Then take me, Leargan."

"Nay. Not until we exchange vows." He sat up, his jaw locked, full lips a hard line. He gently tugged her breastbands back into place and lowered her tunic.

Frustration and desire warred with the hurt that rushed up from her belly, and her vision blurred. Ansley clutched at her shirt and balled the fabric with tight fists.

Leargan emitted several curses.

She gasped. He'd never spoken like that around her.

"Please don't look at me like that," he begged. "I'm not rejecting you. I don't want to hurt you. I just want to do things right for once in my life."

For once in his life? What does that mean?

He urged her into his arms, and she snuggled into the muscled wall of his chest, helpless to resist him, like always.

"Let's get married today, then," Ansley whispered.

His face fell, hardened. "We can't."

"Why?" Eyes narrowed, her instincts flared.

He's hiding something.

Leargan-her-betrothed receded, and suddenly, the warrior captain of Cera's guard sat holding her stiffly against him.

"I want you to have a proper wedding. Not a rushed ceremony so I can get you into bed. That's not me." His words were sincere, but was there more to it? His expression was implacable.

Is there something to worry about?

The night of proposal rushed back, and Ansley's worry about Leargan's motives haunted her, but she ignored them. "It's not only you. I want to be your wife."

Mouth softening, he offered a small smile. "I want that, too. But it's nothing we can't wait for. Besides, with Avril's situation—"

Guilt jumped up from nowhere and she looked down. "You're right, of course."

His warm hands cupped her cheek and tilted her face up. "I don't want to be right." He pressed a tender kiss to her lips. "It's only for right now. But I still want to spend the day with you. And I still want to hold you."

She smiled, nestling closer and sighing against him. Minutes passed and a companionable silence settled over them.

Ali's wuffs and water splashing were the only sounds other than the occasional duck call.

"Are you hungry for food now?" Leargan asked.

Ansley nodded and pulled away to meet his eyes. "I suppose we should eat."

He gently released her, shuffling to the basket of food. "I'll get meat, bread, cheese and wine out."

"All right." She put her hand down to the blanket and was greeted by something cool and wet squishing between her fingers. "Oh, no."

His dark eyes shot to hers. "What's wrong?"

"We smashed the grapes!" She held up a purple stained palm.

Leargan threw his head back and laughed.

She couldn't help but grin.

Chapter Thirteen

Evening approached and Ansley didn't want to leave Leargan's arms. But his obvious reluctance to wrap up their day warmed her heart. They packed up the basket and rolled up the furs, continuing to chat as they had all afternoon.

He'd made her laugh, talking about his childhood, growing up with many of the knights of Cera's guard. Leargan saw them as his brothers. He was charming and funny, and by the time she attached the blanket to Caide's saddle, Ansley was even more in love with him than she'd been before.

"I don't want to go back," she murmured.

He was at her side in seconds, pulling her into his arms and pressing a quick kiss to her mouth. "I'd stay out here forever with you."

She grinned, shifting into his chest. Her stomach fluttered as she stared into his eyes. What did he feel for her? Of course, he wanted her. But when he said things that took her breath, made her weak in the knees, and looked at her like *that*, was it foolish to think he could care for her?

Ansley's heart skipped, and she tore her gaze away before she lost herself even more. "We probably *should* go," she whispered.

He released her after another quick kiss. "We've been gone a while."

"Probably missed evening meal," she said, swinging herself onto Caide's saddle.

Leargan flashed a grin. "That just means we'll have to sneak into the kitchens."

She laughed. "Morag thinks I'm sweet. I'm sure all *I*

have to do is ask politely."

"You *are* sweet." His eyes darkened, and his stare gained intensity.

She looked away as her cheeks scorched. "We'd better get back. I don't want Cera to worry."

The ride back was quick and mostly silent, but it was companionable.

Ali darted back and forth on the road in front of them, her spirits much higher than when they'd left late morning. Chasing ducks and playing in the water had been great fun for her bondmate.

Regret settled over her even before they gave their horses over at the stables. Ansley didn't want to be without Leargan for the rest of the night, but he wouldn't come to her room.

"Are you hungry?" He settled his hand at the small of her back as they headed to the vast guest wing.

"No, actually, I'd like a bath in front of a warm fire."

"Ah, you didn't get too cold?" Concern clouded his deep brown gaze.

She shook her head. "Nay."

Ali sidled down the hallway and Ansley skimmed her hand through ebony fur as the wolf passed her.

"Ansley! I've been looking everywhere for you!" Aimil rounded the corner, throwing her hands up in the air, olive complexion flushed pink.

Ansley shot a look at Leargan before meeting her friend's gaze. Her stomach dipped. "What's wrong?"

"Cera's having the baby!" She stopped in front of them, sucking in a breath. Her smile widened to a grin as she studied Ansley and Leargan, one delicate brow arched. "Hello, Sir Leargan."

Her knight inclined his head, slipping his arm around Ansley's shoulders and pulling her tight to his side.

Aimil had enjoyed her *I-told-you-so's* when Ansley had told her two best friends about their betrothal.

Heat crept up her neck and Ansley cleared her throat.

"Is Cera all right?"

"Aye." She nodded. "She sent Jorrin for Tristan some time ago, but now she's asking for you and me."

"Me?" Ansley swallowed.

Could she stand being *in* the room when Cera's baby came? She'd never been very good at blood and messiness.

Besides, Morag probably wouldn't like it, if Cera hadn't kicked her out. It was against decorum for an unmarried woman to witness a birth.

"Aye," Aimil said, grabbing her arm. "Let's go. Leargan, you can come too, I guess. Someone has to keep Jorrin in line. Cera threatened to throw him out of the room." She shook her head, laughter in her voice. "Cera's temper is very much present."

When they made it to the door that led into the duke and duchess' suite, Jorrin was indeed in the corridor. His high cheekbones were flushed with color, and his blue eyes wide. The lord was frantic. Pacing, shoving his hand through his dark hair.

Leargan took a breath. Maybe he could calm his friend after all.

"Jorrin? She actually put you out?" Lady Aimil's dark eyes were wide, mouth a half-agape.

The duke froze, saying nothing as the apple of his throat jumped. He shrugged, averting his gaze.

Isair and Ali greeted each other and lay down in the wide corridor, but no one paid them any attention. Trikser lay not far from the door, staring as if he could see through it.

How'd they managed to get Lady Cera's bondmate to leave her side?

"C'mon, Ansley," Lady Aimil said quietly, taking her hand and slipping into the room.

Leargan took a step forward and squeezed his lord's forearm. "I can't know what you're going through, but I'm sure it'll be all right, Jorrin."

When had he finally conceded to calling the man by his given name?

The duke had chided him for months about it. They were friends as much as lord to captain. It was comfortable, as relaxed as their relationship.

Morag of course, would say it was improper, but he rarely paid her any attention anyway. She'd have to be content that he'd never address Jorrin without *my lord*, in front of their men.

The duke took a breath and met his eyes. "She's in so much pain…I can't stand it."

"Tristan's in there, right?" Leargan asked.

"Yes."

"Then it'll be fine. We all trust him with our lives; let's not stop now."

Jorrin gave him a grateful smile. "I just didn't think…it's hard watching her hurt." He looked at his hands, palms wide. "I can't do anything for her. All my magic, and I have nothing." He winced. As an empath, he would literally feel what his wife felt.

He echoed the wince, grateful he didn't have to suffer other people's emotions like the duke always had to. Especially the woman he loved.

"That's what Tristan's for, my friend. His magic will ease her. Don't feel bad that yours is different. As I understand it, pain is how babies come into the world. She's young and strong, and nothing will happen to either of them."

"Thank you, Leargan. I needed someone to talk some sense into me."

"Lady Dagget said as much. But I didn't think your wife would actually throw you out of the room." Leargan chuckled.

He grinned and shrugged. "She simply suggested — through clenched teeth — that I get some fresh air."

"Are you going back in?"

"Perhaps in a bit. Morag and Neomi are in there, along with Tristan and now Ansley and Aimil…it's a bit crowded."

"I'm surprised the duchess allowed Morag."

"I think Neomi tried to send her away, but she wouldn't go," Jorrin said, referring to his wife's lady's maid. "Cera's too busy to fuss her out."

"Yet she had time to throw her husband out." He grinned.

"Thanks for putting it that way." The duke flashed a sheepish smile. "Oh, congratulations on your betrothal. With Avril's situation, proper acknowledgment fell to the wayside. Sorry about that. I hope Ansley wasn't upset."

"Thank you, and no she wasn't. I don't think it's necessary to announce formally." Leargan waved his hand.

Dark brow up, his lord studied him until he squirmed. "Did you tell her about the scroll?"

"Nay."

"So she has no idea her father will be here soon?"

Leargan scowled. "Nay."

"Well, you'd better tell her before she finds out and thinks you only want to marry her because King Nathal ordered it. That will hurt her." Jorrin smirked. "Women are funny like that."

He dragged his hand down his face.

"That isn't the *only* reason you asked for her hand, is it?"

"Of course not," he bit out.

The duke's gaze was appraising, and Leargan averted his eyes from the blue stare.

Why do I want to marry her?

He wanted her physically, but he'd spoken the truth when he'd told Jorrin he didn't want a marriage without love.

What exactly did he feel for Ansley?

Desire. More than any other woman. Ever. Her

passion equaled his. They'd suit each other well, and King Nathal, a man who'd always been a father to him, had chosen her for him.

That was all he needed to know.

He pushed away thoughts and feelings he didn't want to acknowledge and shook his head.

Not now.

"Then why?" Jorrin stared.

Don't ask questions you can feel the answers to. But Leargan couldn't say that. "Ansley is mine."

His friend's eyes narrowed. "You'd better explain everything before they get here. She might want to know her wedding is about a sevenday away."

The door to the duke and duchess' chamber opened, and he was grateful for the distraction.

Ansley smiled at him before looking at Jorrin. "Cera is asking for you."

The duke nodded thanks and disappeared into the room.

She stayed in the corridor, hands clasped together in front of her.

"You're not going back in?"

"It's pretty intense in there." She took a step toward him.

He reached for her hand and entwined their fingers. "Everything all right?"

"Aye. She's pushing. Won't be long now."

Leargan leaned over and kissed her cheek. "I promise I'll stay by your side when our first child is born." Something about Ansley, round with his child made his heart pound. He *wanted* it, almost as much as he wanted *her*.

Her eyes widened and she blushed the most delicious shade of pink.

He brushed his lips against hers, pulling her to him.

She offered him a tremulous smile.

"Did I scare you?" Leargan whispered.

"Nay..."

"You do want children?"

"Oh, aye." Ansley nodded.

He smiled. She would have *his* children. *Why does that feel so right?* "Good. So do I." He couldn't keep his hands off her, so children were inevitable anyway.

"How many?" She snuggled closer.

"I hadn't thought about it." He shrugged. "Definitely a little lad with your eyes."

Ansley looked down, cheeks even more crimson, but he guided her face back up, making her meet his eyes.

"I don't want you to be uncomfortable around me."

"I…I'm not. Especially after today."

"Good," Leargan whispered against her lips.

She opened for him, and he tasted her fully. Their tongues mingled and coherent thought fled. He deepened the kiss.

Until Ansley pulled away from him, glaring to the right.

Ali growled again, yellow eyes sharp, glowing.

"Stop it, now."

The wolf whined and laid her great head back down on the floor.

Leargan relaxed and felt Ansley loosen against him. "Thanks. Can we leave her out of the room on our wedding night?" He was only half-joking.

She looked into his eyes. "She won't hurt you."

"I know. But she hasn't seen you naked in my arms yet." He swallowed hard.

Why did you say that?

He must be a glutton for punishment.

She trembled against his chest. "I haven't seen that yet, either."

Biting back a groan, he ignored the longing in her tone. He was determined to be honorable. Especially since her father and the king would be there soon.

How could he explain everything to her?

Leargan wanted her to understand that he *wanted* to marry her, not because the king had ordered it. *Coward.* "You will. I promise. But I want to do things right."

"What I feel is right."

Blessed Spirit, she's going to kill me.

"It's good to know my feelings aren't one-sided," he managed, but his words cracked.

Ansley froze in his arms, stiff against him. She swallowed, making him want to kiss her throat.

"Are you all right?"

What did I say? Had he upset her?

"Aye...I'm fine."

"It's a boy!" Lady Aimil threw the door open. "Come see him, he's gorgeous!"

Chapter Fourteen

nsley exchanged a look with Leargan, and they both grinned.

Morag and Neomi, Cera's lady's maid, gathered soiled linens and blankets, and an empty bucket. Wearing wide smiles and bustling around the room, it was hard to tell if they would ever tire.

The duke stood next to the bed, tears glistening on his cheeks.

Ansley smiled as he leaned down to kiss his wife.

Tristan sat in a chair not far from the hearth, wiping sweat from his brow. He was pale, but Aimil had told her when he used his healing magic, the larger the injury, the more physically it affected him. Healing someone from a birth was a likely serious thing.

Her Ascovan friend stood behind her husband, rubbing his shoulders and whispering to him.

Cera was propped against her pillows, cradling a small bundle and wearing a brilliant smile as she looked down at her baby.

Ansley glanced at Leargan, smiling at the wonder in his dark eyes.

He entwined their fingers and squeezed, then pressed a kiss to her cheek.

"Come here, come see him," Cera whispered.

They walked to the bed, the captain pulling his hand out of hers so he could embrace Jorrin. The murmur of their hushed deep voices teased her ears, but Ansley only had eyes for the baby.

The duchess' curly red hair covered his small head, and her fingers itched to see if it was as soft as it looked.

His cheeks were full and pink, his little rosebud mouth peaceful while he slept in his mother's arms, and his ears tapered like his father's. Tiny hands peaked from beneath the blanket he was swaddled in.

Ansley had never seen a more beautiful creature. "Oh, Cera, he's gorgeous." She reached to touch his curls. *Downy soft.*

Her friend looked up, her gray eyes shining. "Thanks, Ans. Do you want to hold him?"

"Sure." She leaned down and gently took the baby into her arms.

He stirred in his sleep but didn't wake, and Ansley kissed his soft little cheek.

"What's his name?" Leargan asked softly, appearing at her shoulder.

"Fallon Braylen," Lord Jorrin said.

Ansley smiled. They'd borrowed letters from both their fathers' names to form their son's. A tribute both men would approve of.

"Lord Fallon Aldern," her betrothed whispered.

The duke and duchess both beamed.

"Your father would be proud." She gently handed little Fallon back to his mother.

Eyes misty, Cera nodded, and her husband squeezed her shoulder.

"Oh, sorry..." Ansley whispered. Last thing she wanted was to make her friend cry.

"No, no it's fine. I just wish they all could see him."

"They can, from wherever they are, love." The duke caressed his wife's cheek.

"Thank you." She stared up at him.

Ansley shifted at Leargan's side.

The couple was looking at each other as if they were the only ones in the room.

"Tristan, are you all right?" Leargan asked. He must've sensed her discomfort, unless he felt the same way.

"Aye." The healer gestured with his hand. Like when he'd fixed Avril; Aimil's husband didn't like the attention on himself. "I'll be fine. Won't have trouble sleeping, though."

"Have a rough night, did you?" Cera teased, causing them all to laugh.

"Hey, I healed you all the way. As if you were never pregnant. Your body doesn't know the difference, except you'll be able to nurse him. Other than that, you're as good as new. No soreness, bleeding, the after birth complaints of most women." Tristan winked.

"I am grateful, honestly." She smiled sweetly. "Much better than having to heal on my own."

Little Fallon shifted in her arms letting out a wail.

The three men in the room winced.

"I think that's our cue to find our chambers," Aimil said, a hand on her rounding tummy.

"Aye, I agree." Leargan shot a look at the healer. "Tristan, do you need assistance?"

"Nay, I'm fine, but thanks." He rose from the chair.

The duke walked them to the door. Fallon was already quieting as Cera started to nurse. "Thank you all for tonight."

"Congratulations, Lord Aldern," Ansley whispered.

"Just Jorrin," he chided gently. "And congratulations to you, too."

"Thank you." She leaned into Leargan and he shot an arm around her shoulders.

"See you all tomorrow...or the next day..." he said, closing the door after Cera's wolf slipped past them, heading inside.

"We never did offer proper congratulations, Ansley," Tristan said.

Aimil beamed from his side, her arm around his waist.

"It's fine, really." She wanted to bury her face against her betrothed. Her cheeks burned as she met the healer's warm hazel eyes.

"Leargan's a good man, I'm sure he'll make you happy. I know he'll be very happy with you."

"Aye, I've no doubt," Leargan said.

Ansley glanced at her knight, almost undone by the tenderness in his eyes. She locked her knees to keep them from wobbling. "Thank you."

"Well, good night. Though it's not all that late, I need to get to my bed before I fall over. I'll follow Jorrin's sentiment…see you tomorrow, or the next day." He winked when his wife giggled.

"I'll walk you to your room…again," Leargan said, laughter in his tone, after the other couple disappeared in the opposite direction.

Ansley couldn't keep her eyes off him as they walked down the corridor arm and arm. She wanted to say so much, but words evaporated before they were born.

He'd told Tristan he had no doubt she'd make him happy. Was it true or just small talk for a man who obviously loved his wife?

Shivering, she leaned into him.

Leargan squeezed her against his side, saying nothing.

They arrived much too soon. She shifted, biting her bottom lip. She didn't want him to leave.

"Good night, Ansley." He opened the door.

Ali rushed into the room and immediately jumped onto the large bed, lying in the middle.

They exchanged a wry grin.

"I guess I'll make sure she's out hunting on our wedding night," she said.

He chuckled. "I'd appreciate it."

"Good night, Leargan." Ansley took a step closer and rested a hand on his chest. Looking into his dark eyes, she leaned up.

Leargan lowered his head and met her halfway, kissing her until she was dizzy. His arms went around her, holding her against his chest as her knees weakened.

She wanted him to spend the night in her room, but he'd decline.

How many times did she have to tell him she didn't want to wait? Would the man even take her if she stripped naked before him?

"You'd better go inside," he breathed against her lips, panting hard against her breasts.

She nodded, brushing her lips against his just one last time.

Leargan groaned. "You're killing me, Ansley." His intense gaze bored into hers.

She stared, saying nothing. Then she grinned. "I'm sorry." Without another word, she closed the door, leaving him standing in the corridor, wide-eyed, and open-mouthed. Ansley leaned on the door, sucking in a breath and giggling when she heard his laugh from the corridor.

Chapter Fifteen

vril watched Sir Roduch shift in the chair, arms crossed over his broad chest. His head was tilted to one side and his eyes were shut, but there was no way he was asleep.

Or comfortable.

She stopped herself from reaching for him; which was odd, considering she'd been plastered to him for most of the day. In his arms, against his wall of a chest.

His hands on hers, on her lower back, her arm, even the barest brush of her wrist.

It was rare the knight wasn't touching her when they were together. It didn't make her uncomfortable or scare her. It made Avril crave him.

That afternoon, she'd walked the gardens with him, holding one of his large hands, their fingers entwined.

Warm. Safe.

She'd never felt so free in her life.

If she could stay at Castle Aldern, she could get back to feeling like herself…someone she'd lost track of the day Tynan had taken her to his home when she was fourteen.

Avril shivered. She crushed her eyes against the memories of that night…her wedding night.

Tynan's offensive breath on her face and his rough lips bruising hers. His hands smashing her breasts. His obese body on top of hers, forcing her legs open. The agony when he'd shoved his member into her, tearing her virginity away.

She'd screamed and her new husband had slapped her. He'd told her she liked what he was doing to her. Tynan had thrust into her, over and over, the pain excruciating.

Avril had kept her eyes clenched shut the whole time.

Then he'd beat her when she'd sobbed afterward. Physically thrown her away from him. Tynan had hit her with a bathing linen he'd tossed, and demanded she clean up the blood and change his sheets. He hadn't even given her access to water or the chance to bathe.

Her parents had given her to a monster.

Tynan had paid them more gold than her father had made in the entire previous turn. Her family needed that money. With four younger siblings to feed, she couldn't go back, or her brothers and sister would starve. Her father's injured leg meant he couldn't farm anymore, and the oldest of the boys hadn't yet been three and ten; too young to run the farm.

She'd had to stay with her husband to save her family. At the expense of everything Avril had ever held dear.

All for her damn magic. Visions, prophecies, all forced at her husband's behest, instead of coming naturally as the Blessed Spirit intended.

Sick—sometimes deathly ill—was how she'd lived the past four turns. Weak, with barely enough recovery time before he'd make her do it again.

More. Tynan always wanted more. Information, gold, power, sex. Ways to use what she saw against their neighbors so he could get their land. Promise them something and blackmail them into being beholden to him. And he wasn't even a lord. Despite what he'd told them all.

He'd killed his family—the rightful cousin who was supposed to own his land. Tynan had made the whole family—wife, husband and two children—ill, kept them ill while he '*cared for them*' so he could inherit the place she'd eventually lived with him.

Only Avril saw that he'd poisoned them.

Bastard. She loved Sir Roduch's name for Tynan Mont.

"Avril?" Her knight shot straight up, fair brows

drawn tight as he stared in the dimness of her room. "Are you all right?"

She nodded, heart pounding. He'd startled her, but she still wasn't afraid of him. Guilt crept up from the pit of her stomach. Even though she'd told Sir Roduch's captain, the healing lord, and the duke about what her husband had done to her, she'd never mentioned her magic. Never mentioned the crimes Tynan had committed against others because of her gift.

Or is it a curse?

She was safe at Castle Aldern, and no one would use her magic without her knowledge, or against her, but somehow the words wouldn't form to tell him.

Avril was more than her magic. She wanted Sir Roduch to see that. Wanted him to know *her*.

Care for her?

She swallowed and sucked in a breath, then sat up, leaning into the headboard. "I am."

"Good." He sighed and his big shoulders loosened.

She stared until the big knight shifted in the chair, dropping his arms, hands in his lap. "Sir Roduch…"

He leaned in, making her stomach flutter. "Aye, lass?"

"Do you want to sleep with me?" She forced the words out before she lost her nerve. Her tummy did a backflip.

"Avril…I don't think…"

"Wait." She put her palm up and took a deep breath. "I mean, *sleep* in this bed with me."

"Are you sure?" Eyes wide, his face was open, sincere. It would crush him if she changed her mind.

"That chair can't be comfortable. You've been sleeping there more than a sevenday."

"It's not comfortable," Sir Roduch admitted, averting his gaze.

"I'm not afraid of you," Avril whispered.

It's true.

She wished for eloquent words to explain herself, but

nothing came. She wanted to be with him. Wanted him to hold her.

"You mean that?" he breathed.

"I mean it. Please share my bed. I know you'll not touch me. I know you wouldn't rape me."

"Never." Sir Roduch stood and made a fist, vehemence coming from his whole being. He shed his boots and sat gingerly on the edge of the bed. A move that belied his size. His eyes locked onto hers. "Are you sure about this?"

Roduch looked down at her, holding his breath for her answer. He never would've guessed, in a million turns, she'd ask him to share her bed — not even if he'd had a vision about it.

It was true the chair was killing him, but he'd vowed not to leave her side. Except for the headwoman, everyone respected his decision.

Avril would let him know when she was ready for him to leave her room, but for now she was stuck with him.

He wanted her *stuck* with him forever, but he wouldn't push her.

"I'm sure," she whispered.

It'd take everything he was made of not to touch her at all, but he wouldn't. Roduch forced himself to not even reach for her hand. "You trust me?"

"Yes," she answered without hesitation.

She trusted him?

"I'm glad to hear it." He lay down next to her very slowly.

The bed was oversized. Even with his large frame, they wouldn't have to touch unless they wanted to. No doubt he *wanted* to, but she wasn't ready, so he'd keep his hands to himself.

"Sir Roduch?" Avril's sweet voice jolted him.

He'd been frozen, stiff as a board. Forcing a breath, he

made himself relax enough to answer her. "Aye?"

"Would it be all right if I moved closer to you?"

He nodded. Couldn't find his voice.

She scooted closer, until her head rested against his shoulder, the length of her body lightly touching his side. He wanted to take her into his arms but stopped himself.

"You're so warm," she murmured. "Can you hold me?" Her whisper was very low.

"Aye, lass, but only if you stop calling me *sir*." Heart leaping to his throat, Roduch pulled her to him.

Her nod was shy, and she burrowed her face into his neck. Avril twined her legs with his, her small knee on his thigh.

His breath startled when she nearly bumped his tender parts. His manhood already liked the idea of their bodies close. If she touched him, even by accident and stirred arousal, she'd yank away from him, and that was the last thing Roduch wanted. Holding her felt damn good.

He needed to ask about her magic, but how could he bring it up? He'd been biding his time for days. At best, it was going to be an uncomfortable conversation. But he'd promised Leargan he'd find out the reason behind her hiding it, to see what dangers were before them.

Roduch cleared his throat and pulled her even closer. "Avril…"

She smiled as she lifted her head from his chest, meeting his eyes in the dimness of her rooms. "Roduch."

His heart skipped at his name on her lips. She'd finally dropped the *sir*. "Before we met, did you know me?"

Dark brow furrowed, she shook her head, her mass of curls shifting. "What d'you mean?"

He closed his eyes, swallowing again. If he admitted his visions, he damn sure couldn't tell her she was meant to be his. She was nowhere near ready. "I…" He averted his gaze and cursed himself.

"Roduch?"

"When I saw you on the road, I knew you." Rushing the words, he watched emotions flicker over her face, but she didn't pull away.

Good.

"What do you mean?" Avril repeated.

"Since I was a lad, I've…had…visions. Of you." He rubbed her back, willing her to stay calm, not pull away from him.

Rearing back, she studied his face. Silence descended. "You're not lying," she breathed finally.

"No. I'd never lie to you."

"But…how? I sense no magic in you. I can *always* sense magic." Her emerald eyes shot open wide, and she slapped her hand over her mouth.

Roduch reached for her wrist, gently pulling it away from her face. "It's all right, Avril. You can sense magic? Is that what your powers are?" He pressed a kiss to her knuckles.

She shook her head, but didn't move away from his chest. "I—"

"You can tell me. No one will hurt you here. I will protect you forever."

"I get visions." The whisper was so low, he almost missed it. "Powerful visions. Sometimes of the future. Sometimes the past. But when I look at someone, I can *know* them. In and out. Strengths and weaknesses, wants, desires." She paused, a tear working its way down her cheek.

"I get visions, too," Roduch whispered. "But only of you. I only see you." He cupped her cheeks, thumbing her tears away.

"It's not possible. I didn't know you before that night on the road."

"I can't explain it, lo—lass." His heart skipped, and his chest tightened. He couldn't call her *love*. It'd definitely upset her right now.

"I sense no magic in you, Roduch." She leaned down,

cupping his face with her small hands. She stared into his eyes.

He had to restrain himself from yanking her down and tasting her mouth. His manhood stirred, and threatening to lop it off did nothing to soften his budding erection.

"Can you feel that?" Avril asked.

"Feel what?"

"I'm probing you. With magic." She stared until sweat beaded her forehead.

"I feel nothing but your body on mine."

"No tingles?"

Not the ones you're referring to. "Nothing, lass."

Avril collapsed onto his chest, blowing out a breath.

Roduch caught her up, wiping the moisture from her brow.

"I don't understand," she whispered.

"Neither do I, but I speak true, Avril. I've been seeing you in my dreams since I was a child."

She met his eyes, biting her bottom lip. "I was destined to come to you?"

"Aye, I believe so." His heart sped up again. "Why did you hide your magic from the lords and my captain, lass?"

She averted her gaze, but he drew her face back to his. "I had to."

"Why?"

"Tynan..."

"He used your magic?"

"For himself."

Understanding dawned as she shut down. Avril wasn't ready to talk about it. Her bastard husband had forced her visions, but to what end? And how did one even force magic?

No matter how Roduch had tried over the turns, he could never see Avril on his own demand. His visions came at their own will, *his* be damned.

And why had she said he had no magic? "I need to know, Avril."

"I know." She quivered in his arms, her voice barely a whisper.

Regret hit him in a wave. He didn't want to cause her more strife. Roduch wanted to relieve her pain. *Always.* Take care of her. *Forever.* "I won't push you, but I need to know. Before we can arrest the bastard."

"Can we talk in the morning? I will even speak to your captain and the duke. I just…can't right now. I need you to hold me."

"Lass…" His heart dropped to his stomach when her eyes watered again.

Was she manipulating him? *Nay.* She was genuinely shaking in his arms.

Damn that bastard to hell and back.

"I'm sorry, Roduch."

"It'll be fine, lass. There's always tomorrow. Come here." He pulled her up his body, aching to kiss her mouth. Diverting his lips, he pressed a kiss to her forehead instead.

She flashed a smile that had his stomach flipping as she snuggled closer. Avril rested her head on his chest, her hand tucked next to her cheek.

Roduch rubbed her back until her breathing fell into a deep, even rhythm.

His foundling shifted closer in her sleep, her knee brushing his manhood, which shot to hard and throbbing in about two seconds.

He shook his head, willing it soft.

Roduch groaned. Should've stayed in the chair.

He would've had a better chance at real sleep.

Chapter Sixteen

No amount of battery, intimidation, or gold was getting Tynan anywhere, no matter how many inns in Greenwald he'd visited. He paced in the room he'd rented at the *White Sage Pub*, but that wasn't helping, either.

A ruckus outside the open window had him glancing down and scowling when he saw what the fuss was about.

Knights.

The group was a half-dozen strong, mail and armor clad, flying the pale green and silver flag of the Province, the seal of a howling white wolf depicted on it. Only a few of them wore helms. They observed the evening market crowd, nodding to the people as they rode slowly.

"What the hell?" Tynan asked the empty room, staring at the procession moving down the main thoroughfare.

"Nothing's wrong." A female voice pulled him from his thoughts, and he glared at the maid, who'd entered his room without permission. "They often patrol Greenwald Main in addition to the Provost's marshals. Lord Aldern cares for his people."

Tynan glared, and the smile fell from her face.

She stilled in the doorway, and his eyes rested on the tray in her arms, the full trencher of food. Steam wafted from the baked tuber, as well as the slab of gravy-covered meat. His stomach snarled, reminding him his last meal had been very early that morning. But she didn't have to know that.

"Did I call for you?" he barked.

"I'm sorry, milord. Your man bid me permission to

come up." She lowered her head.

Damn Harlan.

Tynan's gaze traveled her frame. Too round at the hip, but she might do for his aching cock. It'd been too long. Maybe he should thank his steward for the gift. "Where are my men?"

"They dine below, milord."

"Shut the door and place the tray on the table," he commanded.

"Milord?"

"Do it and come here."

The girl set the tray down as instructed, but squared her shoulders and glared. "I am not a whore. If you want one, I can get you one."

"I didn't ask for another. I told you to come here," Tynan growled.

"My father owns this place."

"I don't recall asking. I own vast properties and have much gold."

She didn't even flinch at his honest brag.

He stalked over and closed the door, but was careful not to slam it.

The girl was small, like Avril, but that was where the comparison stopped. Her hair was blonde, eyes blue, and her body too fulsome.

He yanked the kerchief covering her fair locks. She whimpered when Tynan leaned in to inhale her scent. She smelled good. Clean. Like an expensive whore should. When he rested his hands on her shoulders, she started to shake. "I don't want your cunt. I want your mouth."

"I'm married."

Ah, so the hips were due to something Avril had failed to do for him. This one had given her husband children.

"And? Your husband knows you work in an inn. Surely I'm not the first man to require your services."

"My father *owns* my place of employ. I'm not a whore.

Let me get Betha for you. She's our most popular." Big tears made tracks down her cheeks, but her voice was steady.

That just turned him on more. "You will suck my cock. And I will pay for you."

Her eyes widened and she shook her head.

His erection strained his breeches. Tynan guided her hand to his crotch, groaning when her palm made contact. He rocked his hips into her hand. His member throbbed when the girl whimpered.

"I thought you were in search of your lost wife, milord."

"You do not speak of her unless you have information to help my quest. Have you seen her?" He grabbed her shoulders and shook her.

"No, milord. I remember everyone. She has not come into the *White Sage*. But I can help you. I will help you. Please, don't force me. I know people that can ask around. I can get someone to help find her. Someone who knows the Province better than anyone. Please let me go downstairs."

Begging made his blood boil and his cock pulse. He liked it best when Avril had pleaded for him to stop. Pity, his wife hadn't done that for turns.

"Get on your knees, and I won't kill you."

Sucking in a big sniffle, the girl did what he'd ordered, but she trembled from head to toe, quietly sobbing.

Both made him want her more.

"Open my belt. Touch me. Stroke me. Suck me. Show me you're married. Show me you know your way around a man."

The wench whimpered, but reached for his belt. When his buckle lay open, she slowly tugged the ties on his breeches open without being told.

Tynan patted her head. "Good girl. You follow commands well. I bet your husband enjoys you. If you're good, I will thank him with more coin."

"Your supper is getting cold," she whispered, her face soaked with tears.

"Yours is waiting to be released. Do it now. You're too slow." Actually, the anticipation made him harder.

He watched her plump lips, imagined her tongue moving up and down him in rhythm with her hand. He'd come in that luscious mouth, his seed would slide down her throat.

A shudder racked his frame and Tynan waited for her fingers to bare him, encircle him.

Right when she finally brushed his bare skin, the door to his room was thrown open.

"Sire." Harlan panted, his chest heaving. Thick salt and pepper hair stood up at all angles from his run up the stairs. The steward looked at the girl, then back at Tynan and bowed deeply. "My apologies, sire. I had no idea you were indisposed."

"What the hell is it, Harlan?" he barked.

"We must leave now."

"Why?"

"Your wife has been seen."

Chapter Seventeen

After leaving Jorrin's ledger room, Ansley consumed Leargan's thoughts, because of Avril's latest recital. She'd been through much too much for a girl of eight and ten. He couldn't stop seeing his betrothed's teal gaze, her smile, or hearing Ansley's laughter as the lass had confessed all her bastard former husband had done with her magic.

If someone so much as looked at Ansley with ill intentions, he'd kill them.

Tynan Mont was a murderer, rapist and master manipulator. He needed to pay, and he *would*. There was a place for him in Dread Valley, the penal territory of the continent, located in the south eastern most Province, Dalunas. The place was a sevenday and a half ride at best, but Leargan would love to be the one to slap the manacles on the bastard and lead the charge.

If he could keep Roduch from killing him. He hadn't broached the subject just yet, but he was going to attempt to leave his friend out of the arrest entirely. He smirked. If they knocked the big knight out and left in the dead of the night, *maybe* it would work. Roduch was going to fight him on it, without a doubt. Probably would ignore a direct order from Jorrin.

Even if his friend didn't realize it yet, he was in love with Avril. It was written all over the knight's face. They might not have known each other long, but it didn't matter. He looked at her the way Jorrin and Tristan looked at their wives.

Seeing the large rock-steady man an emotional wreck over a lass should've shaken Leargan in his boots. But it only made him think of Ansley.

He needed to see her now.

"She's in the tub." Daicy pulled the door to the guest chamber shut. "I was just going to get fresh bathing linens."

His blood warmed and rushed in his ears; he fought for coherent thought.

Ansley. Naked.

"I'll be right back," the maid said, disappearing around the corner in the wide corridor. The nearest supply closet wasn't far.

Shifting on his feet, he warred with what he wanted and what was right. His manhood stirred at the mere thought of his betrothed bared to him.

Their picnic flickered to his mind. Leargan had touched her, tasted her perfect breasts that day. How he'd had the control to *stop* still shocked him. He wouldn't survive that again.

Leave. Now. Before you can't.

"Here you go, sir." Daicy pushed two fresh bathsheets in to his chest.

"W-w-what?" *Stuttering?* He cleared his throat.

"The soap's right next to her, but she's about done."

He looked at the soft material in his arms, then back into the maid's dancing brown eyes. No words came. Heat crept up his neck.

"You'd better get in there. Mistress Ansley's going to get cold."

"We can't have that." His voice cracked.

Daicy winked and curtseyed before she headed away from him, whistling.

He gave up on the idea of leaving and slipped into Ansley's room. Leargan heard the menacing growl the same moment as the splash and feminine yelp. He whirled and backed up until he hit the door, eyes locked onto the ebony wolf.

Ali stalked him.

"Ali, no!" Ansley's order froze her bondmate before him.

The she-wolf whined but didn't take her yellow eyes off him. After a few softer commands, she plastered her tail between her legs and sprinted to her mistress.

Ansley smoothed a hand down the her bond's back, whispering until Ali licked her cheek and lay down by the friendly fire, claiming the hearth like normal. Then his betrothed looked at him. "Leargan?"

He shook himself. Still in the bath. Naked from head to toe. His erection went from half-mast to full steam ahead.

She didn't look away, though her cheeks went crimson.

"Ansley…" Leargan croaked. He couldn't tear his gaze from her shimmery wet flesh.

She drew her knees to her chest, wrapping her arms around herself, but offered a shy smile.

"She *is* going to eat me one of these days," he said, trying to grasp for some control. He gestured to the wolf, but took a step toward Ansley.

She laughed, and it took his breath away. "Well…you came into my room, unannounced, and I'm…" She gestured to the tub. Then she tilted her head to one side, a twinkle in her teal eyes. "It's funny, she never growls at Daicy."

"Daicy said you were almost done." Words fell from his mouth. He couldn't even respond to her jibe. Leargan waved the clean bathsheets. "She gave me these."

"Oh, is that right?" Ansley grinned.

"Aye." He stared.

Virgin. Leave now. You need to leave.

His arousal throbbed, helping him ignore his conscience. Why hadn't he left before Daicy had come back with the bathing linens?

"Why do you think Ali only growls at you?" She arched an eyebrow.

She was the most adorable thing he'd ever seen. He wanted her even more.

He shrugged. "I have no idea. I'm harmless." Leargan grinned at her rich peel of laughter.

"That, Sir Leargan, I do not believe at all."

He winked and closed the distance to the wooden tub.

She stood, her cheeks reddening even more.

His chest tightened and he gave up on trying not to stare. She was gorgeous, and she was *his*. His breath caught as he perused her.

The water sloshed in the tub, taking his attention. Leargan's gaze followed the curve of her right calf, pausing at her knee, then continuing up to her thighs, his heartbeat increasing as he went. He stopped when his eyes rested on the red curls at the apex of her thighs.

He could see her, *all* of her. His imagination hadn't done her justice.

Ansley wrapped her arms around her slim waist. Her breasts were large and inviting, and her hips curved subtly. Memories teased of how they felt pressing into his, moving against him, under him, the day they'd gone to the lake.

"I should go," he breathed.

She was *perfect*.

His cock pulsed, threatening to punch through his breeches. Leargan needed to go, before he couldn't. But repetition of the idea did nothing to make it sink in.

It's already too late.

"Aye, you should." Her voice shuddered with obvious desire, and her eyes were already heavy-lidded, darker.

"Aye, I should," he repeated lamely. Instead of turning tail, he lifted one of the bathsheets, shaking it open and holding it wide. The other one hit the floor, but neither of them grabbed it.

"I don't want you to," she whispered. Ansley stepped out of the tub, raising her arms and grinning. "Are you going to dry me?"

Leargan forced himself to wrap the material around her slim form, struggling for normal breath.

What the hell is wrong with me?

He'd seen naked women before. Touched them…had more than he could name. Why was Ansley Fraser rocking him to his core?

Her shoulders glistened with water droplets in the dim candlelight of her room, and he wiped them dry with his hands. He drew her to his chest, the drying sheet between them.

The heat of her damp breasts sank into the soft fabric of the pale blue tunic he'd donned after his own bath.

She pressed forward, encircling his neck with her arms.

The bathsheet fell to the floor.

Leargan groaned and lowered his head.

Ansley met him halfway, kissing him back; opening for him, and their tongues dueled.

He had to have her. He crushed her to him, molding her body to his. Resistance was futile. Leargan wanted her more than he'd ever wanted a woman.

His betrothed was right; there was no reason to wait until they were wed. He'd make her belong to him right then and there.

"We shouldn't do this." Reason broke into his head, and he panted against her.

"We'll be married, will we not?"

"Of course."

Ansley's eyes lit up, and she gave a brilliant smile that set his heart off again. "Then what does it matter, now or then?"

"Because I always try to do the right thing. And taking a maid's innocence outside of marriage isn't exactly proper, love."

She froze in his arms. Her smile fell off, expression sobering. "Love?"

"Aye." Leargan pressed a quick kiss to her mouth. "My betrothed, my love."

Her eyes searched his face, her lips parting as if she was going to say something.

Ali broke their silence, answering a series of low howls coming from the corridor.

Ansley glanced over her shoulder. "I'll let her out. Sounds like Trik and Isair are calling. They probably want to hunt."

The black she-wolf darted to the door at the same time as she did, naked as the day she was born.

He stalked her movements. Graceful. Gorgeous. His hands itched to touch her all over. Follow the curve of her bottom, thighs and calves. Taste every inch of her skin.

The chamber door shut.

His gaze darted to her peaked dusky nipples, and he swallowed back a groan. "Come here. Now."

Ansley threw herself into his arms.

Leargan caught her up, claiming her mouth as she wrapped herself around him, pushing her softness into every inch of his hardness.

She moaned as their tongues mated, and he kissed her harder. It continued until she was wriggling and whimpering.

He quaked from the struggle for control.

Slow down. She's innocent

Leargan tore away as her nails sank into his shoulders. Ansley's ragged breath tickled his cheek. He rested his forehead against hers, sucking in air. "I need you. Blessed Spirit, I *need* you, but there's no hurry. We have all night."

She pulled back, studying him. "You'll stay with me all night?"

"You couldn't make me leave."

Her legs slipped to the floor, but he held her up, pinned to him.

She leaned away, tugging at his belt. "I want to see

you, Leargan."

He smiled at the blush that kissed her already-pink cheeks, and helped her open the buckle. When she reached for the ties on his breeches, he grabbed her wrists. "I'm going to make it special for you."

"I don't doubt it, but it'll be special because it's *you*." Ansley met his eyes.

He couldn't tear his gaze away. Words deserted him. Leargan drew her back to him and kissed her tenderly, trying to convey all he couldn't say.

Her eyes were misty when it ended, but her lips curved in a wobbly smile. "I want to see you," she repeated.

He stepped back and ripped his tunic over his head, throwing it down.

Her warm palms were on him in seconds.

Leargan shivered, he couldn't help it. Her touch burned him up from the inside out. He prayed for control while his erection kicked, threatening to blow its top off.

What are you? A virgin of seven and ten?

She hadn't even touched him *there*.

Feather-light fingers traced the defined lines of his pectoral and abdominal muscles, and he tried not to squirm. There was no reason the woman he would marry couldn't touch him. Leargan groaned.

Ansley stilled. "Did I hurt you?"

"No…"

"What's wrong?"

"You're killing me. I want you. The more you touch me, the more I'm on fire for you."

She looked away, but he cupped her cheeks and kissed her. Her hands brushed his belly and settled at his hips, jerking the soft leather of his tan breeches. "These have to go," she whispered.

Chuckling, he grabbed his waistband, lowering one side. "What do you want, love?"

Ansley set her hands on her bare hips.

Leargan tried not to stare at her sex.

"You. Naked."

"Ah." He fought for a serious expression. "And then what?"

She glared, taking a step forward. "You'll make me say it?" Her whisper belied the expression marring her face.

He chuckled again.

"Wretch," Ansley said.

"Oh, all right, love." He pushed his breeches off his hips and slipped out of his boots. Leargan kicked them away and stepped out of the brushed leather. Her gaze devoured him, and he had the urge to gulp. His manhood liked the perusal, springing forward and aching even more. "Love, you're killing me."

"How? We're not even touching."

"The way you're looking at me doesn't bode well for my stamina."

When she came closer and smiled, Leargan hauled her into his arms.

They both gasped when naked flesh came together, his blunt nipples tingling and hardening when hers touched them.

He inhaled the flowery scent of her damp hair when Ansley pressed closer. "Blessed Spirit, I *need* you. I need you so badly," he whispered into her ear, echoing the tremors that shook her against him.

She looped her arms around his neck as he scooped her up and took her to the oversized bed. He kissed her, setting her down in the middle of the fluffy sleeping furs and following her down.

Leargan deepened the kiss and shoved his tongue into her mouth, tasting her until his pulse roared in his temples. When they parted, it was only to force air into his lungs. His gaze raked her whole body, and she made no effort to cover herself. "You're so beautiful."

"With freckles and all?" Ansley whispered.

"Aye, with freckles and all." He spread warm kisses down her neck and settled himself over her, pushing her thighs wider with his knee.

She stilled beneath him.

He didn't want to see fear in her eyes. He'd never been with a virgin, but Leargan could be a gentle lover. He *would* be, to show her how much she meant to him. He wouldn't hurt her; he'd make it good for her, too. "Are you afraid?"

"Nay. Just nervous."

"I'll be gentle, love. I promise. I'd never hurt you."

"I know, Leargan," Ansley whispered.

"It may hurt at first, but I'll go slow."

She pulled him down. Their mouths met, and he let her control their kiss as he lowered his weight on top of her, his erection trapped pleasantly against her sex.

Ansley pushed up, rocking against him until they settled into a gentle rhythm that mimicked lovemaking. She writhed and wiggled, throwing her head back and whimpering. "More…Leargan, you're making me ache."

She wasn't the only one. If he didn't calm himself, one thrust and it'd be over. Leargan leaned away, running his hands over her breasts and down her belly, dragging two fingers down further, parting her silky folds. He bit his lip to stave off a moan, and teased the sensitive cluster of nerves at the top of her sex until Ansley called his name. She was already wet for him.

"Please…I'm ready," she begged.

"I need to taste you first," he whispered against her belly. Leargan dragged his tongue around her navel, nipping and kissing his way lower.

She fidgeted and buried her hands in his hair, tugging when he nibbled her inner thigh. He urged her to open wider for him. At the first swipe of his tongue on her sex, she whimpered, lifting her head from the pillows.

"What're you doing?" Ansley gasped, trying to sit up.

He put a gentle hand to her stomach. "Relax, love, it's

all right. I'll make you feel good."

She shuddered, but nodded, propping herself on her elbows, her teal stare scorching him.

Maintaining eye contact, Leargan licked her.

Ansley screamed, falling flat to the bed and reaching for him.

He gently pushed her hands away after kissing them. He dragged his tongue up and down her center, pulling her into his mouth, parting her and probing inside until she yanked his hair.

Leargan chuckled against her heated skin and her whole form quavered with the vibration. When he sucked her nub, her hips came off the bed. He held her still, giving her no mercy. He wanted her to climax before he joined them. Show her what orgasm was like before her first time making love.

He didn't have long to wait.

Ansley cried out and arched. She opened her mouth, as if to speak, but he shook his head.

"Shhh, love. Relax. Let go. Just feel. Come for me." Pushing his fingertip inside, Leargan groaned as her muscles stiffened. Her core latched on, contracting and releasing as her pleasure washed over them both.

She was tight, hot, and soaking wet…for *him*.

He slipped behind her, holding her, caressing her as she rode the wave of intensity out.

Ansley turned her face and crushed her lips into his.

Leargan didn't hesitate to kiss her back, swallowing her moan. He pushed her into the bed, spreading her thighs wide. Keeping their mouths fused, he gripped his erection and teased up and down her sex.

They both shivered.

He broke the kiss, panting.

She was gorgeous in passion, long red hair spread on her pillows; skin flushed glossy and teal eyes heavy.

He had to clear his throat. "Are you ready?"

Ansley nodded, resting her hands on his biceps.

Leargan shifted forward, sinking into her slowly. He gripped her hips to steady her, and tilted up with each disappearing inch.

She was very still, her eyes going wider the further he went.

He closed his own, unable to bear hurting her, and shoved forward, breaching the resistance of her virginity.

Ansley cried out and clung to him. Her nails bit into his skin, but he didn't care if she drew blood. She had to be all right.

"Love, I'm sorry," he breathed. "Do you want to stop?"

She shook her head, but tears gathered at the corners of her eyes. "I don't want to stop." She wiggled, and he bit back a gasp.

So tight. Mine.

Ansley belonged to him now.

"Be still, love. Give it a moment. I don't want to hurt you."

"I want to be with you, make you feel good."

"Blessed Spirit, you already have. You *are*."

Shoving upward, she whined, but Leargan rocked back into her, grunting as pleasure hit him. His body screamed to propel forward hard, claim her, but he went slowly, gingerly thrusting, until her expression told him discomfort was gone.

Ansley started to move with him, meeting his thrusts and she snaked her arms around him. She urged him to her, slanting her lips over his, until the kiss mirrored his plunges, both picking up speed at her demand.

Slow and steady was rejected by her pelvis shoving into his over and over. Leargan lost himself to their rhythm, kissing her even deeper as he moved in and out of her.

Her hands slipped over his shoulders and down his back, settled on his rear end, kneading, asking for more.

It was too much; the sensations washing over him

pitched him over the edge. Ecstasy so powerful his blood boiled.

Ansley tore her mouth away and screamed his name, pressing her full breasts into his chest. Her core clutched him tight as orgasm hit.

Leargan buried his face against her neck; his spine tingled. He froze as his release shot into her, his erection spasming as her sex tightened and loosened in waves. He groaned into her overheated skin.

She quivered in his arms, wrapping her legs around his waist.

He collapsed on top of her, sweat covering them both. He struggled for breath and coherent thought as Ansley shifted beneath him, shooting a tremor up his spine.

What the hell just happened?

Lovemaking had never been like that. *Ever.*

She caressed his stubbled cheek, offering a small smile when their eyes met.

He held her hand to his face as his mind raced. "Are you all right?"

"Aye. Are you?"

He nodded and slipped from her body. After a fortifying breath, he rolled to the bed, pulling her into his chest. Leargan kissed her temple, then rained soft kisses over her face until she giggled.

Ansley nestled close and pressed her lips to his in what melted into a tender lingering kiss. Their tongues brushed, danced and melded, but there was no urgency. Just her mouth against his, searing his soul.

She was his.

Forever.

Leargan swallowed, heart cantering. "You're mine, Ansley."

She kissed his chin, then his neck, a smile playing at her kiss-swollen mouth. "Are you mine?"

"Aye, always."

Silence descended until she squirmed against his side.

He framed her cheeks and made her meet his gaze. Her gorgeous eyes were misty. "Are you all right?" he asked again.

"Aye."

There was more there, but her expression was guarded, so he let it go, planting a soft kiss to her lips. "If you say so," he whispered.

"I do say so." Her voice wobbled.

Leargan cleared his throat. "I'll get something to clean us up." Without waiting for an answer, he skidded from her bed, wincing at the blood on his softening shaft, even his thighs.

It was *real*. Her innocence was gone. but she was his now. No other man would touch her, make love to her.

Dipping a small corner of linen in the cooling bath water, he washed himself facing away from her, then rinsed the cloth and returned to the bed, wiping blood away from her inner thighs and sex, gently cleansing her.

When their eyes met, Ansley blushed scarlet, but he smiled. He tossed the rag over his shoulder and crawled into the bed, tugging her to him. "Don't be embarrassed after what we shared."

"I'm not." She snuggled into his chest after he pulled the sleeping furs over them. "You'll sleep with me?"

"All night, love. I want to hold you."

Ansley smiled closed her eyes, resting her head on his chest with a sigh. Soon her breathing became deep and even.

Leargan smoothed her long hair, following the curve of her shoulder and dragging his hand down the soft skin of her back. She was so soft, supple. Fantastic beneath his fingertips.

His breath exited on a whoosh. He closed his eyes, contentment and *rightness* washing over him along with instant sleepiness he didn't fight.

Ansley's bed is where I belong.

"I love you," she muttered in her sleep.

He smiled. He'd never had a more pleasant dream.

Chapter Eighteen

nsley was warm all over. She snuggled closer to the source of heat and felt strong arms encircle her. She smiled against a fully-muscled chest. His clean scent tickled her nose as she inhaled, and she kissed the nearest skin.

What a wonderful dream.

Warm fingertips tugged her face up, and his lips captured hers. She opened to the insistent push of his tongue. They both shivered.

She arched into his hard chest, rubbing until her nipples peaked. Ansley kissed him harder, swallowing his groan as their tongues danced.

Desire pooled low in her belly and she swayed as heat shot lower, enhancing the pleasant ache already between her legs.

His hands slid down her back, cupping her bottom. An erection brushed her sex and she throbbed in answer, opening her legs at his urging so he could move closer. The tip of his manhood parted her wet folds as he rocked into her, but didn't enter.

More. She needed more.

Ansley moaned. She'd never had a dream so real. She *ached* for him to join them, make them one. Push inside her.

"Hmmm…Ansley," Leargan whispered against her lips.

Her eyes flew open at his familiar voice. Memories flooded and she flushed to her toes.

Leargan was in her bed.

They'd made love.

The pleasant ache between her legs wasn't imagined.

I love you. She bit back the words, chiding herself. He'd said he *needed* her. Called her '*love*' a few times, but it was a common term of affection. It meant nothing.

Ansley had given him her innocence, and she didn't regret it. But it would've meant so much more if he loved her too. She swallowed and pressed her lips to his. She couldn't tell him how she felt, but she could show him with her body.

He wouldn't tell her no. Wanting her wasn't exactly love, but he'd care for her, and he'd marry her as promised.

She'd have to worry about her heart later.

Ansley needed Leargan like she needed to breathe.

He rolled them and groaned again, pressing her into the bed. Her betrothed deepened their kiss and settled his weight on top of her.

She rubbed her tongue against his, kissing him back with all her might as she wrapped her arms and legs around him. His erection burned her inner thigh, and she writhed. He wasn't in the right place. Ansley needed him inside her.

Leargan had come into her room the previous night, long dark hair damp from his bath, and clothing casual, a simple blue tunic and soft tan breeches encasing his powerful thighs.

Ansley had wanted him even more than she had before. He'd been approachable; even more gorgeous. Although he hadn't said if he'd come to see her with a purpose, she hadn't been about to let him leave without taking her.

No more rejections.

Leargan might have great control, but he was still a man.

Naked had done the trick. She'd have to thank Daicy.

His hands cupped her bottom and pulled her pelvis flush to his. He pressed into her, moving back and forth, but didn't enter.

Ansley broke their kiss, throwing her head back and

moaning his name. "Please…please. I…I…need…"

"I want you." He panted over her, his long hair tickling.

She froze at the tenderness she saw in the dark pools of his eyes. "Have me, please. Take me." Ansley shoved her sex against his.

"Are you too sore?" The concern in his voice made her heart skip. Leargan caressed her cheek.

"You're killing me," she whispered.

A slow heated smile curved his lips as the phrase he'd uttered so many times fell from her lips.

Ansley would've mustered a retort, but he gave her what they both wanted, and gently slid inside her. Gasping, she grasped his biceps as he stilled.

Unlike the pain of first penetration last night, this didn't hurt. She was sore, but not in a bad way. Stretched, filled. *Complete.* As close to him as she could get. And throbbing, since he hadn't started to move. "Leargan…" She shifted.

"Love…don't do that," he breathed.

"Then move…please move…" She lifted her hips and rocked under him, tilting to take him deeper.

"Wanted…to…make sure…you're…all right…"

In answer, Ansley drove up again.

Finally, her lover grunted and thrust forward on a moan.

Leargan devoured her mouth, kissing her into oblivion as he found a comfortable rhythm.

She held him tight to her, moving with him, under him, making noises into their endless kisses. Her blood sang in her ears as he took them higher.

Restlessness rolled over her, and her body twitched, then began to tighten like last night. Pleasure hit her in waves. A cry broke from her lips and she threw her head back, whispering his name over and over. Ansley had no control over her taut muscles.

Her love buried his face against her neck and

plastered her to his chest, hovering above her. His erection jerked inside her; he too found release. Warmth settled low in her belly and she shivered in his arms.

Leargan collapsed on top of her.

Ansley loved his weight. She spread kisses all over his neck and shoulder and held him tight, not ready for their bodies to be parted. Blessed Spirit, she loved him. It was becoming more and more difficult to hold it inside. She sighed into his neck, running her hands down his sweat-dampened back, following the curve of his rear end and as much of his muscular thigh as she could reach.

Springy hair greeted her fingertips, and Leargan shook against her breasts, his face still hidden against her. "Ansley." His warm breath tickled her skin.

She brought her hands back up, running her fingers through his long hair, and squeezed him tighter.

Leargan chuckled and she felt the rumble against her. "I need to breathe, love." He lifted his head and their gazes collided, his dark eyes dancing.

"Sorry." Ansley shivered when he traced her kiss-swollen lips with his finger.

His expression sobered, and his gaze bored into her. "You're mine, Ansley."

He said that last night, too.

Her heart stuttered. He'd told her he was *hers,* too.

"Aye," she whispered.

"Say it."

"Leargan?" She stared up at him.

"Tell me you're mine, Ansley." His tone was a mixture of an order…and something else. Almost a plea?

"I'm yours. Always." She couldn't look away.

His eyes spoke of tenderness and heat, but what else? Was she foolish to think there was more?

Leargan took her mouth in answer, kissing her until her already-languid form slipped into bonelessness. Her legs fell to the bed. He flipped their positions, Ansley landing on top.

She snuggled into his muscled chest, molding herself to him; playing with the sparse coarse hair between his blunt nipples.

"I could stay here all day with you." He ran his hands over her hair.

"Aye, I never want to leave this bed."

Chuckling, he pressed a kiss to her forehead. "Unfortunately, I have duties."

Ansley ignored the wave of disappointment that threated to crash over her. Leargan was right. They couldn't languish in bed all day, regardless of what they both wanted.

They'd be missed. They weren't married yet. He had no reason to be in her room this early in the morning.

"What's wrong?" he whispered, cupping her cheeks.

"N-n-nothing."

His gaze roved her face. "You don't regret it, do you?"

"Blessed Spirit, how could I? I l—" Words rushed, heat crept up her neck, searing her cheeks. She'd almost told him she loved him, *again*. "Nay. I don't regret it."

"Ansley?" Something in his tone made her meet his eyes.

Since when did Sir Leargan Tegran, brave knight and Captain of the Aldern personal guard, need reassurance?

Evidently, right now.

"I don't regret giving myself to you. *Ever*. I Promise."

His shoulders relaxed into the bed linens. "I want you to know it was special to me. It was…" With his brow knitted, he was vulnerable and adorable.

She leaned in and kissed him.

Leargan moaned into her mouth, shoving his tongue against hers and yanking her closer.

Ansley fell into his chest, her arm scrambling for purchase. Her fingertips brushed the tip of his erection. She quivered. He wanted her again. The feeling was mutual.

She pulled away from his kiss, panting hard. "My first

time was very special." She lavished warm wet kisses around his mouth. "As was my second."

Cupping a breast, he thumbed her nipple until it peaked, and she gasped.

One corner of Leargan's mouth shot up. "How was your third?"

"Show me," she demanded.

Cera laughed as she circled Ansley, her sword high. "What d'you mean, it's not fair?"

"It's magic." She gripped the hilt of her weapon tighter. The sword was familiar in her hands. *Feels good.*

Her father had told her many a time she'd been born with a sword in her hands, Ansley's weapon of choice. She'd always been the best of the female Riders.

Too bad the duchess had almost equal skills.

"I'm starting to regret Tristan healing you completely," she muttered.

Her friend laughed again and rushed her, but Ansley twisted her body away and avoided contact.

Men clapped, and someone whistled.

She tried to pretend most of the personal guard, as well as a good-sized group of men-at-arms didn't line the fence of the fighting yard.

Why did I agree to spar?

Cera had declared she needed some air. She'd left little Fallon with her lady's maid, Neomi, and challenged Ansley to a duel. Actually, she'd guilted her, stating — whining, really — about how long she'd been cooped up in the castle.

When the duchess had reminded her of a time she'd beat her in a match at Spring Training a few turns back — in front of new Rider recruits no less — Ansley couldn't say nay.

No one beat her with a sword.

Much like Cera's skills with the bow.

Now she regretted her pride, even though the male eyes were filled with admiration. She didn't like being the center of attention. Never had.

The clash of metal on metal jolted her, and she locked her arms so Cera wouldn't knock her over.

"Concentrate, Ans. Or are you rusty?" her friend smirked.

Ansley snarled and pushed the duchess off, stalking and circling her.

Ali echoed her growl from the tree line, and she hushed her mentally. Her bond knew Cera wouldn't hurt her; she'd seen them spar and train more times than Ansley could count. The she-wolf was just being antsy because Ansley was distracted, not focused on the fight.

"I'm not rusty; *you* are." She pushed forward, thrusting her sword.

The duchess widened her stance and met Ansley's strike, hitting her weapon away from her body. "All right, you got me. That could've been a cut."

"One point for Ansley, love! C'mon, you can do better than that," Jorrin shouted.

Cera growled. "I'll get her."

"Don't let her talk to you like that, Ansley," Leargan yelled.

When Ansley swung her body back around, she spotted Jorrin and Leargan bumping shoulders and grinning. Like they were vying against each other as they cheered them on.

Her heart flipped and she chided herself to concentrate. She flashed a feral grin. "Dare you." She dashed toward her opponent.

Cera raised her magic sword, and the glow around the weapon went radiant as her powers surged. It bled out, surrounding her form too, like an aura.

"That's *cheating*."

The duchess flashed a grin.

Ansley didn't let the magic stop her, although she had

to squint against the brightness. She crashed her sword into her friend's, and Cera stumbled back. She made two long slices in front of her torso. If they'd been fighting for their lives, her strikes would've killed.

Her instinct was to stop the duchess from toppling over, but she didn't. A sparring match was a sparring match, after all.

Cera tumbled to the ground and winced as her rear end hit. Dirt puffed into the air around her breech-clad legs.

Men gasped, then clapped. Some chuckled, but when she glanced over her shoulder, all Ansley could see was rapt attention.

Leargan beamed and hit Jorrin's shoulder. When his eyes found hers, he pumped his fist.

She turned back to Cera, tapping the crown of her head with the tip of her weapon. "*That's* what you get for cheating, my lady. Dead dead dead."

The duchess mock-glared but couldn't quite hold back her smile. "Yeah, yeah, I guess so. But you never said no magic."

She shook her head and sheathed her sword, then offered her hand. "I thought it was inferred."

Cera grinned as she helped her gain her feet. "Sorry."

Rolling her eyes, Ansley failed to bite back a grin of her own. "You're so sincere."

Her friend bowed and sheathed her magic sword. She thrust out her hand. "Thank you for the sparring match. I defer to your greatness with the sword."

Ansley ignored the teasing tone and squeezed her fingers, beaming. "That just made it worth it. Thanks."

Jorrin whistled long and slow from the fence. "We'd better call Gamel to write that on parchment. Cera used the word '*defer*' and '*greatness*' in the same sentence."

She giggled when the duchess glared at her husband.

Leargan threw his arm around Ansley's shoulders when they reached the men, and a tremor slid down her spine. The heat of his side against her seeped through her jerkin.

Them entwined in her bed and that morning flashed into her mind, and she swallowed as her body warmed.

"That was great fun, love." The duke pressed a kiss to Cera's cheek.

Her friend nodded. "I agree. Ansley and I need to spar more often."

"You only want to so you can learn to beat me, Ceralda Aldern." Ansley giggled again.

"Not true," the duchess said, but she was grinning from ear to ear.

"You were fantastic, love," Leargan whispered in Ansley's ear.

She shivered as his warm breath tickled. "Thank you. I bet I could defeat you, too." She doubted it, though. He was stronger, larger, and fantastic with a sword.

Her betrothed arched a dark eyebrow, but the carefree smile he wore made her heart stutter.

Jorrin whistled. "You going to let her challenge you like that, Captain?"

"Oh, I'll get her later." Leargan winked.

Jorrin and Cera laughed.

Ansley's limbs warmed and her cheeks seared.

Blessed Spirit, I hope so.

Chapter Nineteen

h e was absolutely crazy. Officially lost his mind. Roduch sighed, tucking his free hand behind his head. He winced when he knocked his knuckles on the wooden headboard. They smarted, but perhaps a little pain would do him good.

I shouldn't be in this room. She's fine.

His room wasn't far.

Avril could stay on her own. At least overnight. She was stronger now.

He didn't *want* to leave her.

Staying is dangerous.

Roduch tried for the hundredth time to convince himself to leave — unsuccessfully. When he looked down at Avril sleeping peacefully, head on his chest, tiny fist tucked next to her cheek, he lost his resolve again. His heart surged and ached at the same time. Although he'd had visions of her as his wife, he'd never fathomed he could feel so much for her in such a short period of time.

Just over a sevenday, and he was lost to her. Head over heels in love, as the lasses would say.

She wasn't ready for that. And not touching her, not kissing her, was *killing* him.

The fourth night of him sleeping — or not so much — in her bed, with her *whole form* touching his, tested his restraint.

More than tested it.

Roduch loved her. He wanted her. And he wanted to show her.

He stared at the wide arched ceiling, his body as tight as a bow string — one part in particular. No ability to sleep, despite the desire to do so.

He'd get knocked on his arse on the fighting yard in the morning.

Glancing at the chair he'd spent those nights in, he growled. The damn thing had the nerve to look inviting. Or was it just amused?

Inanimate objects having emotions? You have *lost it.*

Avril sighed in her sleep and nestled even closer. Roduch sucked in a breath as her bent knee brushed his erection.

He hardened even more, straining against the softest breeches he could find to sleep in. If he'd been in his own room, his own bed, he'd have been naked, as he always slept. That of course, wouldn't work in his love's bed. He cursed himself to keep his thoughts coherent—and above the waist.

"Hmm…Roduch," Avril muttered.

He froze, heart fluttering. Roduch reached down, brushing her dark curls out of her face.

She smiled in her sleep.

Damn, he wanted—no, *needed*—to kiss her. He settled for touching his lips to the top of her head, smiling as he inhaled the sweet scent of her hair. Blessed Spirit, he wanted her.

He slid a hand down inside the sleeping furs, then to his pants, and shifted the material to alleviate some of the pressure, but his arousal only throbbed more. Roduch groaned.

Avril lifted her head, blinking and fighting a yawn as their eyes met.

"I'm sorry, lo—lass, I didn't mean to wake you." He bit back a cringe—had almost called her *love*. Again.

"Are you all right?" she whispered, her voice thick with sleep.

He forced a smile and nodded. She was too sleepy to catch his slip, but he couldn't exactly tell her what his *issue* was. "Aye. Go back to sleep."

"Only if you do." She gave a smile that had his stomach flipping.

"Are you all right?" Roduch caressed her soft cheek.

Avril was sleep-warm and adorable. He wanted her even more.

"Yes…why?" she asked, dark eyebrows drawing together.

Do not *kiss her.*

"You said my name."

"I…don't…remember." Her face tilted toward his.

Roduch dipped his head down, but stopped himself.

Her eyes widened. She'd not missed his intent.

She'll pull away now.

He couldn't bear to see fear in her emerald eyes. He winced, cursing himself to hell and back, then crushed his eyes shut.

When he opened them, Avril's face was very close to his, her small hands gripping his tunic to haul her body closer.

His heart sped up as she slanted her lips, less than an inch from brushing his. "Avril?"

"Don't you want to kiss me?"

When Roduch cupped her cheeks, she leaned in, closing her eyes.

Blessed Spirit, help me.

"Aye. But I don't want to scare you."

Seconds passed, and she met his gaze, her full tempting mouth curving in a soft smile. "What if I want you to kiss me?"

Roduch swallowed. She *wanted* him to kiss her? "Well, I suppose I'd have to oblige, since my lady wishes it." His voice was too husky, making his jest fall off a bit.

"Kiss me, Roduch."

Slow.

It was what she needed.

Tender. Careful.

He needed to treat her like the innocent she truly was.

Show her what he felt for her. Show her what real intimacy was all about. Intention and thought fled when his lips touched hers. Soft and so sweet he had to have more. Roduch had to have *her*. He groaned when she opened for him, and slipped his tongue in her mouth without hesitation.

Avril didn't hesitate either, which only made his blood run hotter.

She kissed him back fervently, their tongues dueling, then melding, and she snaked her arms around his neck to move closer, pressing her mouth even harder against his.

Small, firm, perfect breasts flattened against his chest as she lay completely on top of him, and Roduch wrapped his arms around her. He caressed her back, then followed the curve of her bottom.

His manhood pulsated; there was no way she couldn't feel him against her.

He squeezed her rear end, shifting her so she straddled him.

Her sleeping chemise rose up around her waist. Her thinly covered sex landed on his. Roduch moved under her, his hands shooting down her thighs and calves. Her skin was soft, smooth and warm.

More.

Avril whimpered into his mouth, and his hands shot up her back. He buried his fingertips in her mess of curls, tugging her even closer as his grip settled at the back of her neck. He devoured her mouth, but she was right with him, kissing him with a surprising fierceness.

He had to get inside her. *Now.*

Roduch's pulse roared in his ears as she rocked in his lap, and his spine tingled like he was about to climax.

Small hands on his stubbled cheeks jolted him. Her touch burned, but he craved more.

So real. Feels so good.

Fighting a tremor, he gripped her waist. He needed to flip them, needed her beneath him so he could get inside her like he had so many times before.

Wait. This isn't a dream. This is real.

He was in Avril's bed in the guest wing of Castle Aldern.

This was their *first* kiss. She wasn't ready to make love.

What the hell is wrong with me?

Roduch was no better than her bastard former husband. He broke away.

You are the worst kind of wretch.

He lifted her gently off him, setting her on the bed. He panted against the headboard, struggling for breath and coherent thought. "You taste better than in my visions. You feel better in my arms," he blurted.

"Then what's wrong?" Avril's emerald eyes went wide. Her breasts rose and fell as she too panted, her gorgeous ivory skin flushed with color, lips kiss-swollen. Her nipples were peaked, pushing against the thin material of her chemise.

"Nothing…" Roduch groaned.

"Why did you stop?"

"Because, love…" He flinched. No way he could avoid the term of endearment after what they'd shared. *She is my love.* "I want you."

Confusion flickered in her beautiful eyes, then rolled over her expression. She averted her gaze. "I'm not a virgin." Wringing her hands on her lap, Avril worried her bottom lip. Her voice dripped shame.

He cursed. Roduch couldn't calm his roiling anger at her bastard former husband. He cupped her cheeks and forced her to meet his eyes. "But you *are*, love."

Her eyes clouded with tears and she shook her head. "I…I'm not. I'm…damaged goods."

"Avril, no!" He'd *never* let her think she'd been ruined.

She was perfect. She was *his*.

"You've never willingly given yourself to a man, so

you *are* innocent, and I'll treat you as such. I won't pressure you into anything you're not ready for."

Her tears spilled over, and he thumbed them away. "So…you'd want me anyway? Even though Tynan…"

Roduch growled and silenced her with his lips.

Avril clung to him, balling his tunic as she moved her mouth under his, pushing closer until he put his arms around her.

He kissed her deeply and thoroughly, ignoring the insistent throb of his body. He wouldn't take her tonight, even if she said she was ready.

She sighed when they parted, but stayed plastered to his chest. "Roduch?"

"Aye?"

"Thank you."

"For what?"

"Saying you want me," Avril whispered.

He rubbed her back in large soothing circles, nestling their bodies down under the thick sleeping furs. "I do want you." It'd probably petrify her if she knew just how badly.

"I…" She looked down, but then took a deep breath and met his eyes. "I want you, too."

Roduch's breath caught.

What? Had she just said she *wanted* him? After what she'd been through?

"Avril, I…" He swallowed hard.

She presented a shy smile and pressed her lips to his. It was sweet, and much too short. "I'm nervous. It's new for me. But it's how I feel. Honestly. If my body burning and aching for you is *want.*"

He nodded. "It is. That's desire, love."

"Then…I want you, Roduch."

His admiration for her shot up. Avril was the bravest lass he'd ever known. He kissed her forehead, gathering her closer still. "Tell me when you're ready. I'll be here. Waiting for you. Always."

A brilliant grin bloomed and she nodded.

Roduch's head spun. The smile was reminiscent of his visions. "I'll do anything for you, Avril."
He bit his tongue to keep *'I love you'* from tumbling out. She wasn't ready for that, either.

"You really had visions of me?" Her whisper was low, her tone as curious as her expression.

"Aye. Since I was a lad of about seven."

"Seven? I was much younger than that when I had my first vision."

"What do you think that means?"

"I'm not sure." Avril cocked her head to one side, green gaze boring into him. "I sense nothing from you. *Nothing.* I've always been able to sense magic."

"Perhaps we should ask Lucan what he thinks. One of his gifts is understanding the nature of magic. I swear to you, I've been seeing you most of my life."

She winced. "Looking at Lucan hurts."

"What do you mean?"

"I see auras. His is so bright, he hurts my eyes. Makes my magic ache. He's so powerful. I've never met someone with so much magic." She sounded fascinated, and it made him frown.

Roduch chided himself. He was jealous of a lad of four and ten?

Avril smiled and it had his heart tripping all over again. "He wants to be a knight so badly. I hope he succeeds."

"How do you know?"

She frowned and looked away. Moments went by before she spoke. "I didn't invade his privacy. I promise. It's just… He wants it so badly, my magic just picked it up. I didn't have to concentrate to see or anything."

"I'm not mad, love."

"I won't use my magic to hurt anyone. *Ever.* But sometimes I see things. Not only about people, but…I…see *things.*"

"Things?" Roduch asked.

"Premonitions. Sometimes I know when something will happen."

"That's happened to me a few times in my life."

She scooted closer, studying his face. "When?"

"Once when I was a page, I dreamt of a rockslide where a lad was hurt. It happened the next day. I felt terrible for not telling anyone. Other times it's just been a sense, or a flash, nothing solid. I also dreamt of Lord Varthan killing Lady Cera's family before it happened. I acted, but we were too late."

Her eyes clouded with tears, and he wiped them away.

"I saw that as well. Tynan believed me, but didn't care. I wanted to tell *someone*. I…couldn't do anything about it." Avril shook her head, frowning. "I suppose the Blessed Spirit punished me. I couldn't sleep for over a sevenday. The visions haunted me."

"Neither could I. I had the same dream over and over again."

She blinked. "Tell me."

Roduch explained as much as he could remember about the dream of the dark man and his shades. All dead now, and the better for it. The dream had been flashes of rage, fire, rape and magic. And death. Visions of blood and the deaths of good people. All for Lady Cera's magic sword, and lust for power.

Avril gasped. "Mine was the same. To the last detail."

"We had the same dream? Over and over again, no less. How could this even be?"

"I don't know. Can you call on your magic? Force a vision?"

"Never. I've tried many times to see you," he said.

"I don't know anyone who can't use their magic when they want to."

"I only ever wanted to see *you*. Other than that, my so-called magic never mattered to me."

Avril cuddled closer. "I think we need to talk to

Lucan. You're right about that."

"Aye, love."

Meeting his eyes, she smiled. "I like when you call me '*love*'."

"Good, because I like calling you '*love*'."

Chapter Twenty

The lad's face scrunched up even though his eyes were closed, and his fingers around Roduch's hand tightened. Sweat broke out on his forehead, and his dark hair was damp. His already-glowing skin increased in radiance and Roduch had to squint to keep looking at him.

Avril sucked in an audible breath and crushed her eyes shut.

They had their hands joined, and were sitting in a semi-circle on the floor of her guest room. Lucan had explained he needed room to work, and needed them all touching.

Roduch's gut told him to make Lucan stop whatever was doing, but when Avril squeezed his hand as if she'd read his mind, he made himself relax. He loosened his shoulders and sat taller.

After minutes that felt like hours, Greenwald's knighted mage opened his eyes. He sucked in air, his narrow chest rising and falling. "I sense…"

"Go on," Roduch urged. He and Avril exchanged a glance. He looked back at Lucan.

"Nothing."

"Nothing?" Avril's voice was a squeak.

His stomach flipped and he looked into her green eyes, then at the lad for the third time. They both had dark hair, green eyes. The two could be siblings.

"No magic in Roduch," Lucan said. "No *magical* reason for him to have been having visions of you, Avril. Let alone for turns, like he did." He released each of their hands, but Avril didn't separate herself from Roduch. "I probed until my head spun." Searching for magic—and understanding it—were what the lad did best. "It doesn't matter how far I tried to delve. I see yours. Not his."

"It was hard to look at you," she whispered.

He cringed. "I know. The more I use, the brighter I get. Your aura is the same way; your skin just doesn't glow like mine. Or Tristan's when he heals."

"My aura glows?"

"Aye, anyone who can read auras would have no problem seeing it. It brightens and changes colors, depending on what you're doing with your magic and how you *feel* about it."

Surprise dominated Avril's expression "You know a lot about magic."

The lad blushed. "Cera's cousin, Lord Avery is a magic scholar, as well as a mage. We study old magic books together via an open-window spell. We can see each other through any flat surface to have a lesson, even though he's in Tarvis. He's helping me learn about my powers."

"Lord Lenore is a good man," Roduch said.

Lucan smiled and nodded, but looked back at Avril. "Don't worry, it's not abnormal that you can't see your own aura, even in a mirror, though Blessed Spirit knows you have strong magic."

It was Avril's turn to blush. She scooted closer to Roduch, and he disengaged their hands and threw his arm around her slender shoulders. She was leery of her magic.

His gut told him she was rarely seen for being herself. Her parents had practically *sold* her to her former husband for her abilities. "What about me?" Roduch asked.

"I wouldn't know the reason, logically or magically, but maybe *her* magic was the cause. Somehow, Avril was projecting her gift onto you, even though you were far away geographically, and even though she hadn't a clue she was doing so. I'll talk to Avery tonight and see what he thinks, but it's the only thing that makes even the smallest bit of sense to me."

Avril locked eyes with him, but Roduch didn't have a word to say on the matter.

Silence descended.

Lucan cocked his head to one side, as if deep in thought. "This is proof."

"Proof of what?" she asked.

"Fate is real. The Blessed Spirit guides us, even if we don't always know the reasons."

The lad grinned, and when Avril's mouth turned up in a shy smile, Roduch's heart sped up.

"Fate," he whispered.

"I believe we're not supposed to understand everything. If we did, *faith* would be affected." Lucan's voice was low, then his expression clouded. "We have to have faith, or we won't survive."

Roduch squeezed the lad's forearm. No doubt he was thinking of that bastard, Varthan. "Thank you, Lucan."

The lad nodded, his green eyes wide. "Anytime, Roduch."

"You're a good man, Sir Lucan," Avril said.

Lucan reddened to the tips of his ears, but his smile could've split his face.

"Thank you for restoring *my* faith," she whispered.

Roduch smiled at them both. "Just what I wanted to hear."

Ansley's laughter made him smile, until he came closer and spotted who she was laughing and talking with near the personal guard's table in the great hall.

A wave of jealousy hit him in the chest. He wanted to smash Alasdair's face in.

The tall dark-haired man was the eldest of the twelve, at thirty turns old. Alasdair was handsome; women gravitated to him. It didn't matter that the knight was exceedingly loyal to Leargan.

Ansley was his, *damn it.*

It was no secret they were betrothed, so why was Alasdair talking to her?

Jolting in his boots, Leargan shook his head. *What's wrong with me?*

She'd never betray him with another man; he knew it as sure as he knew how to breathe. And for that matter, Alasdair wouldn't touch another man's woman. He might be loose with his favors, but never with an attached woman, even if *she* pursued him.

His longtime friend saw him first, over Ansley's red head, and he offered a nod. "Captain."

Leargan ordered himself to relax and pushed away the urge to snatch her tight to his side. "Morning, Alas. Ansley." Her name came harsher than he'd intended.

She turned, giving him a brilliant smile that said she wasn't bothered by his bark, or she'd missed it.

He blew out a breath when Alasdair winked.

"Good morning," Ansley said. She was at his side in seconds.

He craved touching her, as if he hadn't left her bed less than an hour ago. Leargan dropped a kiss on her cheek, throwing an arm around her shoulders. He resisted the urge to gather her to him take her mouth properly.

How could he *need* her so much? He'd taken her no less than three times during the night.

"Alasdair was just telling me some stories about when you were little." Ansley grinned.

The knight had been raised as a foster child at Castle Rowan in Terraquist, as had Leargan, and several of the other members of his guard. Alasdair was seven turns his senior, but they'd spent a great deal of time together growing up.

Leargan could only imagine what he'd told her. Most of the things they'd done together involved mischief. Some of which should never be uttered. *Ever.* He met Alas' dancing blue eyes. "Please don't tell me you told her about the stables."

The knight burst out laughing, but shook his head. "I'd almost forgotten about that."

"What happened at the stables?" Ansley asked.

"Never mind, love." He bit back a groan. Had walked right into that.

"Oh, come now, Captain. She'll be your wife; she needs to know *all* about you." Alasdair beamed.

"Yes, Captain. I *need* to know." She tugged on his arm, meeting his gaze. The smile on her full mouth took his breath away.

He cleared his throat and glanced at his friend. "Well, what *did* you tell her?"

"About the time we got caught peeping in the servant lasses' bath house."

"Ah!" Leargan chuckled. "I took the fall for you and a few older ones, if you recall. I was only ten turns old. I didn't even know what I was looking at."

"Oh no. It may well have been my idea, but you were there all the way, Captain."

Leargan laughed again, and Ansley broke out into a fit of giggles. "The king himself tanned my hide that time," he admitted, wincing. "But I was still mostly innocent."

Alasdair made a weak protest, but chuckled. "I suppose you'll accuse me of corrupting you. Introducing you to the lasses at far too young an age?"

"Corrupting me? I've never thought about it that way."

His fellow knight winked.

A time in a tavern—nay—many times, in *many* taverns, danced into his mind. Perhaps, Alasdair *had* tried to corrupt him. Especially when he'd taken him to that place in Terraquist Main at age five and ten to '*become a man*'. His betrothed did *not* need to know about any of that.

"Well, I guess that's good." Alasdair grinned. "I'd hate for any of that to come back on me now."

"I'm very….curious, Leargan," Ansley said.

He met her eyes. "Then you'll just have to wonder, my love."

Alasdair snorted. "That, Mistress Ansley, is our dear captain exercising discretion."

"You are correct." Leargan bowed, winking at his redhead. "The better part of valor, or so they say."

She giggled again, her eyes dancing. "I suppose there's always later, Alasdair."

The tall knight nodded. "Of course, I wouldn't want to disappoint my captain's bride." He made a show of bowing, and pressed a kiss into her knuckles.

Ansley threw her head back and laughed again, her cheeks pink.

Leargan fought shifting on his feet.

She's so gorgeous.

Their eyes locked. Alasdair, the great hall and the voices surrounding them faded. There was only his betrothed and her teal eyes. He needed to kiss her. Hold her. Take her to his room. Or her room. *Where* mattered not; he just needed her *now*.

"It was nice talking to you, Mistress Fraser." Alasdair's voice destroyed the moment and Leargan jumped.

Her long red plait swung over her shoulder as Ansley shot a glance to his friend. "Just Ansley, Alasdair, please. And it was my pleasure. I'll find you later for more Leargan stories. I very much enjoyed them."

Leargan growled. "I'll order him to keep his mouth shut."

"I *have* heard women are more attracted to mystery men." The knight's words were wrapped in laughter.

"That depends on the man," Ansley shot back.

His heart picked up speed as he watched her banter with his friend. Not that he'd seen her speak with them all, but his men had quickly accepted her *and* her place at his side. She fit in well at Greenwald as a whole. It was right. *Perfect.*

They hadn't discussed it yet, but after they married, Leargan wouldn't force her to leave the King's Riders unless she wanted to. He'd even bid the king to let her stay in Greenwald. Surely, King Nathal wouldn't require her to remain living in Terraquist.

But being away from him...on the road, on a long message run?

Ali would protect her of course, but even the thought of missing her made him ache. On the other hand, it could be prudent to have an official king's messenger nearby. He should run the idea by King Nathal.

"Well, I shall see you on the fighting grounds, Captain," Alasdair said, inclining his head.

"Aye." Leargan nodded.

"Ansley, it was a pleasure." His friend and fellow knight bowed to his betrothed.

"Likewise," Ansley said, grinning. She shot a look to Leargan. "Later," she whispered loudly.

Alas chuckled but said nothing as he turned on his heel to go.

"What a catch he'll be for someone."

Alas with only one woman? If she only knew.

Leargan snorted. "He's trouble." He took her hand and entwined their fingers, as they too, headed out of the great hall.

"I hope you're really not bothered by him sharing stories with me," Ansley said.

"No, no, love." They paused in the corridor, and he cupped her face.

"Good, because I very much enjoyed learning about you as a lad."

"I can tell you about that, you know," he said.

"Oh, I know."

Leargan smiled. "I really should go." He pulled her into his arms.

Ansley leaned up to brush her lips against his.

He bit back a groan. The touch wasn't enough. Niall

could run things for a while, couldn't he?

Roduch and Lucan were going to be arriving late, anyway. The big knight had told him the lad was going to probe Avril's magic.

"Then go."

Her voice grounded him, and Leargan chided himself for irresponsibility.

"I'll meet you for midday meal?" she asked.

"I'd like that." Unable to help himself, he leaned down for a quick kiss.

Ansley moved her lips under his.

He slipped his tongue into her mouth without thought, falling into her as she wrapped her arms around him and kissed him harder.

Their tongues danced and dueled, and Leargan groaned, his breeches already unbearably tight. A voice reminded him he had duties to attend to. He tore his mouth from hers, panting against her full breasts.

His betrothed's breath was just as ragged, as she rested her forehead against his. Her cheeks were flushed pink, her lips kiss-swollen.

He swallowed another groan, his arousal pulsing.

"Go with your men," Ansley breathed.

"Aye, I've got to. But we'll finish this later."

"At midday?" Delicate fiery brow arched, she pulled back, a smile playing at her mouth.

"You're determined to kill me, aren't you?"

She pressed a hard fast kiss to his lips and giggled. "Nay, Captain." Her plait danced around her back as she shook her head. "Have a good morning." Ansley hugged him tight.

"You, as well, love."

Ansley grinned again, and then her expression sobered. "I know you're training, but be careful, all right?"

"Always."

"Well, Cera's waiting for me in the Duchess Solar..."

"Go." Leargan reluctantly released her. The reward

was watching her hips sway as she headed down the corridor. His stomached flipped when she threw a smile over her shoulder.

Chapter Twenty-one

nsley watched Cera grin at the tiny infant in her arms and couldn't help the smile that curved her own lips. He was absolutely beautiful. Dark red curls clung around his tapered ears, and his eyes were as blue as his father's. He had his mother's finger in his little fist as he snuggled close to her breast.

Fallon had hollered something fierce when Cera had changed his diaper, but nursing had quieted him. The duchess had just smiled and cooed at him, whispering words of love. Calm and endearing, she showered him with kisses and nestled him close.

Ansley had never seen her tough, always-in-charge-friend like she was with her son. Cera had matured and grown, maybe even softened a bit. She was already a wonderful mother. Her gray eyes shone every time she gazed at the baby.

She wanted that, too. She wanted it with Leargan.

Could I be pregnant?

A tremor shot down her spine. If he'd already gotten her with child, they'd need to marry as soon as possible. They'd made love so many times she'd lost count.

Other than the night Fallon was born, they hadn't discussed children, but Leargan made no efforts to prevent pregnancy. Every time, his release had been inside her. If not now, it was only a matter of time before they created a child. Ansley was as insatiable as Leargan.

Heart stuttering, her hand hovered over her lower stomach. When was the last time she'd bled?

"Why are you so quiet?" Cera asked, looking up from burping her little son. Streaming light in the warm bright room made her dark red hair shine, appearing a lighter hue. She wore a simple pale gray dress that brought out the color of her eyes, the long loose curly waves of her hair surrounding her like an aura. Feminine and gorgeous. And so happy, she exuded it.

Most of the time her friend wore breeches and a tunic, like the day when they'd sparred. It was odd seeing her *'dressed like a girl,'* as Cera would say.

Since Ansley had been in Greenwald, she'd seen the duchess in more gowns than she'd seen her wear in all their turns together as Riders.

"Just thinking," Ansley said. She scooted her chair closer and caressed the baby's downy curls. Her fingertips brushed one of his little tapered ears.

Fallon was soft and warm and perfect.

"About Leargan? Or babies?" Cera asked slyly, waggling her eyebrows.

Heat crept up her neck but she met her friend's gray eyes. "Maybe both."

The duchess stared. Slowly, a knowing smile curved her full mouth. "Is there a reason to be thinking about babies?"

Ansley averted her gaze, her cheeks burning. She squirmed in her chair.

Cera laughed. "Ansley! Why didn't you tell me?"

"I'm not ashamed. I love him."

"Who said anything about being ashamed? I'm happy for you."

"Good," she whispered, releasing a breath.

"So why're you thinking about babies? Want one so soon?" She winked.

"I wouldn't mind…once we're wed. But I wonder what Leargan would think…"

"He asked you to marry him. He probably wouldn't mind how soon it was, but your father might."

"What d'you mean?" Ansley asked.

Cera winced, but schooled her expression fast. "He

didn't." The whisper was so low she almost missed it.

Leaning forward, she cocked her head to one side. "What're you talking about? Who didn't what?"

"He didn't tell you?" Her friend scrunched up her nose. Her cheeks were bright pink, and she tried to hide her face behind her son's small form.

"*Who*? Tell me *what*?"

"Never mind." She shook her head.

"You can't do that, Cera."

"Do what?"

Cera's words were a fair representation of *innocent*, but Ansley didn't fall for it for a second. She glared. "Tell me what you're talking about. Now."

She threw her head back and sighed. When their eyes met, her friend opened her mouth as if to speak, then paused. "It's not my place to tell you, Ans."

"Nay. You don't get to do that. And don't you *dare* sit there and '*Ans*' me. Spill it, Ceralda Aldern."

"I can't." Red curls danced about her shoulders when the duchess shook her head again.

"Why not?"

"Ansley, I love you. You know that, right? You're a sister to me."

Frowning, Ansley leaned forward even more, only inches from Cera and Fallon. "Aye. You and Aimil both are my sisters in all but blood."

Cera's smile was soft, but with a touch of sadness. "Because I love you, I can't tell you. You need to talk to your betrothed."

"What?"

"Promise me you'll *listen* to him."

"Cera—"

Her friend gripped her hand and squeezed. "*Promise* me. Don't be stubborn like I was."

"What the hell does that mean?" she snapped. Frustration made her gut roil.

"Ansley." Her name was a warning, and Cera's eyes

flashed. "Quit digging. I wouldn't have brought it up, if I knew you hadn't a clue."

Brought what up?

Ansley dragged her hand down her face and sighed. She'd get nothing further from the duchess. "You'd better be glad you're holding a baby."

Cera laughed.

She stared at her longtime friend and former fellow Senior Rider.

What does she know? Do I need to worry? Aye. Something's wrong.

Promise she'd *listen* to Leargan?

"Is it bad, Cera? Tell me that." Her voice cracked.

The duchess' expression sobered, her face drawn and concerned. Fallon started to fuss and she rocked him absently as she studied Ansley. "Remember you love him, Ansley."

"Remember I love him? *That* bad, huh?" She shot to her feet, making a tight fist. "I'll see you at evening meal."

"Where are you going?"

"To do what you told me to do."

"Now?"

Ansley shrugged. "Why wait?"

Not giving her friend a chance to respond, she rushed from the Duchess Solar, almost running Aimil and Avril down when she rounded the corner. Throwing a hasty apology over her shoulder, she continued on her way, meeting her wolf in the courtyard.

If Leargan was hiding something, it wouldn't be for long.

Sweat poured down his brow. Leargan's chest heaved as he regulated his breathing and gripped his sword tighter. His tunic and jerkin long discarded, and the fall breeze tickled his naked skin, relieving some of the heat the workout brought on.

Alasdair and Niall circled him. Either could strike.

He'd already eliminated Roduch from their charge. The big blond knight was nursing his head not too far away. Leargan had drawn blood, but Tristan was on hand, and there wasn't any serious damage.

Roduch had actually apologized and promised he'd be more vigilant next time. It was odd for his friend to falter enough to take a hit.

Maybe the man's mind was on Avril.

Like Leargan's mind was on Ansley.

Dangerous for them both.

He needed to know the outcome of the magic meeting, but it would hold until later.

Leargan regrouped in front of the two knights he still faced, chanting *train like you fight; fight like you train.* Ansley's father, Sir Murdoch, had drilled it into their heads.

The rest of the personal guard, as well as castle men-at-arms, all watched with rapt expressions. The three lads, Brodic, Lucan and Alaric stared; leaning forward as they, too studied the scene. There might as well have been a spectator area of the fighting grounds. Even Jorrin and Tristan lined the wooden fence.

No one else was sparring with swords and spears, or firing off arrows. He wouldn't be surprised if they'd started a pool of wagering.

He thrived on the group assault. Darting, attacking and repositioning. Planning the take-down. It kept him sharp and made victory sweeter when he triumphed. And he was damn good at it.

Niall lunged and Leargan dodged, turning away neatly, then right back, sweeping his Second's legs out from under him. The knight landed on the ground with a *thud*, breath whooshing as the air was knocked from his lungs.

Alasdair took the opportunity and charged Leargan. The knight's sword hit with a clang. He jumped back, but

Alas mirrored his movements, swinging his sword harder. The second hit jarred his arms all the way to his shoulders, but Leargan held steady. He'd not lose the upper hand.

He grunted, shoving toward his friend's broad chest instead of pulling back.

Alasdair planted his boots in the dirt and absorbed the impact. His blue eyes were intense, and he was drenched in sweat, too.

Blades knocked as Alas pressed him back, but Leargan spun away, thrusting at the knight's sword. He was right behind him, charging again.

Leargan ducked, rolling away.

Alasdair over-rotated as he followed, tripping and going down hard.

He saw his chance and hit his feet running, attacking from his position on the ground. But his opponent wasn't done. Alas was strong. He heaved Leargan away; they locked swords from the ground.

Alas kicked him.

His shin smarted as is friend's boot made purchase, but he leaned in, pushing at him as the kn ght struggled to keep his arms locked and tried to scoot backwards.

Alasdair's hand shot out, grabbing his wrist and yanking Leargan down.

Unable to stop his momentum, he tumbled, weapon flying from his hand.

Alas managed to toss his out of the way as well, the cool metal brushing Leargan's bare arm as he landed on top of the other knight.

They made eye contact and Alasdair grinned.

"What the hell was that?" He rolled his back to the ground, panting.

"My attempt at hand-to-hand?" Alas chucked, shrugging as he sat up. He wiped dirt and sweat from his forehead with the bottom of his tunic.

Leargan took a deep breath, smiling at the laugher and comments from the surrounding men. "You just didn't want to get your arse kicked."

"I'll never admit defeat." His friend hopped to his feet and offered his hand.

"Or you could kill me now, since I'm already on the ground."

"Where would the fun be in that?"

He chuckled and let the man yank him up. "For a moment, I thought you wanted to wrestle."

Alasdair made a show of looking him up and down. "Captain, you're not the usual type I like to *wrestle* with."

Leargan retrieved his sword from the ground and sheathed it. "That's what you call it? I think you're doing it wrong."

The men within earshot laughed.

"I don't do it wrong." Alas sheathed his sword and winked.

He shook his head and made his way to the fence, joining Tristan and Jorrin.

"Good show out there," the duke said. "Good job, Captain."

"Thanks, my lord," Leargan said.

Brodic appeared, offering a cleaning linen, a skin of water and a fresh ivory tunic.

Leargan muttered thanks to his squire and took a swig of water, slinging the tunic on the fence. Cool liquid quenched his dry throat, and he took a second drink before drying his face and patting his chest with the soft cloth. "Alas tried to pull one over on me."

"Anything to survive in a fight." Tristan's hazel eyes danced.

"Aye. It does make sense to be versatile," Leargan said.

Niall barked for the men to resume sparring, and Roduch called for the lads to join him.

Leargan stood with the two lords in a companionable silence, watching the large, blond warrior tower over the three lads as he demonstrated the new sword techniques they were working on for the sevenday. Brodic already knew most of what Roduch was teaching, but Leargan's squire was just as absorbed in the knight's words as the other two lads.

Good.

"Did you speak with Lucan?" Jorrin asked, following his gaze.

"Nay, did you?"

The duke nodded. "The boy declared Roduch has no magic."

"Really? What about his visions?"

"Lucan said he thinks somehow Avril's magic was affecting Roduch," Tristan said, expression thoughtful.

"What do you two think?"

"I don't know *what* to think," Jorrin said.

Tristan muttered agreement.

"Perhaps it really is fate?" Leargan mused. Neither lord remarked. "Any news on Tynan Mont?"

"He was spotted in Greenwald Main," Tristan said.

"Shall we seize him there?" Leargan asked.

"Well, my watchers think he's gone home. So, we probably missed an opportunity. Then again, it's probably safer to approach his lands. He doesn't know we're coming. He hasn't learned where she is—at least from the questions he was asking—so ambush at his holding has less risk. There's always a place for him to disappear in the center of the Province, especially at market."

"You're pretty good, my lord."

Jorrin laughed and winked. "I do try."

The loud clop of galloping hooves had him glancing over his shoulder. Both lords followed his gaze.

"The horse is the wrong color, as is the wolf, so it's your redhead, not mine," Jorrin said.

Tristan chuckled.

Why's Ansley coming to the training grounds?

It was much too early for midday meal. He watched her pull her white gelding to a stop, agitation fairly rolling off her.

What's wrong?

She dismounted, and one of his men took her horse, leading Caide to the other horses.

Ansley stood, wringing her hands in front of her. Dressed in dark brown breeches, and a pale green embroidered tunic, her thick red plait swung over her shoulder.

Leargan's stomach fluttered.

Gorgeous. Mine.

They made eye contact, and his feet carried him to her of their own accord.

Ali sat next to her, regarding him with the same wariness in her yellow eyes as always, but the wolf didn't move.

Neither did his betrothed.

"Leargan…" Her voice was soaked in worry.

"Love?" Striving for normal, he ignored the uneasiness in her expression. Leargan pulled the fresh tunic over his head and yanked it into place.

Shame, because Ansley had been staring at his bare chest.

"I need to talk to you."

"Something wrong?" he asked.

"I'm not sure." She worried her bottom lip.

Leargan took a step closer. He wanted to hold her. Comfort her; wipe that look off her face. He pulled her into his arms, kissing the top of her head and inhaling her clean floral scent. Rightness settled over him. Although they hadn't been lovers for very long, she was familiar against him. *Perfect.* "Ansley, what's wrong?"

"Is there something you're keeping from me?"

Damn.

His heart plummeted to his stomach and heat crept up his neck.

Her eyes widened as their gazes collided, and he cursed himself to hell and back. It must've been written all over his face.

"What is it?" she whispered.

Leargan didn't like the hurt in her expression.

Why hadn't he told her about the scroll from the start?

Because she never would have agreed to marry you.

He couldn't lie to her; that would make it worse in the end. Would she still marry him? What if she changed her mind?

Nay. Ansley is mine.

Leargan had always prided himself on his honor. He'd have to tell her the truth and hope for the best. He'd never want her to marry him against her will, despite the king's order. He'd taken her innocence. He was obligated to marry her now.

But he *wanted* to marry her. Wanted to go to sleep every night with her in his arms. Make love to her and wake with her in his bed. At his side. He wanted it with all his heart.

My heart?

He pushed away the realization. Didn't want to ponder what it could mean, what he knew deep down that it meant.

"Leargan?" Ansley whispered. Her teal gaze was so wounded. She'd taken his silence as dishonesty.

He couldn't stand it. Lowering his head, Leargan captured her lips.

Her arms tightened around him, and she opened for him as she always did, pressing her lush body closer.

Ribald comments and laughter from his men distracted him, and he pulled away gently before he could lose his head to their kiss.

She blushed scarlet, and he held her closer when she buried her face against his neck.

"I'll tell you everything when we're alone."

Ansley lifted her head; her eyes were misty.

"Oh, love."

She didn't even know what he was keeping from her,

yet he was already making her cry.

Wretch. The worst kind of liar.

Leargan cupped her face and thumbed her tears away. "Let's go back to the castle. We can talk about this now."

Ansley shook her head. "No, it's fine. I'm fine. Finish your duties."

"No, Ansley. We'll go now."

Chapter Twenty-Two

The ride back was fast and silent; Leargan stewed in his own head.

Blessed Spirit, let me find the right words. Please let her understand.

She had to marry him. There was no other choice. He *needed* her like he needed to breathe.

Still Ansley said nothing as he guided her down the corridor to her quarters in the guest wing. The suite had quickly become *theirs*. He'd made love to her every night in there, except for one clandestine afternoon tryst in his quarters.

Her hand shook as she reached for the door.

Leargan sucked in a breath and pushed it open, gesturing for her to precede him.

Her bondmate darted in front of them both, bounding over to the oversized bed and claiming its center.

He bit back a glare, but it didn't matter. It wasn't like Ansley was going to jump naked into his arms after what he had to confess. Actually, he'd be lucky if Ali didn't attack him when he was through.

His betrothed stared intently at her wolf. She was thought-sending.

Leargan guided her to the chairs by the hearth, gripping her hand as soon as they were seated facing each other, their knees almost touching.

The scroll burned a hole in his pocket, and he swallowed back a wince, shooting another plea to the Blessed Spirit. He'd taken to carrying it daily. Hadn't even questioned why. Maybe subconsciously he'd been waiting for her to confront him. "Ansley…"

Their gazes collided.

Pain. All he could see was agony in her blue-green depths.

His words dissolved. He fought the urge to pull her onto his lap and kiss her senseless.

"What is it, Leargan?" she whispered, averting her face.

He leaned in, cupping her cheeks, forcing her to look at him. How was he supposed to start? Leargan couldn't let words tumble from his mouth without control or thought. He had to explain the scroll before he showed it to her.

She had a right to see it, but he had to tell her how he felt. It wasn't an *order* from his king anymore. It was his greatest need to have her. Hold her. Marry her.

"Do you know why you were sent here?"

Red eyebrows drawn tight, she stared. "Aye. I brought a message, as is my duty, as a Senior King's Rider."

"Aye, that's what you were told."

"What do you mean?"

Leargan inhaled. "Who asked you to deliver the message?"

"King Nathal himself."

"Did you read it?"

Ansley yanked away. "I would *never* do such a thing. Honor, as well as the Rider Oath, is just as important to me as your code as a knight."

"I'm sorry, love. I meant no offense." He reached for her hand, and she let him entwine their fingers.

Her shoulders loosened as she settled back into the ornately carved chair.

"What did he tell you of the message?" Leargan asked.

"Nothing I didn't need to know. He said it was urgent, so I rushed here. That's all my duty allows. It's not my place to question an order or message, especially from

King Nathal." She cocked her head to the side, eyes narrowed. "What does this have to do with us?"

"Nothing. Everything," he muttered. She studied him; he tried not to squirm. "Ansley, I know we haven't known each other for very long, but it doesn't matter. I want to marry you."

"As I do you. As we will," Ansley said cautiously, her words drawn out, question in her voice.

"Honestly, I want to marry you more than I've ever wanted anything in my life," he confessed, pressing a kiss to her knuckles. "But I have to share something with you, because you've the right to know of it."

Her gorgeous smile was short lived, and she swallowed, making him want to kiss her throat. "All right..."Ansley's eyes widened, when he dug the scroll from his pocket and tried to hand it to her.

His hand shook as made no moves to grab the infernal thing. "Read it, love. I need you to read it "

"But it was for Lord Aldern. Why do you have it?" Ansley's fingers trembled as she reached for the parchment that'd once been in her care.

His words were rushed and he perched on the edge of his seat. "He gave it to me. Read it, and you'll see why."

Dread rolled over her. Her stomach clenched, threatening to reject the meal she'd had less than two hours before.

Something's very wrong.

She didn't want to read the words on the scroll. Wouldn't like whatever it said. Her gut told her as much.

Leargan sucked in a breath when she opened it, but Ansley forced her gaze to stay on the message she'd delivered.

King Nathal's hand was neat. She'd recognize his tight perfectly-formed letters anywhere.

Pain constricted her chest and she gasped as the

words sank in. The dagger sank in deeper with every sentence. The creamy color of the stiff parchment blurred as hot tears cascaded down her cheeks.

Ansley choked when her eyes focused on the word *order.*

Skimming it a second, then a third time changed *nothing.* Her world crashed down, as if the walls of the guest suite were alive, crushing her, crumbling. Weight settled over her body, stealing her every breath. She fought through agony. If she let go, she'd pass out.

Leargan doesn't really want me.

Her father and the king, along with her betrothed himself, had done nothing but deceive her.

Cera and Jorrin, too. Did Aimil and Tristan know as well? Had her captain, Sir Artair, helped with the plan, too?

I was the only one in the dark.

Tricked. By the people she cared about the most.

Leargan would've never pursued her if not for the small piece of parchment in her quaking hands. He would've never kissed her in the corridor. Never asked her to marry him, or taken her on a picnic.

No wonder he'd resisted making love. Guilt. *He'd honestly felt guilty.*

She was an *obligation.*

Nothing more. An order to be fulfilled.

He *always* obeyed orders. Especially from the king. It wasn't in Leargan's makeup to disobey.

Everything they had was a lie. Biting back a sob, Ansley fought doubling over in the chair. The scroll slipped from her fingers and hit the floor with a dull *plop.*

It is too good to be true.

She should've listened to the warning in the back of her head the night he'd proposed.

Ali let out a low keen from the bed.

She shot her a look and quick thought-send to stay put, fighting for composure. *I'm fine. I'll be fine, Ali, my love.*

I will always have you.

Her bondmate sent feelings of comfort and love. The she-wolf couldn't comprehend the *why* of her pain, but she knew what love and hurt were through their magic. She felt her pain and wanted it to stop.

Ansley clutched her wolf's feelings with both hands and wrapped them around herself through their magic. Ali was the only thing that would get her through.

Leargan said nothing, and she couldn't look at him.

She couldn't marry him now.

I love him. Had for turns. But he didn't love her. Not once had he uttered the words she longed to hear.

What if she was carrying his child? Her body flushed, heart quickening again.

Ansley would leave in the morning. Go home to Terraquist. If there was a child, she'd raise it; hold it dear. Have a piece of him. He didn't need to know. She'd never get away from him, if he knew.

She'd just be a bigger *obligation.*

"Love, talk to me," Leargan urged.

Her gaze shot to his. "Why do you call me *'love'*?"

His gorgeous dark eyes widened, confusion consuming his handsome face. "Because you *are* my love, Ansley." He reached for her, but she shook her head, scooting her chair back.

"Nay." Ansley swallowed back a sob, shaking her head again. "I'm not." His mouth opened, but she plowed on, not giving him a chance to speak. "I'll tell my father you're released from obligation. I'll explain things to the king. You won't have to follow an order you have no desire for. Marriage won't be forced on either of us. Our betrothal is no more."

Leargan glared. "Are you calling me a liar?"

She looked away. Her whole body tremored, even her teeth rattled. Tears clouded her vision again.

"Did you not listen to what I said?" His tone was low and deadly. "I want to marry you. You can't believe after all we've shared, I don't want you?"

Hope leapt up, but she quashed it. She was nothing but the fulfillment of an order.

Duty.

He was all about his duty to the king.

"You don't have to say those things. It's the king's plan. I understand now. I'll speak to my father. I'll tell him I've released you."

"Dammit, Ansley! I don't want to be *released*. I meant what I said. You'll be my wife. King Nathal may've started this, but it has nothing to do with *us*."

"You don't really want me," she whispered, barely able to shove the words past the lump in her throat.

Why was he so blinded to his duty he couldn't tell her the truth? This wasn't about *her*. He didn't love her. He didn't really want to marry her.

Leargan stood and yanked her out of the chair, plastering her to his chest as he claimed her mouth. Hard and demanding, this kiss was different than the tender heat she was used to from him. He bruised her mouth as his lips moved over hers. His tongue invaded, and Ansley melted into his chest on a moan. He forced her to open for him like she always did on her own.

Her body warmed, and liquid desire settled between her legs. She *ached* for him.

His erection pressed into her thigh and she nestled even closer to his chest.

Ali lunged from the bed, gnashing teeth and growling.

Leargan jumped away from Ansley as her bondmate backed her former betrothed into the hearth.

"Ali. No!" She slipped between them before her wolf could hurt the man she'd always love. Ansley cupped her bond's jowls and stared into her yellow eyes. *Leargan didn't hurt me, love. I promise. Get on the bed. Now.* She caressed the she-wolf's great head.

Ali obeyed, but whined, tail plastered between her

legs even as she leapt to the sleeping furs.

Leargan's body remained tight and he slowly moved away from the fireplace.

She tracked him, glaring. "Don't touch me like that anymore," she ordered. Ansley wished the scroll had never happened. Wished she could rush back into his arms. That she could kiss him, and they could fall into her bed entwined like they'd done so many times before.

That's done now. Forever.

"Why?" He stopped not far from the door, one eyebrow lifted, and the corner of his mouth up.

Her heart stuttered as she regarded him.

A hardened knight, a warrior was staring at her, not Leargan, her tender lover.

Pain threatened to overtake her. Her tongue swept over her bottom lip, stomach flipping when she tasted him there. His scent clung to her tunic. Sweat from training, as well as the clean masculine musk that was just *him*. It didn't disgust her, she wanted to cling to it, wrap herself in him.

When she'd seen him shirtless on the fighting grounds, shiny with sweat, Ansley's insides had become mush. No matter how many times she'd seen the defined muscles of his chest, touched them, tasted them, she'd never get enough of him.

Now...*now* that would be a thing of the past. A memory to cling to. A sob escaped and she covered her mouth with her hand.

His expression hardened. "You like what I do to you, and we both know it."

A hot flush crept up her neck and settled in her cheeks, starting the slow burn of desire all over again.

Leargan took a step toward her. "Deny it, Ansley. Deny you want me."

Ali growled low in her throat, but Ansley stopped her with a quick mental command. "That...that...doesn't matter anymore." She couldn't deny she wanted him. She always had. Her body always would; no matter that her heart knew better.

His gaze bored into her, neither of them moved.

She gasped. "That's it…isn't it?"

"What?"

"That's *why* you're insisting on marrying me."

"What nonsense are you thinking now?"

Ansley cringed at his hurtful words. "Because of what happened between us, you think you *have* to marry me. Well, you don't. I won't mention it to my father or the king."

"That's *not* why I want to marry you."

She could feel the heat coming off his body. Ached for him. To be in his arms. For everything to be all right. Believe the words coming out of his mouth, but she couldn't. "Then, why?" *You don't love me.* Tears scalded her cheeks and she swiped at her face. "I won't tell them I'm no longer a virgin. You don't have to do the *honorable* thing, Leargan."

"Dammit! I'm a lot of things, but I'm not a liar." Leargan's fists were clenched tightly at his sides, his high cheekbones flushed with color.

Ali growled again, but neither of them acknowledged her.

Ansley shook her head, averting her gaze. He *was* a liar. He'd kept the scroll from her.

"All your denials may be for naught. Did you think about that?" His voice was low and serious.

"What d'you mean?" She met his gaze against her will, and sank into his dark eyes.

"*Lie* to your father and tell him you have no desire to marry me. If he asks, lie about us making love. Then in a few months when your belly rounds, try the lie again, and see what he says. Knowing your father's temper, he'll lead an army here to skin my hide. But you'd better tell him it was *you* who refused *me*. No matter what, I'll still want *you*. Even if you think it's forced at your father's hand, *I* still want *you*."

Her hand instinctively covered her womb. "I'm not carrying your child."

"Are you sure?"

"Aye." The confidence in her tone was forced. They both knew it was too soon to tell.

"You *will* remain in Greenwald until you know for sure. I have that much of a right."

Anger boiled up and she glared. How *dare* he order her around like one of his men? "I won't marry you, even if I am having your child."

"If you *are* having my child, you *will* marry me." Leargan looked her up and down.

She flushed, rage battling desire for him. "I will not." Ansley crossed her arms over her breasts.

"We'll see what your father or the king has to say about that." His eyes narrowed, and he mirrored her stance.

"I have no intention of telling either of them."

"Deny *everything* for as long as you can. They'll be here soon enough."

"I'm not afraid to tell my father, or the king, for that matter, how I really feel." She scowled.

"Of that I have no doubt. I promise, if you carry my child, you *will* marry me."

"I. Will. Not."

"Fine. When *my* child is born, you'll give it to *me*."

Ansley gasped. "You're a cruel bastard. I can't believe I gave myself to you. Get out of my rooms."

"What's cruel about it? That's how it's commonly done, is it not? *Bastard* children are raised by their father. Especially he has more standing. I'm a knight."

She plastered her hand to her lower stomach and crushed her eyes shut. He was right, on both counts. If she was pregnant, their child would be a bastard. Born out of wedlock. He had position. Once a King's Knight, now he was the Captain of a Province personal guard. Ansley didn't have a legal shot if he pressed the issue. Denying he was the father would do no good; a healer could confirm the blood tie.

"If I can't have you, I *will* have my child," Leargan barked.

Ansley dragged her hands down her cheeks, growling.

Ali echoed with a snarl of her own.

She was tempted to let her pounce. Her bond wouldn't need much encouragement. "Get out. I don't want to see you ever again, Sir Leargan Tegran."

Emotions she couldn't name flickered across his face before he tightened. Jaw clenched, full mouth a hard line, his eyes narrowed.

"I hate you," Ansley whispered.

He said nothing, but nodded curtly. Just turned on his heel like a soldier about to march in formation. Heading for the door, Leargan didn't even look over his shoulder as he left.

Every step tore another piece from her heart. By the time he shut the door without a sound, Ansley's chest was flayed open, her heart lying in chunks on the floor.

Tears poured down her cheeks, and she collapsed to her knees. Sobs wracked her body as she sank to the floor.

Ali rushed to her, and she threw her arms around her wolf, burying her face in the soft black mane.

She didn't know Leargan at all. He'd threatened to take their child away if she wouldn't marry him. How could he be so cruel? She'd never see such hardness in his eyes.

His smiling, laughing face danced into her mind, and she fell apart all over again, squeezing Ali tight.

Her wolf whined.

"Sorry," Ansley dragged herself off the floor and crawled onto her bed.

The she-wolf jumped up and burrowed against her. Her bondmate whimpered, licking her hands when Ansley buried her face in the pillow that still smelled like him.

Fool. Idiot. Everything had been too good to be true.

The only man she'd ever loved didn't want her. He'd only been interested in her because the king had *ordered* it.

Ansley couldn't regret making love with Leargan, not really. She loved him, and what'd happened between them had been wonderful.

More than wonderful...it'd been perfect. So *right*. Even more so, if they'd actually made a child, even by accident.

She wanted his child, damn him.

Damn honor, duty and *obligation*.

Damn Leargan, and damn love, because it led to no good.

Chapter Twenty-Three

Leargan looked down into the stein, swirling the ale around. The rest of the day had been a blur. He'd never made it back to the training grounds. Instead, he'd gone to the armory to hide out, under the guise of inventorying weapons.

Jorrin had asked him to find out how many swords they needed over a month ago. He'd put it off, busy with other duties.

He could've sent one of the guard to handle things, but he was glad he hadn't. Now, at least, he could present the half-elfin duke with adequate numbers.

Brodic had come to find him, but he'd wanted to be alone, so he'd sent the lad on his way. Told him to tell Jorrin of his task. Refused the request of assistance. His squire's gray eyes had held concern, but he didn't ask any questions. He never would.

Leargan was relieved he'd been capable of holding his tongue and not snapping at the lad who so obviously idolized him. The affection his squire had for him was mutual. They'd been together a long time; turns…but he felt closer to *her*.

What exactly came out of my mouth in Ansley's rooms?

Regret settled over him. And *pain*. How could he hurt so much? A gaping hole resided in his chest as sure as if he'd been run through.

Closing his eyes, he cursed himself to hell and back, but all he could see was Ansley.

Misty teal eyes full of agony and accusation. And the tears. Each one coursing down her cheeks had killed him a little more.

He'd intentionally hurt her with the words that had flown out of his mouth.

I am a bastard.

Take her child away from her? He'd never do such a thing. Family meant too much to him. He'd lost his parents before age five. If it wasn't for King Nathal taking him back to Terraquist after the battle that had split Ascova into two Provinces, he'd have been nothing more than street trash. If he'd survived.

A family of his own was supposed to be different. *Would be different.* Cherished. Loved. Always. He'd raise their children *with* her. If there *was* a child. The idea didn't scare him. It made his heart speed and his stomach flip, but he *wanted* a child with Ansley.

Leargan hadn't been careful with her. He'd given her his seed more times than he could count. It hadn't mattered. Because she was his.

Or was.

"Dammit." He downed the contents of the large stein in one gulp. After slamming the thick mug on the table, he poured himself another, his head already spinning. He wasn't a heavy drinker, but welcomed oblivion. His chest was tight, breathing still hurt.

Getting sloshed wasn't working.

He was alone in the great hall because of the late hour, and the vast room was dim. Only a few candles still lit, and the fire in the large hearth waning. Leargan had shooed the last servant away what seemed hours ago, promising to bank the fire. Company wasn't welcome, even from any of his brothers. It was easier to wallow without an audience.

Neither Jorrin, nor Tristan had checked on him at any point either, but that was all right. He'd deal with the inevitable questions later. No doubt their wives would find out what'd happened.

He scowled as a door opened to his left. Not the main entrance of the great hall, but a door that led to the kitchens. Leargan sighed when he recognized the old steward, and fought to remember the man's name through his alcohol muddled mind.

Nothing. Other than he'd come out of retirement to train Gamel, the very young head steward from Lady's Cera's uncle's household in Tarvis.

Gamel's father was the head steward of Castle Lenore, so he'd been raised for the trade, but needed some guidance. Very bright, but barely eighteen. Also newly betrothed to Lady Cera's handmaiden, Neomi.

Thinking of another happy couple made his temples ache. Leargan dragged his hand down his face and tried to look invisible. He didn't want company from the old steward any more than anyone else.

"Captain," the elderly man inclined his head as he came closer to the table.

He groaned. Obviously the man hadn't seen the black cloud over his head.

Manners, you do *have manners.*

"Hello, Steward." Leargan lifted his cup as his unwanted companion took a seat. "Care for a drink?"

The older man smiled, shaking his head. His long white hair shifted about his shoulders. "No, thank you. I overindulged when I was a young man, so now I stay away from the stuff."

He nodded, straightening his shoulders.

The steward had to be close to eighty turns old, if not more. The man deserved respect, though Leargan had a feeling he'd just been offered a subtle admonition. He met pale blue eyes and forced a smile.

"Keir, Captain," the elderly man said softly, offering a large wrinkled hand.

Leargan gave a firm shake that was returned with the same vigor. The steward was strong, despite his age. His presence was calming, and he released a breath he'd not realized he'd been holding.

The man's brown tunic was filled out by still-broad shoulders. Keir was tall and slim, but his frame suggested he'd been full of muscle when he was younger. Soldier-sized, more than the build of a castle steward. His face was lined, but his skin had a nice bronze tone, as if he spent a great deal of time outside.

The eyes regarding him could see right through him.

He squirmed, clearing his throat. "Hello, Keir." The old steward smiled and Leargan relaxed, chiding himself to sit still. "What's keeping you from your bed this late evening?"

"Ah, I find the older I get, the less I'm able to sleep. I often walk the castle corridors until sleep decides to claim me. What has you out of yours?" Keir studied Leargan from his seat across the table.

"I wouldn't know where to start."

Why the hell did I say that? He didn't know this man.

Keir's smile was sad.

Silence descended, and the old steward's gaze bore into him.

"You know, lad, I can tell you all about loss. The Blessed Spirit claimed the love of my life three turns ago. In a way, I'm glad she didn't have to endure the devastation of our family. Varthan killed my son and grandson." He paused, his blue eyes misty, and cleared his throat. "I've served the Ryhans as my father, and his father before him. I couldn't refuse Lady Cera when she had need of me. I've spent my life in these halls. Shared good times as well as bad, but Castle Ryhan — Castle Aldern now — has always been filled with love."

What am I supposed to say?

Leargan averted his gaze and sipped ale, ignoring how his heart sped up.

"My point is, lad, no matter what happened, life is too short to leave things in shambles. Mend things, and don't lose her."

Was he that transparent that an old man, who'd never said more than two words to him, could see his disaster with Ansley?

He bit the inside of his cheek and closed his eyes. He opened his mouth, but didn't know what to say, so he snapped it shut, still avoiding the elderly steward's gaze.

A strong, comforting grip on his forearm brought his face around. "I'm not trying to pry, lad. It's just, when you're as old as I am, you don't want to see a good man make avoidable mistakes."

"Thank you." Leargan forced words out of his mouth.

"Do you want to talk about it?"

The quiet inquiry made him swallow against a sudden lump in his throat. Did he? How could he tell a complete stranger the love of his life hated him?

He gasped.

"Lad?" Keir's soft concerned voice made him jump.

Their gazes collided.

"I love her."

The old steward patted his arm and smiled. "Aye."

"Blessed Spirit, I *love* her," Leargan whispered.

Of *course* he loved her. Why hadn't it occurred to him before now?

I'm a complete idiot.

Keir's chuckle pulled him from his chaotic thoughts. "Sometimes these things are apparent to those around us before light dawns on our own heads."

He stared. No doubt the old man hit the nail on the head. He was too stunned to be embarrassed.

"Tell her you love her, Captain."

Leargan loved Ansley. Agony threatened to double him over. The revelation would get him nowhere. She still hated him. "She's refused me."

"I thought you were betrothed?" Pale eyebrows drew tight.

"We *were*," His voice cracked.

Keir sighed. "Not an easy thing to tear asunder. Speak to her, lad. Bare your heart. Something that seems more difficult than fighting a whole army on your own, but necessary."

Leargan bit back the denial that hovered on his tongue. Since when was he afraid of anything?

"I believe the Blessed Spirit gives us *one*," the old steward said.

"One?"

"One soul to match ours. One soul, one person, meant for each of us. If you've found yours, you can't let her go, Captain."

"Aye," he breathed. He didn't have the bollocks to ask how he could get her back.

The elderly man's gaze drew him in, and he leaned forward.

"Tell her you love her, lad, and all will right itself."

No it won't.

He'd already told her he wanted to marry her. She'd all but called him a liar.

"I have to go," Leargan muttered, popping to his feet. His head spun and he had to clutch the back of his chair to stay upright.

Damn ale.

"All right."

"Thank you, Keir."

The old steward nodded. "Will you be able to make it back to your quarters?"

"Aye."

"I'll bank the fire."

"Thank you. I'd almost forgotten."

"It's not a problem."

He nodded and turned to go, his heart thundering.

Ansley.

Keir's words bounced around in his mind.

How could one simple phrase fix anything? Was it really over? Was she gone from his arms for good?

"Captain?"

Leargan glanced over his shoulder. "Aye?"

"Though the subject matter pains, it was nice talking to you."

Managing a genuine smile, he bowed to the elderly man. "The feeling is mutual."

Keir's warm smile was all the answer he got.

Although his own chambers were on the opposite side of the vast castle, in the soldier's wing, Leargan found himself outside her guest suite. He stared at the polished dark wood, his gut clenching.

She had to want him. She had to marry him...*love* him.

Did Ansley love him? Why hadn't she said so?

Why would she?

"You threatened her in the worst way possible," he whispered. His head spun, and it had little to do with ingesting alcohol.

He lifted a hand, made a fist, then faltered. She had nothing more to say to him tonight. Disturbing her would be for naught. It wasn't like he could rush into her rooms and declare his love for her.

Ansley wouldn't believe *that* any more than she'd believed his honest desire to marry her.

Leargan shook his head, laying his palm flat on her door and sucking in a breath.

My fault.

All he wanted to do was hold her, but she'd never allow it.

What am I supposed to do now?

Chapter Twenty-four

"Sir Leargan?" The voice was familiar, but he couldn't place it.

His head spun, or maybe sloshed. *Floated?*

A hand shook his shoulder, and Leargan winced, temples throbbing.

"Sir Leargan?" This time the voice was more insistent.

"I'm awake!" he roared, regretting it immediately as his brain protested. He cracked one eye open and saw a familiar pair of worried gray ones.

"Are you all right, Captain?" Brodic's fair eyebrows were drawn tight. The lad leaned in, wringing his hands.

"Brodic, I'm not dead. Back up."

"It speaks. I suppose that means he's all right," Jorrin said from somewhere in his room.

"Aye, he said he's not dead. That's something," Tristan answered.

Two deep chuckles greeted his aching ears. He cringed as he failed at his first attempt to sit up. He batted away Brodic's helpful hands. "I'm glad I could *entertain* you, my lords."

They both laughed again.

Leargan forced his stomach muscles to respond, jolting upright. The room spun. His head screamed a protest, and he fell against his thick wooden headboard. He made tight fists of his ivory bed linens, but it didn't help. His temples pulsed and he blinked to clear his vision, but his squire appeared in triplicate before his eyes. He groaned and covered his face with both hands.

"Hangovers are nasty little things, wouldn't you say, Tristan?" Jorrin asked.

"Aye, that they are, Jorrin."

He growled. "Now they're discussing me as if I'm not even in the room," he muttered, making eye contact with Brodic.

His squire shifted from foot to foot, saying nothing.

"Why don't you fetch some food, Brodic? Make sure there's bread and water, too," Jorrin said before Leargan could reassure them all he was fine.

The lad jumped, and gave a hasty nod before bowing and rushing from the room.

He dragged his hand down his face, scratching his stubble. "I see loyalty has its limits."

"He looks to you like a father," the duke admonished. "He's worried about you."

Guilt crept up from the pit of his stomach. Jorrin was right. Brodic was a good lad, an excellent squire and would make a hell of a knight when he earned it. He didn't praise him nearly enough. Leargan loved the lad.

Ansley.

He loved her, too. For all the good it was doing him. He sucked in a breath, closing his eyes.

Get yourself together. There's an empath in the room.

And *she* was the last thing he wanted to think about, let alone talk about. Especially with Jorrin and Tristan.

"Why are you radiating hurt?" the duke asked.

Dammit.

He didn't have a chance. Leargan shrugged, averting his bleary gaze from the two men before either could call him a liar.

In the short time he'd known them, he'd grown as close to them as he was to the men of the personal guard he'd grown up with.

"Nice try," Jorrin whispered. "I'd not wanted to pry yesterday, but what happened?"

"And why do you have a hangover?" Tristan asked in the same gentle tone. "You're not prone to overindulgence."

"Why are you two in my room? Since we're all asking questions," Leargan countered, trying to frown. He crossed his arms over his chest, but the movement jarred his head.

"Because you didn't come to the great hall to break your fast. You didn't show up for briefing when the castle men-at-arms changed guard, *and* you didn't show up on the training grounds. Niall said he hadn't heard from you, either. When Brodic asked if *we'd* seen you, Jorrin and I knew there was a problem," Tristan said.

"We came here after Ansley said you weren't in her chambers," the duke said.

Her name on Jorrin's tongue made his heart stutter, but he ignored it. "What? What time is it?"

"Almost noon," Tristan said.

"Noon? Blessed Spirit!" Leargan jumped up.

Bad idea.

He wobbled on his feet, then landed hard on his arse on the edge of his bed. He moaned and grabbed his head with both hands. He'd never be right again.

"Here, let me fix that." The healing lord was at his side in seconds, gripping his shoulders. Tristan steadied him, then pressed a hand to his forehead.

Warmth spread downward, and he slipped his eyes closed as he concentrated on Tristan's gentle touch on his stubbled cheeks. His head stopped throbbing. Like a veil was lifting, discomfort and fuzziness receded. A languorous heat settled over his body and his muscles felt loose and refreshed, like he'd just gotten out of the bath after a good long soak. Moments felt like hours, but when he met the lord's hazel eyes, his friend smiled.

Sweat beaded the younger man's forehead, but he wasn't pale like Leargan had seen him after a big healing job.

He squared his shoulders, sucking in one deep breath, then another. He forced a smile for Tristan and Jorrin's benefit. With a clear head only came pain full force.

Ansley.

His chest constricted and he fought the urge to double over. Gone was the pleasant feeling in his limbs.

"Better?" Tristan asked.

Nay. "Aye." Leargan nodded. "But fixing the result of my poor choice is a waste of your healing touch."

His smile was sad. "There's more where that came from, but I do regret not being able to mend your heart."

He cursed under his breath, looking away as the lord slid onto a chair at the table next to the wide hearth in his room. Leargan couldn't look at Jorrin until he gathered his wits. Damn empathic magic was too much. A man couldn't keep his feelings private. "You said you saw Ansley? How is she?"

"She looked like hell, frankly," the duke said, one dark eyebrow up, cocking his head to one side. "Like she'd been crying all night."

Leargan winced. "She probably had been."

The door opened, and his squire appeared with a well-laden tray.

Jorrin took a seat next to Tristan as Brodic set the food down. The scent of fresh warm bread and thick stew tickled his nose.

Thank the Blessed Spirit the healer had cleared his head, or his stomach would have rejected the delicious meal. "Thanks, Brodic." He joined the lords.

The duke poured a glass of water and handed it to Leargan.

Brodic gasped and hurried forward to stop Jorrin from serving, but he shook his head. The lad's chest rose as if he'd taken a breath, his cheeks pink.

"Are the men still on the grounds?" Leargan asked.

"Yes." Jorrin tore a piece of bread from the small loaf and took a bite.

"Brodic, get your horse and join Alaric and Lucan with Roduch. You have training, lad," Leargan said.

His squire's eyes lit up and he jumped, blond curls

bobbing when he gave a curt nod. "Aye, sir."

Leargan exchanged amused glances with the two lords.

Brodic flashed an unabashed grin and started to rush from the room, only to hurry back to the table with a belated bow.

"Good lad." Leargan chuckled after Brodic had closed the door.

"Aye, he is," Tristan said.

The half-elfin lord nodded as he ate, but his blue gaze was keen.

Leargan took a sip of water and steeled himself for spilling his guts. He reached for the spoon on the trencher and dug into the stew. But as he glanced over the normally appetizing meat and vegetables, his stomach roiled. "I told her everything yesterday, and now she won't marry me."

His friends said nothing, but both wore pained expressions. Of course they could understand what he was going through, they both loved their wives. Tristan and Jorrin were lucky; their lasses loved them back.

The story poured out, his heart pounding harder with every word of his confession.

Gossiping. Like a woman. Really?

"Do the honorable thing?" Jorrin asked.

He nodded, giving his friend a long look.

The duke's eyes widened the moment he'd comprehended.

"She practically accused me of taking her innocence so she'd have to marry me." Leargan's voice cracked. He scooted to the edge of the chair, then took a bite of bread to play it off. He hurt, and Jorrin's expression shouted that his empathic lord knew it. "It gets worse."

Tristan squeezed his forearm in comfort, hazel gaze warm.

Leargan told them the worst thing he'd said to her. That he'd take their child, if she was pregnant.

"Awww, hell." Jorrin shook his head.

"Oh my," Tristan muttered. "We have a mess, don't we? Her father and the king will be here any day now."

"Any day now?" Leargan croaked.

"We received word yesterday," the duke said.

"And you didn't tell me?" he demanded.

"I thought it best you come clean first." Jorrin crossed his arms over his broad chest.

"Oh. Aye. *That* did me a lot of good. She told me she hated me."

"Damn, Leargan. You've dug yourself a hole."

"I'll say," Tristan said.

He cringed, shoving his hand through his long hair. "The worst part is, after I left her chambers, I realized just how big of an idiot I really am."

"You love her," Jorrin breathed.

He nodded, biting back the hundredth wince of the day. The lord felt his love for Ansley. Too bad *she* couldn't.

Empathic magic had always fascinated and petrified him. People were *always* feeling something. If Leargan had such powers, he'd have to be a hermit in some isolated mountain somewhere. He'd been told than Jorrin's powers paled in comparison to his father, Braedon's. How could either of them stand being around people?

"Aye, I love her." Saying it out loud was worse. Daggers stabbed his heart with every breath. He wanted to rub the spot, but forced himself to sit still.

"Then tell her," Tristan said.

"I'm pretty sure it'd fall on deaf ears. She told me she never wanted to see me again, in addition to the lovely, '*I hate you, Leargan.*'"

"You *are* a bigger idiot than you thought," Jorrin muttered.

He tried not to bristle. "What?"

"She loves you," Tristan said. Jorrin shot him a look that Leargan didn't miss, but the healer shrugged. "He might as well know the truth."

The duke sighed.

"Truth?" His stomach jumped.

"Ansley told Aimil she loves you," Tristan said.

"She *what*?" Leargan whispered. At another time, he might've been amused that he and the two lords *were* actually gossiping like women.

Ansley *loved* him? She'd called him a liar…but she loved him?

Leargan looked from Jorrin to Tristan and back again. "She told Cera, as well."

"Then why didn't *she* tell me?" He made a fist.

"Did you give her a chance? Besides threatening to take her child away, what else did you say?" Tristan asked gently. "Empty threat or not, that wouldn't tempt her to speak words of love to you."

Heat shot up his neck and he averted his gaze. "She asked me why I wanted to marry her, and I couldn't answer her." Leargan closed his eyes.

"Awww, hell," Jorrin repeated.

"I'm a complete idiot."

"I won't disagree, but there *is* an upside to all this," the duke said, a ghost of a smile playing at his lips.

"What could *that* possibly be?"

"You still have a day or two to fix your mess." His voice was much too bright.

Tristan chuckled.

Leargan glared at them both.

Chapter Twenty-Five

"They're going to arrest him today!" Avril burst into the Duchess Solar, relief washing over her. She couldn't hold back her slow smile.

No fear.

She wasn't afraid of Tynan anymore.

Soldiers were mounting up at this very moment, to be led by Sir Leargan and Lord Aldern themselves.

Her knight had fought to be included. His captain and the duke couldn't stop him. Avril's heart had dropped to her stomach when she'd witnessed the argument between Roduch, his captain, and the duke.

He'd vowed he would refuse a direct order, no matter the punishment, if they left him behind. After a heavy sigh, Sir Leargan had made him swear an oath against killing Tynan and relented, with the begrudged approval of the Duke of Greenwald.

They were going to march on her former husband's holding and arrest him. Throw him in Castle Aldern's dungeons. Hopefully, throw away the key.

Lord Aldern had told her he'd sent people to subtly assess Tynan. He'd gone to Greenwald Main to search for her, but after staying for several days at several inns, he'd gone back home.

She'd told them all she knew about the holding to help strategize and protect themselves.

Then when the king arrived, Tynan Mont would have a trial.

Roduch had said there was a place for him in Dread Valley, the penal territory in the far off Province of Dalunas. Her knight also said '*the bastard*' deserved death over prison, but Avril was fine with either. As long as he stayed locked away forever and she never had to see him again.

He'd pay for *all* his crimes, murder, blackmail, theft of land and holdings, in addition to his treatment of her. Violating their marriage agreement.

Too bad it's not illegal to misuse magic. It should be.

Her eyes darted around the lovely bright room.

Mistress Ansley was alone, sitting by one of the many windows, with her face tilted down toward the courtyard.

Something's wrong.

Avril squinted, concentrating to access her magic. The older girl's aura throbbed, a mixture of pale blue sadness and white hot pain. It fluctuated, other emotions floating in and out, interwoven. A rainbow of unpleasantness.

With a wince, she smoothed the front of the green gown; one of the four Lady Cera had gifted her. It was shimmery and soft, and needed no straightening, but nerves and sympathy crept up from the pit of her stomach, replacing her joy that her former husband was about to be captured.

What'd happened to the normally bubbly redhead? Since Roduch had talked her into spending time with the ladies, Avril had made three fast friends. The three young women had welcomed her with open arms. Actually, even the staff of the castle had been nothing but friendly and kind.

Meara, the maid she'd met on her first day was rarely far from her side, seeing to her every need. She also considered her a friend.

Along with Ladies Cera and Aimil, and Mistress Ansley, Avril spent a great deal of time in the Duchess Solar. Laughter and lightheartedness. Something that was a shocking change in her life. All the pain was fading into the background. Her new friends…and her new love were helping her forget…heal.

Roduch.

Sleeping in his arms every night, kissing him…it was new for her, but she wanted more. Her heart leapt. Avril was falling for him.

Roduch hadn't pushed her. Staunch that he'd be waiting when *she* was ready, but he'd made it plain he wanted her. Could he be feeling for her what she was starting to for him?

She sucked in a breath, stomach fluttering. It was to ponder later. Something was wrong with her new friend. Avril loved talking to Mistress Ansley, with her thick northern accent—not unlike her knight's—and Lady Aimil, with the southern lilt, since she'd come from Ascova.

"Mistress Ansley?" Avril ventured but didn't move closer. She didn't need magic to know the King's Rider wanted to be alone.

"Hi, Avril," she said, but didn't look over her shoulder. The redhead's aura flickered and turned white. Something was hurting her.

"Did you hear what I said?" Avril asked.

"Aye. I see the men in the courtyard right now. I'm relieved for you."

She slipped closer, following her friend's gaze. Roduch's tall form was next to a huge blue roan stallion, his large hands on the reins as he waited to mount up.

The captain's dark head was bent with the duke's.

Mistress Ansley's gaze was glued on the two men.

"Are you all right?" Avril asked.

Misty, blue-green eyes met hers as she looked away from the scene below.

Avril sat next to her friend, heart skipping. She'd come to care about her very much in a short amount of time. Mistress Ansley had saved her. Shown her what a strong woman was.

"I'm fine." The girl averted her gaze.

She said nothing about the lie, but sighed. "I know we haven't known each other very long, but I'm here if you want to talk about it. If not, that's fine, too."

One corner of her mouth up, the Mistress Ansley met her eyes again. "Thanks. You've been through too much to endure my issues as well, but I very much appreciate the offer."

She shook her head, smiling softly. "I'm fine, I promise. Just know I'm here for you." She wanted to reach for her hand but stopped herself.

Touching people was still difficult. Although she'd not forced her magic since she'd come to Castle Aldern, she didn't always have warning when a vision was going to present itself, and touch was a trigger. Avril wouldn't want to see anything of Mistress Ansley's future without being asked to look.

Funny, as much as Roduch had touched her, it hadn't happened with him. And they still hadn't figured out why he'd been seeing her since he was a boy. Lady Cera's cousin, Lord Avery, hadn't been able to find anything in any magic tomes. He agreed with Lucan; theirs was a case of true, divine fate.

Faith and love.

Avril would grasp it with both hands and hold on with all her might.

"I appreciate it. Really," her new friend whispered. Mistress Ansley reached for her hand and squeezed.

She accepted the gesture, but her head spun as the familiar sense of a premonition crept up, then engulfed her. The present fell away, and two unknown figures shimmered into her mind's eye, wavering at first, but finally coming into focus.

Her body heated and her magic surged.

Sir Leargan and Mistress Ansley were standing, hands joined and facing each other. Gazing into each other's eyes as if there was no one else on the continent. Avril gasped as love washed over her. Their love for each other. Feelings of *forever.*

Her friend was dressed in wedding attire, a gorgeous,

lavish gown the pale green of Greenwald. Her red hair was braided intricately, and she wore a traditional wedding crown of woven flowers.

The knight was dressed in shiny decorative armor one would never fight in, the howling white wolf of Greenwald etched and painted in color on his chest plate.

Avril's heart pounded as she comprehended the scene before her. The vision was surrounded in the pale purple aura of things yet to come. She was looking at the future. Mistress Ansley and Sir Leargan's wedding.

As quickly as the vision started, it began to fade, the couple flickering as they went, as soon as Sir Leargan leaned down for a kiss.

Dissipating magic made her head spin, and she reclined in the chair, taking a deep breath when her shoulders hit the carved wood.

"Avril? Are you all right?"

Her friend's sadness washed over her when they made eye contact again, pulling Avril back to the here and now. So opposite of the vision.

She squeezed Mistress Ansley's forearm and smiled. Peace settled over her, and she wished she could project it onto the Rider like the healer could. "Yes, I'm fine. And you will be, too."

Her teal eyes widened and she swallowed.

Avril wouldn't reveal the vision, since it was unplanned, unrequested, but she wanted her friend to feel better with all her heart. "Truly, Mistress Ansley. It *will* be all right. Better. It'll be as it *should* be."

Her stare burned. Like she was trying to make sense of the reassurance.

"Trust me."

Puzzlement settled over the redhead's expression, but she nodded; saying nothing even though her lips parted.

The sound of scraping nails made Avril glance over her shoulder.

Ali, Mistress Ansley's large black she-wolf, made her

way across the solar, heading straight for them.

She reminded herself her friend's bondmate would never harm her and forced herself to sit still.

The beast gave her a onceover that had her stomach jumping as she stopped between them. She bumped her mistress' hands with her large head, then sat on her hindquarters with a slight wag of her tail.

Mistress Ansley smiled and obeyed, burying her hands in the wolf's thick dark fur. Her still-visible aura shifted, the multifaceted pale colors of love weaving in.

Avril could see the magic of their bond, appearing as a thick gold rope as well as Ali's much less complicated aura, which was also made up of pastel colors. "She looks soft."

Mistress Ansley looked up. "She is. You can touch her. She likes affection."

She reached out, praying her hand wouldn't shake, and rested her fingers on the wolf's back.

Ali looked at her, but Avril averted her gaze. Eye contact with a wolf meant an assertion of dominance. She swallowed back a gasp.

"Avril, it's all right. She likes that you're petting her."

Slowly, she turned back to the animal that weighed more than she did. She smiled and stroked the ebony fur on Ali's head.

The big she-wolf leaned into her hand.

"See? She likes you."

Avril grinned. "Good. I've never seen a wolf up close before coming here. The first time I saw Trikser, I screamed and jumped into Roduch's arms. We were walking down the corridor on the way to the great hall."

Mistress Ansley laughed, but the sadness didn't leave her teal eyes. "I bet it was disconcerting. Minding your own business and there's a wild animal not five feet down the hallway."

Giggling, Avril nodded. "Yes. Then I saw Ali *and* Isair. Of course, Roduch explained things to me, but it was still a shock. *Three* wolves in a castle."

"Cera tells me Morag will never accept it."

"I like Headwoman Morag."

"Aye, as do I. But she's too conservative for Cera's tastes."

"And always will be," Lady Cera said, sauntering into the room with her son in her arms.

Avril grinned. She loved holding little Lord Fallon.

"You don't even know of whom I speak," Mistress Ansley said. At least she was smiling. For the first time, her aura brightened. A happy peach color came to the forefront. She was happy to see Lady Cera and the baby.

Lady Aimil slid from behind Lady Cera into the doorway, grinning. "Morag," she said at the same time the duchess did.

The four of them shared a laugh.

Fallon must not have liked their joke, because he let out a wail, but his mother propped him higher on her shoulder and rubbed his back. The little one quieted, and Avril couldn't help but stare.

Sadness and regret washed over her and she fought a frown. She wanted a child. She wasn't sorry she'd never had Tynan's children…he would've treated them as badly as he had her, but she would've loved any child she'd bore.

With her knight…she had a second chance. But was he throwing *his* chance at fatherhood away if he stayed with her?

Tynan had shoved his seed into her over and over during the course of their four turn marriage. Never had she conceived.

Was there something wrong with her? Could she even have children?

Roduch's blond hair and crystal blue eyes floated into her mind. She was dark…he was light. What would their child look like?

"Avril?" Lady Cera sat as Lady Aimil took Lord Fallon into her arms and rocked him by the hearth.

A warm, inviting fire burned brightly.

"I'm fine, my lady."

The duchess smiled. "Good. I'd worried a bit. Today's a big day. Don't fret. You won't even see him, all right?"

"I know, my lady. I'm not frightened." She nodded for effect, her breath exiting on a whoosh. Those words were *true*.

She wasn't afraid of Tynan Mont and it was *glorious*.

Lady Cera and Mistress Ansley looked at each other. Some sort of non-verbal communication passed between them, but Mistress Ansley averted her gaze, busying herself with her bondmate. Her aura throbbed, turning bright white again. She was hurting. Badly.

Avril's heart ached. She wished she could reveal the vision, but would it help, or make her doubt the truth? Things would work out as they were supposed to. Her visions were never wrong.

The redheaded Rider was sweet and genuine. But, what could've happened? And why did the duchess look vexed with her? Concern was in Lady Cera's expression, too, but the color of her aura confirmed she was frustrated with her friend when she concentrated enough to make it visible. The duchess had more magic than Ansley, so the colors glowed brighter.

Lord Fallon let out a wail loud enough to break glass, and their collective gazes shot to Lady Aimil struggling to rock him. "See, Cera? I told you he doesn't like me."

Chuckling as she rose to her feet, Lady Cera shook her head and retrieved her son. "He likes you just fine. He's just fussy this morning. Fed and changed, and he still gave me a hard time. Until Jorrin held him and calmed him. Temporarily, obviously."

The duke had time for babies? Lord Jorrin was a good man. He loved his wife and child.

Avril wanted nothing more in her own life. A husband who loved her, cared for her. Did she have that chance with her knight? Was she crazy to contemplate marriage again?

"I hope this doesn't mean I won't be any good at this." Lady Aimil rubbed her rounded tummy and took a seat not far from them.

"Now you're just being silly," Mistress Ansley said, leaning forward and squeezing Lady Aimil's hand.

"You'll be a fine mama." Lady Cera rocked her baby and did a turn around the room. She didn't sit again until Lord Fallon burrowed into her breast and closed his vivid blue eyes. She rubbed his back, then her gray gaze bored into Avril. "Are you sure you're all right?"

"Yes, my lady. I'm honestly relieved."

"You won't have to testify in front of him at the trial," the duchess said. "Jorrin told me your statement was documented when you told him, and witnessed by Tristan and Leargan. If King Nathal has further questions, he'll speak to you in private."

Heart thundering, Avril forced a nod. Talk to the king? She'd need Roduch by her side.

"Don't worry about it." Lady Cera's smile was warm. "King Nathal's a great man. He might be huge…bigger than Roduch, but he'd never hurt you. And he *will* make that bastard pay. I promise."

Neither Mistress Ansley, nor Lady Aimil looked surprised at the Lady of Greenwald's harsh language.

"Will he put up a fight, I wonder?" Mistress Ansley worried her bottom lip.

"It's nothing they can't handle," Lady Cera said. "And Lucan's going, so I'm not worried about them."

"They are strong knights," Avril whispered.

"Only men," Mistress Ansley said sharply, looking out the window as she scratched her bondmate between the ears. "Fallible."

"Ansley." Lady Cera frowned.

She ignored the duchess, eyes on the now-empty courtyard.

Avril's former husband was essentially a coward, but

would he be foolish enough to act aggressively against Lord Aldern and his men?

Tynan didn't like being backed into a corner. He was unpredictable when things didn't go his way. He'd boasted being trained with a sword, but she'd never seen him fight, or even spar. Her former husband did have a small armory, though. He'd probably order Harlan to defend him. That was the coward's way out, was it not?

Harlan could refuse. Hopefully he *would*. The older man and his wife had never been anything but kind to her. Avril cared for them and their three sons a great deal.

Blessed Spirit keep them safe.

Perhaps she'd get a chance to see them again, and thank them for all they'd done for her. But she needed Roduch to come back to her safe and sound as well. She clung to her earlier words.

She *wasn't* afraid of Tynan Mont. He had no hold over her anymore. Soon, he'd be in the dungeons of the castle that was starting to feel like home.

Then, Avril would be back in the arms of the man she was falling in love with.

Chapter Twenty-Six

"**S**ire, there is a large group of men approaching." Harlan's voice was breathless, his formerly muscle-packed chest heaving. He bent at the waist, hands resting heavily on his knees as he tried to catch his breath.

"What?" Tynan snapped, popping up from his ornate throne in the great hall. He'd been supervising the wood mage reforming the arch that led into the large room.

The man was using his magic to etch in the embossed design Tynan had chosen. It would depict a fox hunt when it was done.

Then they'd talk about the murals he wanted on the ceiling. The mage was talented, and could infuse color into the wood he shaped. It would appear as if it'd been painted, but would be perfect, and permanent.

"Men. A group of men. Knights. The sun glinted off armor as I observed from the tower."

"Knights?" He narrowed his eyes as his gut screamed that his little bitch wife had something to do with the men on his property. Cursing savagely, he planned her death. Torture was in order.

When he found her, that is. He'd spent days in Greenwald Main.

Nothing.

Avril wasn't there.

After questioning the Kenrick boy, he'd gotten the child to admit he hadn't seen Avril, but someone who'd *reminded* him of her. He'd sworn the boy to secrecy regarding his wife's disappearance and sent him home with bruises, along with a tithe demand for wasting his time. A feast's worth of food had arrived less than an hour later, with sincere apologies from the boy's father, one of Tynan's tenants.

"Get rid of them," he barked.

"Aye, Sire." With a nod, his steward turned on his heel, hurrying out of the hall with the same speed of his arrival.

What the hell could knights want with him? What had Avril done?

Not ten minutes later, he heard the clang of metal and steps of booted feet.

"Master Tynan Mont!" The shout said they were headed toward him.

Damn it, Harlan is useless.

He trotted down the dais, and froze by a long table, his hand on the back of the head chair.

The wood mage peered over his shoulder, a sheen of sweat bright on his forehead, his shaggy blond locks slick as well. "Master? Not *lord?*"

"Leave," Tynan snarled.

Without so much as a bow, the wood mage slipped from the soon-to-be great hall, the advancing men paying him no attention.

Harlan simpered in front of the group, walking backwards as the men continued forward as a unit, ignoring him.

They were indeed knights, armor-covered from head to foot. Some had swords drawn.

Before his eyes, they fanned out, blocking all exits, and stopping at intervals around the perimeter of the space.

Three continued to walk toward him, one slightly in front of the other two, dressed from head to foot in the pale green and silver of Greenwald. The seal of the Province, a howling white wolf standing in front of a green flag, was etched into his decorative chest plate.

"What the hell is going on here?" Tynan swallowed,

squaring his shoulders and trying to look taller than his five feet three inches.

The fair-haired knight on the right was a big son of a bitch. He glared, one corner of his mouth lifted in a snarl. He drew his sword, eyes scorching.

"Are you Master Tynan Mont?" the one in the middle asked.

Tynan's eyes shot to him. His ears were long and tapered, like an elf's, but he was very tall. Although not as tall as the blond knight, he was broad, his presence was commanding. He was probably half-elfin.

Wait…half-elfin…what the hell *was the Duke of Greenwald doing in his home?*

"Lord Aldern?"

"Are you Master Tynan Mont?" he repeated, an edge to his voice. He had a wide scroll in his hand, and a sword sheathed at his side.

Tynan didn't answer. His eyes swept over the third man, as well as the rest of the soldiers in his great hall. His heart plummeted to his stomach.

This is about more than my wife.

The third man in front of him, dark haired like the duke, had a Greenwald-silver captain epaulet on the shoulder of his chest piece. His sword was also drawn, his expression fierce.

As Tynan's gaze raked over the big one again, he fought the urge to squirm.

The man's chiseled beardless face was intense, as if he was daring him to doing something attack-worthy. Hostility rolled off him.

Why?

He didn't know him…had never seen him before.

"Sire, I'm sorry," Harlan said, studying his boots.

"Leave us."

"Sire?" Lord Aldern asked before his steward could move, one dark eyebrow arched when Tynan met his eyes. "You've not the rank for such an honorific." He raised a hand, and Harlan froze near the table.

Duke or not, how dare he seek to override his order? "Who are *you* to tell me how my steward is to address *me*?" He glared.

"*He's* the Duke of Greenwald, so you need to watch your tone, *Master* Mont," the dark haired one said, northern accent evident with each word.

"I meant no offense, Captain," Tynan said, inclining his head.

The blond one muttered something that sounded like, "The hell you didn't."

He ignored him and looked at his liege lord. "How many I help you, Lord Aldern?" He made his tone as even as he could muster and bowed at the waist.

"Please confirm your identity." The captain took a step forward.

"I am Tynan Mont, master of all you see here."

"Tynan Mont." Lord Aldern cleared his throat as he opened the scroll.

His heart thundered as he watched the parchment unravel.

"You are under arrest for murder, blackmail, theft, abuse, misappropriation of land and coin, and breech of your marriage contract. You will be taken into custody, offered the choice of Advocate and put to trial for your crimes."

"Avril," Tynan bit out.

"You *do not* say her name," the big blond one growled.

Anger boiled up from his gut. "That little whore. Little. Lying. *Whore*," he spat. He glared at the duke, then the captain. Wouldn't let Avril do this to him. Tynan lunged forward, making a grab for the hilt of the captain's sword.

Taken off guard, the man stumbled. Their hands collided as Tynan's grip made purchase, and they wrestled until he'd gained the weapon from him.

The captain scrambled to remain on his feet, but

Tynan rushed him, slashing at him with his own sword.

He managed to make a swipe at the younger man's face before he was wrenched off his feet. The blade flew from his hand, clattering to the floor.

Tynan winced.

Better not scratch my tile.

He'd special ordered it from the southern continent. There was nothing in the north like it.

The big blond knight slid behind him, wrenching his arm up and back. He pushed down until Tynan had no choice but to fall to his knees.

He tried to pull free, to no avail. The large man's grip was like a vise. "Unhand me. Now," he commanded.

The only answer he got was a tighter grip on his arm.

Tynan winced and called the big bastard every name he could think of, but when he glanced up, the knight had the nerve to grin at him.

"Easy, Roduch," the captain said softly. "You'll break his arm." He'd regained his balance, and seemed unbothered by the attack. The man bent to retrieve his sword, but a small trickle of blood was visible on his forehead.

Good, I got him.

Satisfaction rolled over Tynan, and he smirked at the captain. If the man noticed, he ignored him.

Roduch growled again, saying nothing. His impossibly large hand didn't loosen at all. "I promised not to kill him. Never said I wouldn't maim him."

His gaze shot to his eyes. "Promise not to kill me? Why?"

The knight didn't answer him.

"Master Mont, I am adding assault of my captain to your list of charges," the duke said, his jaw clenched, eyes narrowed.

"Slander is how you run your Province!" Tynan shouted. "I'm being victimized because of a lying little whore!" He was ripped up off his feet and flipped around so fast his head spun. Having no choice but to stare into the huge knight's pale blue eyes, he had a prime view of a hard forehead slamming into his.

Agony exploded and his head reeled.

Then the world went black.

Blessed Spirit he wanted to kill him. Why had Roduch given his word to his captain and the duke he would not?

The bastard was now '*the little bastard.*' Portly and short, he had to be five and forty turns old. Tynan Mont wasn't much to look at. At All. Yet he'd *terrorized* the love of Roduch's life for *four* turns? Beat her, raped her?

Tynan Mont needed to *die.*

If possible, his blood boiled even more when he'd laid eyes on Avril's former husband than when she'd retold what she'd endured. He was a tiny shite. Why was he able to hold so many people under his thumb?

Magic.

Not even his own.

Growling, he looked down at the man's crumpled form on the too-shiny ornately tiled floor.

If one looked around the hall—hell, the whole property—it was no secret how the man used the gold he'd misappropriated. He was trying to make his home even more lavish than Castle Aldern.

"Roduch." Leargan shook his head, but his captain's expression looked as if he was torn between irritation and pride.

He shrugged. "I didn't kill him. The headache he'll have when he wakes isn't nearly enough justice."

"One drop of water in a vast bucket, I agree," Lord Aldern said.

"Alas, Bowen, come retrieve the scum," Leargan ordered. "There are shackles with his name on it outside."

Roduch locked eyes with his captain and smirked. "Don't trust me to take him to the cart?"

"Not for a moment." The ghost of a smile playing at his lips as he sheathed his sword.

He stared at his longtime friend and fellow knight. "I appreciate your honesty."

Blood trickled down Leargan's cheek, and the captain wiped it away. His hand jerked, so Roduch didn't ask if he was well; irritation rolled off the man. It wasn't often his captain was taken off guard.

Who would've thought the little shite was brave enough, anyway?

Alasdair chuckled, hooking one strong arm under one of Tynan Mont's.

Bowen winked as he grabbed the bastard's other one, and they lifted his torso off the floor. At least they dragged him along the tile as they took him away. Hopefully they'd rip is fine breeches and skin his knees, but even that wasn't enough.

Gelding him right then and there might be. Roduch would volunteer his weapon and hand for that duty in about two seconds flat. No sterilization of the blade by fire, either. Who needed to stop bleeding?

Leargan gripped his forearm and squeezed.

Lord Aldern stepped over to the cowering steward.

Roduch nodded thanks. After giving the captain a onceover, his stomach fluttered.

Something's wrong.

More than the cut he'd received from Avril's former husband. Despite the gravity of their mission, Leargan had been too quiet on the ride.

"What's wrong?" Roduch asked. "We got what we came for, and no one was seriously harmed."

A slight shake of his head said Leargan didn't want to talk about it, and confirmed it had nothing to do with apprehending Tynan Mont.

He gave him a squeeze. "Well, if you've need of me, I've two ears."

"Thank you." The knight averted his gaze, but gave a

curt nod.

Even before they could mount up, people—whole families really—poured into the small courtyard of the property, gasping and whispering. Even outright shouting as their landlord was manacled to the wooden cart.

Their expressions held relief; their yells were of thanks, not outrage. If nothing else, that only doomed Avril's former husband even more.

Now most of the personal guard, as well as Lord Aldern himself, could be called witnesses against Tynan Mont's tyranny.

When the half-elfin duke made it to his mare, they started whispering about his presence.

"I'll have to address them," the duke said to the captain.

Leargan nodded and swung himself into Fia's saddle.

He rode toward the people, Leargan close by to protect Lord Aldern if necessary. The crowd parted and encircled them while the rest of the guard watched.

Roduch stayed close to the cart with the unconscious bastard. Although Tynan Mont's people had no love lost on him, he wasn't about to take any chances. If the man woke, he'd make sure he stayed put. Better yet, he'd knock him out again. Two headaches were better than one.

"Tynan Mont is under arrest," Lord Aldern said, his voice loud and clear.

No gasps greeted their ears. Only smiles and more relief.

"This holding is now under the care and control of Master Harlan Pelham. He'll be your temporary landlord, if you were beholden to *Master* Mont. However, if your contracts to that effect were because of blackmail, you are now free. You owe Master Pelham nothing more. Ever." The duke smiled and his gaze appeared to sweep the crowd.

Many of the men threw arms in the air. Women wept and swept children up in their arms. Couples embraced and some even kissed. Though Roduch was no empath, he could feel their relief, their joy.

Lord Aldern cleared his throat and they settled, their gazes once again locked onto him. "I owe you all an apology."

Now there were a few gasps, but the duke inclined his head to the people.

"I say so because I knew not what was going on here, and I should have. As Duke of Greenwald, you're all my responsibility. This went on too long. I'm deeply sorry. If Tynan Mont stole from you in the way of material things, you have my permission—and understanding from Master Pelham—to retrieve these items. If he stole your coin, you will be repaid, if it's from my own coffers. I promise you this."

More gasps, and the people hung on the duke's every word.

"There will be a trial. You'll all have the opportunity to testify if you see fit, but no one will be forced. A messenger will inform you before the trial commences. Once again, I'm sorry this happened in my Province."

It was a while before they were able to take their leave. Each and every one of Tynan's tenants wanted to thank the duke personally, and Lord Aldern obliged.

When they were on the road again, Roduch road abreast the cart, but he wasn't too far away to hear his captain teasing the duke.

"That was well said, my lord."

"You think so? I'm not fond of these things. I never know what to say."

They went back and forth, until they both ended up laughing.

"I bet Lord Tristan will be sorry he missed it," Leargan said.

Roduch shook his head, giving into a small smile as they continued to banter.

Alasdair added his voice as well, everyone in earshot

giving into chuckles at his wit—or what Leargan would call, smart-arsed comments.

Glancing at Tynan Mont's still form, Roduch snarled silently. He still wanted to kill the bastard. But they'd set out to arrest him and they had.

There was a place in the dungeon ready to claim him.

Now Avril could truly move on with her life.

Chapter Twenty-Seven

orrin stood next to Tristan and Leargan as they watched the approach of the king and his entourage from the high wall of Castle Aldern. Even now, after almost a turn being the Duke of Greenwald, the *official* name change rocked him.

For generations Cera's childhood home had been called Castle Ryhan, her maiden surname, like all castles on the continent were named after the holding family. But *she'd* pushed for the official change after they'd married. As long as his line — starting with Fallon — held Greenwald, the castle would remain named after Jorrin's family.

Astonishing.

The love of his life caught his eye, the sun glinting off her dark red locks. Her curls were loose today, swaying with the unusually warm fall breeze as she stood with her two best friends not far from him, the captain and Tristan.

Cera fidgeted in the gorgeous rust gown she'd donned for the king's arrival. The dress was one the queen had given her the night they'd gotten betrothed — much to her chagrin at the time. It was embroidered with silver roses, the corseted bodice cut too low for Jorrin's liking. Especially since she was nursing their son and her breasts were fuller than normal.

Growling to himself, he wanted to go inside and find a shawl to wrap her in, but she'd know why in an instant and fuss at him.

Her body was even shapelier than before, all delicious curves carrying Fallon had gifted her with. Although their son was only a fortnight old, thanks to Tristan, her body was able to make love with no pain, and he could barely keep his hands to himself. Despite fatigue from being up with a newborn every few hours overnight, his wife was right there with him.

Tristan had learned healing magic that would prevent pregnancy. They wouldn't add to their family again until they wanted to, no matter how many times they were together.

For health reasons, the spell needed to be released every few months. After giving the woman's cycle time to regulate—as the healer had put it—the spell could be replaced and last up to four months.

Women were flocking to him from all over the Province.

"Put your tongue back in your head," Leargan muttered, following Jorrin's gaze to where the three women stood as they looked down to watch the procession headed toward the castle.

All three wolves were close by, lying next to each other. Ali napped, Trik's head was up, looking around the battlement, and Isair appeared to be bored, giving a canine sigh as she laid her head on her paws.

"I'm married to a beautiful woman." Jorrin kept his tone light, but when he made eye contact with his captain, his smile faded. His magic tingled with Leargan's dark emotions.

Pain, regret and guilt rolled off his friend.

Nothing had changed between his captain and the lovely Ansley, and they were both worse for the wear.

Leargan glanced at his betrothed, but when she looked over her shoulder and their gazes met, they both averted their eyes. The captain made tight fists and pinned them to his sides.

Jorrin's heart ached, but he couldn't help him now. Leargan had to help himself out of his mess.

Cera had been glued to his arm, and Aimil had also been with Tristan, until about ten minutes before. When Ansley and Ali had arrived on the wall.

The wives had left their husbands, glaring at Leargan and joining the Ansley, linking arms and exchanging smiles.

But the Rider had wilted when she'd seen the captain. Her emotions made Jorrin's limbs ache, his fingers tingle.

She echoed how Leargan felt, and it made his empathic magic scream.

They both felt horrible. So why couldn't they fix it? They only had to speak to each other.

Jorrin's wife had laid into Leargan the night before. The tongue lashing was good enough to make him wince and look for blood; she'd shredded Leargan so badly.

Cera had been honest, and harsh.

His captain had sat head bowed, dark hair covering his face like a curtain. Uttering, "I know" and "aye" from time to time.

Jorrin's eyes swept the approaching group and he swallowed a sigh. Whatever Leargan had planned— Blessed Spirit let the man have a *plan*—he was going to leave him to it.

They had bigger things to worry about than heartbreak. He had to brief the king on Avril's situation and get Tynan Mont's trial handled.

The bastard had declined all three Advocates Jorrin had recruited from Greenwald Main—one of which was the famous Atticus Brehon, a man so accomplished at the law that King Nathal had used his services to settle disputes from time to time. People sought him from all over both continents.

Atticus was a good man, so Jorrin had been surprised he'd even be interested in the case, but the duke wasn't going to exclude the Advocate—also the head of the law school in Greenwald Main—because over all, the man was fair. Justice was in his magic and in his blood.

Tynan Mont was an arrogant idiot.

Jorrin had no issues with letting the trial duties fall to King Nathal. Not that he didn't feel he could handle it, but he couldn't remain impartial. He already cared a great deal for Avril. Wanted Tynan Mont to *suffer*. He'd castrate him if Roduch didn't beat him to it.

The big knight loved the girl. Whether or not he'd told her, Jorrin had no idea, but he sensed love every time he'd been in the same room as the two of them. Avril felt the same way, which was a shock, considering what she'd been through, but he wished them all the happiness in the world. They both deserved it.

If the king hadn't already been on his way to Castle Aldern, he would've *had* to preside over things, but would gladly relinquish his right as Tynan Mont's liege lord to a higher power.

Seeing the look on the bastard's face when the king faced off with him would be worth it, for one. Hopefully, Tynan Mont squirmed in his seat when he had to look *up* at King Nathal's more than six and a half foot frame.

Jorrin stared down at the procession as it slowly made its way over the drawbridge, and into the outer courtyard of the castle grounds.

King Nathal was visible; his large body overshadowing most of the men he rode with.

"Where is the famous Sir Murdoch?" Jorrin asked.

The captain of the king's personal guard had been away on official business when the king and his men had helped them defeat Varthan, so he'd never met the man.

"Riding to the king's right," Tristan said, pointing to a huge man with long red hair and a beard.

"Blessed Spirit, he's almost as big as the king," Jorrin said.

Leargan groaned.

He bit back a smile and arched an eyebrow. "Is this man fond of you?"

Several snickers were covered with coughs when the captain glowered at him.

"Aye. He used to be my captain, after all. I'm fond of him, as well."

"Good thing," he whispered, leaning in. "Maybe you'll keep your hide intact, then."

His captain glared.

Tristan chuckled, patting Leargan's back. "Not sure about that. He's got quite a temper, especially where his only child is concerned."

"I'll tell him the truth." His voice was low enough for only Jorrin and Tristan's ears, and very serious.

Regret from the healer made Jorrin's magic prickle.

"I'm sorry," Tristan whispered. "I shouldn't tease. This is a serious matter."

"I meant to tease, but I'm sorry, too. Honestly." He reached for Leargan's forearm and squeezed. "I believe it will work out."

His captain nodded. "It has to." Pain flared in his dark eyes.

Jorrin swallowed a wince. He and Tristan exchanged a look.

"They're through the gates," Cera announced. "We should go down to the great hall. Morag should have everything set up by now."

Ladies Cera and Aimil walked arm and arm with Ansley in front of them as they headed down the corridor to the great hall.

Leargan's heart burned, speeding up, spreading pain across his chest until his arms shook. He made tight fists at his sides. Every attempt he'd made to speak to her had been rejected.

Daicy guarded Ansley's door as well as Ali could, glaring so hard it scorched no matter the distance.

The first time, the maid *had* asked her if she wanted to talk to him, but now she wouldn't even do that. She'd stare, hands on hips, silently daring him to come closer.

He'd never been a coward before, but the half-fear of a petite maid was cutting it close.

Respecting Ansley's hurt and anger was killing him. Would he ever touch her again? Perhaps the king's arrival wouldn't help anything. Was she lost to him? *Nay.* Everything would be fine.

It had to be.

Morag and her many maids met them in the great hall, lined up and ready to serve. A fine repast already lay on well-laden tables.

There would be a feast that night for evening meal, so the midday food was on the light side, but should still satisfy the king and his men after a long ride.

The headwoman's fussing about *the beasts* made Leargan glance in her direction.

Lady Cera was on her in a second, cancelling Morag's *order* for the three wolves to exit the hall. His lady liked her bondmate close—not that he blamed her.

Only moments later, Trikser, Isair and Ali all plopped down by the main hearth—no doubt at the bidding of their mistresses—but Leargan didn't miss Morag's glare of disapproval.

His men were starting to assemble as well, each giving him a curt nod as they passed.

Laith, the youngest of the personal guard—at nineteen turns old—winked at Meara, one of the maids. The fair-haired knight bowed in front of her and kissed her knuckles after she'd set two baskets of sweet rolls on the personal guard's table.

With a giggle, the girl blushed and twirled away, a wide smile on her face, flashing dimples.

Laith regarded her with a grin and his brother, Merrick, slapped him on the back.

Even Laith has a woman?

Envy curled Leargan's gut.

Searching Ansley out against his will, his gaze collided with hers, but she looked away so fast her long red plait jolted like a whip.

She was clustered close to Ladies Cera and Aimil, and

the duchess shot him a glare before squeezing Ansley's forearm.

Damn, he had to fix things. Lady Cera had summoned him to Jorrin's ledger room last night for a sound tongue lashing that'd made him feel about five turns old.

He'd sat there and taken it, because he didn't have the guts to admit the embarrassment that had come hand in hand, or the lack of desire to speak to *the* Lady of Greenwald about his very personal problem.

What was he supposed to say?

Jorrin — the traitor — had stood in the corner, a cringe on his face the whole time. Silent. *Coward.* At least there hadn't been any other witnesses.

King Nathal dominated — by sheer size and booming voice — as he entered the great hall of Castle Aldern, a smile on his bearded face. His tawny hair was helm-mussed, and the men with him were as just as boisterous, laughter in their conversation as they strode forward to meet everyone. The man who'd raised him appeared to be in a good mood.

The king wore no armor, but was covered in the bright blue of Terraquist — breeches and tunic. He wore a silver doublet with his seal stitched into it. The lion was roaring, surrounded by a shield and a blue flag. He was dressed for a celebration.

Leargan groaned.

My wedding.

Sir Murdoch wasn't far behind, along with the rest of the men — which numbered about a dozen. Not all of them were the king's personal guard, of course. King Nathal had left probably half in Terraquist to protect his family while he was away. Leargan would do the same, if he and Jorrin had to leave for any length of time.

Loud voices, along with pats on shoulders and backs ran rampant as the king's men greeted Leargan's. They hadn't seen each other in some time, and both Kale and Teagan — two of the knights of the Greenwald personal guard—were saluting their fathers.

A smile played at Leargan's lips despite the pain in his heart. Family reunions were a good thing.

No one had approached him just yet, where he stood by the dais, but he surveyed the crowd. The king was hugging Lady Cera. His eyes rested on Avril and Roduch.

The tiny lass stood shyly by his side while the big warrior clasped the forearm of Sir Renen, one of knights of the king's personal guard. The man was blood kin to Roduch. His friend had squired for the older knight when they were lads.

Avril and Roduch's hands were entwined. Her mess of dark curls had been tamed, intricately braided, with a pearled comb and flowers woven in. It made her look even younger. Beautiful and innocent.

Roduch slipped an arm around her shoulders. Even from the distance he was standing, Leargan saw the blush light her cheeks as the big man introduced her to his cousin. But her smile was sweet, welcoming. It was good to see no fear in her expression.

She still stayed away from men other than Roduch, but she was warming up slowly, and Avril spent time with the ladies of Greenwald. The girl was safe now, and she finally seemed to feel so, too.

The trial would help—hopefully. The bastard would pay. Perhaps the king would require gelding as a part of his punishment. King Nathal had always been an outspoken protector of women. Tynan Mont would be punished. Severely.

Avril and Roduch were gazing at each other before Sir Renen as if they were the only two in the room. Roduch's cousin had a smile of indulgence on his bearded face.

Leargan's heart skipped and he frowned.

When would he stop hurting?

Never.

A glimpse of red hair caught his attention and he glanced away from the budding new couple.

Ansley darted across the great hall, practically throwing herself into her father's arms.

The large knight caught her up, his face a mask of surprise as he pulled her closer to his massive chest. His tunic only partially muffled her sobs.

Oh, hell.

Leargan gulped.

Chapter Twenty-Eight

As Ansley pressed ever closer to his chest, Murdoch tightened his arms around her. His daughter had never been one for frivolous tears. She wasn't crying out of the joy of seeing him; it hadn't been long since they'd last parted.

She buried her face against him, and he rubbed her back, waiting for her to calm so he could meet the blue-green eyes that matched his own.

Find out what had upset her.

Destroy it.

Murdoch caught Nathal's eye. The king stared, a fair eyebrow arched. He gave a half-shrug, pulling his lass even closer. "What's wrong, love?" he whispered just above her ear.

Ansley shook her head, her thick plait jumping across her back and brushing his wrists.

He felt eyes on them and looked up, inadvertently meeting the gaze of his only child's intended.

Sir Leargan Tegran's face was a mask of pain for only seconds before the young captain schooled his expression and inclined his head.

Murdoch narrowed his eyes, growling deep in his throat. The lad had made his Ansley cry. He'd always been fond of Leargan.

Blessed Spirit, I hope I don't have to kill him.

"Not now, Da," Ansley whispered.

Their gazes collided. Tears stained her cheeks, and he frowned.

"I'm all right, Da, really." She nodded for effect, but he didn't believe it for a second.

He tucked her into his side and strode forward, giving his daughter the choice of moving her feet or getting dragged.

"Da!"

Murdoch ignored her squawk and kept walking. He'd get to the bottom of things. *Now.*

"It's good to see you, Sir Murdoch," the lad said, thrusting his hand out for a shake.

He looked Leargan up and down, not acknowledging the younger captain's courtesy. "It's yet to be decided if the same can be said of you."

"Da!" His lass' sharp admonition came with a gasp, but Leargan didn't react.

Nor did he squirm as Murdoch stared him down. In that, he respected Leargan a touch.

His daughter pulled on his arm, but he didn't look away from the young man he'd practically raised. "What have you done to my daughter?"

Ansley sputtered.

"I want to marry your daughter, sir." Leargan's tone was even; calm. The lad looked away from him, staring at Ansley, but she averted her gaze.

"That is why I have come."

"She's refused me, sir."

Why in the world would she refuse the lad she was in love with?

Murdoch arched an eyebrow and spared Ansley a glance.

She glared back, defiance flaring in her teal eyes. His daughter slipped from his grip and squared her shoulders, her mouth a hard line.

Who was this lass—this *woman*—standing before him? Certainly not his daughter.

Ansley had always been on the timid side. Confident and capable of fulfilling her duties as a Senior King's Rider, but not aggressive. That was what'd made the decision for him to get her a bondmate—Murdoch didn't worry so much when she was away; Ali was at her side.

Timid was absent in the female before him. She looked ready to give him a piece of her mind. Something she'd never done before.

They had a rather open relationship, but his daughter had always been respectful, dutiful. Never raised her voice, or spoken crossly to him. It was good to see she had some of her mother's fire after all.

"Daughter, is this true?"

Ansley narrowed her eyes and lifted her chin. "Aye. I won't have a husband forced on me. I've no use for a man who doesn't want me."

The lad snorted.

His daughter scowled.

"Hmmm…" He looked from one to the other, stroking his beard. "What has happened here?" he muttered, more to himself than to Leargan or Ansley. "Well, I have come for a wedding, and a wedding we shall have." Making eye contact with his only child, he dared her to contradict him.

Pain marked her beautiful face, and Murdoch's chest tightened. This was real, not his lassie being stubborn. She was hurting.

Leargan's expression mirrored his daughter's.

What the hell happened between them?

"I need some time to sort this out," Murdoch said.

"Good," Leargan said

"There's nothing to sort," Ansley snapped at the same time.

Scheming. The look on his face told Ansley her father was scheming. Like King Nathal, it put him at his most dangerous.

She'd rather face him with a sword than let him meddle in her love life — or lack thereof.

Sir Murdoch had never been a man to be trifled with.

If she was Leargan, she would've been shaking in her boots when the huge man regarded her with the keen stare he currently appraised her former betrothed with.

Ansley sucked in a breath at the reminder that things were irrevocably damaged with Leargan. She trembled, planting tight fists at her sides.

"Neither of you will speak?" her father asked.

She met Leargan's eyes, ignoring the agony there and averting her gaze. Her heart thumped.

His pain was as real as hers. Why?

He doesn't love me.

How could *he* look so hurt?

He'd betrayed her, not the other way around. And her father was *mistaken*, if he thought she would still marry Leargan.

"There's nothing to say," she whispered. She'd pull him aside later, explain to him in privacy of her intentions. Ansley would appeal to his heart. After all, he'd loved her mother. He wouldn't force her to marry a man who didn't love her.

No matter how *she* felt.

Murdoch knew how she felt about Leargan. She'd been furious with him — still was for the most part — for his role in her delivery of the scroll and the king's order. No doubt the whole damned thing was his idea.

She'd been determined to give him a piece of her mind, hold it together long enough to do what she needed to do. But when her father had entered the great hall, hurt had assaulted her, and she *needed* her da. Needed him to hold her, comfort her. So she'd run into his arms like she hadn't done since she was a small child.

His surprise had been evident, but Murdoch had held her tight without question. That was always her da, though. He'd be there for her no matter what.

Ansley's mother, Marael, had been the love of her father's life. She'd passed away when Ansley was only eleven from a mystery fever that had stumped even royal healers. Murdoch had been devastated.

Not fully understanding why she'd lost a parent, she'd clung to the only one she'd had left. He'd raised her on his own, and they'd grown very close. At fourteen, she'd joined the King's Rider's. Her father had been so proud of her.

"I will speak to the king." Her father's deep voice pulled her from her thoughts, and Ansley locked gazes with him.

"Da…"

He didn't pause. Turning on his heel, he left her with Leargan.

Alone.

She frantically glanced around, but failed to locate anyone who could save her. Cera was directing maids, Aimil stood arm in arm with her husband, speaking to two of the king's knights.

Panic rolled over her. Ali whined from the hearth, but Ansley sent her a quick thought-send to stay put.

"I miss you." Leargan's pained whisper bought her head around.

Their eyes met and held.

Angry tears burned her eyes, and she blinked them away. She would *not* let him see her cry again. "Even if you get your way, I will hate you for the rest of our lives. It won't take you long to resent me, either. Marrying me to follow *orders* isn't good for either of us."

She tried not to remember the terror that had hit when Cera had told her Avril's former husband had *attacked* him when they'd arrested him. She made herself look away from the urge to search his forehead for a mark, even though Tristan had long since healed him. It hadn't been serious, and Leargan hadn't been otherwise harmed, anyway.

I don't care.

But she did.

His dark eyes blazed with ire and he made a fist. "It's

not like that. How many times do I have to tell you that?"

Her teeth sank into her bottom lip to stave off more tears.

Rage. She needed to be angry. It wasn't working.

"I've never lied to you," he insisted.

Ansley closed her eyes, ignoring his urgent voice. "You lied about the scroll."

Leargan stepped toward her; she could feel the heat coming off his body and ached for him, cursing her traitorous desire. For his arms around her. For his lips against hers.

"Nay. I told you the truth about it. I only regret that it wasn't from the start." He grabbed her arm. "I'm sorry for the things I said out of anger."

Yanking away from his grasp, Ansley glared. "Don't touch me."

He dropped his hand to his side, his face a mask of undisguised pain. "I'm sorry. No matter what you think, I *am* sorry for what I said."

She shook her head.

Gazes scorched from all directions, and a hush had fallen over the great hall. *Everyone* watched them. Heat snaked up her neck and seared her cheeks, as embarrassment threatened to swallow her whole. Their very private situation was now *public.*

The urge to flee was overwhelming.

"Leargan." The king's booming voice made her jump. "Come speak to me, lad."

With one last glance filled with accusation and hurt, the man she loved left her side to obey his king.

Again.

Ansley ran from the great hall, tears scalding her cheeks.

Chapter Twenty-Nine

She'd run as soon as his back was turned.

Leargan's heart broke all over again, but he forced his feet toward the man who raised him instead of running after her like he wanted to. His eyes rested on her father, and he winced at Sir Murdoch's murderous expression.

King Nathal stepped in front of his captain, blocking Leargan from view. Surprise washed over him when the king pulled him in for a quick, but tight embrace. "It's good to see you, lad." The king's voice in his ear was accompanied by an affectionate pat on the back that almost knocked him over.

He forced a smile, meeting the king's pale blue eyes and trying to forget some hurt. Being away from the big man had made Leargan forget just how large the king was. Seven inches past six feet made him feel short at his height of six feet, one inch. Tristan was his height; Jorrin a few inches taller. That was what he'd grown accustomed to.

Looking *up* at King Nathal brought back memories.

The king smiled back, his tawny, shoulder-length hair as wild as a lion's mane, and dancing around his shoulders. His gaze was warm.

Emotion tightened Leargan's chest, and he struggled for breath. He wanted the king to fix all his problems. He'd ordered them to marry, after all.

If Ansley approached her father, and Sir Murdoch agreed with her refusal, only one thing would change the older captain's mind.

Revealing that Leargan had taken her innocence.

That was a problem, too. Being totally honest *would*

force their marriage to happen — if Sir Murdoch didn't kill him. Ansley would hate him even more.

He loved her. Needed her to want him as much as he wanted her. His wife. The only woman he wanted to marry. Pain clenched his gut and he swallowed hard against the lump in his throat.

His foster father's expression slid from friendly to concerned.

Jorrin, standing with Tristan and Aimil in the periphery, cringed. The duke wasn't all that close, but evidently King Nathal could see Leargan's pain and his lord could *feel* it.

"Walk with me, lad," King Nathal said, his tone a gentle order. He threw his arm around Leargan's shoulders.

Sir Murdoch took a step forward to join them, but the king shook his head.

"I need to speak with the lad alone, Murdoch. We'll join you later."

The scowl on his face was as big as the Province, but Ansley's father nodded.

They headed to Lady Cera's garden. It was large, and because of its maze-like pathways, private.

"Arriving in Greenwald wasn't exactly as I'd imagined." King Nathal regarded him seriously, but one corner of his mouth was up. His familiar thick northern brogue made Leargan ache for Terraquist.

He'd been born in South Ascova, but the king had brought him to Terraquist after he'd been orphaned during the battle. Raised him as a warrior, a knight.

"Well, lad…you're awfully quiet."

Leargan glanced away. "I've really messed things up, Majesty."

"Lad, look at me and tell me what happened."

He focused on the order, sucked in a breath and met the king's eyes. Leargan opened his mouth to speak. No words came. Was he really about to air what happened with *the king*? He cleared his throat. "I wanted to thank you."

"Whatever for?" King Nathal's bushy brow arched.

"For choosing her for me."

"Oh. You'll have to thank Murdoch. The whole thing was his idea." He smiled, his broad shoulders relaxing.

Damn. What can I say to that?

"He was afraid she'd never marry if it wasn't you, lad." The king squeezed his shoulder.

Leargan closed his eyes. Even her father knew how Ansley felt about him. No wonder she didn't believe him. She must've thought his proposal was too good to be true. Then she'd been crushed when he'd revealed the scroll. The idiot that he was, he hadn't known his own heart until he'd lost her. "Maybe I can thank him. But right now, I think he'd rather kill me than listen to a word I have to say."

King Nathal's chuckle made warmth rush his neck. "I doubt it's that serious, lad."

Disagreeing with the man who'd raised him wasn't something he was used to, but Leargan shook his head. "You've not heard what happened."

"Tell me."

"I love her, your Majesty," he blurted.

The king said nothing, but nodded.

Words tumbled from his mouth. He couldn't look at the king when he confessed the threat that'd torn her heart out, but King Nathal offered no judgment. The comforting grip on his forearm remained steady as the big man listened. His expression was troubled, but he let Leargan get everything out.

His chest shook with the last of his recital.

"Well, it's a mess, aye," King Nathal said, but there was no admonition in his voice.

They sighed at the same time.

"Not that I blame her, but she won't believe a word I say. Even if I tell her how I feel, she'd call me a liar again."

"We'll get it all sorted, lad."

"I don't see how," Leargan said. He tried to banish the hopelessness washing over him. "When Sir Murdoch finds out we've already been intimate, he'll either kill me or force her to marry me. I wouldn't be opposed to him forcing the issue — after all, she'd be my wife — but Ansley would take issue. She'd probably run away."

The king chuckled, shaking his head. "My Senior Riders are made up of stubborn lasses. It's a handy thing when they're dealing with life on the road. Not so much when it comes to marrying them. Blessed Spirit forbid if they perceive an order."

He frowned. "But it was an order."

"Aye, for *your* purposes. I'd hoped you could have affection for her, because I knew you wouldn't refuse me. It looks like that worked out, at least."

"It's done me no good," he whispered.

He knows me well.

Leargan couldn't be angry for the *disguised* order. After all, he'd accepted the words of the scroll almost immediately, despite expressing frustration to Jorrin.

Orders were duty. Not to be questioned.

Even in matters of the heart. Marriages were arranged for alliances all the time, after all. *Love* was rarely considered in the world of nobility and knights, but the king loved his queen. He was surrounded by strong marriages filled with love.

He ached for the same with Ansley.

"All is not lost, lad." King Nathal patted his shoulder. "But Murdoch doesn't need to know his daughter is no longer a maid. That, we will keep between us. The rest, we will reveal. He has a chance to get through to her. They are very much alike. From that display earlier, I'd say even their tempers are similar." He grinned and Leargan scowled.

There's nothing amusing, dammit.

"I was prepared to confess all, actually, so he could

get us to the altar quickly, but I don't want her against her will. I'll do as you suggest, Majesty."

"And I will do my best to keep your hide intact." The king laughed again.

He winced.

"Come now, Leargan, you've always had a sense of humor." The big man was crestfallen when their eyes met.

"Aye. When I don't fear I *need* someone to keep my hide intact."

King Nathal clapped him on the back, almost knocking him off balance.

Leargan groaned and the king threw his head back and bellowed with more laughter.

Chapter Thirty

The room spun, and Ansley grabbed the back of the chair to steady herself. She blinked to clear her vision. Swallowed against the sudden lump in her throat.

What's wrong with me?

Ali whined, and she glanced in the wolf's direction. Once again, her bondmate had claimed the large hearth in the guest room.

"I'm fine, Ali."

But am I?

She needed to get dressed. Her father would be there soon to escort her to the feast.

Ansley glanced at the gorgeous dark green gown on her bed. Cera had had it made for her just a few days ago, and had surprised her with it the previous night in the Duchess Solar.

The bodice was a cut a bit lower than she was used to, but it was her favorite shade of green; the hunter green hue of the Senior Riders.

Cera's gown maker had outdone herself. Beautiful large golden roses were stitched across the corset. Ansley caressed the shimmery fabric. The skirt was full and would flow when she walked.

The former Senior Rider duchess was infamous for her dislike of all things feminine, but she had good taste in gowns. The dress was perfect. She loved it.

A knock on the door made her look up. "Come in."

Daicy grinned, her brown eyes dancing, pretty face lit up. She exuded joy.

She couldn't help the smile that curved her lips.

"What are you so excited about?"

"Everyone is in such a good mood. The king and his men are so friendly."

Ansley laughed, feeling a weight lift off her, despite the negative interaction with Leargan in the great hall. Daicy had been her constant champion since she'd discovered the truth. A new — but true — friend. "Do I get a hint that perhaps a certain one of the king's men is friendly?"

The maid grinned again, but her cheeks were pink. "Actually…not one of the king's men. One of ours."

"O-o-urs?"

"Yes, Mistress Ansley. You belong in Greenwald." Daicy nodded, meeting her gaze.

Pain gripped her chest and threated to bowl her over. She didn't belong in Greenwald. Because Leargan didn't want her.

Ansley looked away. She sucked in a breath and cleared her throat. *Normal.* She needed normal. "So, who's the lucky man?"

"Merrick." The maid fairly sighed his name.

"He's very handsome."

Sir Merrick, one of the knights of Cera's personal guard, wasn't as tall as Leargan, but he had pretty green eyes and fair hair, like his younger brother, Laith. The brothers had been raised like Leargan, by King Nathal in Terraquist, groomed to be knights. From what Ansley knew of him, Merrick was a jester like Alasdair.

Daicy's smile faded, and her teeth sank into her full bottom lip. "I'm sorry. I…don't want to make you sad…"

"No, no. Don't be silly, I'm fine." She mustered a weak smile.

Silence fell, and the maid looked away first, her nod making her ponytail bob.

Neither of them had fallen for Ansley's statement.

"Well, let's get you dressed," she announced, rubbing her palms together, a smile back in place.

"Aye. I don't want to be late. My father's escorting me."

"Your da, mistress?" Daicy asked, raising an eyebrow. Her tone made it plain Sir Murdoch Fraser was the wrong choice.

Funny, since she'd been the one to keep Leargan *away* from her. Had she changed her mind about the captain? The maid knew Ansley loved him. Perhaps budding feelings for Merrick had made her reassess things.

"Aye, and he's always been fond of punctuality. So we'd better get moving." Ansley made a grab for the dress and missed. The bed spun along with her head, and she reeled, rocking back on her heels.

Daicy gripped her forearm; it was the only thing that kept her on her feet. "Are you all right?" Her brown eyes were concerned.

"Aye…aye…" Nodding made her head somersault.

The maid's eyes darted all over Ansley's face and body. "Perhaps you should lie down."

"Nay. I need to dress. Cera had this gown made for me. I need to go to the feast. My da will be here any moment. Everyone's expecting me."

"Shall I fetch Lord Dagget?"

"I'm fine. I skipped midday meal, that's all. I broke my fast very early this morning."

"All right." Daicy's voice shouted she didn't believe Ansley, though the maid would never call her a liar.

Needing a distraction, she picked up the gown, holding it up to her body. "I'll need help lacing this."

The maid's chest rose and fell as if she had taken a deep breath. However, her expression was still much too worried for Ansley's liking. "That's what I'm here for. Then we'll do your hair. How would you like it?"

Her instinct was to say *down*. Leargan loved to run his hands through it.

She met Daicy's gaze and ignored the pain that crept up from her gut, scalding her from the inside out. "Up. Can you do any special braids?"

"Of course. I can even weave flowers in if you like."

Ansley tried to stave off tears. She needed to forget about Leargan.

Like that would ever happen.

Ali whined, and she mentally shushed her, praying to the Blessed Spirit she would make it through this night.

The second knock at the door came only moments after Daicy had taken her leave, and Ansley sucked in a breath. For a split second, she wished Leargan was standing in the corridor waiting for her. Sense descended with the pain, and she panted as she went to let her father in, her head spinning all over again.

It's the braids.

Maybe Daicy had pulled too tightly.

The gorgeous style was reminiscent of something Queen Morghyn would've done to her flaxen locks; intricate braids crossing and crisscrossing each other, some up, some left down, with flowers woven in above her ears and down her back.

Beautiful.

And she looked fantastic in the dress. It brought out the color of her eyes and pushed her breasts up. Ansley looked like a lady. Too bad she didn't feel like one.

The longer it'd taken to get ready, the more she wanted to avoid the feast—and Leargan. Her bed looked inviting. Curling up with Ali was all she desired at the moment. However, she'd spoken the truth to Daicy; she *was* expected in the great hall. And she was hungry.

"Oh, lass. You look beautiful. If your coloring was hers, I'd think your mother was looking back at me." Her father's voice was thick, his teal eyes misty.

Ansley's heart ached for a reason other than Leargan.

Mother.

She'd been so young when she'd died. Her mother

had been tall and slender, with blonde hair and brown eyes. Gorgeous. And her father had adored his wife.

Ansley nodded, chewing her bottom lip, unable to speak for a moment. After chiding herself to pull it together, she looked her father up and down, smiling. "You don't look so bad yourself, Captain."

Dressed in a fine dark brown doublet and matching breeches, he had a fancy decorative dirk at his waist instead of his usual broad sword, and his normally unruly red hair was straight and combed, bound by a leather strap at the back of his neck. Murdoch had even trimmed his beard. Her father looked turns younger.

Handsome.

"Thank you." He gave a lopsided smile and offered his arm.

She stared, freezing in the doorway.

Leargan.

It was the other captain's arm she should be on. The man she loved. Right?

His dark eyes had been full of so much pain that afternoon in the great hall. Had it been real?

I miss you. His words reverberated in her head and she fought the urge to close her eyes. Ansley missed him, too. So much.

"Are you all right, love?" her father asked.

His deep voice jolted her, and she reached for him, movements jerky. "Aye." Ansley cleared her throat. "I'm fine, Da."

"Love…"

She swallowed a groan.

He didn't continue until their eyes met. "What happened between you and Leargan?"

Her vision blurred and she averted her gaze until a large calloused hand gently forced her chin back around. "Nothing, Da."

"Nonsense, lass."

Ansley clenched her jaw and pushed his fingers away

from her face. "I don't wish to discuss it."

Murdoch grunted, narrowing his eyes.

She squirmed. "Let's just enjoy the feast. Can you let it go? Please?"

"For now," her father allowed.

Her stomach fluttered.

That was too easy.

Sir Murdoch Fraser *didn't* let things go.

Ansley stared into eyes that matched her own.

"You cannot avoid things forever." *You will talk to me,* was implied.

She sighed and ignored the unspoken promise. Hadn't bought very much time. "How's Xander?" she blurted.

Murdoch harrumphed, but a ghost of a smile played at his lips. "The same mangy flea-ridden, oversized tomcat he always is."

Ansley gave a genuine grin. Her father would never admit it, but the orange and gold striped cat she'd rescued thirteen long turns ago was more Murdoch's cat than he'd ever been Ansley's.

He'd attached himself to her father not long after she'd brought him home. Tolerated her as a child, but Xander had always been all about her da. He always purred louder for her father than she'd ever coaxed even from lavish affection.

When she'd bonded with Ali, Xander had totally ignored her. Then again, Ali had been rather obnoxious to the cat as a cub.

"I miss him," she said.

Her father grunted. "I don't see why. He's getting crotchety in his old age."

Ansley giggled and patted her father's broad chest. "Even more like you, huh, Da?"

Murdoch threw his head back and bellowed a laugh. "I should've thrown him out of the cottage turns ago."

It was an empty threat and they both knew it. Her

father's blue-green eyes danced when their gazes met. No doubt Xander slept with her father in his bed. But she wasn't brave enough to remark on it.

"Let's go, Da." She did want to enjoy the evening. Ansley would have to stick to her father like glue to avoid Leargan.

Ignoring the agony that threatened to cave her chest, she stood tiptoed to press a kiss to her father's bearded cheek before they headed down the corridor.

Chapter Thirty-one

nsley allowed her father to walk her to the dais, kissing him on the cheek again before he bowed to her, Cera and Aimil, then took his leave. The duchess beamed, and Aimil waved as Ansley took her seat next to them.

"Hello there," Cera said, grinning. The duchess' expression was much too cunning, disguised by the friendly smile.

What's she up to?

As Ansley and her father had passed by Leargan, she hadn't missed that his dress-doublet was dark green with stitched gold embossed accents. They were matched. Having couples dress alike was something Queen Morghyn was fond of doing.

Cera and was supposed to be on *her* side. Aimil, too. They were *supposed* to be as mad at Leargan as Ansley was.

She'd gotten over her hurt regarding Cera knowing about the scroll rather quickly. After all, they'd been friends — more like sisters — since they were fourteen.

They'd taken turns holding her while she cried the first night, and then the second after Leargan had betrayed her.

Ansley's stomach tightened.

Not now. I will have *a pleasant evening.*

"What's wrong?" Cera's whisper snapped her back into her own skin.

"Nothing. I'm fine." Both of her friends' expressions spoke of their disbelief, which Ansley ignored. "Thank you for the gown. I truly love it."

"You're welcome."

The two ladies also wore new gowns for the occasion, and of course, looked stunning, even seated.

Cera wore Greenwald colors. Her dress pale green, with intricate silver lace lining the edges of her corseted bodice and waist.

Aimil's garment also denoted her Province of birth; an Ascovan deep red gown with a navy blue sash at the waist, accentuating her pregnancy, but it just made her glow.

"Have you seen Avril? I put her in light blue since she said that was her favorite. I personally think it has something to do with the color of Roduch's eyes. No matter, she looks gorgeous. As do you, Ansley." Cera reached for her hand.

"You both do, as well."

The duchess grinned and Aimil nodded thanks.

"Oh, there's Avril," Aimil gestured toward the personal guard's table.

Ansley smiled when the younger girl caught her eye and inclined her head. She returned the gesture.

Avril *did* look stunning in the pale blue gown. Happy. The dress shimmered, the material iridescent as it caught the light. Cera had done well for the girl. She stayed close to Roduch, smiling when the large knight leaned down to press a kiss to her cheek. Like Leargan, the blond warrior's decorative dress matched Avril.

Ansley ignored Leargan, even as her eyes zoned in on him against her will. He was talking to Dallon and Alasdair.

"It'll be all right, Ans." Cera squeezed her arm.

She bit her lip to stave off tears and met her friend's gray eyes. She *had* to stop being so transparent.

Aimil smiled and patted her hand.

Ansley reached for a goblet and sipped wine, needing a distraction. Sweetness exploded on her tongue and warmth spread as she swallowed. "I will have a good time tonight."

"Aye. We all will," Aimil said. Her dark gaze wandered, and Ansley's followed, resting on the duke and Tristan as they entered the great hall. Both wore doublets that matched their wives.

Ansley groaned.

"What?" Cera asked, eyes wide and a fair impression of innocence.

"Matching," Ansley said.

Aimil giggled.

"As you well know, I stole the idea from the queen. But there's no harm in matching those who belong together." Her eyes spoke volumes.

A lump rose in Ansley's throat and her breath caught. *Nay.*

Wasn't Cera on her side? Hadn't she been mad at Leargan just that morning? Why had her friend changed her mind?

Aimil cleared her throat, judiciously averting her gaze.

Aimil, too?

Ansley closed her eyes, sucking in air for the hundredth time that night. Her chest ached, heart pounded.

Am I on my own?

"Good evening, my love," Jorrin said, dropping a kiss on his wife's cheek when he'd stepped up to her chair.

Cera's warm smile could have split her face.

"Hello, Ansley, Aimil." The duke inclined his head and winked. Tall and broad, the pale green hue of Greenwald looked good on him, making the sapphire of his eyes even more startling. Tapered ears and high cheekbones added to his attraction. His ebony hair was a little mussed, as if he'd come in from the wind.

Jorrin was beyond handsome, but the way he and Cera were looking at each other made Ansley hurt even more.

For one not born to nobility, he looked the part.

However, from what Ansley had heard and seen since coming to Greenwald, her friend's husband made a fine duke.

"Where did my husband suddenly disappear to?" Aimil asked.

She was hit with another pang of envy, then berated herself as guilt crept up from the pit of her stomach. Her friends were *happy*.

That really is a good thing.

"I believe one of the maids had need of him for a sick child. He said he'd be right back."

"Whose child is ill?" Cera's words held concern.

"I'm not sure, but he or she will be healed shortly. No worries, love."

"You're right, of course. I don't like the idea of any child being sick."

"Tristan will make sure no one else falls ill," Aimil said.

After everyone had gathered in the great hall, the duke stood and gave welcome for the king and his men.

King Nathal also spoke, and Ansley's heart pounded with every word. Would he announce her betrothal?

She'd heard about Cera and Jorrin's formal betrothal being decreed at a feast celebrating the defeat of Lord Varthan. It was common knowledge she and Leargan *had been* betrothed, but she didn't want the painful reminder of why her father and the king had come to Greenwald. Her respiration didn't return to normal until all the men were seated. He'd not said a word.

Before long, all of Morag's women poured into the great hall with laden trays.

Ansley looked at the steaming cut of steak on her plate. The tempting scent teased her nose, and she couldn't wait to enjoy it. She glanced at her father, who was seated next to her, and exchanged a smile with him.

Reaching for her knife, she made quick work of slicing the tender meat. She placed a piece in her mouth, ready to savor the flavor on her tongue. Bile rose and she fought the urge to vomit. After chewing quickly, she forced it down her throat, unable to hold back a cough that sounded more like a choke.

Alarmed gazes darted her way, and her father's large hand swallowed her shoulder. "Are you all right?" he demanded.

"Do you need me?" Tristan asked.

She cleared her throat and accepted the goblet of water Cera pressed into her hand. "Nay, but thank you."

At the same time, her father barked, "Aye."

"I'm fine, Da." Ansley ignored his searching gaze as heat settled in her cheeks.

"Are you sure?" Murdoch asked.

"Aye. It went down the wrong way. Finish eating." She grabbed her fork. Wanted everyone to stop staring—especially Leargan. Although she'd not looked in his direction, she could *feel* the worry in his dark gaze.

He was seated next to the king, three chairs away and across the table. It didn't matter how far away he was. Ansley *always* knew where Leargan was.

Dammit.

She studied the contents of her plate, but her appetite was gone.

Cera patted her hand, and their eyes met. Concern wasn't the only thing in her friend's steel gaze, but she ignored the obvious questions.

Her stomach rebelled against the two following attempts at eating the steak, so Ansley gave up.

What's wrong with me?

Sipping water helped, and she was able to eat two slices of warm bread.

Laughter and lively conversation surrounded her, but Ansley sank into her chair, her body heavy and hungry, despite her lack of desire—or apparent ability—to eat. Since when did she have a finicky tummy?

The duchess kept shooting her looks, her expression

calculating, but she did her best to disregard her.

Over and over, Ansley's gaze collided with Leargan's. Hurt rushed her every time. His dark eyes were bothered, questioning, but she didn't let it affect her.

She didn't speak much, answering when someone spoke to her, and forcing a smile when required. Perhaps everyone believed she was having a pleasant evening.

When the music started, people drifted from the tables to the dance floor, couples holding each other close. She looked away from happy smiles and kisses pressed to cheeks, sweet looks passing between men and women, even those she called friends.

Pretended not to watch Leargan as he rose and pushed his chair in, slipping from the dais behind the king and her father. The three of them stayed together, stopping by the personal guard's table to talk to Niall and his wife.

One of the younger men of the personal guard—Ansley thought his name was Teagan—stepped over to join them, one of the king's men with him. The knight looked enough like Teagan to be his father.

Aimil's giggle caught her attention as Tristan bowed lavishly and bid her to dance.

Cera and Jorrin also headed to the dance floor, exchanging a loving smile that made her feel even worse.

So much for a nice evening.

"Mistress Ansley."

She met a pair of leaf green eyes and managed a genuine smile for the young knighted mage. "Sir Lucan." Ansley inclined her head.

His cheeks went pink. "I was wondering…would dance with me?"

"Aye, I'd like that." She rose and placed her hand in the lad's.

His blush deepened, but he gave a half bow and led her to the dance floor, stopping not far from Jorrin and Cera.

The duchess caught her eye over his head and

winked.

The song was a slow love ballad and Ansley looked away from her friend, tucked into her husband's chest, his arms holding her close. She focused on the lad trying to pull her to him, and gave Lucan an encouraging smile.

His awkwardness was endearing. She took his hand and gently settled at her waist. Lucan jumped, but moved closer as they swayed. He averted his gaze, and she grinned.

He was almost as tall as her five feet ten inches, but his frame was slender. She sensed strength in him and not just magic. Lucan was building muscle with training. He'd only fill out with age. Handsome and sincere, he was a sweet lad that would no doubt become a good man.

They found a rhythm soon, and Ansley found herself thoroughly enjoying his company. Lucan was soft spoken, but witty and funny, and she danced with him through the next two songs, too.

Her father stepped in after that, and she liked dancing with him as well. Although he was a knight, he'd never been much of a courtier, so Murdoch was almost as awkward as the lad had been, in a different way. But it was very nice of her father to take time to dance with her.

Unwillingly, her gaze kept finding Leargan. He danced with no one, but he was moving about the room, talking to anyone and everyone who stopped him or called with a smile. His position as captain of Cera's guard made his company desirable, as much as who he was as a person.

However, she didn't see him speak with any females alone. If he was waiting for an opportunity to ask her to dance, he was going to be disappointed. It mattered not if the whole room knew them betrothed. Ansley wouldn't be that close to the man she was no longer going to marry. Her heart would be unable to endure it.

Before she could take a seat, Alasdair asked her to dance, bowing with a charming flourish that made her grin. She couldn't refuse him or the twinkle in his blue eyes. He was very handsome in his blue doublet and fine navy breeches.

He pulled her close to his well-muscled chest, and Ansley pretended not to feel Leargan's fiery gaze as they twirled past him.

Alasdair's touch was firm, but nowhere near inappropriate, yet jealousy was written all over Leargan's face. Alas was either ignoring his captain or didn't notice.

He sat with a few men of the personal guard, watching.

She couldn't look away either, no matter how she ordered herself to do so. Distraction caused her to miss a dance step and nearly tromped Alasdair's foot only halfway through the lively tune. Her face warmed when she met his blue gaze and she apologized.

He wore a lopsided grin. "No problem." He steadied her with a hand on her forearm. "Are you all right?"

Ansley nodded.

The knight's gaze became troubled and he studied her face. "Let's get you in a chair and something to drink. You look flushed."

"I do?"

"Aye. Are you sure you're all right?"

Nodding again made the room spin, and Alasdair slipped an arm around her shoulders, pinning her to his side.

"Easy." He guided her off the dance floor and pressed her into the nearest chair. "I'm getting Lord Dagget."

Before she could protest, the knight disappeared into the crowd.

Cera appeared in front of her, a goblet in her hand. "Ans, are you all right? Alasdair said you almost fainted."

"I did not."

"You *are* pale. Here. Water."

"I've been dancing for over an hour. I'm fine. Everyone needs to quit fussing over me."

The duchess' expression brooked no argument, so

Ansley took the water and sipped.

"I'm fine," she repeated feebly. A yawn took her by surprise as fatigue made her limbs heavy. "I think I'll just go to bed."

Her friend studied her, then nodded. "Jorrin," Cera called. In a moment, the half-elfin duke appeared at his wife's side. "Can you escort Ansley to her room?"

"Sure, love."

Ansley sputtered. "I'll find my da."

Cera's gaze swept the great hall. "Sir Murdoch isn't here."

She groaned. The king and Leargan were missing from view as well. That couldn't be good. "Well, it's not necessary. I can find my own quarters." The great hall whirled as she stood.

The duke grabbed her arm, the only thing that kept her from landing in a heap on the floor. "Whoa."

"Looks like it is necessary." Cera's tone was worried and her brow knitted tight.

She didn't like the appraising expression that settled on the duchess' face, though the redhead said nothing.

"Let's get you to your room." Jorrin tucked her hand into his elbow and threw a glance at his wife.

She had no energy to argue, so Ansley sighed. She was tired and hungry. The long day and light meal was getting to her. Obviously she was coming down with something.

Cera looped her arm in her free one, and the duke and duchess escorted her from the great hall.

Ansley wouldn't have been able to get away if she'd tried.

Jorrin bid her goodnight and excused himself, letting Ali slip out of her rooms as he left. Her wolf would find Trikser and Isair and the three would likely go hunting.

She didn't fight Cera helping her undress, yawning as soon as her sleeping chemise replaced the gown and settled over her body.

"In bed with you." Her friend tucked her in as if she was a child.

"Tell my father I'm fine, please," Ansley said with another wide yawn. "I don't want him bursting in here."

"You should see Tristan in the morning."

"Just tired. Be fine with a good night's sleep. Long day." She ignored the disagreement in her expression.

Cera's mouth opened and closed, as if she was going to say something, but changed her mind. She gave a curt nod. "Goodnight, Ans. Sleep tight."

"Goodnight. Tell Jorrin thanks. And I really did have a lovely time."

"I will, and I'm glad. Sweet dreams."

"Thanks," Ansley muttered.

She was asleep before Cera even closed the chamber door.

Chapter Thirty-Two

Lucan he could handle. But Alasdair?

Logic told Leargan his friend had innocent intentions in asking Ansley to dance, but seeing her in another man's arms—even on a dance floor—grated. He growled.

Artan paused. "Captain?" The gruff voice of his friend had his head swinging around.

What had the knight said, anyway?

He met Artan's dark eyes, avoiding the burn scar that consumed the right side of his face.

The man didn't like eye contact—even from a longtime companion. The whole right side of the knight's body was scarred from burns—his own fire magic gone horribly wrong when they were small lads.

Artan was from Ascova, brought back to Terraquist by the king, like Leargan. A man of few words, but he'd always been a friend. Always fought by his side.

"Sorry," Leargan said.

"Alas isn't foolish enough to try to take your woman."

Damn.

He'd noticed where Leargan's gaze had been glued since Alasdair had approached the love of his life. He cleared his throat. "I know."

"You should go get her."

He muttered a nonresponse, and the knight said nothing more, swirling the ale in the stein in front of him before taking a sip.

Kale and Bowen were seated next to them, engaged in a lively conversation that neither Leargan nor Artan was a part of.

Teagan had left the table moments before with his father, Tarmon, one of the king's knights.

Padraig and Niall were dancing with their wives.

Roduch and Avril had retired for the night. The trial was in the morning, and despite the joyous feast, no doubt it weighed heavily on their minds.

Dallon, too, was gone. Probably curled up with a willing woman somewhere.

It was surprising Artan had even attended the feast. The knight wasn't known for being social. Beyond time spent training with the knights of the guard, he stayed in his quarters. Kept to himself. Because of his scars, he never bathed with the men after a long day on the fighting yard. He never accompanied their brothers when they went wenching.

Artan's dark eyes darted to the left and Leargan couldn't help but follow. A petite, fair-haired maid placed empty trenchers on a tray. When she looked their direction, she flashed a shy smile. His friend stared at the pretty girl.

Shock rolled over Leargan. She'd been looking at *Artan,* not Leargan. Wearing a smile, not a cringe, as she regarded him. Locked eyes with him.

Good for Artan.

He was a fine knight, a hell of a warrior, and a good man. People tended to retreat from him, not giving him a chance, judging the scars. Especially women. Personality kept most females in fear of him. His friend had become gruff over the turns.

If the girl could see the man, not the horrid markings on the knight's body, good for her. Good for *them.* Let Artan, too find someone in Greenwald.

Leargan fought the urge to close his eyes as pain rolled over him in waves.

Ansley.

She still moved with Alas on the dance floor, graceful and elegant despite the required speed of the lively group song. At least he didn't have to endure watching his friend hold her close during a love ballad.

His breath had caught when he'd seen her enter the great hall on her father's arm.

Gorgeous. Her hair was in intricate braids, and Ansley's gown a dark green, the same color of the soft doublet Jorrin had insisted he wear to the feast. Lord Aldern had showed up at his door, pushing the garment at him, ignoring his questions.

Obviously, Lady Cera had taken a page from Queen Morghyn's book and matched them.

Too bad Ansley hated him.

Hadn't spoken a word to him all night, even during the meal at the head table on the dais.

Leargan's heart had stopped when she'd appeared to choke. He'd wanted to rush to her side. But her father was right there—proving to be an oversized buffer—and he hadn't been able to get close to her all evening.

Not that she'd let him anyway. Ansley had made it clear that afternoon that she still thought he was a liar.

Still hated him.

"Leargan." The king's deep voice took his attention.

"Sire?" His legs pushed him to standing of their own accord.

Sir Murdoch was at the king's side. Both men appraised him. The king's expression held concern, but Ansley's father's was tight, suspicious.

"Come, lad." King Nathal beckoned with his hand.

Leargan looked away, meeting Artan's dark eyes, but the other knight only inclined his head. A gesture he returned as he left the table, nodding to Bowen and Kale as well.

He gulped, then chided himself.

It's not like King Nathal will let him kill you.

But he felt as if was headed to the gallows as he walked to Jorrin's ledger room with two very large men.

"So, what's this all about?" Sir Murdoch asked

without preamble, glaring at Leargan.

King Nathal cleared his throat as he settled in Jorrin's chair. "Your lass is stubborn." He gestured for them to sit.

Leargan was antsy, but one didn't refuse the king, so he sat in the very chair he'd been in when the duke had presented him with the scroll.

Ansley's father remained standing, his thick arms crossed over his impossibly broad chest. Sir Murdoch made a face that he couldn't decipher, then gave a curt nod. "She is much like her father."

The king chuckled.

He sucked in a breath, but his former captain didn't relax as he looked to him, and back at King Nathal.

Should he say something?

Nay.

King Nathal seemed like he was going to lead the conversation, and Leargan was happy to let him do so.

"Ansley believes that Leargan's intentions are solely because of my disguised order."

Leargan cleared his throat and Ansley's father's teal gaze shot to him. "I was less than upfront about the scroll…the order."

"I suspected she wouldn't take too kindly to my interference," Sir Murdoch said, "But the lass is my heart, and I want her happy. I thought *you* could make that happen." The last part of his statement was an accusation.

He bit back a wince. *Truth.* Time to tell his former captain the truth. "I want to make her happy, sir. I love her."

The man gave a curt nod. "Good."

That was *it*? Only one word to say about an uncomfortable confession?

Leargan blinked. Searching for the right words, he forced his mouth to remain moving. "She feels if I was dishonest about the scroll, I don't actually want the marriage, or her. I was honest with her *before* I gave it to her. I told her I *wanted* to marry her. I've never lied to her."

"And?" Her father's one word was demand and order at the same time.

"She doesn't believe me. All but called me a liar. Convinced I'm only following orders." His gaze darted to the king, but the man only nodded encouragingly. "She was furious with us all, Lady Cera and Jorrin, too. Forgiven some, obviously."

Too bad I wasn't included.

"Would expect no less from my lass." One corner of Sir Murdoch's mouth rose, and Leargan wanted to growl.

He's amused?

He took a deep breath, then another and closed his eyes. Weakness was something these two men had trained him to *never* show. But here he was, about to *beg* his former captain's help. "I don't know what to do. I want to marry her." Leargan dropped his voice. "I love Ansley more than my own life."

King Nathal reached for his forearm and squeezed.

He gave his foster father a grateful nod and met Sir Murdoch's eyes. For the first time, he read sympathy in the man's gaze. At least his former captain knew he was sincere. Believed he loved Ansley. Would help him get her back?

"If I order her to marry you, she'd likely run away." He stroked his neatly trimmed red beard.

"Aye, I agree." The king's tone was thoughtful.

"You'll have to wait until she comes to you, lad," his would-be-father-by-marriage said.

"What?"

"Ansley will have to come to you—but she will, have no doubt," her father insisted.

Leargan sagged, the high back of the chair biting into his shoulders, but he clung to the sting. Needed it. No way he could sit and do nothing. He wanted Ansley by his side, in his arms, in his bed. He missed her so much he ached.

"Hear me out, lad," Sir Murdoch said softly. "I know my daughter. She loves you, which is why I proposed this whole thing—though I had no idea you both would turn it into such a debacle. Ansley's stubborn, but she's smart as well. She won't be able to ignore her feelings for you forever."

"How long do I wait? I can't do *nothing*." Desperation was almost enough to make him come clean about taking Ansley's innocence—almost.

Her father would either kill him or have them before a priest within the hour. The king's plan was more prudent for his hide. Leargan didn't want her forced—no matter how much he wanted her. She'd hate him for the rest of their lives, as Ansley had so aptly said that afternoon.

"You have made it clear how you feel, lad." King Nathal gave him another squeeze. "Let things fall into place, now."

"How?" His eyes darted back and forth between the two men.

"I shall talk to her lad, worry not. You have my support."

Leargan reached for Sir Murdoch's outstretched hand and shook it, relief washing over him.

"You have mine as well," King Nathal said.

"Thank you, Sir Murdoch, your Majesty." He was able to give a genuine smile.

"You're welcome, lad. If I didn't believe you'd make a fine husband for my daughter, I would've never suggested it."

He flushed with pleasure. He was in the same room with his old mentor, not his beloved's angry father. All was not lost after all.

How long before Ansley felt the same and was back in his arms?

Chapter Thirty-three

Roduch's leg jumped. He swallowed a gulp and shifted in his chair. As the second round of nerves rose from the pit of his stomach, he landed a hand so hard on his thigh it smarted, but he clung to the sting.

Leargan said nothing as he caught his captain's gaze, but his eyes were calm. The younger man inclined his head and Roduch took a deep breath, chiding himself to sit still.

What was keeping the king? The waiting was killing him.

Half the Province was already assembled in the great hall.

The little bastard's trial would be public, and many of his victims had filed into Castle Aldern to witness his demise.

Avril had testified to the king privately, with only King Nathal, the duke, and Roduch present. No one wanted to put more pressure on her than necessary, and she'd been petrified when she'd seen the king up close.

King Nathal was a huge man, both in physical body, and in personality. He'd been very gentle with her, but it'd taken quite a bit of coaxing to get her to relax even a little bit.

Roduch had held her hand with his arm around her shoulders the whole time. She'd leaned into him and spoken softly. But no tears this time. He'd been proud of her for that.

The king had been stoic in reaction to her words, but Roduch had known the big man for a long time.

King Nathal was angry. Seething; although beyond

the clenched bearded jaw and blazing pale blue eyes, he'd held himself back as to not scare the lass.

Hopefully, it had sealed Tynan Mont's fate.

Death sentences were rare, but the penal territory on the continent, in the Province of Dalunas, was widely known for its cruelty. Just the place for the little bastard.

In Dread Valley—as it'd been dubbed by inhabitants—Tynan Mont would be clothed and fed, sheltered in a tent. The rest would be up to him, including getting along with his *neighbors*. Would the coward even last a sevenday?

The sorry excuse for a man had made Avril's life a living hell for four turns. Someone in Dalunas needed to return the favor. Even show him what being on the receiving end of rape was like. Women were not sent to Dread Valley. The men housed there *made do.* Just what Tynan Mont needed.

Lords Dagget and Aldern arrived together, both returning Roduch's nod as they took their seats next to him and the captain, to the right of the dais, among the group of chairs designated for them away from the rest.

The healer would testify to Avril's wounds—old and new—the night she'd been found.

"It'll be all right, Roduch." Lord Aldern's voice took his attention. No doubt the empathic duke could feel his nerves.

"Aye," he muttered.

"Should be quick, too," Lord Aldern said.

Roduch nodded, ignoring the low voices of his lords and captain as they discussed what was to come, and his eyes swept the great hall. The normal rows of tables had been replaced with chairs for spectators.

Two tables had been placed horizontally in front of the dais, opposite of their normal direction. Seated at one, Keir, the old steward, was next to Gamel, the lad he was training to be the head steward of Greenwald. They were setting up parchments and inkwells and other utensils required for the official recording of the trial.

Wax for the king's seal was already being heated. Roduch couldn't wait to see it on Tynan Mont's proclamation of doom.

"Who's going to advocate for the bastard?" He glanced back at the duke.

The duke snorted. "I gathered three from Greenwald Main, Atticus Brehon included. Mont declined all choices."

"Atticus Brehon himself?" Roduch whispered.

"Evidently the man wasn't *adequate*." Lord Dagget smirked.

"So…he doesn't have an Advocate?" He met the duke's eyes. Shock rolled over him. Tynan Mont was stupider than he'd imagined.

"No. He chose to represent himself."

"What an idiot," Leargan said, shaking his head.

"King Nathal will still be fair," Lord Aldern said.

"Of course," Roduch said.

Silence descended with the arrival of the king. He sauntered up the main aisle with determination written over his face, his tawny hair shifting as he moved. King Nathal was dressed elegantly in the blue and gold colors of Terraquist, the roaring lion of his seal etched into his decorative chest plate.

Sir Murdoch was at his right, a hand on the hilt of his massive sword. The Terraquist blue over tunic marked him as one of King Nathal's personal guard, but the gold woven rope shoulder knot denoted his rank of captain.

The king and his captain nodded to Roduch and his companions before they both went up the stairs to the dais. The head table had been removed like the rest, and King Nathal took the lone chair at its center.

Sir Murdoch stood beside him as still as a statue, expression implacable.

They didn't have to wait long for Tynan Mont. The clinking of chains and shuffling feet entered the great hall as a commotion breaking the relative quiet.

Dallon and Merrick were on either side of the short portly man, each with a grip on his upper arms. He wasn't fighting them, but his expression was dark.

Alasdair and Laith trailed behind, hands on swords and ready to act if necessary.

Blessed Spirit, Roduch wanted to pound the little bastard. The rough handling on the day they'd arrested him hadn't been nearly enough.

"This is outrageous! Malicious slander," Tynan Mont sputtered as the knights forced him into a chair at the table opposite the stewards in front of the dais. His shackles clanged as they bumped the hard wood.

Merrick and Dallon stayed close, both ignoring the little bastard's open glare.

Alasdair and Laith flanked them, all four knights lined up and ready to pound Avril's former husband.

Good thing Leargan had forbidden Roduch from being one of Tynan Mont's escorts.

"You will get your chance to speak. That time is not now," King Nathal boomed from the dais.

Tynan Mont jumped in the chair, paling.

It gave Roduch some satisfaction.

"Where is the whore wench, anyway? Don't I have a right to face my accuser? Lying bitch."

Roduch growled.

His captain and Lord Aldern gripped his forearms, keeping him in his seat.

"Easy," Leargan whispered. "Let King Nathal lead. You know he's more than capable."

"Silence, Master Mont, or I shall have you silenced." The king's roar had Roduch's breath exiting on a whoosh.

Avril's former husband sank down in the chair.

Merrick cracked his knuckles, and Dallon shifted closer to the coward, resting a hand on the back of his chair.

Good.

His brothers were ready. Probably wouldn't even require the king's order.

"Who is your Advocate, Master Mont?" the king asked when the room had quieted.

"I do not have one, your Majesty."

"Why is that? I was informed that Lord Aldern, Duke of Greenwald and your liege lord, presented you will several candidates."

"No, your Majesty."

"Nay?" King Nathal raised a thick tawny eyebrow. "Are you calling Lord Aldern a liar?"

A murmur went through the crowd. There were a few muffled laughs.

"N-n-n-o," Tynan Mont stammered. "They did not please, Majesty."

"Very well," the king said. "Are you ready to hear your charges?"

"Lies," the bastard yelled.

The king leaned forward, his expression deadly, eyes locked onto Tynan Mont. "*I* am the one who decides what is a lie, Master Mont."

"Yes, your Majesty," the little bastard demurred, visibly shaking. He lowered his head.

King Nathal gestured to the two stewards.

Keir rose, clearing his throat and unrolling a large scroll. He faced Tynan Mont, squaring his aged shoulders as he stood tall. "Master Tynan Mont of Greenwald, you are hereby charged with murder of your blood kin with the purposes of forging inheritance, blackmail of those beholden to you, theft from the same by means of misappropriation of gold and goods along the misuse of magic that is not your own. You are also charged with breaking your marriage contract of your child bride, Avril Larange. Your written agreement to consummate your marriage upon your wife reaching the age of eight and ten was egregiously disregarded. You are also being charged with repeated rapes, physical abuse and neglect of your considered wife." The old steward sat as the crowd in the great hall gasped and whispered, his pose as regal as the king's.

The lad, Gamel, paled out beside him.

"How do you answer these charges, Master Mont?" the king asked, his booming voice once again causing Avril's former husband to jump.

"I was presented with documentation that my marriage has been dissolved by my liege lord." His tone referencing Lord Aldern was an implied insult.

"You have not answered your charges." King Nathal's voice was hard and his eyes narrowed.

"I am innocent. I have been slandered by the barren whore I had as wife."

Roduch snarled and shot to his feet, his sword half-drawn.

"Silence," the king roared at the same time.

Lord Aldern and Leargan rose, pressing him back into the chair after Lord Dagget disarmed him.

Tynan Mont's gaze locked onto him, scorching with its intensity.

Roduch glared right back, daring the man to make a move. Any of his brothers would knock him on his arse.

"It is the law that any underage person, male *or* female given in marriage prior to the legal age has the right to renounce their marriage when they reach eighteen turns old. Your former wife's choice to do so has *nothing* to do with your charges. Understand that, here and now," King Nathal commanded.

"Is adultery not a crime?" Tynan Mont demanded, his eyes still boring into Roduch's.

Roduch growled, but stayed seated, hands of his captain and the duke resting on his shoulders.

"As there has been no evidence of infidelity, you shall not further slander Avril Larange in my presence," the king ordered.

The trial progressed, and Leargan was called by the king and questioned about finding Avril with Ansley on the road, and confirmed that she'd called for help.

Ansley had also testified privately to the king, so she was also spared public questioning.

After the captain, Lord Dagget testified about her injuries, including the evidence he'd discovered about the rapes, and the two broken ribs that had gone untreated, in addition to the broken nose and fresh wounds covering her body that night.

"Master Mont," Lord Dagget said, "I found no physical evidence that Mistress Larange is barren. So, it looks as if *you* are the problem."

Tynan Mont's face reddened and the little bastard glared at the healing lord.

Lord Dagget rose and bowed as the king dismissed him.

Roduch smiled. It was good to know the gentle healing lord could be intentionally vindictive when necessary.

As Harlan Pelham and his wife answered King Nathal's summons to testify, their former employer's eyes shot daggers even before they spoke.

Dallon shifted on his feet, *'accidently'* knocking the little bastard in the back of the head.

Roduch bit back a grin, but Tynan turned his glare on his brother instead of the man's former steward and his trembling wife.

The king stood and bowed at the conclusion of all testimony and the reading of written statements from other witnesses and victims, retreating from the great hall to make his decision.

Roduch closed his eyes, trying not to hear Avril screaming in his mind while trapped underneath that piece of trash. He didn't want to see her, scared and small, cowering after a rape, enduring a beating. It hurt too much.

He shook the thoughts from his head, focusing on the rise of voices in the great hall as everyone speculated. The buzz of conversation in the large room was loud, and he sat on the edge of his seat, staring at Avril's former husband. He wanted to pound his face in—no he wanted to geld him and watch him bleed out. Roduch made a fist and growled.

"Easy," Lord Aldern said, resting a hand on his forearm. "He'll get what is coming to him." The duke's expression was pained.

"I'm counting on it." Roduch nodded and forced himself to calm. His emotions were affecting the duke.

"I have no doubt," Lord Dagget said.

He locked onto the healer's hazel eyes and leaned toward the lord. "Did you mean what you said? That Avril can have children?"

"Aye. I saw nothing in her body keeping her from it. The...rapes..." Lord Dagget winced, "did no permanent physical damage."

"So why didn't she...conceive...all this time?" The words were hard for him to get out. His heart thumped, his chest aching.

"Sometimes it's better to leave some questions up to the Blessed Spirit," Lord Dagget said gently.

"Take things slow with her, Roduch," Lord Aldern said, squeezing his forearm.

The healer nodded agreement, but his captain wore a soft smile, as if Leargan expected nothing else.

"I am." He looked away before glancing back at his lords and captain. "It wouldn't have mattered, you know. I would still want her; even if she couldn't give me children, but it's a relief to know the little bastard didn't take that from her."

Lord Dagget smiled, and Lord Aldern gave him an approving nod.

Leargan patted his forearm.

Emotion threatened to choke him. Roduch blinked and swallowed against the sudden lump in his throat. Blessed Spirit, he loved her. He wanted nothing more than to care for her for the rest of their lives.

Less than an hour later, King Nathal and his captain

strode back into the hall.

The king spoke to Keir and Gamel before whirling around in front of the dais, not mounting the three steps or taking a seat. He raised his chin and squared his wide shoulders, speaking without preamble. "Tynan Mont, I sentence you to no less than thirty turns at the work camp in the penal territory of the Province of Dalunas."

Tynan Mont gasped, his eyes as wide as saucers.

"That amount of time will not replace the lives of your cousin and his family that you stole, but you will have plenty of time to contemplate it. As you know, your marriage has been dissolved, so you are a free man." There were several snickers in the large room. "Since you are the last of your line, your land is forfeit from your family and formally awarded to Master Harlan Pelham and his line in perpetuity. You are never to regain it. If you should make your way back into the borders of Greenwald upon your release in *thirty turns* time, you are to have nothing to do with your former wife, Mistress Avril Larange. You shall never be permitted to hold land on my continent again."

Avril's former husband sputtered, shaking his head and making two tight fists. His shackles rattled.

"Be very well informed, and relieved, that gelding is not a part of my proclamation, Master Mont. I take the mistreatment of women *very* seriously."

The sorry excuse for a man gulped.

"Take him back to the dungeon," King Nathal commanded.

Chains clanged and clinked as Merrick and Dallon dragged the little bastard out of the chair. Tynan Mont was in a shocked stupor, being shoved forward to shuffle his feet.

Alasdair and Laith brought up the rear, and soon they were out of sight.

The crowd started to file out, excited conversations and loud voices dwindling as the great hall emptied.

"I want to be among those that take him to Dalunas,"

Roduch said as he gained his feet. He looked at Lord Aldern, and then at the king.

"That will be up to Lord Aldern," King Nathal said, his voice kind.

"Of course, Roduch," the half-elfin duke said quickly.

He nodded in appreciation and glanced at his captain.

Leargan tilted his head, studying him, but finally, his captain inclined his head.

Roduch released the breath he'd not realized he'd been holding.

"The journey is long. Would you not rather stay with your lass?" The king stepped closer to them.

"I need to see this through. I need to see him interred at Dalunas." He made a fist.

"Very well." One corner of King Nathal's mouth shot up.

"If you'll all excuse me, I need to find Avril," Roduch said.

"She's with Ansley," Sir Murdoch supplied.

Roduch nodded thanks before rushing out of the great hall. He heard a few chuckles.

Chapter Thirty-four

Leargan sighed, leaning against the fence surrounding the training ground, watching his men pair off with the king's men to spar. He'd been invited to join them of course, but he was too busy sulking.

King Nathal, Sir Murdoch and their entourage had been in Greenwald a full sevenday, allowing time to inform the penal territory of its new prisoner's advent; the king had sent a messenger the very day of the trial.

Hell, he was surprised Ansley hadn't volunteered to take Tynan's proclamation and sentence parchment. It was a sure way to stay away from him, but King Nathal had summoned another Senior Rider, a man named Simond. He'd been off to Dalunas without even staying for a meal at Castle Aldern.

She hadn't even looked at him since the night of the feast, even when they'd been in the same room. If her father *had* talked to her, nothing had come of it.

They still weren't married. It was killing him.

Everyone knew she'd rejected him, even if they didn't know why. Worse were the sympathetic looks and sad smiles *everyone* shared with him. Pats on the shoulders and back. He was so transparent, Leargan was surprised no one had given him the *there's-more-than-one-sword-in-the-armory* speech.

He'd always been a private person, but now his love life—or lack thereof—was *very* public. He cringed and gripped the hilt of his sword, growling to himself. He was restless.

Leargan needed...*Ansley*. Since that wasn't possible,

he needed to get away. Get some air. Something to focus on so he could clear his head.

Duties. They'd always saved him before.

He scanned the fighting yard, failing to spot Jorrin or the king. Niall and Sir Murdoch, even Roduch, were no long in sight either. "Damn," he muttered.

Am I too late?

Leargan shoved off the fence, sprinting to where Fia was tied. Without a word to any of his men, he mounted as fast as he could, then kicked his mare toward the castle. "Let's go, lass."

She nickered as she took off, in her element. Her powerful muscles rippled under his thighs and he urged her even faster.

His beloved mount could benefit from getting away, too. It'd been a while since they'd run free together.

He jumped off her back even before they'd stopped in front of the stables, shoving Fia's reins at the surprised lad that'd rushed to meet them in the courtyard. She tossed her head, but the stable boy gained control quickly, and Leargan didn't look back as he ran for the castle.

As he skidded to a stop, he almost toppled over in front of Jorrin's ledger room door. He wrenched it open. Several heads shot up, but he didn't pause as he rushed into the room. "I'm going. As a matter of fact, I'll lead." Leargan caught Niall's eye.

One of his Second's eyebrows shot up, but his shoulders loosened.

The knight was supposed to lead the party to Dalunas. But he could stay in Greenwald with his wife. No doubt Lyde would appreciate him taking her husband's place. The journey would be long and arduous. Likely more than a fortnight total.

Two sevendays I can forget about Ansley.

He sucked in a breath and squared his shoulders, standing taller.

"Leargan?" King Nathal was the first to speak,

crossing his arms over his broad chest.

"I need to lead my men. Niall, you stay here. As my Second. As you should." Leargan looked at his duke, then back at the king. "It makes more sense for me to go. I'm captain."

Surprise and hope rippled across Niall's face. But his longtime friend locked blue eyes with him. "I don't shirk my duties."

"I know. Not saying that. It just…makes more sense for me to go."

You have Lyde. I have…no one.

He ignored the tightness in his chest, blaming it on his sprint into the castle.

His Second stared, gaze intense. His friend knew exactly why he'd volunteered to go, but said nothing. When Niall inclined his head, Leargan smiled and looked at the king.

"I have no issue with this change," King Nathal said. "Jorrin?"

"It is fine with me." The half-elfin duke shrugged.

"When do we leave?" Leargan asked.

Roduch smiled, reclining in the chair he was occupying.

Sir Murdoch and Tristan regarded him silently, both wore expressions of concern.

Leargan ignored them, making eye contact with the man who'd raised him.

"At dawn," the king said. "Murdoch has some route recommendations." He gestured to the detailed map of the Provinces laid out on Jorrin's desk.

"Looks like we have some things to discuss then," Leargan said.

The king nodded.

Sir Murdoch started talking and pointing to landmarks.

Leargan's heart sped up.

Blessed Spirit, please let this work.

"Frankly, Cera, I don't care." Ansley strove for nonchalance when she was really falling apart inside.

The duchess gave her a long look and Aimil snorted from her chair by the fireplace in the Duchess Solar.

Great, she hadn't fooled either of them.

"Well, I thought you'd want to know. Dalunas is a long, hard ride. They'll likely be gone more than a fortnight."

She shrugged, not answering. Maybe by the time Leargan got back, she'd be in Terraquist with her father, forgetting about him. She averted her eyes from her friend's keen gray gaze.

Cera rocked her fussy son and silence fell over them.

Ansley shifted in the chair and ignored the book she'd been pretending to read as Cera nursed Fallon and Aimil was attempting some sort of needlework.

"You two are supposed to be on my side." Her voice was feeble to even her own ears, and she frowned. She swallowed against the lump in her throat and snapped the book closed, rising to go to one of the many windows overlooking the courtyard. Her eyes smarted and she blinked.

She was *so* done with tears.

In her peripheral vision, she noticed Cera set the baby in a rocking cradle by the warm blaze, after pressing a kiss to his dark red curls. Soon, the duchess enfolded her in a hug from behind.

Sighing, Ansley leaned into her as Cera's arms settled around her waist. "Thanks," she whispered.

In less than a minute, Aimil joined their hug, both of them holding her tight.

"We *are* on your side," Cera whispered close to her ear. "But I see two of my friends hurting."

"I'm not talking about this."

Neither of them pushed her; just squeezed her in

comfort.

Ansley closed her eyes, determined not to cry. She'd been in this position, bawling while her best friends held her, too much as of late.

When will it stop?

"I didn't tell you to upset you, but now you've some time to think about things," Cera said.

"There's nothing to think about." She pulled away, whirling to meet the duchess's gaze. "I don't want to talk about this."

Aimil frowned, resting a hand on her rounded tummy.

Cera sighed, her brow knitted tight. "Ansley—"

"Hello." Avril's soft voice caused all three of them to glance to the doorway. She smiled, but it was sad, and guilt crept up from the pit of Ansley's stomach.

The girl had been through so much.

"I'm sorry, Ansley. My issues took your man away." The petite beauty slipped into the warm bright room.

How long was she there?

"He's not my man," she said quickly.

Avril's dark curls danced about her shoulders as she came to them.

"You are at fault for *nothing*," Ansley said, and tears once again threatened. "Leargan is Cera's captain and he…" Her vision blurred, and Avril reached for her.

The gesture surprised her, but she didn't turn the girl away when Avril hugged her tight.

"It'll be all right," she whispered.

Ansley sniffed and pulled back, swiping at her nose. "Aye."

"Everyone and everything will be fine," the duchess said, handing Ansley a soft corner of linen to wipe her face.

They all found chairs around the warm fire, Cera rocking her son's cradle gently. Ansley didn't bother to retrieve the discarded book, but Aimil returned to her project.

"At any rate, I am sorry," Avril whispered, looking into the fire.

The younger girl wasn't apologizing for Leargan being gone, but Ansley ignored that knowledge and forced words out. "There's nothing for you to be sorry about. That man is getting *exactly* what he deserves, and Leargan," her voice broke, but she made herself continue, "is a fine knight. It makes sense that he led his men. It makes sense that Roduch and Lucan went, too."

Avril looked down. Her chest rose and fell as if she'd taken a breath, then she locked her emerald gaze with hers. "Thank you for being so gracious."

"Heh. I'm not gracious."

"I miss Roduch already, very much," she said, cheeks pink.

"You care for him," Cera said.

Avril beamed.

Aimil laughed. "I think that's a yes."

"I…more than care for him," the girl said softly.

Ansley fought the urge to close her eyes as pain hit her in waves.

You're a wretch. Happiness for them should be first and foremost.

She *was* happy for Roduch and Avril. She was just sad for her and Leargan. Guilt warred with envy. Her stomach clenched.

"Good. You deserve a real man," Cera said.

"Thank you." Avril looked down again. "He's so gentle and patient with me…I don't know how I would've survived this without him."

"Roduch is strong and steady. He'll be at your side always," Aimil said.

"I've always been very fond of him." The duchess smiled.

"As have I," Ansley said.

The girl's expression was genuine and open. With her riot of ebony curls loose, and beautiful green eyes bright, she was about as relaxed as she'd ever seen her.

"Thank you," Ansley whispered. "You've made me feel better."

"That's what friends are for." Cera reached for her hand and squeezed.

"I've never really had friends." Avril gazed at each of them. "I'm glad I have some now, and I'm grateful you're letting me stay here, Lady Cera."

The duchess inclined her head. "I'm glad you want to stay."

"I want to stay wherever Roduch is," she admitted, cheeks crimson again.

"Well, I'm glad to hear that, too," Cera said.

Fallon started to squall, and his mother scooped him up, rocking him and whispering until he quieted.

"Even crying, he's beautiful," Avril said.

"Thanks." Cera smiled again as she settled her son against her.

"What do you want, Lady Aimil?" Avril asked. "A boy or a girl?"

Aimil smiled, resting a hand on her tummy. "It doesn't matter to me, but I'm sure Tristan would like a son."

"How about a daughter, to grow up and marry Fallon?" Cera winked.

They all laughed.

"That would be fine, too." Aimil grinned.

Leargan's hurtful threat danced into her mind as she listened to her friends' conversation. She watched Cera stare at the babe in her arms, a warm smile curving her friend's lips.

A little lad with dark hair and big brown eyes running into her open arms popped into her head. Her heart skipped and she frowned.

Nay. That would only make things worse, even if she wanted Leargan's child.

He'd left without saying goodbye. Not that Ansley

had really expected him to reach out to her, but it hurt. Dalunas was far away, and the journey could be dangerous.

What if something happened?

Wait. Forget it.

She didn't care, anyway.

Liar.

"Are you all right, Ansley?" Avril's voice pulled her from her thoughts.

She forced a smile. "Aye, thanks."

"They will come home to us," the girl said, a soft smile on her full mouth.

Ansley flushed. It was like she'd read her mind. "Aye," she muttered.

What else could she say?

Chapter Thirty-Five

nsley counted on her fingertips, sucking in a breath when she came to the undesirable conclusion.

Nay.

Had Leargan cursed her when he'd spoken of a possible child? Or had he just *known*?

Well, there was no *possible* about it. Not even a *probable*. She hadn't bled since the sevenday before she'd been sent to Greenwald.

Dizziness, queasiness, the sporadic inability to hold food down…or not being able to endure *looking* at it from time to time. It all made sense.

She was carrying his child.

Denial hit hard and made her head reel. Her knees buckled and she landed hard on the edge of her bed, chest tight.

Ali whined and nudged her as she scooted closer from her spot on the middle of the sleeping furs.

The caress of her bondmate's head was automatic as tears welled.

Pregnant…carrying *Leargan's* child. The man of her dreams.

Was she happy or sad?

He'd only been gone four days. Ansley missed him so badly she ached. But it wasn't like she'd actually talked to him when he was there, anyway.

Her father was going to kill him if he found out. *When* he found out.

Like he'd said, she couldn't hide the rounding of her belly for the whole of the pregnancy.

If he didn't kill Leargan, Murdoch would drag them in front a priest immediately. She didn't want that...did she? Was she really contemplating raising Leargan's child without him? She closed her eyes, teeth sinking into her bottom lip.

What the hell am I going to do?

The day after the feast, her father and the king had summoned her—cornered her really—to Jorrin's ledger room. Without preamble, Murdoch had told her he supported her marriage to Leargan, and expected them to proceed without delay.

Anger had boiled over, and Ansley had done something she'd never done in her life—yelled at her father. She let him have it, *all* of it. Explained her hurt and shock that he'd meddle in her life when he'd known clearly how she'd felt about Leargan. She hadn't even held her tongue in the presence of the king.

Murdoch had taken her words in stride, crossing his arms over his broad chest, appraising her.

She'd half expected his mouth to be hanging open in shock, but he hadn't said much—neither had King Nathal.

Unfortunately, true to her father's nature, he'd calmly repeated his wish she wed Leargan. That statement was only to be compounded by the fact King Nathal echoed the sentiment. Her da had even had the nerve to tell her it was what *she* wanted.

She'd glared at them both, ignoring the king's *apology* for sending her to Greenwald under the guise of an official message. King Nathal hadn't apologized for *ordering* Leargan to marry her.

Her demand to know if she'd be forced was left unanswered by both oversized men. Her father had spoken his peace. Experience told when he did so, he rarely *ever* changed his mind. Murdoch's feelings on the matter wouldn't differ, no matter how Ansley tried to sway him.

Now...it was different now. There was a child on the way.

She rested a hand over her womb, sucking in a breath, burying her other hand in Ali's thick fur.

The child in her belly had been made in love, even if it was only one-sided. Ansley would love Leargan for the rest of her life…

Tears scalded her cheeks, but she ignored them, hugging her wolf to her side.

Her bond whined and leaned up, licking her face from ear to chin.

"Alllllli," she groaned but was able to give a small smile as she wiped her cheek dry.

The she-wolf thumped her tail on the bed when they made eye contact, and Ansley smirked. Her bondmate was only trying to make her feel better.

She stood and took another deep breath, squaring her shoulders. Cera was expecting her in the Duchess Solar. She needed to pull herself together and pray her stomach remained settled.

Not only was one friend a new mother, the other was carrying a child. Cera and Aimil were intimately familiar with symptoms of pregnancy. If she lost her breakfast when either was in the room, she was doomed. She wasn't ready to tell them.

Definitely didn't want to hear one of Cera's lectures. The duchess had long calmed in her ire about the scroll and Leargan's dishonesty. She wanted Ansley to forgive Leargan.

Ali stayed close as they headed down the corridor to the Duchess Solar. Her emotions took turns shooting up and plummeting. Her bond didn't send any concrete thoughts, but through their magic, Ansley felt her love. Her wolf wrapped her in it like a warm blanket.

She appreciated Ali's silent support, and buried her hand in the she-wolf's thick black fur as they walked.

A wave of nausea hit as soon as she stepped foot in the bright warm room. Ansley ran forward, clutching her stomach and covering her mouth with her free hand.

Looked for something to throw up in.

"Here," Cera said, tossing a small wooden bucket.

She caught it, righted it, and vomited twice. Panted and slid into a seat as the duchess took the bucket away. Thank the Blessed Spirit Cera was the only one in the room.

Ali whined, circling her chair, but Trikser made a wuffing noise from the hearth, and the she-wolf headed over to Cera's bondmate, lying down beside the white wolf.

Ansley thought-sent, admonishing her to stay there. She asserted she was fine, and wiped the moisture from her eyes, glancing up at her friend.

The duchess said nothing, but her gaze was keen. Cera handed her a linen handkerchief and a goblet of water.

"Thanks," Ansley said, sipping water slowly. Her stomach didn't roil or reject it.

Good, a start.

"How long are you going to let this continue?" She cocked her head to the side and sat across from her.

"What?"

Cera gave her a long look. "The king and your father have been here for over a fortnight. That'd make you what...about a month—a month and a half at most—pregnant? You're already sick almost daily. As soon as they get back, tell Leargan and be done with it. Marry the man you love, the father of your child."

Ansley scowled. "Nay." It was no use denying anything. Her friend was much too observant.

"You can't avoid things forever, Ans," she said gently. "I know you're hurt because he kept the scroll from you. And you have *every* right to be upset at the meddling king—I know I was—but it's only a matter of time. Leargan has had *many* talks with your father, and Jorrin told me he's made his intentions to *both* Sir Murdoch and the king very clear. He wants you."

"He doesn't want me; he's following orders. And

besides, he's not even here now. *He* left. *He* volunteered to lead the men."

"Ansley." Cera crossed her arms over her chest.

She winced. The duchess had seen right through her lame attempt at deflection. Ansley wasn't really upset that Leargan had led Tynan Mont's way to prison. It was his job.

"You well know what duty is, and you'd never fault him for it, so nice try. You can't blame him for wanting to see that bastard punished, either. Leargan doesn't lie; has no reason to. If he said he wants you, he wants you. Let this go. Marry him. Be happy. We can even plan the wedding for the day of their return."

Ansley shook her head vigorously.

Cera rolled her eyes. "Your fate is sealed now, anyway. Don't you realize it? Neither the king, nor your father, is stupid. They're both fathers. They *both* know what's going on when a woman can't hold any food and is apparently otherwise healthy. I think you risk Leargan's wellbeing by not being honest. Everyone knows your father's penchant for decorum equals his temper."

Her temples throbbed, and she rubbed them.

Blessed Spirit, Cera's right.

Leargan wasn't a liar. But when he found out about their baby, he *would* insist on marrying her. It was even worse than before.

Duty. Obligation.

Ansley didn't want him like that. She wanted him to want *her.* Needed him to *love* her. Her eyes smarted and she sighed. *No more tears.* "He told me he'd take my child from me."

"He'd never do that to you," Cera said evenly, not even phased by the serious threat. The duchess took a breath, leaning forward to take her hand. "What do you know of Leargan's childhood?"

"He was raised by King Nathal, at Castle Rowan, in Terraquist."

"Right. But, what do you know of his parents?"

"Nothing," Ansley said.

"King Nathal brought Leargan and several other orphaned boys back to Terraquist after the battle of North and South Ascova. The skirmish was quashed quickly, and the control of the Province was put back into Aimil's family's hands, as it should've always been. There were many deaths, including Leargan's parents. His father was a farmer, not a warrior, and only wanted to see his family to safety. Unfortunately, he was struck down. Leargan's mother ran with him in her arms, but didn't get far. She shielded him with her body, saved his life. When King Nathal found him, he was covered in her blood. He was barely four turns old, Ans."

"How do you even know this?"

"Jorrin told me."

"Why are you telling me?"

"I want you to know how important family is to Leargan. He lost his at such a young age. King Nathal raised him, but he's never had a family—blood—of his own. He'll want his child—*your* child—to have both parents."

Ansley averted her gaze. She *hated* how much sense her friend was making. Ignored how her heart hurt for Leargan. Why hadn't *he* ever told her about his parents?

"Leargan's hurting as much as you are," Cera whispered.

"No, he isn't. He doesn't love me."

"Has he told you he doesn't love you?" The duchess' gentle tone brought tears to Ansley's eyes all over again.

"Nay."

"I think he does love you. I also think the way he feels has everything to do with his *volunteering* to be away from you for a sevenday or two. He's hurting, Ans. I don't have to be an empath to know it."

"Then he could've told me instead of lying about the scroll."

"When you confronted him, did he lie?"

She growled, meeting her friend's eyes. "You're supposed to be on *my* side."

Cera quirked a half-smile. "I love you both. You're *both* miserable. It's unnecessary. The moment they get back, tell him you love him. Please." She squeezed Ansley's hand. "Stress is something you don't need. You risk the new life inside you. Do you want this baby?"

She couldn't find her voice, so she just nodded. She wanted her baby—and his father—more than she'd ever wanted anything in her life.

"Good. But your baby will need his father." Cera smiled softly.

Ansley looked down as guilt rushed her. Even before learning about Leargan's past, how could she even have contemplated keeping the man's child from him? It was *wrong*.

Hurt over words he'd flung in anger would never justify it. Besides, he'd already tried to apologize for what he'd said, the day her father and the king had arrived in Greenwald.

Cera was right, about everything, and Ansley *hated* that.

"Is your stubbornness worth life-long unhappiness?" Her voice was just above a whisper. "I know you too well. Even if you left tomorrow and never came back, you'll always love him."

She sighed. *What can I say?*

"Think about your child," the duchess urged. "Would it be fair to keep him or her from Leargan? He's a wonderful man and will be a fantastic father."

She winced, feeling another rush of guilt. "When did you get so wise?"

Cera laughed and rubbed her shoulder. "I don't know about being wise. But I love Jorrin and Fallon more than I ever thought possible. I can't imagine my life without either of them. I think about my parents and sister all the time, but Jorrin and Fallon are my *life*."

"What am I supposed to do? Walk up to him and shout *I love you*? I haven't *really* spoken to him since *before* my father arrived."

"I said some awful things to Jorrin when King Nathal told us to marry and I found out he'd be named Duke of Greenwald. I also made some assumptions that were very wrong. I know admitting you were wrong is tough, but at least it's only to Leargan. He won't say *I-told-you-so*; he's not the type. And I'd bet my best gold coins he loves you. I wouldn't say it if I didn't think it was true."

"Then why didn't he tell me that night?" she whispered. "I asked him why he wanted to marry me, and he *couldn't* answer me. He stared, dumbfounded." Tears spilled, drenching her cheeks. "It…just about killed me. If he loves me…and he'd *told* me, it would've fixed everything. Instead, he threatened to take my child away."

Cera scooted her chair closer and threw an arm around her shoulders. "Maybe he didn't know. Sometimes it takes losing something to tell you how badly you need it…" Their eyes met, and her friend wiped the tears from her cheeks. "I mean, we *are* talking about a man." The duchess grinned.

One corner of Ansley's mouth lifted.

"Oh, look. That was *almost* a smile." She patted her cheek.

Ansley didn't say anything, but their silence was companionable. She sighed and rested her head on her friend's shoulder. "When we made love, he told me he needed me. But I need more than his body. I know he'll love our child. I'm jealous, can you believe it? Leargan will love our baby, but not me." Shrugging, she blinked away new tears.

"Yes, I believe Leargan *will* love your child. But he loves you *already*." Her smile was tender.

Chapter Thirty-Six

Why hadn't he remembered just how damn far away Dalunas was? They'd been gone a whole sevenday. The further from Greenwald they'd gotten, the further Dalunas had seemed. Leargan could've sworn the roads had moved.

He missed Ansley.

Distance was more torture than reprieve. She might not be speaking to him at Castle Aldern, but at least he could lay eyes on her.

Sleep had been elusive every night they'd stopped. When he'd managed to drift off, she haunted his dreams. He'd woken in a cold sweat, his heart pounding, arms empty and aching for her.

Their party *finally* entered Dread Valley's heavily armored gates, passing over two separate draw bridges, a high defense wall, and more than two dozen well-armed guards and marshals.

No one was leaving the place that wasn't supposed to.

The only satisfaction Leargan had was Tynan Mont shrinking down in the prison cart he rode in, lowering his body so only the top of his head was visible through the iron bars.

Avril's former husband was lucky to have made it to the penal territory in one piece. He'd run his mouth the entire way. Gagging him hadn't helped, either.

Roduch's original desire to kill the man wasn't a bad idea.

All his men, including the normally jovial Merrick, had wanted to pound him into the ground. And Leargan had had to threaten Roduch with shackles and disarmament to keep him in his saddle and away from the little bastard.

Waiting in the ledger room for the provost — a burly dark-haired man named Malcolm Graham — to read Tynan Mont's sentencing proclamation was nerve racking.

He was exhausted. His limbs were as heavy as his heart. He wanted to hand Mont over and get out of Dread Valley. The place made his skin crawl.

Leargan wanted to seek a bed. Venue didn't matter, as long as the linens were clean and there was a real pillow.

Malcolm Graham read the mile-long parchment twice, his shaggy brow knitting tighter with each word. At King Nathal's direction, Gamel and Keir had detailed the man's crimes. "So your main talent is blackmail? Murder, too." The man scratched his coal-black beard, gaze boring into Tynan Mont's stooped form. "And you like to torture and rape innocents who are dependent upon you, do you?"

Shoulders caving even further, the sorry excuse for a man lowered his head, his shackles clinking together. Tynan Mont said nothing.

Leargan smirked.

Coward.

Where was the brazen mouth he'd opened freely during their long journey? The gates of Dread Valley had made Tynan Mont a mute.

"Very well. We have a special hell for trash like you." Provost Graham motioned two of his marshals forward.

Dallon and Merrick shoved Tynan Mont.

He stumbled, falling to his knees before the provost.

The burly man looked down at him, wearing a smirk.

The marshals each grabbed Mont by an arm and yanked him to his feet. Avril's former husband yelped, but cut it off quickly.

He flinched as the men jerked him, and they started to walk away. If he didn't move his feet, the shorter man would be dragged.

Roduch harrumphed, crossing his arms over his chest as Mont threw one last look over his shoulder at Leargan and his knights. "Funny, he has nothing to say *now*."

Provost Graham stepped forward, eyes darting to Roduch before meeting Leargan's gaze. "Thank you, Captain Tegran, and thanks to your men and your mage, Sir Lucan, for seeing the prisoner here *safely*." He bowed, a smile on his bearded face. "We shall take over his *care*."

"It was our duty," Leargan said, inclining his head.

"Shall you need lodging for the evening? I can recommend the *Rusty Nail* in Dalunas Main. Funny name, but good food and the prettiest wenches in the Province."

He swallowed against the sudden lump in his throat. He didn't need a *wench*. He needed Ansley. "Thank you. We'll consider it." His voice cracked.

"Mention my name to the innkeeper, Belton Scalar. He'll give you a good rate and his finest rooms. He's my brother-by-marriage."

Their task accomplished, Leargan's men were rowdy as they mounted up.

Dallon, especially, was grousing about their long journey. He declared fine drink and the arms of a willing woman would fix all his troubles.

He glowered from Fia's saddle, trying not to think about Ansley as his brothers quipped at each other on the ride into Dalunas Main.

Leargan glanced around the noisy tavern, pushing away the half-eaten bowl of stew. Hadn't even tasted it anyway. His fatigued body's demands for food had made him shove as much sustenance past his lips as he could stand, but he'd stopped as soon as his stomach had ceased growling.

Two pretty lasses, a redhead and a blonde, had draped themselves all over him as soon as he'd taken a seat with his men, but he'd dismissed them quickly, ignoring pouty lips and low bodices.

He couldn't even look at the girl whose locks reminded him of Ansley's. She'd taken the hint and gone to another table when Merrick, Laith and Roduch also ignored her attentions.

Should he feel better or worse that all three of his brothers were also thinking about women back in Greenwald?

Dallon had snatched the blonde barmaid around the waist, and she currently resided on his lap.

Alasdair had already retired with a beautiful brunette. Knowing Alas, the knight had known of the tavern and the lass long before they'd even set foot in the place. He'd wasted no time pulling her into his arms when they'd walked into the *Rusty Nail.* She'd greeted him enthusiastically and practically dragged him up the stairs that led to the finer rooms.

Lucan was looking around, wide-eyed and pink cheeked at all the bosoms on display. The women in the tavern were indeed pleasing to the eye, just as the provost had said.

Leargan smiled at the lad. Then he thought about Alasdair dragging him into taverns when he was Lucan's age and cringed. The mage was a sweet lad. He needed to hold onto his innocence for a while longer — perhaps turns — until he met the lass he wanted to marry. It meant more that way.

He fought the urge to close his eyes as pain crept up from his gut, and reached for the stein of ale in front of him, chugging. It burned on its way down his throat, but it was already warm and unappetizing. He ached for Ansley.

A feminine laugh took his attention, and Leargan glanced at Dallon and the lass in his arms. The girl's blonde curls were swept up and piled on top of her head. She had big dark brown eyes, and not much of a dress on. She stared at Dallon, and he gazed right back. Obviously, they were quite pleased with each other. As the knight had planned, he wouldn't be sleeping alone — if he'd be *sleeping* at all.

"Are you sure none of your friends need a good woman tonight?" the lass asked, winking and looking at Laith and Merrick in open appreciation.

The fair-haired brothers were no stranger to wenches in taverns, but neither had shown any interest in any women since they'd left Greenwald.

"Sorry, but I have my Meara back in Greenwald," Laith said, downing the last of the ale in his mug. He winked and the girl smiled.

"Daicy would part me with something I'm rather fond of, if I used it elsewhere." Merrick grinned, swaying in his chair.

The knight's head was going to ache all the way back to Greenwald with as much as he'd imbibed.

Roduch and Dallon chuckled and Laith rolled his eyes.

Leargan snorted. Seeing how protective she'd been of Ansley, there was no doubt the petite maid *would* part Merrick from his bollocks if he '*used them elsewhere,*' as he'd said. Daicy definitely had a temper. The girl would also probably not wish it public knowledge that she was sleeping with Merrick, but his friend must care for Daicy. The knight had never been a one-woman kind of man. If he wouldn't touch another lass, it meant something.

Good for them.

He wished them happiness — Laith and Meara, too — he just hurt for himself and Ansley.

"What about the little one? Vera, just over there, has a fondness for virgins." She gestured to a brunette that was currently bending over a young man in an obvious display of her body.

Lucan blushed scarlet and shook his head vigorously.

Dallon's lass smirked, but no one commented on the young mage's virtue or his denial.

"Hmm..." She looked directly at Leargan, and he swallowed a groan. She sized him up, her gaze moving up and down his face.

Could she not take a hint?

"Your captain is a bit broody, but I've a girl in mind." She glanced at Dallon before looking back at Leargan.

"He's attached, as well." Dallon made eye contact with him.

Pain lanced his gut as Ansley's face danced into his mind. He tightened his grip on the stein as the girl on his friend's lap shook her head and gave an over-dramatic sigh.

"What about you, big man?" The lass ran her fingertips down Roduch's chest.

The blond knight shook his head and swatted her hand away.

"Awww," she pouted, her full lips pulling down. "I was curious to see if you were big all over." She winked.

Dallon growled, and the girl giggled as he cupped her face and covered her mouth in a kiss that projected possession.

She kissed him back eagerly.

How much of it was for show, on her part? Did she want Dallon or his coin?

The lass moaned into the knight's mouth, and Leargan tore his eyes away.

"*I* am all the man you need," his friend said.

Lucan shifted in his chair, obviously uncomfortable, so he threw an arm around the lad's shoulders, giving him a squeeze. The young mage relaxed, but averted his gaze from the display.

"Then it is time to show me," the barmaid told Dallon.

The knight scooped her up and stood. She wrapped her arms around his neck, planting another kiss on him. Dallon headed for the stairs, not breaking the lip-lock or even pausing as he ascended with her in his arms.

Roduch shook his head. "I hope my room doesn't back up to his."

Leargan nodded and leaned back in his chair.

Merrick laughed loudly—too loudly—and downed the last of the ale in his mug before slamming it down on the table.

Laith shot his brother an amused look, but said nothing.

"Laith, why don't you help your brother find his bed? Lucan, you too. We're off at dawn, and it's late," Leargan said.

The lad yawned and nodded, scrambling to his feet and smiling. "Night, Leargan, Sir Roduch." Lucan inclined his head.

"Not a bad idea, Captain. C'mon, brother." Laith hauled his older brother to his feet, slipping arm around his shoulders when Merrick swayed.

"Good night, lads," Roduch said, giving their brothers and Lucan a wave.

Leargan echoed the sentiment, watching the knights stumble to the stairwell. Lucan stepped forward, slipping his slim arm around Merrick's waist to assist Laith.

"He's a good lad," Roduch said.

"Aye, he is."

Their eyes met and silence descended, contradicting the noisy tavern. Leargan had always liked Roduch for his quiescence, but his friend was much too intuitive. Instinct told him what the big knight would say before he spoke.

"I'm sure when we get back things will be righted between you two."

"I can only hope."

Why did you say that?

He didn't want to talk about Ansley.

"As I hope things will go well for you and Avril." Leargan needed the focus off of him and the love of his life.

The look his friend gave him shouted he'd missed the mark, but Roduch inclined his head. The big knight was nothing if not polite. "Aye, I hope the same."

"You love her." Had he lost all control of his mind and his mouth?

Are you a lass?

Love was the *last* thing he wanted to talk about.

"Aye," Roduch said simply, smile sliding into a grin. It made him look younger, despite the two sevendays' worth of blond fuzz on his normally clean-shaven face.

"She's been through so much. It's going to be a long road," Leargan said. "But, you're one of the most patient men I know. You'll stay by her side and provide what she needs like you do when you train the lads."

He chuckled. "Love is very different than training youngsters to fight, but thank you, Captain. I appreciate your faith in me."

One corner of his mouth lifted. Was love really all that different from fighting?

Silence fell again, the sounds around them amplifying as he tried not to think about Ansley and all that'd happened between them.

"My visions of Avril...it's hard to believe I have no magic."

"I know, considering your so-called magic saved us so many times, I'm having a hard time with it, as well." Leargan met his friend's pale eyes.

His expression was serious. "In my visions — or whatever they were — she was laughing, more carefree and happy than I've seen her now. And she *loved* me." He sucked in a breath, his large chest heaving. "That hurts...like a physical pain in my chest..."

"Why?"

"Why did I have to meet her now? *After* she had to endure that bastard? Why couldn't I know her before? Why *him*? I could've been the one her father gave her to. *I could've kept her from it...I could've kept that light from being wiped from her face. What if she can't smile like that again? Never laugh, like she did in my visions? What if he killed that in her?" Roduch's expression was wrought with pain, fair brows drawn tight.

Leargan had never seen his friend like this. The big

warrior was always calm, steady, like a rock. Even when they were lads, Roduch never fell apart. He gripped the knight's forearm and squeezed. "How do you know your visions weren't from when she's healed? Not that I'd *ever* wish those horrors on anyone, least of all a beautiful lass one of my brothers is in love with, but what if *you* are the reason she smiled and laughed? What if *you* are the key to that light returning? You'll heal her, my friend. It's already starting."

"I rescued her," he muttered.

"Aye, but that's not the reason she won't stray from your side. She shines when she looks at you. You're just what she needs…and she's just what you need."

Roduch smiled.

His heart ached with envy as he stared at his friend. *Lucky bastard.* "Roduch?" Leargan croaked.

"Aye?" Pale blue eyes searched his face.

"When we get home, tell her how you feel. Hold her and kiss her. When she's ready, wed her."

He grinned again, and nodded curtly, as if he'd issued an order. The big man leaned in, gripping his forearm. "Captain?"

"Aye?"

"You do the same."

Leargan groaned, trying not to think about Ansley.

He failed miserably.

Chapter Thirty-Seven

Why for the Blessed Spirit's sake had she agreed to accompany everyone to greet the men? Ansley didn't want to see Leargan.

Liar.

All right, so she *did* want to see him, but she wouldn't talk to him. She waited for her conscience to contradict her. It didn't, but her chest tightened, heart missing a beat.

She stood stiffly next to Cera and Aimil, ignoring how her father's head was bent low as he spoke to Lords Jorrin, Tristan and the king.

Plotting.

That was all her father was doing lately.

Ansley wished he would just go back to Terraquist.

Of course, Murdoch was as stubborn as she was. When she managed to broach the subject, he'd just assert he wasn't done in Greenwald yet. Sometimes he'd even mutter something about a wedding.

If she threatened to leave on her own, her father would shake his head. He hadn't gone as far as using the word *forbid*, but he did tell her Sir Moray, her captain and leader of the King's Riders, was under instructions to *not* have her back.

Damn my father's meddling.

However, it wasn't like she could continue being a Senior Rider with ease, anyway. Her pregnancy would be showing in a few months, and she couldn't safely go on a long hard ride and not jeopardize her baby. Ansley had spoken to the truth to Cera; she wanted Leargan's child.

His name bounced around in her mind, pain roiling

along with her gut.

What am I going to do?

She'd thought long and hard about Cera's words. It wasn't fair or right to keep Leargan's child from him. But she needed him to love her. She wouldn't marry him because she was carrying his baby.

Refused to be a duty fulfilled. That hadn't changed.

Ansley's eyes swept the courtyard and she pushed the hurt from her mind.

Avril stood not far from the gate, a visible ball of excitement. The girl was as close to the roadway as safely possible, her anticipation of Roduch's advent obvious.

At least Avril's man would be happy to see her.

She sighed, swallowing against the lump in her throat.

"They're coming!" the girl jumped up and down, clapping her hands.

Cera giggled and waved, tugging on Ansley's arm. "C'mon, she's adorable. Don't tell me you can't smile?"

One corner of her mouth lifted, and she glanced at Avril again before meeting the duchess's gray eyes. "Aye, she's adorable. Happy to see the man she loves."

"As you should be," Cera admonished.

She averted her gaze, inadvertently meeting Aimil's dark eyes. Her diminutive friend flashed an encouraging smile.

"There will be a feast tonight; the king practically took over my kitchens to arrange it. Perfect opportunity to speak to Leargan." Cera rocked back on her heels, her expression nonchalant.

Avril made a squealing noise, and Ansley used it as the perfect opportunity to ignore the redhead, eyes landing on her. She was clad in a shiny pale blue dress; the same gown she'd worn to the feast the night the king and his men had arrived. It made her look even more radiant.

The girl launched herself at Roduch, who barely had time to catch her up in his arms after dismounting a large blue roan stallion.

Dark curls loose and flying around her shoulders, Avril initiated a kiss the large blond knight had no problem continuing.

Breathing hurt and Ansley had to look away from them. They looked *happy*. Didn't that just make it worse?

Unfortunately her eyes landed on Fia, Leargan's unusually colored buckskin mare.

Don't look at him. Just...don't...

But she couldn't help it.

He was still in the saddle, sitting low and exuding fatigue. Haggard. Shoulders slumped, a full beard on his normally clean-shaven face.

She wanted to go to him. Touch his cheeks, kiss his lips. Have his arms around her. Greet him with the same enthusiasm Avril had Roduch. Gluing her feet to the ground, Ansley buried her hand in the thick fur of Ali's neck when her bondmate appeared at her side and whined. She blinked away tears, watching the king, her father, and her friends' husbands surround the man she loved as he dismounted.

Pats on the back and vigorous handshakes were exchanged, but he still didn't look her way.

Serves you right, a voice chided, but it didn't lessen the pain. She bit her bottom lip when it wobbled.

Cera reached for her free hand and entwined their fingers, but thank the Blessed Spirit, the duchess stayed silent.

He saw her in his peripheral vision, standing with his ladies and her wolf. Leargan couldn't look at her. Not after the show Avril and Roduch were putting on.

Ansley had made no move to come to him. She hadn't even waved to try to get his attention.

His heart sank to his stomach.

Nothing's changed.

He'd thought of nothing but her on the long ride back—especially after the talk Leargan had had with Roduch at the *Rusty Nail.*

Well, his friend wasn't going to have any problems with *his* follow-through, if that kiss was any indication.

"Leargan?" King Nathal asked.

The concern in his foster father's voice told him it wasn't the first time his name had been called.

"I'm sorry, what was that?" He met the king's eyes.

"Are you hungry, lad? Morag has laid a fine repast," Sir Murdoch said.

He had to look away from the teal eyes that matched the love of his life. His gaze landed on Jorrin, whose expression was tight, pained.

Damn empathic magic.

Leargan squared his shoulders and took a breath. "Honestly, what I want most is a bath and a blade, to shave this roughness from my face."

"And I was going to say you looked dignified." Jorrin grinned.

King Nathal chuckled, and both Sir Murdoch and Tristan grinned.

"No thank you. I'll leave the beards to my elders." He winked.

The king gave a large bark of laughter and hit his shoulder good-naturedly.

Ansley's father grumbled, but still wore a smile.

How he'd managed the joke was a mystery, because it belied Leargan's thoughts and feelings, but it was good to be home.

Home.

The thought jolted him. *Greenwald* was home. It'd only been about a turn, but the Province had replaced Terraquist, the place and people working their way into his heart.

Jorrin and Tristan were as close to him as Niall and Alasdair, and even Roduch. He'd gained two more brothers.

Too bad Ansley was included in his view of *home*.

He should've gone to her as soon as they'd ridden into the courtyard, instead of leaving the first — failed — move to her. Leargan missed her so much. If he would've wrapped her in his arms, would she have shoved him away in a courtyard full of people?

Knowing his stubborn love, probably.

He wanted to kiss her, but at the moment just holding her would've been enough. "Well, I shall meet you all in the great hall. I think I'll be better company clean. Especially before stepping foot in the castle, anyway." He cleared his throat, trying to smile. "Morag is no fan of dust and mud, and I'm no fan of getting fussed at by our headwoman."

King Nathal grinned and clapped him on the back so hard he almost fell over. "Aye. Off with you then, my lad."

Leargan headed to the public baths without a backwards glance. If he looked at her, he'd be even more lost to Ansley than he already was.

Chapter Thirty-eight

Roduch ran his fingers through his hair, liking its shorter length. Now it rested at the base of his neck, closer to his scalp. After a bath, Morag had cut it for him, even though she'd fussed at him the whole time. Told him he'd better marry '*that lass*,' because the headwoman wasn't going to stand by his impropriety any longer.

Grinning, he shook his head and rubbed his jaw, skimming his fingertips along his newly clean-shaven face. He'd gotten as close as he could with a fine blade. Didn't want to abrade Avril's soft skin when he saw her in a bit.

Now that he was cleaned up, he was going to head to her rooms and see if she would dine with him at the personal guard's table in the great hall, or if she would prefer a more private affair as they'd grown accustomed to. Either would be fine with him, although the king and Lady Cera had a feast planned.

Roduch just wanted to be with her.

She'd kissed him. In a public setting. Without a care for the presence of Castle Aldern's residents. His heart leapt. As soon as she was ready, she'd be his. Morag didn't have to worry about that.

A tentative knock on his door had him glancing over his shoulder.

"Roduch?" Even through the thick wood, the voice was unmistakable.

Avril.

What was she doing at his door? He'd never brought her to his small room in the soldier wing of Castle Aldern. As a matter of fact, women were scarce in this part of the castle. A maid or two occasionally, but they had three male servants assigned to see to their needs.

Morag wouldn't allow her maids in the area with single men unsupervised. Unless it was during the day, and the men were out. Married knights, like Padraig and Niall, lived in a different part of Castle Aldern. Most of the men-at-arms didn't live on site, but there were rooms designated for their use when necessary.

His stomach fluttered, his eyes grazing his rustic oversized furnishings. He was surrounded by what he needed. Nothing fancy. Masculine and sparse, his furniture was all dark wood and large.

A desk and chair, bed, big chest at the end of it, and one other chair by the window. Much different than Avril's lavish guest room.

Roduch didn't even have an armoire to hang garments.

"Are you in there? Sir Lucan told me this was your room."

Her voice jolted him and he rushed to the door, wrenching it open.

Their eyes locked and Avril smiled up at him.

The smile from his visions. Open and honestly happy. She exuded joy, her skin creamy, healthy, and her riot of curls loose and dancing around her shoulders.

Perhaps his captain was right; he was helping her heal.

She'd changed into a dark green gown that made her emerald eyes shine. Her small breasts were pushed up by the corset.

Roduch wanted to growl. No other man would be permitted to look there. His hands itched to touch her, hold her, continue the kiss she'd planted on him in the courtyard.

Avril was so gorgeous it took his breath away.

"Are you going to invite me in?"

He suppressed the urge to jump and made himself

nod. His voice had deserted him.

When she slipped past him, he managed to close the door behind her, only to watch her peruse his room in silence, running her small hands over his things. Avril stared at the oversized bed large enough for his six foot five inch frame, her cheeks reddening to her ears.

Roduch needed to say something—*anything*—but seeing her among his things was so enchanting, words dissolved before they were born.

Avril in his quarters was *right.*

He couldn't tear his eyes away.

"I like your room very much. It's so…you." She turned to him with another brilliant smile. Avril stopped in front of him, close enough to touch, but too far away for Roduch's liking.

He took a step toward her. "Thank…you." He needed to touch her. After a fortnight of being gone, the small amount of time she'd spent in his arms outside in the courtyard wasn't nearly enough.

She beat him to it, as if she'd read his mind. Reached up, laying her palm flat against his cheek. "You shaved. And cut your hair."

Roduch nodded and put his hand over hers to keep contact. A tremor shot down his spine when she pressed into him instead of pulling away, her small breasts flat against him. He caressed the back of her hand, slowly moving downward, brushing his fingertips against the skin of her wrist, then her forearm.

He slipped his hand into the wide sleeve of her dress, touching the soft skin of her elbow, feeling her shiver. He needed her naked. *Now.*

The tightening in his breeches told him how much his body agreed. But he couldn't do that until she was ready. Wouldn't push her.

Roduch forced his hand to his side and gulped.

Avril's gaze locked onto his. "Why'd you stop? I like when you touch me."

He groaned and tugged her into his arms. She quivered against him, and he squeezed her tight, pressing a kiss to her head instead of taking her mouth like he wanted to. "You trembled. I wasn't sure what it meant."

"I was anticipating more."

His heart fluttered. "Really?"

"Yes. I was hoping you would kiss me again." Her confession was whispered, her face crimson.

How he adored her. "Aye. I'll kiss you any time you want."

"How about now?"

Against his better judgment, Roduch lowered his head and brushed her lips. He needed to keep it simple and tender, to not overwhelm her.

Slow.

But the moment her soft wet mouth started moving under his, he was lost.

Avril opened for him without urging. Their tongues mingled and he kissed her harder. She moaned and pushed closer, reaching up to put her arms around his neck. She was so diminutive she couldn't reach more.

He lifted her off the floor, and her arms went around him. She rocked her hips into his, rubbing his arousal with enough pressure to tease, make him burn.

Roduch tore his mouth away, panting. He couldn't do this to her. "I want you," he breathed, resting his forehead against hers.

"I want you, too." Avril's cheeks were flushed, her expression hazy with passion. "I love you, Roduch."

He froze, staring into her green eyes. His heart tripped. "What?"

Hurt flashed across her beautiful face, and she averted her gaze.

Wrong answer, stupid wretch.

"Avril, I'm sorry," he said quickly, but she wouldn't look at him. He set her to her feet and cupped her face, tilting up until she didn't have a choice but to meet his eyes again. "That came out wrong. You took me by surprise. I never thought you'd say that to me."

"I feel it. It…just came out."

"Good." Roduch read hope in her gorgeous eyes. "I love you, too."

She shrieked and threw herself into his arms.

He chuckled and caught her up, kissing her again, pulling her off the floor again as she clung to him. He kissed her languorously and deeply, exploring her mouth as she did the same with his. The earlier urgency was still there, but rightness settled over him with her in his arms.

Avril was his, and Roduch would never let her go. But he wanted her. He *ached* for her, erection trapped between them.

She wasn't ready.

"We need to stop. I don't want to overwhelm you."

She pulled back, staring at him. "You're not. I love kissing you. I love how it makes me feel."

"I love kissing you, too. I need to be with you, Avril. More than I need to breathe. But even more than that, I need *you* to be ready. Your needs are greater than my own, love. So when it's time, I can show you what making love is. That day is not today."

Her breath was ragged.

Roduch bit back a groan. Wished he could change his mind, but he wouldn't push her.

Avril stared into the crystal blue eyes of the man she loved. "I want to know what making love is like." Words exited her mouth on the breath she was struggling for.

Roduch groaned and closed his eyes.

Now she knew what desire was, what it felt like, but was she ready to take the next step? Her whole body was warm, and the place between her legs ached. Her breasts felt heavy, and her skin itched to have his hands on her.

Was she ready to be with him today? Have his big

body on top of her, his manhood inside her?

She swallowed. Avril wrapped her legs around her love's waist so she could get even closer to him. An erection pushed back, but she wasn't afraid. "I love you, Roduch." She kissed both cheeks and smothered his mouth with tiny wet kisses until her man finally took her lips properly.

His arms shook around her, and he backed up to the bed, his strong—yet gentle—hold on her body never wavering. Roduch sat, settling her on his lap. He yanked his mouth off hers, his massive chest panting against her breasts. "I need to stop now. Before I can't."

Her pulse thundered in her ears and made her head spin. She didn't say anything.

"Avril. What do you want?" His beautiful eyes bored into her.

Was she ready?

Repetition of the question wasn't making an answer materialize.

Avril couldn't find her voice.

Roduch rested his forehead against hers. "I see doubt in your eyes, love." There was no censure in his voice. No judgment, just the patience he always had with her.

Her stomach somersaulted. "What if I don't know? What I want...because I've never experienced it."

He offered a soft smile. "We'll get there, love. I'll show you everything."

"Can you hold me? I want to lay with you like we do in my room."

Roduch kissed her and nodded. Without dislodging her, he scooted back into the large bed, nestling her in his arms and against his chest, his carved wooden headboard at his back. He stroked her shoulders and hair, and Avril rested her head against him. "When you're ready, it doesn't have to be everything at once. There're many ways to make each other feel good without joining bodies fully."

She lifted her head and their eyes met. Her heart

flipped at the love she *felt*. She didn't have to concentrate to see his aura. He glowed with love for *her*.

"We have turns — we have forever. If you'll have me."

Avril froze. Surprise and hope washed over her. His blue eyes were warm and tender. "Yes. A hundred times yes," she blurted. "I mean…if you're asking."

He cupped her face and laughed. "Aye, I'm asking." He pressed his lips to hers. "Avril, will you marry me?"

"Yes!" She wrapped her arms around him, lavishing kisses over his cheeks and forehead, causing him another chuckle.

"I never thought you'd want to remarry." Roduch's voice was low and serious.

She smiled and shook her head. "I'm done with my past. I won't think of anything but my future with you." The smile that curved his lips made her stomach flutter. "I fell in love with you. So yes, I want to marry the man I love. You were meant for me. Your visions prove it."

"Fate. You were meant for me. I wouldn't have it any other way," he whispered.

"And children?"

"Of course. Only if they're yours." Roduch smiled.

Her heart plummeted to her gut. A sharp pain destroyed the languid feeling in her limbs. Avril closed her eyes and looked away.

"What is it?" He tugged on her hand.

"I don't think I can have children."

"Avril, look at me."

She obeyed and their gazes locked.

His expression was so tender it made her love him even more. "You can."

"I'm not sure I…" Avril refused to think of her former husband.

"Lord Dagget said he saw no reason within your body that you cannot. I don't think *you* were the reason that you…failed to conceive."

"He did?" She had to suck in a breath, and her pulse

kicked up.

Roduch nodded.

Avril shrieked and threw her arms around his neck.

He laughed, but it was cut off as she kissed him, deep and urgent.

Their eyes met as the kiss ended and they panted against each other.

"Many things, you said?"

"Aye."

"These things you can show me…can it be today?"

Roduch's gaze raked her face. "Avril?"

"I…want to try. I want to be with you. Can we try?"

The apple of this throat jumped as he swallowed, but her betrothed nodded. "I won't hurt you or do anything you don't want. Anything you're not ready for."

"I know."

"If it becomes too much, at any time, you are to tell me, and we will stop," he said firmly, gripping her shoulders and squeezing. "Promise me, Avril."

"Promise." She nodded and crashed her mouth to his.

He framed her cheeks, preventing her from deepening their kiss. "I love you, Avril."

"I know. Time to show me."

Roduch flashed a grin and fused their mouths.

Chapter Thirty-Nine

Ansley stood outside Leargan's door wringing her hands.

Why is this so hard? Oh, I don't know…maybe because your future and the future of your unborn child is at stake?

She hadn't had the guts to speak to him at the feast. She'd stared at him all evening, looking away whenever their eyes met. And since she'd been watching him so hard, their gazes had collided a great deal.

Like he could see right through me.

Her face had probably been as red as the deeply hued gown Cera had insisted she wear. Red had never been Ansley's color. But the dress was a stunner, for sure. Tight, with a laced corset that pushed her breasts up, and like her green gown from the duchess, lower cut than she was comfortable in. She'd gotten stares all night, and not just from Leargan.

Ansley had hurried back to her room and ripped it off at first chance, settling for a brown earth-toned soft dress she'd begged the steward, Gamel, for from the stores. No corset. It was loose and worn, and she could breathe in it. Which was good, because she needed to breathe right now.

She paced, chiding herself for cowardice. The corridor was empty, because it was very late. Still, she needed to make a decision.

Sooner than later.

If someone saw her alone in the soldier wing — a place where women were scarce — and word got back to her father, Sir Murdoch would take matters into his own hands. A priest would be called even if there was no impropriety witnessed.

She groaned, settling her hand over her lower stomach. Until they were married—if he still wanted to marry her—she and Leargan's child were more than *improper*.

Knock. Make a fist and knock on the door. Right. Now.

All she could manage was to stare at the thick wooden panel. Ansley had never been so close to him, yet so far away.

Cera had insisted Leargan loved her. Why couldn't she find out?

All you have to do is knock. When he opens the door, tell him you love him. That's it.

Thinking about what the duchess had said made too much sense. The time he'd been gone *had* helped clear her head—although she'd missed him so much Ansley ached from it.

She'd called him a liar when he'd said he *wanted* to marry her. What if her hostility and accusation had changed his mind?

What if Leargan doesn't want me anymore?

Would the child in her belly be the only reason he'd marry her? Do *right* by her?

Nay. Ansley didn't want him that way. Her eyes burned and she blinked.

Stop jumping to conclusions and face him. You were wrong.

The knock was low, quick, but it resounded in her ears and in her heart.

She waited. Gulped.

The door remained shut in front of her, and she closed her eyes, struggling for breath as rejection settled over her. Maybe Leargan knew she at the door, and wasn't going to answer.

Should she knock again? Or leave? Could she live with herself if she didn't try?

"Ansley?"

The surprise in his voice had her eyes flying open, her heart thundering in her ears. She opened her mouth to speak, but no words came.

Leargan peeked around the door, head moving back and forth as he scanned the empty corridor. Then he grabbed her wrist and pulled her into his room.

Ansley didn't fight him as her feet shuffled forward.

"It's late…and…" The love of her life shrugged, and she managed a nod. He didn't want to deal with the prospect of her being caught alone with him anymore than she did.

"I…need…to talk to you." She cleared her throat.

He said nothing as his eyes drank her in. Looking her up and down as if he hadn't seen her in turns. The apple of his throat bobbed. "You're so beautiful."

Heat seared her cheeks. Ansley shifted on her feet. She didn't feel beautiful in the plain brown dress; it was more of a shift than a gown.

Leargan's dark gaze bored into her. "I've missed you so much."

"I missed you, too," she whispered, jolting as the confession passed her lips and made him freeze before her.

"Love, I—"

"Leargan, I—" They spoke at the same time. Tears burned her eyes, and she wanted to rush into his arms. He'd called her *love*. Blessed Spirit, she'd missed that.

He reached for her hand, his broad shoulders loosening. "Come, sit with me."

She let him guide her to his bed, and they both perched on its edge.

The bed was probably a bad idea. Ansley avoided looking at his soft sleeping furs and pillows, even though memories assaulted her. They'd only made love in his bed a few times, but she could see it—*feel* it—as if it was yesterday and everything was right between them.

She fell into his eyes as soon as she had the courage to look at his face. So handsome. Stubble graced his cheeks, and she wanted to touch him. Lean in and kiss him, have his strong arms around her. She had to fix things. "I…" She sucked in a breath and swallowed against the lump in her throat.

Leargan's expression was tender as he waited, saying nothing, but her stomach jumped. He'd listen to her.

Which was more than she'd offered him.

He entwined their fingers, and her vision blurred. *Again.* His touch was familiar, but more than that, it was *right.* As *right* as it ever was, as it ever would be.

"I'm sorry," Ansley blurted. She wanted to look away but the dark pools of his eyes drew her in.

"I'm sorry I hurt you," he echoed.

She needed to be with him. *Now.*

Ansley threw her arms around his neck, scooting as close as she could get. Prayed he wouldn't reject her. She buried her face against his tunic, inhaling his familiar scent. Masculine. Clean. *Sandalwood and leather.* Fresh soap coming off his heated skin. She closed her eyes against the tears that wet her cheeks.

Leargan rubbed her back and pulled her flush to his chest. He whispered in her ear, but she couldn't make sense of the words as his heat washed over her.

He hadn't pushed her away.

She felt his lips on her cheek and temple, then the crown of her head. It wasn't enough. Ansley lifted her face, meeting his lips with hers.

He groaned into her mouth as he deepened the kiss, but she let him, slipping her tongue against his.

Need threatened to swallow her whole. Desire set low in her belly; her sex pulsed. It'd been too long. She wanted him.

He tore his mouth away, resting his forehead against hers just when she was getting lost in him. "Wait," he breathed.

"Wait?"

"We need to talk…"

"Later." Ansley pushed forward, trying to kiss him again.

Leargan settled both hands on her shoulders and squeezed. "Nay, love. I have some things I need to say to you." One corner of his mouth lifted.

"Making love won't fix all our problems?"

He chuckled and shook his head. "Would that it could."

She gave a small smile.

His expression sobered and his gaze bore into hers. "I love you."

Ansley froze. He loved her?

He loves me.

Knowing what Cera thought and hearing him *say* it were two different things. "You…love…me."

"Aye. So much…" Leargan smiled. His chest rose and fell against hers.

She whimpered and blinked away more tears. "You really love me…"

"Aye. I love you." Her captain grinned. "Do I have to keep saying it so you'll believe me?"

"I believe you. And I love you, too." She pressed her lips to his, initiating a kiss he quickly took control of. Ansley melted into his chest as he pulled her closer, sliding back onto his bed and settling her on his lap. His erection dug into her, but there was too much fabric between them. "I want you," she panted. "I *need* you…"

"We're not done talking." Leargan's voice went up and down as he struggled to speak.

She rocked in his lap. "After." She leaned back, grabbing the edge of the gown and ripping it up and over her head. She hadn't bothered with breastbands.

He gasped. "Ansley…"

"I just…need to be with you," she whispered, lavishing wet kisses around his mouth.

Leargan shuddered, but pulled her to him instead of pushing her away. "I need to be with you, too. Always."

His lips were warm on her forehead, and he held her close. Then he laid her down on his bed, tugging off the shortpants she'd donned. He held them up. "Love? Men's undergarments?"

Ansley giggled. "They were handy. And I always wear them on long message runs; they're more comfortable."

He shook his head and grinned, tossing her shortpants over his shoulder as if they were offensive. His eyes zoned in on her nudity, and she squirmed, her cheeks hot. His gaze devoured her. "I need you. I love you."

She smiled and reached for him. "I love you, too. Lose the clothes so I can show you how I feel." She pressed a kiss to his hand like he'd done so many times to hers.

"You've always shown me," Leargan whispered, discarding his tunic. "Sorry I was so bad at doing the same for you."

Ansley would've answered, but she couldn't stop staring at his chest. How could he have gotten even more beautiful in their time apart? Her mouth went dry.

He pushed his breeches off his hips slowly, a twinkle in his dark eyes as he watched her stare.

Impatience had her on her knees at the edge of the bed, grabbing his wrist and dragging him closer so she could finish the job herself.

Leargan chuckled, cupping her face and kissing her deeply after stepping out of his breeches and boots.

She sighed against his mouth as their tongues danced. She dragged her fingertips down his chest and stomach, then teased the tip of his erection until he groaned.

He wrapped his arms around her, and they fell onto his bed in a tangle of limbs, their mouths never parting.

Their naked skin met from head to foot and she shivered in anticipation of his touches, kisses, the feel of him inside her.

Leargan pushed her down even further, parting her thighs with a knee as his hands roved her body.

Ansley writhed as he skimmed over her sex with seeking fingers. She rocked, lifting her hips in a demand for more.

He broke the seal of their lips, dragging warm wet kisses down her neck and onto her breasts. He circled and tasted her nipples into taut peaks before suckling her until it drove her mad.

Her core pulsed, begging him to join them. His erection rested against her inner thigh. Hot and hard, but too far from where she needed him. "Leargan," Ansley moaned.

"I know, love. I'm torturing us both."

"I…need…"

"I know." He leaned down and took her mouth in a kiss that curled her toes and made her even hotter for him.

She felt his hand shoot between them, positioning his erection to take her. Then with one long stroke, Leargan joined them, filling her exquisitely and completely. Ansley cried out, lifting to meet his first thrust and entwining their legs so she could move with him. She caressed his back as he conquered her mouth again, kissing her deep and hard, like the movement of his hips.

Their lovemaking was fast and frenzied and exactly what she needed. The reconnection with him was perfect.

"Love, I…" he whispered near her ear.

"I know," she groaned, throwing her head back and closing her eyes as her muscles tightened. She tilted her hips as climax hit her with the force of a storm, her muscles contracting against Leargan, inside and out. She cried out, squeezing his rear end with both hands as he came back to her with a firm thrust.

He called her name and buried his face against her neck, his back stiffening as his release shot into her.

Heavy breathing was all she could hear as her vision cleared. They panted against each other, Leargan still on top of her. She loosened her grip on his buttocks, but ran her hands up and down his damp back until he groaned against the overheated skin of her neck, his warm breath tickling.

When he lifted his head, their eyes met. "I love you, Ansley."

A warm smile curved her lips. "I love you, too."

Leargan stared into her teal eyes. Sweat bathed her forehead. Her cheeks were flushed pink and damp, her freckles prominent. Her lips were swollen from his kisses and her glorious red tresses were spread out on his pillow like they belonged. In his bed. *Always.*

She was his again.

This time, he wasn't going to let her go.

He slipped from her body and rolled over, taking her with him. He kissed her forehead as she nestled close, propping herself on his chest to look down at him.

"I've loved you for turns you know," Ansley whispered, her cheeks even pinker.

Leargan cupped her face before she could avert her gaze. "For turns?"

"Aye. Since I was about eighteen."

Shock rolled over him. He'd seen her in Terraquist, of course. He'd known who she was, but other than polite conversation in passing, had never spoken to her. She was just another Senior King's Rider, but more than that, she was his captain's daughter.

Her father had said he was afraid she wouldn't marry if it wasn't him, but had Sir Murdoch known how long Ansley had loved him?

He could've had her turns ago, in his arms, in his heart. His wife. "Why didn't you approach me, love?" Leargan whispered.

"You never looked at me." Ansley smirked. "I was that lanky freckled redhead, your captain's daughter. I mean, even if you knew that."

He laughed. "I knew who you were, love."

"And never looked at me twice." Her teal gaze challenged him.

He kissed her. "And I was a fool for it. You're gorgeous, and you're mine."

She grinned and snuggled close. When she met his eyes again, her beautiful face was somber. She licked her lips and his heart fluttered. "I'm sorry." She averted her gaze, and he let her. Obviously, his love needed a moment to gather her words. "Sometimes…because of how long I've loved you…you just seem too good to be true. That's why I didn't believe you wanted me. Why I thought I was just an order to you."

"Oh, love."

Their eyes locked and she flashed a watery smile. "It doesn't excuse what I said."

"Nothing compares to what *I* said, Ansley."

"Leargan—"

"Nay. I mean it. What I said to you was *inexcusable*. No matter our situation, it was…unforgivable."

Ansley grinned.

Leargan paused, staring. A smile wasn't unwelcome, but it wasn't exactly what he'd expected in response.

"So, you won't take our child away from me?"

Shame rolled over him, and he looked away, closing his eyes. He felt her hands on his stubbled cheeks, pulling his face back to hers, then her lips on his eyelids and forehead before she pressed a tender kiss to his mouth.

He met that blue-green gaze again.

Ansley quirked a half-smile and kissed him again. "I suppose that was in poor taste. I was…trying to tease you. I need to tell you something." Her face reddened, but she didn't look away.

Leargan's heart started to gallop. "Tell me what?"

Her gorgeous breasts rose and fell against his chest as she inhaled deeply. "You weren't wrong when you spoke of a child."

"What?" His pulse thundered in his ears.

"We're going to have a baby, Leargan."

They stared at each other in silence.

When Ansley smiled, his stomach jumped.

He cupped the back of her head and pulled her gently toward him. She met his mouth with hers, twisting their tongues as he slid his hands down over her shoulders and back, holding her gingerly to him.

She laughed into his kiss. "I won't break."

Panic squeezed his chest. "Blessed Spirit, I took you so roughly—"

"Leargan." Her voice steadied him. "I'm fine. Our child is fine. I promise. You didn't hurt either of us when we made love. You touched me how I wanted you to. Wow, you've paled out..." She caressed his cheeks again, calming him with her touch and small kisses she placed all over his face.

"Promise?" Leargan croaked. He grabbed her wrists.

"Aye. But we'll go see Lord Tristan if you like."

He nodded, his shoulders relaxing into the bed. They sighed at the same time and he stroked her back, holding her closer. "Will you marry me now?"

Ansley studied his face before she spoke. "Because of the baby?"

"Because you both belong to me."

Tears slipped down her cheeks and his heart clenched. "I love you," she whispered.

Thumbing her tears away, he smiled. "I love you, too. But you didn't answer me."

"You didn't answer me, either."

"It's no secret I want this child. I told you from the start that I wanted children. They have to be *your* children, love. The baby isn't why I want to marry you."

"Why do you want me, Leargan?" Ansley quirked one red eyebrow. Her full mouth quivered as if she was fighting a smile.

"Well, you see, I was given this scroll, and there was this order..."

"Wretch!" She pummeled his chest until he caught her wrists and showered kisses over her fists.

When their eyes met, she giggled and he laughed. "I love you, Ansley. I want this child because it belongs to us both."

"Then I have no choice but to marry you, I suppose." She rolled her eyes but scooted closer.

Her mouth hovered over his, teasing, but Leargan closed the distance and tasted her again. It grew desperate and heated in moments. He buried his hand in the soft hair at the back of her neck, holding her closer as she kissed him harder.

His arousal throbbed, trapped pleasantly between them but it wasn't enough. He pulled his mouth from hers before he lost the ability to think. "Did I answer correctly this time?"

"I think so." Ansley straddled him, their bodies coming together in the right places.

They both groaned.

"Did you come back to me because you discovered the presence of our child?" Concentration was difficult as she started to rock, pressing her wet hot sex against his erection.

"Nay." The word was breathless.

"Then why?" He grabbed her hips to hold her still.

She moaned and ground against him.

Leargan's manhood pulsed, but he ignored the demands of his body.

"Because you were miserable."

He arched an eyebrow. "Oh?"

Ansley grinned pure mischief, but said nothing.

"Is that all?" he prompted.

"Nay." She leaned down, her nipples brushing his. She licked his bottom lip.

He groaned. "Wh-wh-what…else?" Running his hands down her back, he followed the curve of her bottom, cupping her with both hands and pulling her down as she rubbed against him again.

She tremored, but sucked in a breath, her lips only millimeters above his. "I was miserable, too." Ansley made a move to kiss him, but Leargan tilted his head away.

"What about now?"

"I'm not miserable, are you?" she panted.

"Nay." *Miserable* couldn't be farther from his current truth. "I don't want to talk right now."

"Then shut up and show me what you'd rather be doing." She braced herself on his chest and sat up.

His retort dissolved on his tongue as she lifted her hips and impaled herself on him.

She wiggled, making them both gasp.

Leargan hauled her down for a kiss and thrust upward to meet her first downward stroke, proving he'd be happy to do just that.

Epilogue

nsley looked down at the two perfect little forms. Brogan slept with his tiny face buried against her breast, his red hair tickling her bare arm as it stood out in several directions. Brynn faced the opposite of her brother, her linen padded rump against Ansley's stomach and her cheek on her forearm as she too, slept. Her sable hair curled at the ends.

Murdoch was proud his grandson was a redhead, going around proclaiming himself *world's-greatest-Grandfa* already. Prattling on and on about what he would teach Brogan, much to Leargan's amused chagrin.

Their daughter wouldn't be slighted by her father in the least. One look from the tiny lass, and Brynn already had the huge man wrapped around her little pinky finger. She could only imagine what it would be like when her children were walking and talking.

Leargan and Ansley had been honest with her father the morning after they'd righted things between them. Admitted she was carrying Leargan's child — children — and that they intended to marry.

Murdoch had ranted and raved, but King Nathal had calmed him, and they'd had a very nice wedding a few days later. Her father had vehemently refused the delay, but Cera had insisted she be given time to arrange an adequate ceremony and celebration feast.

Although he'd grumbled, her father had walked Ansley down the aisle in Castle Aldern's chapel with a smile on his face. He'd never admit it, but his eyes were misty as he'd handed her over to Leargan.

Cera had surprised her with a lavish wedding gown.

The pale green of Greenwald in hue, intricately embroidered as was her friend's favorite style. She'd cried—of course. The duchess had planned the gown sevendays before, and had her dressmaker working on it for almost the same period of time. It was gorgeous and perfect, and Ansley would cherish it always.

Her wedding had been equally perfect. The day almost nine months ago was like yesterday. Just as loving and sweet.

Brynn made a sound in her sleep, and Ansley rocked her daughter, careful not to disturb her napping husband or their son on her other arm. She smiled as the lassie settled, her tiny chest rising and falling in a deep rhythm.

Of course, Cera already had Fallon betrothed to Brynn. Tristan and Aimil had also had a baby girl and named her Aislinn. In turn, the duchess now had her paired with Brogan. When she reminded her friend they'd all married for love and would expect no less for their children, Cera would smile and insist it wouldn't be a problem. Ansley almost asked if the duchess had Gamel draw up marriage contracts.

Two babies were more of a challenge than one. They'd been a surprise. Even Tristan hadn't known she'd carried twins until he'd delivered Brynn, and the healer realized she wasn't yet done giving birth. About ten minutes later, Brogan had graced them with his presence, screaming louder than his sister had.

Leargan joked his son was offended they hadn't known he was there.

The healer speculated Brynn had magic. Her brother did not—or it was much less than hers—so when he'd used his healing touch to track Ansley's health and the health of the babies during the pregnancy, Brynn's magic had called to his and effective masked Brogan.

Raising children with magic might be difficult, but they already sensed magic within little Fallon, so at least Ansley wouldn't be alone.

Ansley loved the twins so much, and even though they were only three sevendays old, she couldn't have imagined her life without them, or their father.

It was like Cera had said; her husband and these children were her *life.*

Leargan shifted in his sleep, and she glanced at him. Since the night of the babies' birth, he'd insisted on getting up when she had to nurse during the night, so he was just as exhausted as Ansley, but it was a good kind of exhausted. It only made her love him more.

Dark eyes fluttering, he sighed as he came around, giving a loud yawn.

"Hey there," she whispered.

His mouth curved in a smile that made her heart skip as he sat up, pressing a tender kiss to her mouth. "Hello, love." He leaned over, kissing his son's little hand and caressing Brynn's downy dark hair before pressing his lips to her tiny cheek, since she was closer.

Ansley smiled. She couldn't get enough of seeing him with their children. "Did you get enough sleep?"

"Aye, what time is it?"

"Late afternoon."

Concern clouded his expression, and his brow knitted. "Did *you* sleep?"

"Aye." She nodded. "The twins woke me not long ago. I fed them and got a bite to eat. Morag brought a tray and fussed at me, of course."

Leargan chuckled, his shoulders relaxing. "What about?"

"Oh, I'm to let Daicy take them to the wet nurse and have a long hot bath. I'm so exhausted because I'm not caring for myself."

Her husband cupped her cheeks and studied her face. "She's got a point, love."

"She does *not.* I can care for our children."

"*We* can care for our children," he said. "But we do have people to help us. People that want to help because they care for us as well."

Ansley leaned over to kiss him. "I love you," she whispered against his lips.

"Good thing. Because I love you, too." He pressed a lingering kiss to her mouth, then gently took their daughter into his arms. Brynn snuggled into his broad chest as if she'd not switched parents. "I love them, too. More than I ever thought possible, Ans."

She rested against him and grinned, nestling their son higher. She loved when Leargan called her by Cera's nickname for her.

"I can't believe Brynn looks so much like me," he mused as he stared into the sleeping little girl's face, running fingertips over her dark hair.

"And Brogan resembles me." Ansley smoothed the tiny lad's wild red locks. No matter what she did, her son's hair preferred to stick out in all directions. When she looked up, her gaze locked with Leargan's. Her heart sped up. Like it always would.

His dark eyes were intense, and she melted instantly. "I need to thank King Nathal for his meddling ways."

"My father, too."

"He gave me you," they whispered at the same time.

Leargan flashed a smile and pulled her closer gently, with one arm. He caressed his son's cheek and kissed Ansley tenderly. "Scroll or not, you and the twins are mine forever," her husband whispered against her mouth.

"Forever," she echoed.

the end

About the Author

Bestselling, award winning author of romantic suspense and epic fantasy romance, C.A. loves to dabble in different genres. If it's a good story, she'll write it, no matter where it seems to fit!

She's a hopeless romantic and always will be. Risking it all for Happily Ever After is what she lives by!

C.A. is originally from Ohio, but got to Texas as soon as she could. She's happily married and has a bachelor's degree in Criminal Justice.

She works with kids when she's not writing.

WEBSITE: www.caszarek.com
BLOG: www.caszarekwriter.blogspot.com/
TWITTER: www.twitter.com/caszarek
INSTAGRAM: www.instagram.com/caszarek
FACEBOOK: http://www.facebook.com/caszarek
GOODREADS:https://www.goodreads.com/author/show/5815085.C_A_Szarek
EMAIL: ca@caszarek.com